SHELTER
OF LEAVES

LENORE H. GAY

She Writes Press, a BookSparks imprint
A Division of SparkPointStudio, LLC.

Published 2016

Printed in the United States of America

ISBN: 978-1-63152-109-6
Library of Congress Control Number: 2016933150

For information, address:
She Writes Press
1563 Solano Ave #546
Berkeley, CA 94707

She Writes Press is a division of SparkPoint Studio, LLC.

This is a work of fiction. Names, characters, places, and incidents either are the product of the author's imagination or are used fictitiously. Any resemblance to actual persons, living or dead, is entirely coincidental.

In memory of my brother,
Allen T. Gay.

CONTENTS

PART ONE

Chapter 1

DOGS OF SANITY

May 26, 2014. Memorial Day.

The last thing Sabine remembered was a flash coming through the window and a shudder like colliding subway cars. She woke sprawled on the floor, unsure where she was. She stumbled to the window. Buildings across the street swayed and her apartment building shook. She ran room to room, avoiding flying glass, yelling. "Go, go, get out before the building collapses!"

At her bedroom door she froze. A backpack hung on the doorknob. As if from a great distance, she watched her hand pick up the backpack, toss in some clothes, then stash notebooks, cell phone, and wallet into the pack's side pockets. She grabbed her jacket and favorite shawl from the closet and sprinted down the hall past the elevators. She lurched for the stairway exit, took the stairs two at a time, and burst out the front door. Against the building she caught her breath; her head pounded and her legs wobbled.

A body splayed across the bottom step. Shreds of green cloth came into focus, hanging from a charred leg. Half of the man's cranium was missing. The mess of skull, pink matter, and blood made Sabine turn away. A dark-green uniform with gold braiding: it was the doorman's. Samuel. Yesterday he'd told her all about taking his aging dog to the vet and they'd reminisced about pets they'd owned as children. Samuel.

She moved closer to his body and searched for something to hold on to, besides his kindness—always smiling, and opening and closing doors for others. She found it in his curled hands. Good-bye, Samuel.

Crumbling buildings. An assault of smoke and sirens. Burnt bodies sprawled on the sidewalk. A white van burned and rocked furiously, a dance of smoke and flames. Across the street a young woman leaned against a building, clutching her entrails, sliding sideways. Sabine staggered through a maze of scorched cars spewing the stench of oil and coolant, the poisoned air of batteries and tires. The reek of gasoline.

She stayed in the street to avoid falling debris. Drowned in panic, she wanted to move fast but couldn't think with the screams of ambulances and fire engines. West could be the safer direction. East might mean people squeezing onto a margin of coastal land, the beach and the ocean thick with drowned people, sluggish waves rolling corpses onto fetid sand. Please don't let me be the sole person left alive. Samuel's gone. What a nice man. She would never know what happened to his dog, his only family. She wondered about her family. Did she have a family?

Out of habit, she flipped open her cell phone and punched the first contact. The name wasn't familiar, but that didn't matter, since the phone didn't have a signal. Did neighbors in her apartment building need help? She couldn't picture anyone; she had no memory of any names. Samuel was the only name she recalled.

Go back and check. She dodged debris all the way back, but couldn't enter the building. The fifth floor was blown open to the street. Her neighbor's apartment looked like a dollhouse living room: black leather furniture, an upended table, a refrigerator on its side. She turned, not wanting to see her personal belongings exposed. Go west.

She wanted a map. If you had a map, you couldn't really be lost.

A black SUV with a rifle stuck out of a back window smashed into an ATM. The SUV backed over a man crossing the street, then leapt forward to ram the machine again. Two men jumped out of the vehicle and rummaged through ATM debris while the driver shoved the rifle out the window. The man the van ran over lay bleeding; she didn't help. Would his raincoat fit her? No, she wouldn't steal a dead man's coat. Relief felt like joy, the robbers in the SUV weren't interested in hurting her.

A cramp caught her gut. No time to lean forward, she vomited onto her clothes.

A wet rag for her shirt and face. She stumbled forward. In a convenience store halfway down the block, she grabbed three packs of baby wipes, packs of gum and Nabs, and oranges and a banana, hoping their thick skins made them safe to eat. From the canned food aisle a teenage boy yelled, "More bombs! Run, run! More bombs!"

A kid wouldn't know about bombs. He wants all the food for himself. She pulled two jars of peanut butter from the shelf.

The image of the boy moved closer, running at her, screaming in her face. Something swung into her vision. Pain in her head, and the white linoleum spun. Then nothing, until she pushed herself off the floor. She stumbled toward cases of water bottles stacked on the floor. She took four bottles and stuffed them into her backpack. No cashier. She took off running.

She slowed her pace, cleaned her face with baby wipes, and dabbed at her shirt. Something had happened back in the grocery store. The wild look on the teenage boy's face when he ran up to her. Too fast to keep track of anything else.

◈

Saturday morning, or maybe Sunday, she woke in a ditch beside a suburban road. Disoriented, lying in dirt and weeds, she mulled over a dream: she'd been wandering through an enormous park resembling DC's Rock Creek Park. Baby carriages flew through the air; children's legs and arms dangled from trees, small skulls surrounding the base of the trees like pale, grotesque flowers. She hadn't cared about the dead children, had been intent only on wandering, looking for more sights.

She was turning into a monster, uninterested in helping and oblivious to dying children. She detested children.

Drink water. Get up. She scrambled out of the ditch, turned her back on the rising sun, and set out. A piece of spearmint gum removed the foul taste in her mouth but not the chemical smell permeating the air. Since leaving the city, she'd discovered neighborhoods untouched by the blasts; in other areas, houses appeared whole but uninhabited. Had people put their cars in the garage, locked their windows and doors, and hidden inside, waiting for the danger to subside?

She came to a well-kept neighborhood and tried to convince herself she'd visited one of the large houses when she was a child. Hard to resist knocking on a door when the angle of a road or a shade of brick on a house stirred dim memories.

Christmas. The season she wanted her country to be celebrating. She didn't want to live through a summer of maimed people and corpses. How wonderful to drive her car into this neighborhood, park, and walk into one of these houses. Her parents, brothers, and sisters were gathered by the Christmas tree. Cinnamon and pine smells. Someone played carols on the piano, like in the movies. She'd entered a happy new life, where the chaos was merely a bad dream.

But she'd never visited these houses, because she didn't have a family. Or, if she did, she had no idea what they looked like, or where they were. If they were even still alive.

Five or six people in a front yard, talking in a tight group. She called out with a wave and walked over to them. She longed to join their picnic, to eat and talk and hear the news. But the adults either frowned or looked at her blankly, and most turned their backs. The first time she was shunned, she'd dismissed the reaction as an aberration. But then it had happened again. Twice children had run to greet her, but were stopped by the adults.

Eight days without much food, weak with hunger and enticed by the smell of hamburgers and steaks on the grills, she had to force herself not to approach anyone. The suburbanites appeared ordinary and sane, yet they gave her furtive glances, some outright stares. They had access to the news and knew things she didn't. It must be Sunday, or Monday. Her body reeked and her hair smelled worse. She ran her hand through the greasy tangles, wondering how she looked. *A wild-eyed hag in eight days.* If a woman walking alone created hostility and suspicion, only eight days—*or was it six or ten days?*—after the explosions, she dreaded what would come.

Find shelter indoors. Keep priorities straight. Do not think about dying. Think about something uplifting. Okay, okay, uplifting: at least I wasn't near a window during the explosion.

She had her life, water, and an intact face.

જી

Two days later, she came upon another wealthy neighborhood with a nearby mall called Avery Old Farms. Few cars passed as she walked through the mall parking lot. The buildings revealed no signs of damage. Inside the grocery store she moved past cash registers, drawn toward a man wearing a Hawaiian shirt because his face appeared soft and smiling. Maybe he could tell her the latest news. But as she drew close, his mumbled, disjointed words frightened her. The man pushed an empty grocery cart, his eyes unfocused.

She backed away and bumped into a cart belonging to a woman and two children who were pulling cans off shelves and throwing them in the cart. Sabine nodded; the woman only turned and screamed at the children, "Hurry the fuck up! Come on!"

Squashed, rotting vegetables littered the floor. The stench of slick broccoli rose when she slipped on a heap of decomposing vegetables. From the dairy case she snatched two big blocks of cheese, then ran to the one open checkout line, where five people stood talking in boisterous voices. Someone approached from behind—too close. Panic flooded her. She fled with the cheese, slowing only to snatch three packs of gum. No one followed.

She walked. Toward dusk she passed a suburban gas station with eight pumps. Hand-painted signs tacked to the pumps read, "No gas. No food. Closed."

She kicked open the restroom door and washed her face, studying her skin, noting the wear and tear of thirty-five years. Could she still pass for twenty-eight? The skin under her eyes had turned dark and puffy, and new lines had formed around her mouth. Her lips were swollen and cracked. She ran her fingers through her hair to work out matted places. *A stinky old dog with mats*. But what did she expect if she didn't comb it? At the next store, she must steal a comb.

In the mirror, her eyes shifted like a crazy person's; she didn't look familiar to herself. Almost like her clone was standing behind her, looking at her with eyes too big for her face.

Behind the station, several crates were piled on the grass. She crouched behind them and ate half a block of New York sharp cheddar. Her head pounded; the echoing throb had lasted two or three days now. At least the sirens had stopped. Ambulances, police cars, or fire engines. How many days had the sirens' screams filled the air, the urgent, intermittent sounds invading her restless sleep? The hospitals might all be in ruins, or full and turning people away. She hoped enough people would be left to dig graves. They'd need pits to hold the corpses, like during a war. The jobs left would be corpse burner, gravedigger, and tomb builder. Burial would be important. Contagious diseases could spread quickly through cities.

She moved out from behind the crates and went to the front of the gas station. She scanned the intersecting roads, checked the traffic and road signs. Two cars passed on the state road and turned onto an interstate ramp about a quarter mile away. Close by, human voices, several people were walking east on the road. She ran to the back of the station, pushed through knee-high brush, and lay flat on the ground. The voices grew louder, but didn't stop at the station and soon faded.

She'd leave the suburbs behind in the morning. They no longer felt safe; she hated them. Using her jacket for a pillow, she slept.

॰॰॰

For two days she trudged along the state road, taking cover whenever she heard a car or human voices. The terrain shifted—rocks littered the pastures and hills, small stone and wood-frame houses angled away from the road. White farmhouses sat on hills shaded by lush trees.

Among the larger houses, a few were abandoned. Curious, she headed toward an eerie-looking one, but the stench of urine and dead bodies—maybe animal, maybe human—forced her back to the road. At the bottom of a hill, a stagnant pond with a broken-down dock, a rowboat, and two rusted motorcycles on their sides in high grass. On a rise the charred remains of a barn. Wind blew high-flying clouds into tatters above distant hills. Nothing but crickets chirping and persistent wind.

Over on the left, something darted behind a hay bale.

She listened. Nothing.

She picked up her pace.

She stopped. There, behind the rock pile in the field: a shadow, then jerky movement. A man ran toward her, carrying an object above his head. A sword? A machete. She ran full out, and he fell in behind her. She pushed herself but was too exhausted to sustain the pace. A few steps behind now. No outrunning him. She jerked to a stop, turned, and faced him.

Wide shoulders, a black beard, wild eyes. Open-mouthed, she stopped and turned.

He shouted, "Gimme, gimme!"

"What?"

His voice rasped; his tongue was swollen. "Water." He dropped the machete and held out his filthy hands.

She opened her pack and shoved a full bottle of water into his hand. "My last bottle."

He wrenched off the top and guzzled it all.

She focused on the machete. She backed away and glanced around. A car; she needed a car.

The man dropped the empty bottle and moved close enough to grab her shoulder.

She screamed and pounded on his chest with both fists.

"I like 'em feisty!" He grinned, fiddled with his fly, then grabbed her arm and pulled her to him. He stank like rotten meat. "Oh baby, baby," he groaned, pushed his groin into hers. He slipped his hand down to his pants. The sound of a zipper opening.

She tried to push him away, but he overpowered her. *Go limp. Let him rub up against you.*

"Good, baby, good. I ain't gonna hurt you. You come on back to my cabin. Yeah," he said, and moved back enough to undo his belt. His stink was unbearable.

Don't move till his pants are down. When his pants dropped to his ankles, Sabine smashed her knee into his groin. He screamed and scrabbled at her as he doubled over and fell.

She grabbed the machete off the ground and with a shout took two swings at his head. One blow hit his neck and he fell. At the first sign of blood, she turned and ran. Looking over her shoulder, she confirmed the man was still on the ground. She crept back, close enough to see blood. A lot of it. She shouted at him but he didn't move. She watched him for maybe a minute. He didn't move.

She took off. Up ahead, the road curved to the right. Around the curve, trees lined both sides of the road. She darted through low scrub and small trees, and kept moving even when the canopy thickened and the light dimmed. Fallen branches slowed her. In a small clearing she allowed herself to rest, stunned that she'd escaped.

She'd run as fast as she could, yet her body was moving through molasses. She rummaged through the pack for the other water bottle. She took small sips, alert for human sounds. *Don't rest for long. People could live in these woods. Catch your breath and go.* Her jeans felt damp.

She'd peed her pants. Her tongue felt sticky and her head pounded. But the machete at her feet filled her with strength—more than strength, a strong need to protect herself. She'd never seen a machete close up before, but she'd practice swinging it until she transformed into a powerful woman. She had to get stronger.

Sounds of small animals in the underbrush. She dug into a jar of peanut butter with two fingers and pushed a chunk in her mouth. The crunchy kind, her favorite.

Machete man wasn't the sneaky type—more the maniac type who attacked head-on. She was almost positive he was dead. But even if he wasn't, she didn't think he'd have the energy for stealthy tracking. Still, she could be wrong. No telling what he'd do.

If she hadn't given the man water, he'd have searched her pack and taken both bottles. These days stealing water was as bad as rape. Taking a person's water could kill. This sounded dramatic, but true. In a single day her world had changed. She'd protect her water and food differently now.

Sudden sounds behind her. She froze, too scared to leave the woods. After a few moments of standing still, she decided to rest awhile. She kicked dead tree limbs out of her way, zipped her jacket, and made a pillow with damp leaves.

⁂

Her head rammed into something solid, and something struck her face. *Be still. Listen.*

A trickle down her cheek; she tasted blood. She reached out her hand and felt the sharp branch of the log that she'd rolled into.

The water bottle lay near and she stroked its sleek, graceful shape. More branches snapping—panicked, she shouldered her pack and felt around for the machete. Definite footsteps moving fast behind her. She took off running. She felt the familiar scratching of brush against her leg; she was nearing another road.

At the road she halted, took a right, and hurried along the road. What day was this? She'd left the apartment a few days ago. No, no, too much had happened. Maybe the explosions happened ten or twelve days ago. And again, the pounding in her head. Woods on one side of the road, fields of stubble on the other. Blue sky with thin red streaks, as if it were dawn—a beach sunrise sky. She loved the beach. But she'd never see the beach again.

Without warning a scrawny dog darted from nowhere and lunged at her. She jumped into a ditch, scooped up a handful of rocks, and aimed at him. He moved off a little way before standing his ground, snarling. She lurched toward him, screamed, and threw more rocks, keeping after him until he slunk into the woods.

The dog could be rabid, he could've bitten her. Yet she felt a pang as it disappeared, because the dog felt familiar. A childhood memory of a dog connected to her mother and father. Then the memory floated off, insubstantial as a cloud. Of course she must have parents somewhere—or had had them, until the explosions came. Even if her memory was shaky these days, she knew she must have parents.

What if machete man was alive and had heard her yelling at the dog? What if he was already tracking her, a bloody rag tied around his head, his mind on revenge?

Stop worrying. Just move.

The few cars she passed had West Virginia license plates. She'd crossed the state line; at least she'd accomplished something. Where could she find maps? Colored lines on paper meant less with the country in upheaval; still, a map would matter if she found someone who knew the area and the safest places to go. Since leaving the city she hadn't seen signs of explosions. And if the explosions had been bombs dropped by planes—well, nothing out here looked worth bombing.

Birds crowded the sky; the inky-colored ravens, crows, and vultures called to each other as they came to feast on bodies that must be near. Around the bend, a car pileup by an interstate off-ramp. The cars had out-of-state plates; they must've tried to detour off the interstate. Vomit rose to the back of throat. She swallowed. Had the highway been blown up? Had the military put up a blockade—did that make sense? What was of military importance, or even symbolic importance, in rural West Virginia? She had no knowledge of the military. Maybe West Virginia was a good place for an installation.

When she reached the number twenty, she stopped counting the vultures walking and flying over the hoods of cars. More vultures poked around inside the automobiles, searching the car carcasses for food. They grunted, barked, and hissed, fighting over food.

If she died right here, winter snow would obliterate her tracks and her body. The vultures and ravens would feast on her, but what difference would another skeleton make?

Her eyes filled, and she wiped her face on her jacket. She wouldn't know anyone out here in the country. How shortsighted she'd been to chase the dog away. The dog was as thirsty and as scared as she was. They could've been company for each other. *Poor Sun Dog.* That had been the dog's name. Sun Dog had waited for her outside a place stinking like a chemistry set, where people ran up and down the halls wearing blue pajamas. A hospital where someone important died when she was a child. *Sun Dog. What a great name for a dog.*

Engine noise in the distance, coming closer, followed by smoke. The sky grew darker, but this was the wrong season for thunder. *No, not the wrong season. Look at the trees, dummy. It must still be June.* But the noise might be from cars over on the interstate. She was leery of the interstate.

Remnants of last year's corn rustled in the fields. If new crops had been planted they hadn't grown much. Maybe it hadn't rained.

The wind through the tattered stalks made a soothing sound. *Focus on the mountains ahead. Walk faster. Forget smoke and noise. Priorities: Water. Food. Shoes.*

Shoes. She backtracked to the wrecked cars and tied a bandana over her mouth and nose—putrid flesh made her gag no matter how many times she came across it—then moved among the cars, glancing inside, focusing on feet and avoiding faces and hands, the most intimate body parts. A woman's legs dangled out of the passenger side of a red car. The hiking shoes on her feet looked to be the right size. Sabine put her hands around a shoe and yanked, pulling off part of the woman's heel with it. She shook the rotted flesh out of the shoe and measured the sole against her own swollen right foot. Almost perfect.

The other shoe came off clean. Brand-new walking shoes, the kind that must have cost two hundred dollars. She needed water to wash the rotten smell out of them. Her own socks smelled rotted too; clean socks were a luxury.

She took a final glance into the red car and spotted a half-empty bottle of water. She drank it all. It helped at first, but then made her thirstier. She checked the car again but didn't see any bottles.

She walked away from the cars, gulped clear air, and tried to stop crying. *Damn it, don't act like a brat, don't snivel and whine.* But, but, this was a real reason to cry. She could cry if she wanted. Who used to yell at her for crying? Probably one of her parents. But they weren't here to yell at her now. And besides, crying could be good news. Tears were made of water. There was a little bit of water in her body.

Keep your mind off crying, off the ache in your head and your dry mouth. She forced herself to think about color. Blue, her favorite. The blue patina on aging Chevies, Caddies, rusted Mustangs, abandoned blue shells of cars, and the sky. Off to the left, a barrel with the words Keep Out. A clump of green along the edge of a fire-blackened field. Someone had torched the field. Ah, there! A scorched tree without leaves. The black streak looked like a lightning strike. There were green buds in the soil at the base of the tree. She knelt

over the tender sprouts and pushed, half-expecting them to disappear, but the seedlings felt solid. Her fingers, when she put them to
her nose, smelled pungent, fresh, and green. The color green had its
own particular smell.

A flash of blue, across the road—the turquoise of an emaciated
child's shorts and halter. The child walked toward her carrying a pitcher
of lemonade. The air didn't stir and the sun burned hot. Summertime.

Next to the road stood a white metal sign peppered with holes
from people using it for target practice. She read aloud, "Welcome
to Big Brook, Home of the Harold County Annual Music Festival.
Population 17,540."

She snorted. "Yeah, right."

Where did the girl with the lemonade go? She forced herself to
think about another color blue, from an Elvis record. She was singing "Blue Moon" on a stage. In the distance, crowds of dead people
clapped and hooted at her off-key singing, a few threw stinking
tomatoes. She bowed—wearing a blue dress, of course.

The prominent blue veins in a lover's hand as he bent over a
notebook in a coffee shop, his silhouette stark against the window.
His long chestnut hair and tight blue T-shirt. Their naked bodies
wrapped around each other. Making love all night, falling asleep
while morning seeped through sheer pink curtains.

The blue of an ocean—except it was not an ocean but rather a
lake, cool and seductive, that lay before her. The bright blue reflected
the sky. Yes! All the water she could hold. She knelt by the lake and
drank, then pulled off her clothes and walked into the cool water,
where she floated and gazed at the sky. Back on shore she washed with
a magic bar of soap and a bottle of shampoo that appeared on the sand
at the lake's edge. She swam and dove under to rinse off. A vulture
dropped a towel and clean clothes. She ignored the vulture, took the
towel and dried off. She washed her socks and scrubbed the rotten
flesh out of her new shoes. The shoes and socks dried themselves,
spinning in circles above her head.

Cross-legged on the ground, she telescoped and studied herself from a distance. Within minutes, the clothes turned into tiny, dark, twittering birds. She giggled until their beaks grew long, sharp, and ominous, and the twitters turned into terrible screeching.

She grabbed her filthy clothes from the birds and hurried away.

When her stomach growled, she thought at first that it was hunger. But then her bowels moved and a hot, foul-smelling liquid ran down her leg. She was sick. *Drink more water to avoid dehydration. Water. Food. Soap. Everything.*

∂

She woke the following morning lying in weeds beside a deserted roadside store. She stayed still, exhausted. Her jeans were stiff with dried diarrhea, but at least the stink wasn't fresh. The lake, the vulture with a towel, and the awful birds were gone. A mirage?

Her head hurt and her face felt tight, dirty, and sunburned. Her feet ached. She whimpered and finished off the last of her water. Her stomach still ached. She dug around in her pack hoping to find some Nabs, anything to eat. Instead she found an old pair of cut-off jeans and a gauzy orange dress, mashed flat. She examined the clothes as if they'd landed from outer space. Summer clothes from a beach trip in another life, a carefree week, so carefree she'd forgotten to unpack. Back when actions didn't have dire consequences.

For the first time, she tried to find her wallet. But it must've fallen out of the pack—no probably the kid in the store took it, after he hit her. Money didn't mean much at the moment, but a driver's license would have; it held information, like her last name.

Since the explosions, her mind had felt slow and confused. Maybe it was shock, or maybe the bash to her head. One thing she did recall: almost three years ago, she'd launched herself into being a missing person without a family. That must've been when she'd shredded her credit cards. Now, she had no place to live.

Chapter 2

WOLF MOON

June 15, 2014.

All morning the trees blurred when Sabine moved her head. She felt herself swaying, almost falling. Maybe she was walking funny. That engine noise again—louder than yesterday, or the day before. A big engine; maybe a tractor? Through the hazy air she picked out a large shape: a red truck headed toward her, bumping across the rutted field, dust rising from its wheels among shriveled beans and ragged corn stalks.

She steadied the machete in front of her. Run and hide? Wave? Before she could decide the truck juddered to a stop in front of her, and the driver cut the engine. The field went silent, followed by cricket sounds. Through the mud-spattered windshield, she saw the faces of two men.

The driver hung out the open window. "You alone?"

His question was so strange she just stared at him. *Careful. Careful. They could be crazy or maybe rapists.* She waited.

"It's okay," the driver said. "We just want to ask some questions."

She moved close enough to see the man in the passenger's seat smiling as he held up open hands to show he was harmless. He wore a red T-shirt.

Hard to think what to do. She didn't move closer but said, "I'm alone. Walking since . . . maybe two weeks. Or three. But no live people for, well, I don't . . . know. Too tired. Walking, things get blurry. A man came at me. But that's over." She squeezed the machete handle.

"My name's Hank Johnson," the driver said. "What's your name?"

"Dunno." *Careful what you say.* "Why do you wanna know?"

"If you're a person, you can name a name. Just trying to get to know you. So, where you from?"

"I live in . . . I *did* live in an apartment. In DC. I walked here. My mind's fuzzy. . . ."

He nodded. "It's okay. A group of us are staying in a house not far from here. Want to come with us?"

"What house?" She inched toward the truck.

Hank said. "A farmhouse near here. Are you hungry?"

"Yes," she said. "And thirsty."

The man in the red shirt wore a baseball cap. He opened the passenger door. Sabine limped to the truck and climbed in without hesitation, because her choices . . . better not to think about choices. She couldn't go on much longer; her body was in ruins. They wouldn't waste a bullet on her if she ran.

The truck cab reeked of cigarette smoke. Her head began pounding, but she was past caring. Then, suddenly, she wanted a cigarette. How many years had it been since she'd smoked?

"This guy here is Sharp," Hank said. He reached across Sharp and handed her a can of Pepsi.

She gulped down half the warm cola and tried to give it back to Hank.

"I drank too much," she apologized, belching. "And I'm filthy. I stink."

"Drink the whole can. We'll keep the windows open." Hank laughed.

"Yeah, you do stink." Sharp pulled his ball cap down over his face and made gagging sounds.

Hank laughed again. "Don't worry, we all stank when we got here." He looked at her. "You've got a big gash on your cheek too, ya know. It's kinda bloody."

Sharp pulled off his cap and ran his hand through his curls.

She took another gulp of soda. "My name's Sabine. I don't remember my last name."

"Sabine's a beautiful name," Hank said. "Don't be scared. We'll get you fixed up with food. Our place is just down the road."

"How many bombs went off near you?" Sharp asked. "Did you walk on the interstates? Did you see many wrecked cars?"

Too many questions. Sabine said nothing.

"You sure you lived in DC?" Hank asked.

Another question.

Hank pulled onto the road and squinted through the windshield. "I'm from DC too. I lived close to the Capitol. Whereabouts did you live?"

"The sidewalks collapsed," Sabine said. "It was hard to walk on the rubble . . . I think near Rock Creek Park?" She closed her eyes. "The buildings were swaying. I got out fast. Cities are the worst, so I went west on back roads. Walking and walking and finally no malls. Fields. A few farms with lanterns, but I couldn't tell if they were safe so I steered clear."

"Smart," Sharp said. "A good survival skill. Few trustworthy people in times like this."

"What day is it? My body feels like I walked a month."

"Today's June 15th," Sharp said. "If you started walking the day of the bombs, May 26th, you walked twenty-one days."

She tried to calculate to see if he was right, but couldn't focus.

"We're gonna stop for the dogs," Hank said.

She wanted to tell them about machete man she'd killed, or probably killed. And the dog she chased away. But the warm truck cab made her drowsy. She eased her head onto Sharp's shoulder.

A voice dictated to her from inside a dream. The stern voice said: *Stop for the dogs. The dogs of sanity. City people won't buy a blue velvet sofa, or take off in a spaceship, or play ball in a city street once they run through tall prairie grass.* A sign, propped in a garbage can, marked the trail to the higher grasses. She peeked inside the can; a rotten pastrami sandwich and a gravy boat lay at the bottom.

Her body shifted when the truck turned onto a bumpy road and her eyes flew open. They stopped at an aluminum farm gate. Sharp got out and hunched over the gate. She couldn't figure what he was doing until he swung it open and Hank drove through. Sharp locked the gate and hopped in the truck. Her head eased back onto his shoulder.

Hank drove a little way, left the engine running, and climbed out. He whistled. In a few minutes, three dogs ran from the woods. The two big ones jumped in the back of the truck. Hank picked up the little dog and put him up there with them.

Hank talked in a low voice. "My Little Gun, and my Big Rom and Big Remus. There, there now, you boys calm down. You boys been good?" His voice was kind, soothing.

They rode up the hill toward a large wood-frame farmhouse in the shade of two giant trees.

"Great dogs with keen noses," Hank said. "They showed up around the time Sharp and I got here. Right starved, so we fed them scraps, then Kate took over feeding them. They never left. Their owners are dead, most likely. These labs are good hunting dogs and the little one's some kind of terrier. Without them, we might've starved. They love riding in the truck."

She fell asleep again and the dream words returned: *On the sign is a map to the outlaw tribe's homeland, called The Dogs of Sanity Lands. A long walk but the destination is worth the walk. The dogs take turns carrying two sticks in their mouths, for talking. Blue raven, wild turkey, and raccoon help you answer riddles before they guide you to the tribe's*

meeting hall. In a circle the dogs' furry shoulders touch. The tribe will ask
questions and only smart dogs can join.

Hank's hand on her shoulder shook her awake. She forced open
her eyes and stared up at him for a few seconds before she recognized
his sandy hair, cut close to his skull like a Marine's.

Her head throbbed as she struggled out of the truck.

He picked up her machete and pack. "I got these."

"Are you a Marine?" she asked.

"A Marine? Nope."

"It's your haircut." Giddy with exhaustion, she laughed. She followed Hank through the backdoor, wondering about the Dogs of
Sanity. Had she seen many dogs while she was walking? Only the
one who resembled Sun Dog, the dog she'd known when she was a
kid.

Sharp was already in the kitchen talking to a woman with a long
blond braid. He asked the woman to give Sabine food. The woman
pointed to a table. Another man walked in, put his hand on her
butt, and squeezed.

"Tommy, stop!" The blond woman pushed away his hand with
a giggle and dished up a bowl of meat stew. Sabine sat at the table,
and the woman put the bowl and a piece of bread with peanut butter
on it in front of her.

"My name's Kate," she said. "This guy"—she pointed to the man
who'd squeezed her—"is Tommy."

Sabine nodded. "Water. Please. Water."

Kate brought water. Sabine drank and handed the glass to
her for more. She brought another glassful, but said, "Go slow on
the water, or you'll throw up. You aren't used to drinking normal
amounts. Same goes for the food."

Sabine tried to sip the water slowly and chew the food with
care, reminding herself not to gobble. When her stomach felt full,
she yawned and swayed with fatigue.

Hank held a candle in a wooden candlestick. He picked up her

pack and machete, and led her to a corner of the kitchen, where a
flight of stairs led up to the second story. At the end of a long hall,
he opened a door and guided her with his hand on the small of her
back. He set the candle on a table by the bed and lit it. He put her
things on the floor.

"We're in the attic," Hank said. "This will be your room. The
bathroom's at the end of the hall, so take the candle when you go.
Even with moonlight through the windows, the hallway's long and
dark. If we have electricity, it'll be in the morning, and you can take
a quick shower then. Someone will get you for breakfast." He flicked
a glance at the candle. "Don't burn the place down. Good night."

He shut the door.

Blow out the candle.

⁓

Sabine woke at dawn to a silent house, her body stiff and head
aching. The stuffy room smelled rank. Her body. She'd fallen asleep
on top of the coverlet, still wearing her filthy jeans and jacket. The
man who'd driven the truck and guided her upstairs? *Hank.* The guy
with sandy hair who looked like a Marine, but said he wasn't.

She rooted in her pack and pulled out her other pair of jeans
and the one T-shirt that didn't smell. With socks and tennis shoes
in hand, she stumbled to the bathroom. She studied the gash on
her face in the cracked bathroom mirror. The bloody line ran from
her temple down her cheek; no more sleeping in leaves in the dark
without checking surroundings first. Still, her cheek didn't hurt as
bad as her big toe.

Soon she would have to sit with strangers at the breakfast table.

While the tennis shoes and socks soaked in water and detergent
from the box under the sink, she drank water from the showerhead,
then sluiced water all over and rubbed at places still caked with
diarrhea. She winced while soaping when she felt the raised skin
of a scar on her stomach, even though the scar no longer hurt. She

hurriedly scrubbed her hair, aware that the warm water might run out; then she quickly soaped and rinsed again.

Still wet, she sat on the toilet and enjoyed the feel of water on her body. She wrapped a warm washcloth around her sore toe and counted to one hundred before taking it off. The toe throbbed when she hurried to her room. She laid her shoes and socks on a towel to dry. Her jacket, jeans, and the coverlet went to the bottom of the armoire against the wall. She'd wash it all later, if the washing machine worked.

Barefooted, she waited for someone to take her to breakfast. She peered out of a window, searching the landscape. Sun shone on a creek running through the field toward the woods. A crumbling barn, a broken-down shed, and a chicken coop stood near the house. A wind turbine spun on the nearest ridge. The dogs barked and ran around the yard. Dogs. What in hell were the Dogs of Sanity? Confused by the dream, she squeezed her eyes tight. If she cried, it would make her head hurt more. If she moved too fast, things went all blurry.

Someone tapped on her door. Hank. He held out a red candle on a saucer and a box of matches. "Your personal candle. You have two. Once you've burned these down to nothing, you can have more."

She put the candle on the dresser.

"You're the last one," Hank said.

"The last what?" Her heart sped up.

"You make nine. The house is full. We won't take in more people, not unless they bring their own food and can shoot straight."

"Oh. Okay." She should ask why they took her in. But not now.

"You had on shoes when you got here."

She pointed to the towel. "I washed them. I pulled them off a dead woman."

"You'll get splinters from these old floors."

"My feet are swollen. My toe even more. My socks were filthy, so I washed them, too."

"Sit."

She sat, and before she could stop him, he knelt and took her foot in his hands. She flinched when he touched her, but let him hold her foot.

He poked around her toes. "The cut's infected. How did you do it?"

"I went after a better spot to wash in this creek, took off my shoes to climb over some rocks. Who knows what filth was in the creek."

He stood and laid his hand on her forehead. "You have a fever. I've got aspirin and antibiotic ointment. I'll get you a tube. I've got toothbrushes and toothpaste, too. Do you need that?"

"I've been chewing gum. A toothbrush and some toothpaste would be great." She looked up at him. "You're a good guy. You're the . . . leader?"

"Kind of. Several of us are. Kate, the woman who fed you, runs the house. Sharp and I take care of the outside, we scrounge food and tools. We check out shooting skills when we take in people, and train the people who need practice. We work on watch teams; the good shots work in teams."

"Guess there's no time for music, or anything fun," she said. "Are we safe here? I'm so tired of walking."

"We're waiting for more information before we decide to stay or leave. To take folks' minds off the heavy stuff, sometimes I read stories after dinner. You hungry?"

"Yes." She laid her hand on his arm. "Thanks."

Hank didn't respond, but she didn't mind. He'd heard her. A wave of gratitude flooded her as she followed him down the creaky back stairs. She leaned against the wall and slid, afraid the steps would blur and she'd fall.

Sabine's heart pounded as she entered the kitchen and slipped into the chair next to Hank. She glanced around: nine people counting herself. Everyone said their names. She nodded, but the names ran through her like water. Except for Sharp, Hank, and Kate. She was the woman with the blond braid. The person in charge of the house.

Hank brought three aspirins and water to the table. Sabine thanked him. Two of the men ate quickly, without talking, then left. Hank said, "They're on watch. You'll learn about chores and the watch."

She served herself a big helping of venison and three small boiled potatoes. Halfway through, she stopped eating to let the food settle. To restrain herself from taking another serving, she put her hands in her lap and touched her stomach. It felt tight with food, yet she wanted to eat all day.

After breakfast Hank pointed to the refrigerator. "Folks—and this includes you, Sabine—there are three pieces of paper tacked on the fridge. The first lays out the rules: No stealing. No going in other people's rooms without permission. No gossip. Report infractions to me, Sharp, or Kate. By the rules you'll see the watch list. If Sharp or I have tested your gun skills and given you the okay, sign up. Tommy and I will walk the watch tonight. The watch is a bear and team people get tired. But after tonight, the schedule's blank."

Hank turned his attention back to Sabine. "A watch team has two people. The teams are armed. We walk the property for eight-, sometimes twelve-hour shifts."

"Got it," she said.

"Sabine still has a fever, most likely from her infected foot," Hank said to the rest of the room. "Today she'll get two small chores. We'll increase her responsibilities when she feels better."

A guy with a mustache took off his ball cap and set it beside his plate, then flashed Sabine an impish grin. "In case you forgot, my name's Tommy." He looked around the table and cocked his head. "Come on, guys. Let's spread out the watch team fun." He acted as if walking the perimeter for hours was like a night at the circus.

Sabine heard murmurs about signing up, but she let the conversations wash over her. She couldn't handle a gun and had nothing to contribute.

The side of her face hurt, which triggered an image of hiding in

the woods, followed by a short film clip of the machete man attack-
ing her again and again. Then his head lying in blood, his eyes open
wide, not seeing the sky. Sabine the killer, who didn't know her last
name.

She copied Hank as he scraped his leftovers into a bucket. She
left her plate on the counter, gave him a nod, and went up the back
stairs. Finally, safe in her room with its comforting slanted walls.
A protected sleeping place. Sleep would help her forget the dead
man. Maybe even bring dreams about her life before the bombs. By
the light outside she guessed it was about nine in the morning. She
wanted to sleep all day and through the night. Enjoy the luxury of
cool, clean sheets.

She'd just drifted off when a sound jerked her awake. The door
opened and Hank appeared. He stood still and glanced around
before approaching her bed.

Sabine sat up, her heart beating faster. But he wasn't interested in her. There was nothing alive behind his eyes. He was a
take-charge kind of man, coiled tight inside. He dropped tubes of
antibiotic cream and toothpaste, along with a toothbrush, on the
foot of her bed and left.

Sabine exhaled with relief, sat up, and rubbed the cream on her
toe and down her cheek. Mysterious Hank. She'd never met anyone
like him, or like Sharp. Had one of them taken her machete? It
wasn't on the floor where her pack still lay. The armoire door stood
open, empty except for her dirty clothes and the coverlet. There was
a small table by the bed, a desk and chair in front of one window,
a wobbly dresser. Nothing else. She'd watched Hank while he was
in her room. Someone must've taken it while she slept. A flash of
anger. Did someone think she planned to murder everyone in their
beds? She'd find the right time to discover who took it. Head on the
pillow, she closed her eyes.

ॐ

For the following three days Sabine dozed off and on, waking around meal times. In the kitchen, Hank or Kate would feel her head and give her aspirin when it hurt, even when she didn't have a fever. Sometimes she wasn't hungry, and she lay in bed while the others ate, staring at the walls and out the window in a dreamy daze, trying to make her old apartment or images of her parents materialize.

On the fourth morning she felt energetic and her forehead felt cool. She crept down the back stairs.

The backdoor stood open. Hank, Sharp, and some other people stood around a pickup truck talking about the engine. She sat on the stoop and watched. No one noticed her or tried to start a conversation. She didn't know some of their names and they didn't ask hers. Maybe Hank had told people she was crazy and they planned to kick her out, so they shouldn't bother talking with her. She felt insubstantial, unwanted.

Yet Hank and Sharp could've raped and killed her in the field where they found her. Was she somehow special? Or were they being kind because they saw her as a loser who had lost her memory? What were their intentions? Maybe someone had taken her machete intending to use it on her. *No, that doesn't make sense.* They had guns—and anyway, what reason would they have? *Stop acting like a loser. You have to smile, act friendly and happy to be here.*

The guy with a mustache, Tommy, joined the others. When he glanced over at the porch, she smiled and he flashed a grin. Maybe they weren't conspiring, just busy. After all, they had more important issues than a crazy woman with a bad memory.

Inside she made a peanut butter sandwich for herself and ate it hanging over the sink. When she finished eating, she'd look for Kate and offer to help her fix lunch. Voices coming down the hall, moving to the veranda. She stuffed the last of the sandwich in her mouth, crept to the living room, and opened the window a few inches. She flattened against the wall so they couldn't see her. Hank discussed the day's foray. "Today we need canned tuna, Spam, and salmon, or whatever you can find. Also kerosene for the lanterns, and gas for the blue truck."

"Like gluttons, we ate both the hams that were curing in the shed," Sharp said. "From now on, we eat only fresh meat we kill or canned meat. It's summer—we should eat more vegetables, corn, and potatoes. The shed's nothing but rubble, so we won't be smoking meat."

Sabine left the window, forced herself to amble outside and sit in a rocker.

Hank was saying, "No worries about meat, Sharp. Let's hunt today. You with me in the blue truck. No one rides in back; we gotta leave room for a big deer, cause I'm feeling lucky. Tommy, can you take a look at the red truck and try to fix it? It's not for shit. Jen and Paul will go out on watch."

Which guy was Paul? The redheaded boy who was pulling a cap out of his pocket. Hank had told her he'd arrived the day before she did. Jen must be the short young woman she'd noticed yesterday.

Sharp called the dogs. "Gun, Rom, Reeeemus! Gun, Rom, Reeeemus!" The dogs came running on the first call, and just like before, the two big ones jumped right into the truck. Sharp picked up the little dog and put him in the back with them.

At the bottom of the hill, the truck stopped, and Sharp jumped out to unlock and relock the gate padlocks. Kate told her they might come back at lunchtime, but usually they were gone until three or four. The truck turned left and moved down the state road.

Sabine loved the quiet field in front of the house. It was restful. And after the crisis—and it would end eventually, wouldn't it?—she would remember Sharp. Not only because he'd rescued her. Today the handsome man wore a red work shirt instead of a T-shirt. She supposed he always rode shotgun.

Before Hank pulled away, Sharp had looked at Sabine directly, out the truck window. She'd smiled, but he'd merely nodded with a bored expression. She'd glanced away as if his snub meant nothing.

Women probably came on to Sharp all the time. Sabine's mind was full of holes, she looked like shit, and she had probably killed a man. Why would Sharp be interested in her? And why should she bother? Even with the watch teams, the farmhouse could be overrun with refugees and they could be blown away while sleeping in their beds.

⚘

By late morning the farm had electricity. Sabine emptied her pack onto her bed and surveyed her possessions. The orange dress, two thick notebooks, a cell phone, two pairs of jeans, three T-shirts, and a few pairs of socks and underwear. A lightweight jacket and her wonderful red shawl, which she'd wash by hand. She got her dirty clothes and coverlet and put everything except what she was wearing in the washing machine. When they were done, she hung them on the clothesline in the yard and wandered to the barn.

She stopped by the doors. Too eerie and dark inside, with a strong manure smell. She walked to the rickety garage. Plenty of junk piled at one end, and along one side, piles of plastic garbage bags full of paper to burn in the fireplace. Nothing promising, until she noticed an old pickup truck. Did it still run? Probably not. Someone would've checked it out already.

Two men's loud voices at the water pump. At the word "bombs" Sabine stepped into the shadow of the garage door. The tall skinny man repeated, "Bombs. What do you know? In college I researched dirty bombs. Dirty bombs scare people, and you don't need planes."

The man with a blond ponytail stopped soaping his face. "Damn. Today's a hot one. I'll need another washing later."

The tall skinny man repeated himself.

"Sol, my man, you don't have a grasp on what happened," blond ponytail said. "You read some articles. Big deal. Maybe what happened is bigger than bombs in major cities." He pulled off his shirt and wiped his chest with a towel, dropped his jeans and wiped his

legs. A bowie knife was strapped to his calf. He stood spread-eagle
and dried his face and hair.

Sol ducked under the pump, let water run over his shoulders
and head. "Nah. Just a few big cities got hit. That's probably it." He
toweled his head.

"Then how come most of my family's dead and Barnville's in
ruins?" blond ponytail demanded. "And what about the empty houses
and farms we passed on the way here? Explain that to me, boy genius."

"Your farm must be near some kind of secret installation." Sol
shrugged as if he didn't believe his own explanation.

She waited until the men went inside before stepping out from
the shadows. Why attack a rural area? It was all scary, and even scar-
ier because she couldn't fit the pieces together. *Don't be a jerk, but
don't worry about being friendly. Ask questions and snoop for information.*

She retreated to her room, grabbing two clean water bottles on
the way. They both went in her backpack, which she stowed in the
armoire. Ready in case of an emergency.

❧

The blond man from the pump wasn't at the lunch table. When
he did finally arrive he mumbled an excuse for coming in late, but
no one seemed to notice. He sat down next to Sabine and his arm
brushed hers when he served himself.

"What's your name?" she asked him. "Sorry. I'm having memory
problems." She took two pieces of rabbit and handed the platter to
him.

"Jude. Jude Smoot. And you're Sabine, the woman without a
last name." He smelled like soap and sounded like a hillbilly, with
his wonderful foreign accent.

"You're from around here?" she asked.

"A town about fifty miles away, called Barnville."

"I live in DC . . . or I did, but my apartment building's gone,"
Sabine said. "It collapsed after a bomb exploded nearby."

Jude gazed straight at her. Pale eyebrows, long blond hair tied back with a leather string. One of his eyes was pale blue, the other brown. Exotic. Everything she knew about men who lived in the mountains came from TV Westerns and cartoons. Farmers, hunters, and trappers went to small-town parades and cookouts with moonshine and pigs roasting on spits. Some of the men yelled at their tired-looking wives while their kids ran around the yard yelling and hitting things with sticks. Big families where kids could be Cub Scout–4H types, or bullies, or both. The men, and the women, had leathery faces. They wore ball caps and cowboy hats, convincing themselves the brims protected them. She'd read in the newspaper once that farmers were at high risk for melanoma.

Everything she was thinking sounded awful, she realized, feeling squirmy. She would never say any of it out loud. Jude's eyes didn't reveal anything about his personality, yet she wondered what else might be different about him. She liked his slow-talking drawl and his polite, kind manner. Next mealtime she'd sit at the table early and slip her jacket on the chair to her right. Maybe he'd figure out what she wanted. She hoped he'd treat her like an ordinary person, not a crazy person. He was cute. She'd flirt with him and find out about the other people living at the farm.

She hated mirrors, because she couldn't predict what she'd see these days. What might a mirror reveal that she needed to keep hidden? She must do more than drag a comb through her hair and yank out knots. Find shampoo. Shreds of a bar of soap smelled nice, but left her hair limp. She hated the smell of dirty hair; after those twenty-one days of walking, clean hair now felt as important to her as a clean body did.

꙾

That night Sabine lay in bed planning the best times of day to snoop and take advantage of eavesdropping opportunities. She'd liked spying on people ever since she was a kid—that she could remember. She'd loved to ferret out secrets, and her family had been full of them. Snooping and eavesdropping took less energy than trying to wheedle secrets from people who didn't want to tell them. Yet she risked making incorrect assumptions if she didn't ask questions.

From the small room downstairs she could eavesdrop on people in the living room. Hank and Kate would be her first targets. Kate was in charge of the house, which didn't sound as important as Hank's decision-making. Sabine was wary of Kate, she had some sort of alliance with Hank. Sex, or something else, even though Tommy was her boyfriend, or so she claimed.

Sharp was sitting on Sabine's other side. She had already served herself two small slices of venison, but now, before she could stop herself, she said, "Kate, could you pass the meat?"

Kate pushed the platter in her direction.

Sharp looked at Sabine's plate. "Take all the food you want."

Surprised Sharp had spoken to her, her cheeks grew hot. She took another slice of venison, some more green beans, and a small portion of the fried potatoes and onions, which were greasy and fragrant.

"You walked a long way with little or no food," Sharp said. "You could use more flesh on your bones."

"Thanks," she said. Nothing else to say.

Sharp didn't talk much but when he did, people paid attention. His confident manner and deep, articulate voice reminded Sabine of a radio announcer. Sharp mostly hung around with Hank, the two often laughing at private jokes. She spotted them often, walking through the fields together. Whenever she felt Sharp watching her, she put a sway in her hips and slowed her pace, hoping he'd catch up with her. But so far he hadn't. Other than Sharp, Jude was the most interesting man at the farmhouse.

Sabine rested her elbows on the wobbly table in her room. It swayed in a rhythm almost as comforting as a rocking chair. With its slanted walls, the attic room felt familiar and cozy. If she had any ugly attic memories, they would have emerged by now, and none had. Nothing bad had ever happened to her in an attic.

The rocky land surrounding the house was more rugged than she had expected. The state license plates read "Wild and Wonderful." But dwelling on license plates led Sabine to recall decomposing bodies in abandoned cars, and she had to picture a restraining hand in front of her face to quell the images of bodies. The mountains reminded her of a Cherokee warrior on the cover of a coffee table book. The Cherokee people had been the first in the Great Smoky Mountains, and had named them so because they appeared to emit smoke. The Cherokee studied the moon, tying its cycles to crops and their cycles of hunger and satiation; their celebrations permeated all aspects of their lives. The Appalachian Mountains were softer and rounded. They framed, surrounded, and protected the farm and her new family. Everyone had a story about where they had been and what they'd been doing when the bombs went off—stories of how they'd escaped and come to the farm. But Sabine had only heard a couple of their tales. Some of them had probably told their stories before she arrived.

Chapter 3

REFUGE MOON

July 5, 2014.

The foragers discovered three jars of honey, which was cause for celebration. A tin of cinnamon and jar of honey sat on the breakfast table. Morning sunlight shone through the jar, turning it a caramel color, as luxurious to see as it was to spread on toast. The foragers had fought armed strangers for the kerosene, gas, and food. They gave scant details, and Sabine didn't ask for more, afraid the images would leak into her dreams. But to show interest and gratitude, she forced herself to listen to their foraging stories.

After breakfast she said, "Kate, I've been here since mid-June, and still don't know much about the foragers' routine." She scraped food off dishes into the pail, handed Kate the stack of dirty dishes, and went back to the table.

"Sometimes they come back with full gas cans, occasionally rabbits, on rare days a deer," Kate said. "On lucky days Jen and the men bring a table up from the cellar and set it in the yard. They skin the game, and I make soups and stews. But more and more, they don't bring meat."

"Here. More dishes." Sabine set glasses and silverware on the counter. "The table is clear. I wiped down the table and chairs."

Kate dried her hands. "Sit. I have a request."

Sabine threw the sponge in the sink and sat.

"We need someone to record our experiences," Kate said. "I want you to be our scribe. You've been eating our food, it's past time for you to take on chores. I'm too busy. Describe the farm and our activities and interview everyone. People in the future might discover the log. I have empty notebooks if you need more of them. We'll talk more later, but go on and get started."

"How did you find out I have notebooks?"

"I'm not supposed to talk about the process," Kate said.

Sabine narrowed her eyes. "What do you mean?"

Kate shrugged. "We had to check you out. Someone went through your backpack the night you arrived, while you were sleeping. They found notebooks and scraps of paper with poems. You might not be the best writer in the world, but you're the best we've got."

"Someone searched my pack?" Sabine asked, her face heating. "Do people just wander into *your* room?"

Kate's voice was cool. "We didn't know you. Hank picked you up in a field."

Sabine felt defeated. And she didn't trust Kate's agenda. No matter what Kate told her to do, she'd write what she pleased. *Pacify her. Pretend to do what she asks.*

"Okay," she said. "I'll do it."

She wanted to find out more about the people she was living with anyway. Writing fit with her snooping and might help her find clues, form a line from the city to the farmhouse, and fill in the gaps before the explosions. She'd put off the interviews, though. Those sounded scary. And no one would tell the truth anyway.

⁂

Most nights they gathered in the living room and Paul lit a fire in the oversized fireplace. Sol complained about wasted firewood, since West Virginia nights weren't cool. But warmth and light drew people together. Hank sat in the honored easy chair and read from one of the library's novels. Sabine thought of the big chair as Papa's chair in "Goldilocks and the Three Bears." The Papa feeling was one reason they followed Hank's lead. He read Poe's "The Gold-Bug" and "The Imp of the Perverse." Sabine asked him to read *A Midsummer Night's Dream*, but he rolled his eyes. Sol suggested they each pick a part, pass the book around, and read the play together. Sabine agreed, but no one else did.

"No more reading," Hank said. "Tomorrow night we go over the chores."

The following day, while she and Hank pulled weeds in the garden, he asked her to take notes at the meeting. She mumbled that she didn't want to take notes.

Hank's face flushed. "What? You don't want to? Do it anyway."

She forced herself to look away as if she hadn't heard, or didn't care, how he'd just ordered her around like a bratty child, humiliating her. Kate, Tommy, and Jen were working at the other end of the garden staking pole beans and tomatoes. She didn't think they'd heard, though she wasn't sure.

☙

After dinner that night Sabine brought two candles to the living room to illuminate a writing corner. Hank had told her a good writer listened, watched, and rarely spoke.

Once Hank settled into Papa's chair he said, "People, some of you are slacking, chores aren't getting done. We're not a hotel. We need to see if we can work together, if we can start building a community here, before we have to go somewhere safer."

Kate stood. "The chore list is posted on the refrigerator. Basic chores at the top must be done daily. Big chores at the bottom, once or twice a month. For example, Paul and Tommy just chopped wood, separated it into wet and dry piles, and stacked the piles by the porch. They covered the piles with tarps. This week Jen will remind you all to check the chore list and sign up.

"Sabine, you'll tend the dogs," Kate said. "Fresh water in their bowls twice a day. Let the dogs out in the morning, call them in before dark, and feed them. If the dogs won't come, you have to look for them. Any time you see strangers lurking around, call the dogs in immediately. I mean immediately."

"You already told me this," Sabine said. "Why are you treating me like I can't do this?"

"Because you need repetition," Kate said.

"At home our dogs slept on the porch, on old blankets," Sol broke in. "The dogs dirty up the sofas and shed hair; soon this house is gonna end up smelling like a kennel. Dogs are pack animals and belong outside."

"We can't let them sleep outside," Hank said. "They'll be stolen, or shot and eaten. Once you're here a while, you'll appreciate the dogs. The game population has dwindled. Our dogs are good hunters."

"They'd be good watchdogs at night," Sol said.

"Sometimes we take one dog with us. It depends," Hank said. "Game's scarce. We need to protect our dogs."

"If you see the scrap can full," Kate continued, "take it to the compost pile. Pull weeds, especially while seeds are sprouting and need growing room. Save paper trash to burn in the fireplace. Dust and sweep the first floor and the second-floor hallway. Clean your own room. If you haven't signed up for a chore, do it. The days or nights you're on watch, you won't have a chore." Kate glanced around the room. "Questions?"

Jen, a boyish, grim-looking girl, said, "If Sabine gets tired of feeding the dogs, I'll do it."

"Thanks. Anything else?"

No one spoke. Kate leaned back on the sofa and snuggled with Tommy.

Hank yawned. "Sharp and I found Sabine in a field on June 15th. She was supposed to be the last person we'd take in. Yesterday—which, by the way, was the Fourth of July—Lavinia and Randolph flagged me down on the road." He nodded to the two newcomers, who were sitting together a little apart from the group. "They talked me into letting them join us, at least for a few days."

Hank looked at Jen. "What about you?"

"Been here awhile." Jen crossed her arms. "People know me."

"Doing things together and talking is how you get to understand people." Kate said this with a smirk, like she was talking to a simpleton.

"I don't wanna know more about you people. You can tell about me by how well I handle a gun." Jen chuckled, but when no one laughed with her, her neck turned red.

Tommy broke the silence. "I'm the loudmouth Italian boy. Kate and I planned to live on a farm and have kids one day in the future—and you can bet it wasn't supposed to be like this."

"Since everybody eats, you all know the woman in the kitchen," Kate said. "I taught math at the same high school as Tommy. Before." She raised her head with a tired smile.

"Kate keeps the place running," Hank said.

The freckled, redheaded boy, Paul, sat cross-legged on the floor by Jen. "I'm fifteen. I hitched here from the Upper Peninsula—that's in Michigan. I live with my Pop and Gramps."

"Why here, Paul?" Sol asked. "The UP's remote. Isn't it a good place to be at a time like this?"

Paul shook his head. "It's isolated, but it's also damn cold. A mistake will kill you, and without resources you won't make it. If bombs took out Detroit Metro, what's next? You-all did hear about the airports in Boston, DC, and Atlanta?"

Randolph said, "And perhaps Charleston airport, I'm not—"

"Detroit? That far away?" Tommy asked.

"The point is," Paul interjected, "I gotta locate someone who lives around here. Before it's too late."

"Who?" Sol said.

Paul glared at Sol. "Family business. Okay?" He nudged Jen.

"Okay, okay," she grumbled. "The name's Jen Morgan, I'm twenty-five, from a wide place in the road, down in Kentucky. I graduated high school, and could've gone to college on a basketball scholarship. Yeah, I'm real short, but I'm real fast. I wanna stay with you folks, so if we have to leave, I'll come along. After this bomb stuff blows over, I'm heading out West to take up bull riding."

Sabine could imagine Jen in a cowboy hat and boots, reveling in bull riding and roping. But Jen was naive to think this chaos would just "blow over."

"What's your story?" Jen frowned at Randolph and Lavinia. "You-all don't look like the type to enjoy farm living."

Though she acted like a simple country girl, Sabine thought that under the bluster, Jen was astute.

Randolph and Lavinia sat in ladder-back chairs, shoulders touching. "I'm Randolph Edward Lewis, IV. I'm from Richmond, where I still live." He looked like a middle-aged banker with his bald head, paunch, and Ben Franklin glasses. "Before grad school I was in banking."

Bingo, Sabine thought.

"Now I'm an electrical engineer. This is Lavinia Milvain, my fiancée. She's also from Richmond."

Lavinia didn't speak. She was a gaunt woman in her twenties with short, pale hair. Sabine wondered if she had cancer, or maybe anorexia. She looked out of place in her long yellow skirt with a ruffled hem and its matching blouse; everyone else here wore shorts or jeans. Jen had spoken the truth: these two did not look like they would enjoy farm living.

"Tell them what you do, Lala," Randolph said. "It's interesting."

Lavinia kept inspecting her feet.

"Since she finished prep school, Lala has been training show horses," Randolph said. "She gives riding lessons on a farm outside Richmond. Not a working farm, of course. The farm has two stables for horses and riding rings. I own a few show horses. And horses are how we met." Randolph patted Lavinia's hand.

Hank pointed to Sharp.

"Malcolm Sharp, I live in Quantico."

"Sharp's your last name," Jen said. "And all this time I thought Sharp was your nickname because you're a great shot. Are you Special Ops?"

Hank turned to Sol. "Want to go next?"

"Wait!" Sol said. "Sharp hasn't told us anything."

"I'm just a regular guy who repairs appliances," Sharp said. "I work out at the gym. Friends come over to my place for pizza and beer and we play poker or watch a ball game."

Sabine coughed to stifle a laugh. Appliances? She didn't have any idea what Sharp did, but he was more fit than most men and she couldn't imagine him in a shop tinkering with toasters and making house calls to repair refrigerators. Sharp was military, possibly something secret. He had a cold way of piercing through your eyes, right into your brain. Hank got the same look, at times.

She also wondered why Sharp always wore red shirts, but of course, she wouldn't ask. Too personal.

"If you don't live on base, why Quantico? The town's a dump," Sol said.

"My family's from Northern Virginia." Sharp kept his eyes on the fire, his mouth clamped shut.

Hank glanced at Sol, who rose from his chair. "Solomon Henley. Thirty-one, and too old to be working at a pizza place. I've put myself through two years of community college. This coming fall I'll transfer to Charlottesville to finish undergrad at the university there, then start grad school in business. That is, if the university's open. I come from a farm family. I have two brothers." Sol gave a little bow. His attempt to charm surprised Sabine.

"Thanks, Sol," Hank said. "Sabine?"

Everyone sat in silence, expectant. They were accustomed to her not talking.

"I'm from DC," Sabine said. "After an explosion, my building started falling apart. I ran out the door and headed west, figuring it was the safest place. End of story." She looked around and blurted out, "Jude, what about you?"

Jude cocked his head. Sabine thought he wanted her to keep talking.

"My last name's Smoot," he said. "If I sound like a hillbilly farmer, it's cause I am. I'm from a nearby town called Barnville. A bomb exploded near my house, killing my family, except me and Dad. I don't understand why. My dad's missing."

Sabine was shocked. Jude had just told everyone his family had been killed by a bomb. With no emotion at all.

"It's the way of God," Sol said in a soft voice.

"It's a dumb way," Sabine whispered to Sol.

Jude seemed to notice everyone's bewildered expressions. "I don't mean why my *family*," Jude said. "I mean, why blow up Barn-ville? There's nothing important there."

"Sugar Grove's in Pendelton County?" Hank asked. "Isn't there a naval facility called Sugar Grove near you? Maybe it's still operational."

"Sugar Grove closed when I was a kid," Jude said. "A big deal, because local folks lost civilian jobs. You mean you think it didn't really close, and maybe it was connected to the bombs?" He covered his face, as if expecting a blow.

"Hell, I don't know," Hank said. "I just read about it once."

Sabine wondered why Hank would know about Sugar Grove, an obscure base that closed years ago. Hank and Sharp palled around all the time. Sharp was from Quantico and Hank lived in DC. He and Sharp were involved in something. Maybe the CIA?

"It makes sense that bombs exploded in airports, big cities, and banks," Sabine said. "But why a small town in West Virginia?" She kept her focus on Jude, who was staring at the floor.

Randolph sat up straight in his chair. "We may never find out."

"Maybe there's a grand plan and we're too close to see it yet," Tommy said.

"Perhaps, perhaps." Randolph's face sagged into the face of an old man.

"No grand plan." Sabine said. "Just pick a target and convince fifty people to strap on explosives, visit the Capitol, airports, and train stations. Carry a suitcase with a bomb through a stadium, leave the suitcase on a bleacher, and head to the refreshment stand. Send sick people carrying airborne viruses, like pneumonic plague or SARS, to walk through malls."

"I get the point," Tommy said, frowning.

Kate patted Tommy's leg and said to Hank, "Fill in the newcomers."

"Sharp and I were in DC when it happened." Hank's voice came out smooth. "Loading camping gear before daybreak, we heard a roar and the sky lit up white. A blast from around George-town, another one close to Capitol Hill. Sharp yelled: 'Let's go! Before the whole city blows. Before gridlock.' Sharp drove. It was a spooky race through dark, empty streets. Going south, we kept hearing explosions behind us. We took Route 50 and turned onto 17th. At a gas station, the self-serve pumps were closed, and the guy only let us have a quarter tank of gas. In the little grocery we bought lots of food. Sharp wheeled the cart to the truck, we unloaded the groceries, shoved the cart on top of the groceries, and took off."

Sabine looked around the room. Everyone was mesmerized by Hank's story.

"We ran out of gas and left my old Ford truck about sixteen miles back. Cars were moving, but we couldn't hitchhike with groceries.

Some stations had already put up out-of-gas signs. Folks were lining up at the open stations and stores."

"You can bet they're not lining up anymore," Tommy said.

Hank nodded. "By this point city people will have run out of food and gas. All hell's probably breaking loose."

"In DC people were already looting the day of the bombs," Sabine said. "On the way here I took food and water from grocery stores."

Hank continued, "The damned grocery cart had a front wheel with a mind of its own. Irritating when you're stressed. Sharp and I slept in the woods. The next day we found this place and thought we'd offer to do farm work in exchange for room and board. We yelled and knocked on the door, but got no answer, so we went around the side of the house. That's where we came upon the bodies." He picked up the poker and prodded the fire. "Wild animals and the weather made the bodies hard to identify. Two kids lay side by side, dried blood on their clothes. The girl had freckles and brown curls, and the boy looked like her." Hank fixed his eyes on the fire. "Hidden in leaves we found another little girl, about three. Her arms and legs lay at weird angles, maybe she'd been tossed. An old guy in coveralls lay near a man and woman in work clothes. Probably the grandfather and parents. All their throats and thighs had been slit."

Sabine shuddered, thinking of the machete man. *The throat and thigh slitting? Saving bullets, or not making noise, were they the real reasons? The attackers had cut arteries, so there must have been lots of blood.*

"Sharp and I dug a wide grave and wrapped them in tablecloths," Hank said. "The grave's at the edge of the field, facing east, under two big trees. Sometimes I still hear a certain wind, and a wild hollering gets into my bones through those trees."

"I got here in time to help out on a watch team," Jen said.

"Yep," Hank said. "Jen arrived the same day as Kate and Tommy. Sharp and I could tell Jen was tough."

"Hank," Sol said, "before the bombs, what kind of work did you do?"

Hank didn't respond.

"How long had the tenants been dead?" Sol asked.

"A while, before the bombs," Hank said. "The bodies had deteriorated."

"So their murders weren't connected to the bombs?" Sol frowned.

Hank shrugged. "The day after we found the bodies, Sharp and I worked in what was left of their garden. We were mixing barn manure into the soil when these two came up the driveway like ragged orphans." He pointed to Tommy and Kate.

Kate and Tommy raised their joined hands. Kate giggled.

Sabine was surprised at the giggle from solemn, bossy Kate.

"The same day, May 28th, that Kate and Tommy came, Jen pounded on the backdoor at dusk," Hank continued. "When I opened the door the first thing she said was, 'I brought my own guns.' And, lemme say she's good with those guns. Then, on June 5th, Sol and this goofball Jude Smoot rode up the driveway like rodeo boys sittin' high on their horses. Our local boys."

"You're rodeo guys. Bull riders?" Jen leaned forward.

"Nah," Jude said. "I been to rodeos, but never rode in one. I like my bones in one piece. My horse, Dannygolden, I had him for years. Guess what Sol called his horse?" Jude chuckled. "Shadowfax, like Gandalf's horse from *Lord of the Rings.*"

"Cool. I liked those books," Tommy said.

"*Lord of the Rings?*" Jen said. "Sounds religious. My pa dragged me to Harmony Vineyard Church every Sunday till I got lots older and could outrun him. I hate religion."

"Jen, those books aren't about what you think," Tommy said.

"Growing up," Jen said, "it was get a beating or go to church, so I hate religion."

"Why you scowling at me?" Jen asked, pinning Sabine with a glare.

Sabine realized she must've been staring at her. She looked away. "Nothing."

"We pastured our horses in that field." Sol pointed to the window. "The fence is high and the gate's padlocked, but somebody sawed through the fence and stole Shadowfax. For riding, or food, who knows? Jude and I fixed the fence the next day."

"You guys did a good job, too," Hank said.

"Later Dannygolden stepped in a gopher hole and snapped his leg," Sol said, "I had to put him down."

Jude wore a bknife and acted tough. Sabine wondered why he didn't shoot his own horse. Had they eaten the horse meat? What had they done with the carcass? She didn't need to imagine; vultures were everywhere.

Sol wore black jeans and a black shirt, the combination of which made him appear tall and too thin. Sometimes when he acted nice, he came off pedantic. His face wasn't expressive and his mouth hardly moved when he talked. He always looked tired, maybe depressed and haunted by nightmares.

"We're lucky to have this house," Sol said. "Let's set an example of cooperation for each other. If we work together, we'll survive. I think Jihadists, or another radical group, coordinated the attack. Simultaneous bombs exploded in cities all over the country on Memorial Day."

"A jihad can also mean a quest," Tommy said. "It doesn't have to mean what you think. We don't know who was responsible. Maybe radical Islamists; maybe it was homegrown terrorists who communicated with other small groups. There's not enough information yet."

Sol launched into a lecture about dirty bombs.

"Enough, Sol." Sharp's melodious voice cut Sol off.

"Okay, man. I'm just a person who thinks the more information, the better."

Sabine felt bad for Sol. Sharp's tone could be scornful.

"Anyway, this is it," Hank said. "The house can't take in more people."

"Four big bedrooms and a small room at each end of the

second-floor hall," Sabine said. "And my attic room. Seems like more could fit if we wanted . . ."

"It's not about space," Hank said. "It's about food. So no more— unless they're good shots. Who else will volunteer for a watch team?" Hank looked at Sol. "Want to join?"

"I'll consider it." Sol grimaced.

Sabine liked Hank calling Sol's bluff. Sol was quick to complain but short on action. She recalled Sol lecturing Jude at the pump.

Randolph stood. "Hank, a few words beyond our names. Lavinia and I were planning an engagement party, but our plans were thwarted."

"When did you hear the first explosions?" Hank said.

"Monday morning the radio said there were explosions in DC, Miami, and New York. Later, there were at least three explosions around Richmond. Phones and electricity were also down on the West Coast."

"And?" Hank's forehead wrinkled.

Sabine was intrigued by his concern. He must be searching for a specific piece of information.

"The President is probably safe," Randolph said. "FEMA has mobilized in DC and the suburbs. The IAEA released a report saying most bombs were not INDs, improvised nuclear devices."

Hank leaned forward. "Most bombs? But not all bombs?"

"What's IAEA?" Paul asked.

"The International Atomic Energy Agency." Randolph smiled at Paul.

"No reports of planes, so most bombs must've been IEDs," Hank said. "Smaller, easier to handle and conceal in buildings, bridges, and tunnels. The sticky bombs are magnetically adhesive so you can put them in a car, a truck, or a bicycle. And you can control them remotely. Biological or chemical, sometimes they're made with nail heads and razors. They're about creating chaos and fear."

"There are long gas lines, and runs on grocery stores and ATMs all along the East Coast," Randolph said. "The military and police are pushing abandoned cars off the roads around DC—"

"FEMA is supposed to work like this: first they restore power, then communications, and finally transportation," Hank said.

"How do you know that?" Sol asked Hank.

"I'm an info junkie," Hank said. "I read papers and online news."

"Coming out of Detroit, I counted three military convoys," Paul said. "The highways around the cities were totally crazy. I couldn't catch rides. People were suspicious and panicky to get out."

Randolph glared at the floor. Sabine guessed he didn't like being interrupted.

"Panic makes people do crazy stuff." Paul shook his head.

Randolph let out a loud sigh. "Let me finish. Bombs exploded all through Monday, all around the country. My parents, bless their ancient hearts, refused to travel. So Lala and I were Pittsburgh-bound for the engagement party. We detoured due to unforeseen circumstances."

"Nice understatement." Tommy chuckled.

Everybody except Randolph laughed; even Lavinia smiled.

"My motorcycle maneuvers well in traffic," Randolph said, so we managed to avoid jams and wrecks, till a blasted tractor trailer ran us off the road. I couldn't find a service station to repair my bike, so we had to abandon it. And Hank rescued us."

"I can't picture you two on a bike," Tommy said.

Kate hit him on the arm. "Be quiet, you ass." Her whisper was loud enough for everyone to hear.

"Who cares about your damn bike," Jen said. "Most of the East Coast's in a panic and we have to hear you blab about your wedding and your rich-boy bike."

"Officials reiterated the government's functioning," Randolph said, "but I don't believe it. One day the news was about the missing president and vice president. A day later the White House issued a contradictory statement."

"The part about IEDs, and about the president and vice presi-dent, is new information," Hank said. "We've had scant news since mid-June. If we had reliable access to gas, we'd drive farther, try to find more out, but our priority is food, supplies, and keeping the farm safe."

"Far as I heard no group has even taken responsibility for this," Randolph said. "We don't even know the enemy."

"We're lucky the farm family put in a turbine," Sharp said. "Driving around the area I've only seen two, and one of them is here. At least we have intermittent electricity."

"Turbine, or not, we aren't safe!" Jen glowered at Sharp. "We should get the hell out. Every day we see more refugees walking along the roads. How long you think our fence will keep them out? And we can't grow anything once winter comes."

"Go. No one's stopping you," Sharp said.

Jen's face fell. Sabine felt bad for her.

"But I'd miss you on watch," Sharp said. Jen's shoulders relaxed.

Hank said, "Jen, if we have to leave in a hurry, we will. Folks, think about what you want: go with us, or go off on your own? I hope we'll all leave together, but it's your choice." He looked around. "Anyone have more to say before we wrap up?"

No one said anything.

"Okay," Hank said. "If you haven't signed up for chores, or the watch, do it. Good night."

Later, Sabine lay in bed, relieved the bombs weren't nuclear. But what about cannibals and plagues when sanitation broke down? And outside help? Walking to the farm, she'd tried to stay aware of surroundings. If she'd been any slower, the machete man would've gotten her. And any hope she'd had that the government might help had slipped away. FEMA would help the bigger cities, but FEMA wasn't coming to rural West Virginia.

Sol had a point about cooperation, but she didn't want to agree with him about anything. He went around the house picking up dirty coffee cups and moaning like a martyr while he washed them. At the table, he remarked about the boring food and called for more salt. Sabine didn't like Kate much, but she knew she worked hard making do with the food they had. She probably couldn't stand Sol.

Sabine had already broken a rule and snooped in everybody's rooms. The small room at one end of the second floor must be Sol's. Four books stacked on the floor by a tidy single bed, a chest of drawers, and a braided rug. One T-shirt and a change of underwear in the drawers. His jacket hung on a peg in the wall.

❧

Kate hummed as she plowed through the pile of dirty breakfast dishes. Sabine, still intent on her plate of food, recalled the evening she'd arrived, when Kate had given her a kind smile, water, and food. Still, she didn't like or trust the woman.

Kate sat at the table. "Some more about the log. It's important because years from now, people will want to understand what happened in the US. They'll pore over our bones to figure out if a bomb or some plague wiped us out. Or if perhaps we killed each other off." Kate's expression was benign, but panic shot through Sabine's legs and arms like electricity at her words.

"Other countries have been attacked?"

"We've had no contact with the world beyond Canada," Kate said. "Driving out of DC, Hank got a call from a Canadian friend who'd heard about the bombs on the radio. Canada was okay when his friend called, but then cell phone service conked out."

"DC could get bombed again, then people sick with plague will flee to the countryside and infect us."

"Think any of us will ever get to go home?" Sabine asked.

"The cities are in big trouble," Kate said, twisting her braid. "I'll take my chances right here."

"You think we're the smart ones, then? For getting out?"

Kate nodded. "You DC folks were smart to leave. Hank heard rumors when he ran into some friendly scavengers. Cities are a bad place to be right now."

Sabine thought about her family. "Do you ever expect someone to show up here—someone who recognizes you?" she asked.

Kate's head jerked a little. "No."

"Do you hope it'll happen?"

"I never thought about it much till now," she said. "I've got Tommy. My brothers and sisters lived in DC and Northern Virginia. I assume they're dead."

The room tilted at the word "dead." Sabine frowned. "The city was a mess, but parts of the suburbs were okay. People didn't want to help me, but there were people working in their gardens and kids riding bikes along the road. After enough people turned me away I stopped trying, just kept my head down and walked."

Kate didn't respond for a while; then, finally, she said, "You were confused when you got here. The attic was empty so we let you sleep there, hoping the quiet would help you recover. You're lucky to have your own room. Most of us share."

She probably wants a small attic room where she and Hank can meet. "I stay in my room when I'm scared. Some stuff happened that wasn't good."

Kate clenched her fists. "You think you're unique? Scary things happened to all of us."

Ashamed, Sabine felt self-centered, focused only on herself. While she assumed others had suffered, she hadn't asked anyone much about themselves. Before she could stop herself, she said, "I bet you and Tommy have a nice big room. Nobody searches your room or steals stuff from you."

Kate didn't answer.

Sabine felt her voice rise. "You know who stole my machete, don't you?"

Kate pursed her lips; probably she'd expected Sabine to be

grateful about the room. "Don't forget to put your plate on the counter," she said, and walked out.

Sabine hated to get loud, but Kate deserved it. What a bossy bitch. She thought again about the notebooks. Maybe she'd collect the "corpus" of her work—but the word *corpus* brought to mind Memorial Day, the woman across the street leaning against the building, trying to keep her insides from falling out of her body, and Sabine's attention skittered away. She closed her eyes, remembered herself hunched over a school desk in eighth grade, holding a pen like a pro, scribbling an essay. Her finger turning white from pressing hard on her pen, writing fast, before the lunch bell made its clang-clang-clang. Kate could be right; she might make a good scribe after all. But the thought of giving in to Kate, talking with people and describing the farmhouse, made her head buzz with worry and resentment. Asking every person questions didn't sound like fun.

The kitchen's best feature was a map of West Virginia that was taped to one wall. Sabine studied it from her seat at the table. Lines had been drawn on the map with a black magic marker. She wondered what they meant.

Feeling restless, she went outside and yanked at the brass rings on the cellar doors. Dank air rose up the steps. It was too dark to see beyond them. The smell and blackness flooded Sabine with a closed-in feeling, like she was suffocating in a cave. She'd inspect the cellar another time. As she closed the doors, she wondered if she should keep her pack with her. No. Wearing her backpack in the house would draw unwanted attention. But she'd keep it ready to go, just in case.

A large propane tank sat by the back steps. The turbine on the ridge produced electricity, when the wind was up. Limited electricity meant they went to bed early and got up at five or six. Each afternoon at dusk Kate moved along the first-floor hall and lit kerosene lanterns. From the outside the lanterns appeared bright with haloes.

They pushed back the dark until bedtime when another watch team took over.

Sabine was sweeping the kitchen floor when Kate reappeared, ducked into the pantry, and came out with a long apron. Sabine didn't acknowledge her, and Kate made no effort to talk to her; she just moved to the sink, pulled the apron over her neck, and tied the strings around her waist.

As Sabine stared at her back, Kate's body disappeared and the image of another woman in another kitchen emerged. Not a face, but a pair of delicate hands with chipped purple fingernail polish reaching and meeting behind her back and tying apron ties into a perfect bow—a smooth movement, practiced and familiar. Sabine had watched this woman tie an apron many times. The apron was cream-colored and covered with red and pink cabbage roses. The design and material resembled a 1930s slipcover. After she tied the bow, the woman turned around, but the woman's face remained a frustrating blur.

Sabine ran her hand across the table and left. In the library, which she'd come to consider her den and writing room, there was no TV or computer. A dictionary with a worn black cover and gold lettering lay on the desk. It had been published twenty-three years earlier, so it didn't have slang, but she wouldn't be using slang; rather, she'd be looking up words like "scribe." Kate had made the job sound so important. She flipped to the right page and wrote down the two definitions she found there, studying the fascinating pictures of bearded men wearing clerical and court robes. They sat at ornate desks, writing letters or copying documents for kings, queens, and clergy.

Kate managed the house and bossed people around capably. Her accent sounded flat and Midwestern. Yet she diverted questions about herself, engaging in conversation about present problems. Tommy, a flirt and a tease, was the kind of man who pried out secrets. When Kate lectured him about a task, insisting he take out the trash and wagging her finger, he'd take her hand and put the fin-ger in his mouth. When she pulled away, he'd open his mouth and grin. They'd laugh and he'd nuzzle up to her, then they'd kiss and he'd head out the door, yelling over his shoulder, "I'll take the trash out later!" And he would—but on his own timetable. Tommy was an Italian boy with a doting mama, who'd perfected his strategy as a kid. Sabine admired his adroitness. Could she pull off manipulating Kate, divert her from managing Sabine's writing chore?

The library was the quietest room on the first floor, and the view through the window—the field and mountains beyond—helped her feel peaceful. After the snow melted, she'd dress in layers and climb a mountain. At the thought of being up high, seeing more of the land, something opened in her chest—a feeling resembling happiness.

Chapter 4

FORAGE MOON

July 8, 2014.

Hank asked Sabine to go foraging with him. Before they drove off, he checked his list: wire cutters under the driver's seat, a cardboard box and big empty bags in the back of the truck, and three guns behind the backseat. He laid a fourth gun on the seat between them and drove slow down the gravel driveway. At the bottom he told her, "Do the padlocks."

She let out an exaggerated sigh, but did as he asked. Back in the car she said, "It looks weird to have the gate chained up. No other farmhouse has padlocks."

"Other people aren't smart," he said. "You gotta admit, a secure gate slows down intruders. 'Course, if you're a target, they'll get you."

"Did you steal my machete?" She crossed her arms, and waited for Hank's answer. She meant to keep her voice low, but her tone came out shrill.

Hank laughed. "That was yours? I'm skeptical."

"I took it from a man who attacked me on the road."

"You got away?"

"I waited till he pulled down his pants, then I kneed him in the groin, grabbed his machete, and hit his head twice. He bled a lot, and then he didn't move. I think I killed him. I ran like hell and hid in the woods."

"If he attacked you, he deserved to die. You did good, for a woman. Your machete's in a safe place. Don't worry, it'll get used."

"You're nonchalant about killing. Why are you being condescending? Killing's a big deal. Maybe you're used to it, but I'm not. Before the bombs, none of my friends owned a gun. Of course, I don't exactly remember some things."

Hank's eyes widened, and he shook his head.

Sabine wanted to dislike Hank, but she couldn't. He was good-looking, at times personable and polite. A competent, take-charge man, even if sometimes he acted like his mind was not in the room. She felt shy around him when he was remote, as if he were looking through her. But she'd been told she acted remote, too.

He started humming with a song on the silent radio. He put on a good show with a nice falsetto singing voice as they sped along country roads, and then down a four-lane highway. Soon they were pulling into a shopping center parking lot. Hank drove slowly around to the back and came through to the other side. A few cars were scattered around, but most of the stores looked like they'd already been ransacked or boarded up.

Hank stopped the truck, took the gun off the seat, and gave it to her. Then he took it away. "Tell you what," he said, "you come along. Let's see how good you are at looting. Stay no more than four feet away from me. Run if I tell you to run." He handed her a key. "Put the truck key in a safe place. Let's go."

She slid the key in her jeans pocket and waited, but he didn't open the door. He watched the building for a few minutes before finally saying, "Okay. Let's roll."

Her stomach churned walking by his side, hurrying to keep up with his long stride. They negotiated their way through a splintered glass door, then he took her arm and held tight, saying, "Watch it."

He guided her through a second door. The floor was slippery with broken glass.

He glanced around. "Looks like the food's to the right."

They grabbed carts and headed to the first aisle.

"Take the left." He kept his voice low.

She threw big boxes of pasta into the cart, then large cans of tomatoes and several containers of Parmesan cheese. Intent on scanning the rows, she didn't look up until she reached the end of the aisle. Hank's cart stood across from her, half full.

Hank crouched in the open, a gun in his hand. Without looking at her he shouted, "Run!"

Three shots from the back of the store. She froze. In slow motion she reached for an empty cardboard box on the floor and hurled groceries from her cart into it. She lifted the box.

Hank glanced over. "Go, goddamn it, go!"

More shots, men yelling, their voices coming closer. She didn't move. *Don't leave him.*

Hank got off a few shots and hurried to her. He reached for her arm, and she struggled to keep hold of the box as, his other hand on her back, he shoved her toward the door.

She ran. But at the door, she stopped. Hank wasn't behind her. She swiveled around.

Six men were approaching from the back. Hank, still near the registers, crouched and shot at a tall man, who yelled and crashed into a display of cans. A beefy man wearing a bandana and a sneer slowed but didn't have time to aim. Hank got off several shots. The man clutched his gut, blood spurting all over the floor.

As soon as Hank spun around, Sabine jumped through the glass doors. At the truck she unlocked the driver's door and pulled it open, then unlocked her side and scrambled in. Seconds later Hank climbed in and peeled out of the parking lot. When they hit the highway he floored the gas and checked the rearview mirror. "No sign of them yet."

"Four men still standing," she said. "Maybe they stopped to help the other two. But any one of the cars in the lot could be theirs."

Hank's hands were white-knuckled on the steering wheel. "You didn't do what I told you."

"I couldn't leave you. But I got a little food." She laid a shaking hand on the box in her lap.

"You're aware of what they would've done to you, if they caught you?" Hank sounded exasperated. "You can guess. Food isn't worth your life. Keep it in mind, stubborn girl."

She stared out the rear window. "It wasn't like we pulled up in a giant truck intending to take everything. Why did they attack us?"

"Protecting their food supply. There's probably a community of refugees close by. It's not unusual these days."

"Did you kill the man wearing the bandana?" She wanted him to say no.

Hank shrugged. "No hospitals around here. Unless they have a medic or a nurse, he'll bleed to death. I just nicked the other guy, he should be okay."

She glanced in the rearview mirror. "Nothing behind us."

He nodded. "Sucks I couldn't grab some food."

"I hate this. All of it."

"Sabine, we're six weeks into this mess. It's kill or be killed."

But she didn't want to hear it. She wanted him to be sorry he'd shot the men. She wanted him to assure her the chaos would stop. But even a strong guy like him couldn't fix things.

At dinner Hank tapped his glass with a spoon, and everyone stopped talking.

"When Sabine and I were foraging today, we had a nasty surprise at a mall," he said. "The place is called Mountain Rock. If you go east, twenty-five minutes down the two-lane road, then turn right onto a four-lane highway, the mall's right there. I tangled with some guys in the store. I shot two; the one with a bullet to the stomach probably won't make it. They might've seen the blue truck, and could be searching the roads. So anyone who goes out in that truck, be aware. And kudos to Sabine, who grabbed a box of food and helped me."

Startled he mentioned her, she smiled at him, but he didn't notice. Hank could be so secretive; she'd worried that he wouldn't warn them. She felt relieved he had.

"Make sure to park the trucks behind the house," he said. "Throw the big brown tarp over the blue one." He took his empty plate to the sink. "Okay. Night watch, time for you to roll."

❧

From the window in the attic hall Sabine watched Sharp load empty gas cans into the back of the blue truck. Hank was already at the wheel. Sol jumped into the back of the red truck. His agility was appealing, yet she didn't like him. During meals he stared at her, in a way that didn't feel sexual—more like curiosity.

Then there was Jude. Was he interested in her? She wasn't sure.

She walked to the library and opened the window for fresh air. Maybe Jude was working in the garden today. He had strong arms and a bowlegged walk—was built like a cowboy should be. She paced the room, touching books with faded brown, red, and green bindings. Books about farm animals, horses, and agriculture. What livestock the family had been raising was gone, eaten by refugees and vultures. All that remained were the dried-up cow pies in the field, an empty chicken coop behind the ramshackle shed, and the animal bones littering the grounds.

Distracted by thoughts of Jude, she couldn't write. She shut and locked the window, and then, with a final glance to make sure things were in order, she closed the door.

Someone took her hand and she jumped. *Jude.*

He sat by the door in a straight-back chair, a rifle across his knees. "Hey girl! Give me a minute. I'm almost done cleaning my rifle."

"Where did you come from?"

"I figured you'd be in your little room. Got a minute?"

"A minute for what?" she asked, her voice rising slightly.

"Lots of minutes, actually," he said. "Walk with me, I'll show you the woods. I could use a walk. You could, too."

"Okay," she said. "I'll wait for you on the veranda."

"The porch?" He stared into her eyes, his expression challenging.

She felt her face flush. "A veranda's the same as a porch. This is a veranda because it runs the length of the house. It's wider than a porch."

She walked outside and paced the yard in figure eights, wanting to run across the field and collapse on the ground with this man she barely knew lying on top of her. He might crush her, in a good way.

Jude opened the front door. "Ready," he said, buttoning his cotton shirt.

"Isn't it hot in that shirt? It must be seventy out."

"Keeps my knife hidden," Jude said.

"Don't you keep it strapped to your leg?"

"Sometimes my leg, sometimes my waist." He set off at a brisk pace across the field and she matched his stride.

"What are you doing in that room?" he asked. "Alone in there for hours."

"I write," she said. "Piece together images of people, especially my family. I think I had brothers and sisters. I think my last job had something to do with sports. So weird, because I'm not into sports."

"When you got here you were a mouse. Occasionally you popped out a big word, like a schoolteacher, but otherwise . . ."

Sabine shrugged. "I don't like people going through my stuff." She paused. "Kate won't tell me who came in my room and stole my machete. Hank either. Do you know?"

"Whoever was on watch would've searched the pack your first night," Jude said. "You were sleeping like a dead person."

"A dead person, huh? And how would you know?"

He didn't answer. Instead of heading straight for the woods, he turned left, toward the creek, warning, "Watch out for gopher holes."

Once they'd jumped the creek he slowed his pace.

Drop it. He won't tell you anything about the machete. Sabine tried a different subject. "I'm organizing the farm family's library. I found an old dictionary."

"Don't bother," he said, his mouth a straight line. "We're leaving."

"I didn't know leaving was for sure." Despite what Hank had said at the group meeting, she wanted to stay. She understood why heroes and bad guys in spy novels had safe houses.

Jude touched his waist and she wondered if he was checking his knife. "It's just a matter of time," he said. "Everything depends on our borders. We've been paying close attention to the woods. For the past five days we've tried to use three-man watch teams. If we're not safe, we're talking about heading east, around the Virginia Beach area. Hank's idea. He hasn't said why, but I think he wants access to constant news, thinks he has a better chance of that there." He spat and kicked the dirt. "It's uncool to admit, but I don't much care what's going on anywhere else. I'm just trying to stay alive."

Sabine sighed. "Virginia Beach's too far north. We should go way south, where we can grow food year-round."

"You're right. I'm tired of pulling extra duty with the watch team."

"What's changed?"

Jude pointed in the direction of the road. "More refugees and gangs on the road. One of these days, some of 'em will try to take the farm."

"But there's so much land here."

"You city girl." Jude chuckled. "Not all this land's usable. It's hilly and rocky, has poor drainage. The best land has been cleared. We've talked with a few folks. They told stories about farms and pastures raided, livestock slaughtered or stolen. Houses and fields burned to the ground, too, which makes no sense."

"Terrible stuff can linger after bombs," she said. "Parts of the country might not grow anything in our lifetime, with radiation falling on fields and rivers. The wind blowing it around."

He stopped walking. "Radiation? That stuff scares the shit out of me."

"Let's hope Randolph was right. He said the IAEA reported most bombs weren't nuclear. That gives me hope." She took his hand. "Tell me about West Virginia."

"I can't talk about West Virginia," he said, squeezing her hand. "No more than I already have."

"Why not?"

"I don't want to think about my family."

Sabine leaned close to hear, but Jude shook off her hand and moved through the trees at a slow pace.

"Come on," she called after him. "I'll tell you all I remember. 'Course, it's not much." She caught up and pulled on his arm. "Pretty please." She stood in front of him and inched closer until her breasts pushed against his chest.

He flushed but didn't back away.

She looked into his eyes and felt him melting. He put his hands on her shoulders and she came closer. His knife sheath dug into her hip.

"Ah hell, girl. You got me good." He chuckled.

"So I'm a girl? I'm not so young." She pulled back so she could see his face.

"You have a girl's spunk."

"Why, thank you." She grinned. "Come on. Talking about what happened to our families can make us feel better."

"It might make me feel worse."

She pulled down on his hand and they sat on a wide log at the edge of a clearing.

"When the first bomb exploded," he said, "I was in the garden near the house. Mama and the kids were swimming. The river's a quarter mile away. Dad had gone for groceries and a new truck tire, or so he said, but Mama thought he was screwing a town whore. Guess it's useless to worry about that now."

"So your dad's missing?"

"I suppose. If he was in town, he's probably dead."

"How many brothers and sisters do you have?"

"Two younger brothers. An older sister." He glanced around the clearing. "A flash of light covered the sky. I rang the cow bell for them to get in the cellar. Strange lightning. I thought maybe a tornado was coming our way."

"A tornado?"

Jude nodded, passed a hand over his face. "I figured Mama and the kids would come any minute. I took cover in the cellar. Soon as I got down there, the ground shook and I heard windows smashing. I'm crouched on a dirt floor with potatoes, beets, and onions rolling around, waiting for Mama and the kids. The rain didn't come." His eyes filled with tears. "Soon as the wind died away, I hurried down to the river. There they lay—or what was left of them. I held my hand across Mama's neck to feel her pulse, then I sat by the river, looking at my family and thinking about the ways I'd miss each one. But none of it felt real . . . more like a bad movie."

Sabine put a hand on his knee, but said nothing.

"Finally I ran back to the house. A big tree had caved in the porch roof, toys were all over the yard. I packed some clothes, filled five canteens with water, and put food in my saddlebags. Our pigs and chickens were dead. Dannygolden was safe in the barn. I saddled him and rode to town."

"How awful to see the bodies . . ." She trailed off, realizing that nothing she said would be sufficient.

He took a deep breath. "Weren't nothing to do for them. Sirens were blasting off at the volunteer fire station, but it was too late for that."

"You didn't bury them?"

"Nope. I got the hell out. Besides, Mama wouldn't mind lying facing the sky. She loved looking at the sky."

"I was disoriented when I heard the blast," Sabine said. "When I ran outside, the doorman was lying dead on the steps. Steve, or Sam. Something with an 'S.' Samuel. That was it."

"A doorman." Jude darted a look at her. "You must be rich."

"In big cities lots of apartment buildings have doormen. Doesn't mean you're rich."

"I didn't think about Dad till later," Jude said. "I'd been mad at that bastard for so long, I stopped caring."

"I don't believe you." Sabine touched the frown lines between his eyes, noted how the skin around his eyes was creased with fine wrinkles—from working in the sun, gardening, riding a tractor, baling hay, she supposed. "Enough about the past. How old are you?"

"What do you think?"

"First I thought you were a teenager. Now I guess twenty-five."

"Thirty-one." He pulled her hand to his mouth and kissed the palm. "How old are you?"

"Twenty-eight." Her lie came with ease. *Would he believe her?* "The recent past feels hazy. But high school and further back my memory's pretty good. In high school I got demerits and spent Saturday mornings working math problems with a teacher glaring at me and the other offenders."

"I don't see you like that," Jude said, eyebrows raised. "Not at all."

"I wasn't a mouse then. A fortune-teller told me I'd be a great healer. I laughed because I didn't care about healing, or helping, anyone. Nobody helped me. I drank beer, danced on tables at parties, and didn't keep boyfriends long. And I loved hiking and the outdoors. But these days I hate walking outside. All you see is dead people, dead cows, dead dogs . . . I'm a traveler who doesn't have a map leading to anyplace good."

Jude looked down. "I'm a regular country guy."

"You can do better than that."

He rose and set off at such a fast pace she couldn't keep up. They walked single file beside the creek and into the woods. Stopping, he pointed to a stand of birches. "Mama said birches are called trees of desire. They demand light and won't grow in the shade of other trees." His voice sounded soft. "She knew about animals and trees. When she had time, she'd take us kids exploring. Even when I was a teenager I hiked with her."

"Someday you'll teach your children," she said.

The sound of their footsteps was muted by the pine tags and leaves covering the ground. With Jude she didn't feel scared, but if she were alone she'd be thinking about the machete maniac. He'd probably built some ratty hut out of mud and tin in woods like these. Probably raped women in his hut—maybe he still did. But he was more than likely dead. She'd never know.

Jude led her to a giant tree. "My favorite. See those broken limbs? Look up real high. I been studying this tree since Sol and I got here. This stand is well over a hundred years old."

Sabine squinted up at the tree. "Were you with someone before the bombs?"

"Yep, I had a girlfriend. We'd been dating about a year, but not serious. My family needed me at the home place, and you probably think I'm too old to live at home and work the farm, but it's what country people do." He touched the trunk of the tree. "After I packed up and saddled Dannygolden, I rode straight to my girlfriend's house. Nobody there, so I rode to town. Folks were standing around looking at piles of rubble with blank expressions. People crying and screaming. I had no idea where she might be. I couldn't think straight. "In town, I saw all I wanted to see, and I was worried a poison cloud was drifting toward us. So I headed east—and right outside of town I saw a guy stumbling down the road."

"Sol?" Sabine guessed.

Jude nodded. "You ever watch Sol walk? With his long legs he takes big steps, sometimes a little to the left or right, like a spider. He was coming to find me. The two of us were too heavy to both ride Dannygolden far, but by some miracle, Sol spotted a bay grazing in a field. No one around—maybe they fled after the bombs, or were all dead. We sneaked in the barn, stole a bridle and saddle, and took off. Sol left a note saying he'd try to return the horse later. Once we left there, we kept heading east."

"You thought east would be safer?"

"I wasn't thinking clear about anything. I just had to keep moving." Jude paused. "Her name's Laura. My girlfriend—my ex, I guess. I hope she's alive."

Sabine noticed Jude used the present tense, while she'd been doing the opposite, practicing with past tense. When she got more of her memory back, she wanted to be prepared to discover that the people she'd loved were gone. "Laura's a pretty name," she said.

Jude took her by the shoulders and pushed her toward a tree with a wide trunk. He held her face and kissed her from her forehead down to her lips. His cheeks were stubble rough and he smelled like cigarettes. While they kissed, he hummed and moved his lips over her neck. He ran his hands over her back and lower down, pulling her closer, moaning in her ear.

She felt powerful and excited fiddling with the metal buttons on his pants and zipper. She moved her hand inside, down his belly to his erection. She had no birth control and bet he didn't either, but she wasn't concerned—she was probably too malnourished and skinny to get pregnant anyway.

"Over by the pines where the tags are soft," he said.

Hand in hand they moved toward a stand of trees and lay on the tags. Without hesitating, Jude pulled off his pants and dropped the bowie knife beside him. Then he pulled her down and kissed her as if he hadn't kissed anyone in years. He jerked up her shirt and kissed her belly.

She pulled the leather thong out of his hair, took a handful, twisted it, and let it fall. "Your hair feels nice," she said. "It's so long and thick."

He kissed her belly again and again.

"Slow down. I'm not going anywhere," she said with a laugh.

"You're moving pretty fast yourself."

She laughed and took his penis in her hand. "True. True."

The pine tags felt scratchy, but Jude seemed oblivious, and the way he moved her body around, she felt his strength. When he moaned, she thought he'd be easy to please. Their bodies fit, he moved at a slow pace, and she caught the rhythm. If they died in one minute, it would be enough. He didn't hurry. He made it last, and she was glad. He came seconds after she did. He hummed, nuzzled her breasts, and laid kisses along her neck. She felt her own tears, but his eyes were closed and he didn't notice.

He laid his hand on her stomach and felt with his fingertips the ragged welt. "What's that scar?"

"My appendix almost burst. I was fifteen and had surgery."

"Appendix? My sister's burst, but her scar was smaller and lower down."

"I think I'd remember my surgery."

"You sure?" Jude's eyebrows rose.

He didn't believe her, but wouldn't push. She kissed him to cover her nervousness, wishing she could tell the truth about her dead child. But there was too much to tell.

"I wanted you," he said. "Since the first morning you came down from the attic. But you looked through me. If I'd walked in your room naked, you wouldn't have noticed. I worried Sol or Hank, maybe Sharp, would make a pass at you first. I wanted you bad enough to fight Sol, but never Sharp or Hank. Hank's a beast. You seen his stare? Like you can't reason with him and he'd kill you without thinking twice about it. I told myself Hank wasn't interested in you. He likes Kate an awful lot, and you gotta admit, Kate's beautiful." He stopped, then added, "But she's not my type. I

suppose Sharp's like Hank, except more closemouthed, even harder
to read."

"Yeah, Kate's beautiful. I wish I had her blond hair. It's always
clean and shiny."

"Your hair's the color of creamy chocolate. I would've knocked
Sol on his ass for you."

Flattered, Sabine pushed down a smile. "But you and Sol are
friends."

His harsh laugh. "Sol and I have been friends since we were kids.
Makes no difference. Women make trouble between men, that's the
way of things."

"Fighting isn't something I'm used to. Please don't fight with your
friend on my account." She laid her face on his chest. His body was
different from other men she'd dated. He was short, bowlegged, mus-
cular, and blond as a Swede. She felt safe with her head on his strong
chest. "Let's stop talking." She kissed him to close his mouth. Not
many days ago he'd sat by her at the table and they'd talked, getting
to know each other. She'd never moved into sex this fast. Had he?

"If I leave the farm," she said, "I won't come back. And I don't
want to go back to DC either." She basked in the amazing color of
his eyes, ran her hands through his thick, wavy hair.

"Why's that?"

"I don't belong either place. It's beautiful here though. You have
a beautiful state, Mr. Jude Smoot."

They laughed. She loved feeling relaxed with her bright, shiny
man. She needed him; they could all die tomorrow, after all.

He kissed her, and she shut her eyes and made Jude, the trees,
and the ground disappear. She imagined watching the two of them
while she floated above. The man lies on top of the woman. His
pale butt moves up and down. Her thin arms clutch his back. The
man and woman make a rhythm, the same rhythm millions of other
men and women make, and soon their need passes, so the man and
woman move apart—move apart, and become separate people again.

Chapter 5

SHADOW MOON

July 10, 2014.

Sabine prepared three bowls of dog food, then stepped onto the back porch with venison scraps and dried food. Gun's dish stayed by the backdoor. She took the big bowls down the steps and set one on either side of the porch. She called, "Gun, Rom, Reeemus . . . Gun, Rom, Reeeemus . . . dinnertime!"

The dogs scrambled across the yard. Gun flew up the steps and ate with dainty bites. Rom, a black Lab, and Remus, a chocolate Lab, gobbled their food. She played referee on the bottom step until they finished eating.

She petted them all, and tried to hold Gun in her lap but he wiggled out and ran into the yard, sniffing the grass for an old sock he liked to fling around. The Labs slobbered on her hands, their strong tails banging against her legs. She loved this chore, which felt nothing like a chore. When the three dogs ran off, she took the bowls inside.

Hank sat at the table, his chair close to Kate's. Sabine felt their abrupt silence when she walked in. She washed the dog bowls and her hands. "Hank, they're great dogs. You came up with their names?"

Hank ran a hand over his bristly hair. "Gun's full name is Gunther, which means 'warrior' in Scandinavian. I named the Labs after Romulus and Remus, the mythical twin founders of Rome."

"That sound familiar," Sabine said slowly.

"The story goes that the brothers had a dispute over where to situate Rome, and Romulus killed Remus over it."

"The names fit, don't they?" Kate said. "We have to be tough, willing to kill each other, if necessary, to survive."

"Kate," Hank said in a warning tone.

But Sabine wasn't looking at Kate; she was focused on the map on the wall. Part of West Virginia appeared to be missing. Had someone cut the map? Maybe she'd just forgotten what the state looked like.

Kate and Hank sat in silence.

"Yeah, Hank," Sabine said, "good names for the dogs. Well, good night." She hurried down the hall to the veranda, where she knew Jude was waiting.

He took her hand and they walked into the yard to watch the moon. His knife made a bulge at his waist. He was more alert once the sun went down. They didn't even get as far as the field.

❧

She woke from a dream of walking along the beach, dodging starving bodies collapsing like strips of blown tissue paper. She fell back asleep and woke when the sky was still dark. She had something to do before anyone got up for breakfast. She took the back stairs. Yesterday, Kate had asked if she was at work on the log, and she'd lied, said yes. Kate had told her to include a description of the barn, the turbine, and farmhouse. If someone asked why Sabine was poking around, she'd refer them to Kate.

Rummaging through the dining room sideboard, Sabine found a phone with an old-fashioned rotary dial tucked under a tablecloth. She felt silly plugging the phone in the wall receptacle and picking up the receiver. The line was dead, of course. She shoved the phone back in the drawer. No cell phone bills in the pile of old mail she threw in a bag to burn in the fireplace. The farm family didn't appear to have had cell phones, or a computer. But maybe someone had stolen their computer before Hank and Sharp arrived.

From time to time she glanced up. Morning light filtered through the windows now, and she hurried to finish. She opened a box that smelled of lavender. Inside were twelve white candles wrapped in tissue paper. Also in the drawers were a stack of sheets, a pile of cloth napkins, and a couple of yellowed tablecloths full of moth holes. One red-checkered tablecloth was covered with yellow stains. She pictured the farm family's mother laying the checkered cloth over a card table as a special treat for the children, letting them drink milk and eat homemade brownies there.

She took two white candles for her backpack, just in case, then reconsidered and slipped the candles back in the box. If someone searched her room again, they'd find the candles, and she could get thrown out for theft.

Two Hudson River School framed landscapes hung side by side on the opposite wall. Strange in summertime to see an Advent candle holder with three purple candles and one pink one, sitting in the middle of the table. The candles had never been lit. A spot of color through the gloom. If they couldn't scavenge more kerosene, they'd have to start using candlelight.

Kate. Any minute now, she would come down to make coffee and breakfast. Sabine rose to leave before the cook came downstairs. On her way out, Sabine glanced out the window and saw Sharp walking toward the garden, carrying a hoe and wearing a red flannel work shirt. She supposed he'd work until breakfast. But when Kate called everyone for breakfast, Sharp didn't come. Sabine went to the dining room window. He wasn't in the garden. She went outside. From the veranda, only the empty field. Should she look for him? What would she say if she found him? Silly to think of hunting for Sharp.

After breakfast, Sabine opened her notebook. "Okay, how about answering a few questions for the log?" she said to Kate, who was perched on the edge of the sofa across from her in the living room. "Where do you want to start?"

"With Tommy, I suppose," Kate said. "We met two years ago, at the high school where we both taught. We dated about a year then moved in together in Kensington, Maryland. We were visiting friends in DC for the holiday weekend when the explosions came. We always wanted to live on a farm one day. So I guess we're actualizing our goal a few years early." She offered a tiny smile. "We left DC right after the explosions. When we ran out of gas we walked until we saw this picturesque farmhouse and came up the driveway. This was before Hank started padlocking the gate."

"Did you and Tommy help Sharp and Hank bury the bodies?"

"Thank God, no. They'd done that a few days before. Hank told us about it. Gruesome."

"Where did you grow up?"

"Appleton, Illinois."

"Tell me about your family."

"There were six of us kids. My father taught biology at the local university. Mom managed the office at a construction company. They loved the outdoors. Every Fourth of July the whole family took off in our camper and traveled until mid-August. Even when we were teenagers and wanted to stay home and hang with our friends, our parents dragged us off. Imagine, six kids crammed in the car and a camper for five or six weeks. We wrangled the whole time." Kate smiled. "Looking back, I'd give anything . . ."

Sabine waited, but Kate didn't finish the thought.

"In our rush to get out of DC," she said, "Tommy left his cell phone. What a scatterbrain. My battery's long dead. But there's probably no one to call anyway. Paul's was charged when he got here. He and Jen both keep their cells charged. It figures, they're the youngest. But we have no cell reception." She stood. "I've got to go."

"Wait, you're leaving? We just started. Tell me more about your family."

Kate shook her head. "Go talk to someone else."

Sabine yelled after her, "But you were the one who wanted me to do this! Have you changed your mind?"

Kate didn't answer.

Sabine didn't want to chase her. Talking with people who wouldn't say much was a waste. She'd write what she damn well wanted to write. Forget Kate's project.

Sabine pulled on her jacket and hurried into the field. A noise that sounded like a horse whinny came from somewhere, though she couldn't pinpoint the source. *Ridiculous.* She hadn't ever seen horses near the farm, and the ramshackle barn stood vacant, its wide doors hanging off their hinges. She and Jude had gone inside and seen empty horse stalls and birds roosting on the rafters, their droppings covering moldy hay on the floor.

She headed to the barn, but didn't go in because the decay saddened her. She sat on the ground outside, her back against the rough, sun-warmed wood. Out of habit she pulled out her cell phone and, with a surge of hope, flipped it open. After the usual letdown she put it back in her pocket.

Clouds drifted by. The shape of a rabbit merged into the head of a horse. She wished real horses still lived at the farm, grazing in the fields. She conjured an image of a house for a horse. A house crafted from leaves. On a piece of paper she scribbled "The Tale of the Horse and the Shelter of Leaves."

On the way back to the house she felt eyes on her and glanced back. The sun lit up the barn, and a clear shadow moved across the building. Was it a person? She wouldn't tell Jude. He had enough to worry about. But all evening she couldn't shake the ominous, vulnerable feeling the shadow had inspired in her.

When everyone left the breakfast table the next morning, Sabine helped Kate wash dishes, wondering where Kate learned to improvise so skillfully, using a wood stove to cook for such a big group of people.

"By the time you're done washing dishes," she said, "it's almost time to start the next meal. You must get sick of this room."

Kate scrubbed a plate. "My dad wanted us to be champions at fire building, water purifying, and animal tracking. He demonstrated and we practiced. And Mom taught me to shop for food, estimate portions, and cook, for a lot of people on an outdoor grill, a Coleman stove, and a wood stove. My brothers and sisters weren't interested in food, beyond eating it. Kitchen work was a thing Mom and I did together." Kate put down the sponge and faced Sabine with a faraway expression. "Working here reminds me of her. Sometimes I'd rather do something else, but the folks here need someone who knows their way around a kitchen. Plus, at least this way I don't have to take watch. When you're on watch, you never catch up on sleep."

"You think of everything," Sabine said. "Even fresh water. You watch the pump like a hawk."

"Water purification tablets." Kate pointed to a high shelf. "My stash, just in case. When we got here, Tommy and I checked the cellar and found potatoes, carrots, apples, onions, and parsnips, all edible. We found these two big pots I use too, and canning equipment. Tommy dug through junk and found some garden tools."

"I see," Sabine said, but she didn't see, beyond understanding that Kate's parents had taught her practical skills, and she missed them. Did Kate have another message—a judgment that Sabine wasn't contributing enough?

"Want help with drying and putting away?" She tried to appear interested.

"Why put away dishes when I'll use them in a few hours?" Kate shook her head. "Let 'em air-dry."

"To remind you, I have been doing chores," Sabine said. "I sign up every day. I pick up newspapers the foragers leave lying around and stack them by the fireplace. I take the vegetable scraps bucket to the garden for the compost pile, I hoe and pull weeds for one or two hours, I take care of the dogs. I dust and sweep, downstairs and upstairs. And work on the log."

"Yes, you do," Kate said. "But I expect you and the others to do more. I walk around and check. Like my mother did."

Sabine scratched her elbow. "I can't be the only writer here. Lots of people write, especially if they're upset. You've read about those hundred settlers, in the 1500s? They had time to leave two clues: the word CROATOAN carved in a post and the letters CRO carved in a tree."

"You sound like a schoolteacher."

"Like you?' Sabine laughed. "Nope. I hated math and history. You have a master's degree, right? In math?"

Kate nodded.

"I'm familiar with Croatoan because there's a play about it every summer on Roanoke Island. Historians still puzzle over what happened. Humans are curious, which is a good thing."

"You're a real chatterbox today," Kate said. "I've never heard you like this."

Sabine shrugged. "I'm not a chatterbox, I just like to talk sometimes. I write to figure out who I am. I don't care about leaving a record for other people."

"But you must write about this," Kate said. "I can't bear the idea of this farm, especially the people, disappearing. You're our insurance against being forgotten."

"You just told me more about your life, so I'll add it to your interview," Sabine said, wanting to pacify her. "By the way, do you have shampoo? I only have a few pieces of soap."

"In my room. I'm finished here, let's get it." Kate dried a jelly glass and slipped it in her apron pocket. They went up the front stairs and down the hall. Sabine glanced into bedrooms with open doors, but didn't see much.

In Tommy and Kate's room, a double bed with a frayed patchwork quilt and blankets stood against the longest wall. There was a table with spindle legs and two easy chairs, one under each window. Clothes were strewn all over. Kate glanced over at Sabine, saw her noticing.

"Yeah, messy," she said. "I'd like to blame Tommy, but I'm worse. Ignore the mess. I do." Kate kicked at a pile of clothes, then went into the bathroom and came out with a jelly glass full of shampoo. "From my last bottle," she said, handing it over.

"Thanks, Kate," Sabine said. "Don't worry, I'll get us more shampoo. Looting keeps getting easier, though I haven't forgotten the days when taking was called stealing."

Kate nodded, her face grim. "Hopefully we'll get more gas soon, so we can drive farther away, find stores and buildings that haven't been ransacked. I hope we've got enough root vegetables stockpiled to last through the winter and into spring."

"People in DC are much worse off," Sabine said. "So many explosions. I can't imagine what it's like up there."

Kate held up her hand. "Stop. It's not helpful to talk about what happened over and over. Stay focused on the present."

"But—"

"I said stop," Kate said, frowning. "Stay focused on helping around the house."

"I just reminded you I do sign up for chores. Most of the garden stuff I do because others won't." She stifled an urge to throw something at Kate's head, or curse her.

Kate nodded. "I'm aware," she said, her voice softening. "Sorry, I'm just scared. We're worried there will be more attacks."

"What do you mean, 'more'?"

"Haven't you noticed the bullet holes? A patched window in the dining room and one in the living room?"

Sabine started. "Oh. Right."

"It happened before you came."

"I noticed, but it didn't register. Too much going on." There was a box of maps on the floor at Kate's feet. "Exactly where in West Virginia are we?" Sabine asked, pointing to the box. "Show me. The map on the kitchen wall is pretty, but it doesn't show the whole state."

Kate frowned. "We'll talk later."

"Jude's from a town called Barnville," Sabine pressed.

Kate went into the bathroom and closed the door. Sabine reminded herself to act nice and crouched down by the box. It contained AAA maps of Virginia and West Virginia. The maps were smudged with dirt, with red pen marks crisscrossing West Virginia. An escape route, perhaps. Sabine slipped some maps in her waistband and left the room. More maps wouldn't be hard to grab from Kate's room. The woman spent her day preparing food, cleaning or rocking on the veranda, her face as blank as a plate. With her braid falling halfway down her back, her perfect oval face and pouty mouth, she reminded Sabine of a barmaid in an old Western movie.

Chapter 6

BONE MOON

abine raised a living room window to hear the voices coming from the veranda. Paul and Jen were on watch; they sat in straight-back chairs cleaning rifles. No surprise that Jen wasn't following orders to walk the perimeter, but Paul sitting on the veranda was a surprise. He usually worked hard. At least they wore pistols and could move fast. The day Paul arrived, Hank had taken him out in the field to test his skills, and at dinner announced that Paul was a terrific shot and would join the watch.

Outside, she sat on the veranda steps. Paul looked up with a lopsided grin. Lavinia sat apart, her bony hands limp on the arms of the rocker, engrossed in the field. From watching Lavinia at mealtime, Sabine had decided Lavinia didn't have cancer but anorexia. Her emaciated body repulsed Sabine, and the childish nickname Randolph used for her, Lala, irritated her. Randolph must see something was wrong with her. Why didn't he do anything to help her?

Jen started to sing, her eyes closed. Paul joined her in the military tune with a marching cadence, a hut-hut beat. At the end they yelled, "Oh, yeah." In the stillness following, Jen sang a gospel in a solemn voice.

Riveted, Sabine couldn't take her eyes off her. Lavinia stared, open-mouthed. Her shoulder blades jutted through two bulky sweaters. Her face relaxed, she smiled at Jen, a beatific smile. When Jen finished, the hush remained, like after prayers in church. Jen's superior, swaggering attitude and her refusal to divulge information made her hard to like, but she had a voice like a goddamn angel.

"Beautiful, Jen," Sabine said. "Your voice is stunning."

Jen's cheeks pinked up. "Thanks. Time to walk the perimeter." Jen hurried down the steps and called to Paul. "You coming?"

Paul lay down the rifle he'd been cleaning. "Give me a few minutes. Head to the woods and I'll find you." He picked up a pouch of feathers, pulled one out, and attached it to an arrow he took from a pile next to him. Lavinia returned to staring at the field.

Sabine pointed to the arrow. "What are you doing?"

"Grandpa taught me to hunt with a bow and arrow. I wanna keep my skills. I go off sometimes and let loose arrows. Otherwise I don't get to practice, 'cause Hank and I hunt with guns and the dogs."

Paul hurried off the porch, and Sabine was left with Lavinia's vacant silence.

No one had sung or played an instrument until now. Jen's singing had reminded Sabine how much she missed music. Music could crack people open and pull them together.

☙

Sabine was pulling weeds and picking beans in the garden with Paul, Jen, and Sol.

"Paul, it's just me, Sabine, and your buddy Jen," Sol said. "You can tell us why you hitchhiked from the UP. We won't tell."

"Sabine, throw me the trowel," Paul said.

"Come on, man." Sol grinned. Sabine wondered why he wouldn't let go of the subject.

Paul shook his head. "I got my reasons. I told you, it's family business. Not your business."

Sabine glared at Sol until he felt her stare and met her eyes. Then she gave him the finger.

Sol wiped dirt from his jeans. "Screw you, Sabine." He walked back toward the house.

Jen laughed. "Sol can be a real big jerk. He's as bad as my crappy father. But Paul, why didn't someone come with you? I'm surprised they let you hitchhike here all alone."

Paul answered with his charming grin. "Let's just say they didn't notice my empty bed till it was too late. When I could get through, I called and left a message. So they wouldn't worry." He worked the trowel into the dirt, pushing hard.

"Sneaky child," Jen said.

Paul turned away.

Jen touched his arm. "It's cool if you don't wanna say what you're doing here." She started humming.

Sabine stopped picking beans. "Will you sing for us? Anything's fine." Jen and Paul were the youngest, the obvious secret keepers, mistrustful of adult authority. Several times Sabine had felt their quick, hushed silence when she'd come upon them.

Today was no different. Acting as if she hadn't heard Sabine, Jen said, "Hey, Paul, wanna go shoot some arrows?"

Paul rose. "Sure thing."

Jen inspected her stubby fingers, wiped them on her pants, then stood. They left together.

Sabine went back to picking beans.

❧

Sabine flipped through magazines, searching faces, hoping to recognize someone famous or someone she knew. A politician, musician, or writer might be a clue to what kind of life she'd led in DC. A picture could string together associations, like a slide show turning into a movie. If the angry memories returned, her cruel, unforgiving side would emerge. Then Giles would enter her heart, like always, weighing her down like a wet blanket draping her shoulders. Her forced march, the hobbled miles with the sodden blanket, dripping misery. Damn his ghost voice, his gait, his blue eyes. She must stuff him down, and make him stay put.

She threw the magazine on the floor and went to the veranda. Tommy was finishing a joke. Randolph and Sharp stopped laughing when they spotted her.

Tommy grinned up at her in his boyish way. "How you doing?" He tugged at his mustache.

"Where's my machete?" she demanded. "I had it when Sharp and Hank found me. Someone took it the first night I slept here. Remember?"

"Can't say as I do," Tommy said with a sly look at Sharp and Randolph.

"Come on!" Sabine said. "Don't lie. Don't act like a shit."

Tommy laughed. "Okay. I do. Think you can handle a machete?" The men chuckled.

"Think I'm gonna chop off your head?" She couldn't control her voice.

"A guy's never sure what an angry woman might do." Tommy laughed, and Sharp smiled, taunting. His amusement made Sabine angrier.

She smacked the back of Tommy's head as hard as she could. "Go to hell." She registered a startled look on Sharp's face before she stomped off the porch. She ran to her room and checked on the backpack. Everything was still there. She paced; any minute, someone would come. Tommy would tell Jude and Hank. She dreaded what Hank would say. Would they kick her out? Her head hurt again. She lay on her bed.

❧

The smell of fried onions wafted through the window. Dusk had darkened the field. She must've slept through lunch. Tommy would humiliate her at dinner. She delayed going downstairs, but was too hungry not to go.

When everyone had gathered, Sabine sat by Jude, and he squeezed her hand. Someone had told him; his look was puzzled and concerned. She hoped he didn't think she was crazy. She couldn't stop glancing at Tommy, but he was flirting with Kate and never met her eyes.

After dinner, she and Jude sat on the veranda. The field was washed pale by the full moon.

"I'm not in the habit of hitting people," she said. "Tommy pushed me. He teased me like he does, and giggled like a little shit. He has no idea what happened on the way here, and no idea what the machete meant to me. He mocked me."

"You're lucky it was Tommy," Jude said. "Hank? You might be in trouble. Soon as we got back from foraging, Sharp told me what happened. He laughed and said you were more amusing than scary. Tommy shrugged and said no harm done. He realized he'd said something that pissed you off, but couldn't figure out what."

"Tommy's no idiot. He was pushing my buttons on purpose."

Jude put his arm around her. She pushed him away. "I came with a machete. Where is it? It's mine, and I want it back."

"It's okay. Nothing's going to happen to you with Sharp and Hank around. And what's so important about a machete, anyway?"

"On the way, on the road, a man swinging a machete came running out of a field and tried to rape me. I let him come close and drop his pants, then I kneed him in the crotch, grabbed his machete, and whacked him a couple times. He fell and blood gushed out of his head. I probably killed him, but I'm not sure, 'cause I ran like a bat outta hell."

"That's real bad."

"Bad for me, or him? I didn't mean to kill him."

Jude tried to hug her, but she pushed him away.

"You'll get away with it," he said. "The law's useless these days."

"The law?" She almost screamed the words. "Screw the law. He was a crazy man. He runs at me with a machete and tries to rip my clothes off, what am I supposed to do, smile?"

"You're right, you're right," he said, putting up his hands in surrender. "It's self-defense. Why didn't you tell me before? You've had a rough time."

"It was self-defense; I've never attacked anyone."

"Please tell me why you didn't talk to me about the man with the machete?" Jude said.

"Too awful," she said. "And that's my way. Forget bad things and move on."

⁂

They gathered in the living room. Kate worked at lighting a fire, then Hank stood in front of the fireplace, where he made announcements. Except for the crackling fire, the room was silent. "Some of you might have noticed us washing a long time at the pump this afternoon. Tommy, Sharp, and I had to kill three men on our way out the gate today. It happened so fast we didn't have time to discuss anything. They were waiting at the foot of the driveway. A couple didn't die easy."

"The foot of our driveway?" Jen said, sitting straight up in her chair. "Why didn't you alert us? Paul and I were on watch, in the woods."

"Like I said, it happened fast," Hank said. "They were hiding in scrub below the gate, and must've come on foot. I was driving, with Sharp in the middle. Tommy was on shotgun and spotted them half a second before they started shooting."

"Lucky for us they were terrible shots," Tommy said. "We checked their clothes when it was over, but didn't find anything worth taking." He went silent. He had dark circles under his eyes, short on sleep from too many nights on watch.

"Their faces were red and their bodies were sweaty," Sharp said.

"Their lips were cracked. Mucus, some kinda goo coming out their eyes and noses. Some type of fever."

"A fever? Oh, god." Lavinia folded her arms.

"Did anybody hear the shots?" Sabine asked.

"Popping sounds," Lavinia said. "Thought it was a truck backfiring."

Kate shook her head. "I was doing dishes and the washing machine was running."

"Why didn't you come back and warn the people inside?" Jen balled up her fists and paced.

"Don't worry, we washed our clothes, then rinsed them in bleach," Sharp said.

"I mean it! Why did you wait till now?" Jen focused on Hank, but his face remained impassive.

"Jen and Paul were on watch, they're good with guns," Sharp said. "After we moved the bodies we scouted along the road, but didn't see more men. So we drove back to an abandoned cabin we noticed yesterday, hoping to find more guns, maybe even a tank of propane. But the trip was a waste of time; all we found were jars of disgusting preserves and a quilt the mice hadn't finished shredding."

"Should we keep putting a third person on watch?" Randolph asked.

Hank shrugged. "People are too tired to keep up this way. Unless you want to volunteer as a third . . ."

"I'm a terrible shot," Randolph said. "Weak eyes." He tapped his glasses with a sheepish expression.

Hank glanced around the room. "Okay. I'm finished."

"Wait." Randolph's voice rose. "I can't shoot, but I'll come as the third person. I see distance better than close up. I'll carry a gun and look menacing."

Hank smiled. "Thanks. Let's talk strategy in the morning."

Randolph nodded. Lavinia touched his arm and smiled.

People left the room, and Sabine sidled up to Hank. "I keep putting off asking you. Remember the time you took me foraging?"

"Yeah," he said. "You did great, except you were jumpy."

"An understatement. I've never hung around with people who own guns. Can you teach me to shoot?"

Hank's eyebrows went up. "You've never shot a gun? Guess I'll never put you on watch."

"You know I can't," she said, laughing. "But I can swing a machete."

"I'd be glad to teach you," Hank said. "We just have to find time and enough daylight hours. A gun's more useful than a machete."

"Why did you take me foraging, anyway?"

"Curiosity," he said. "You made it a long way by yourself. No car, no horse. Alone, on foot, which takes guts. You come off as fragile, and even a little crazy. But you aren't."

"You think that?" She felt her cheeks grow hot. "Thanks."

"You're welcome." He put a hand on her shoulder.

She walked away pleased and embarrassed, though she hadn't yet forgotten his "not bad for a woman" remark about machete man. Still, he kept the farm together. He was part of her new family. She wanted to hug him, but felt too shy.

Hank would teach her to shoot. She didn't have much interest in learning; it was fear that had driven her to ask. She'd never be good like Jen and the men, but she could learn the basics. They might come in useful some day.

What if she remembered the people from her past, then discovered they were all dead? What if she and the others at the farm all starved during the winter, or a gang attacked them, and the marauders threw their bones in the field? With bones already littering the field and the farm family's bones buried in the front yard, what were a few more?

Through the library window, an image crossed the barn, followed by a booming sound that jarred her back to the room. She blinked and peered through the window; she couldn't see anything that hadn't already been there. An acidic taste rose in her throat and she swallowed. A foulness spread through her body. At the field's edge, the creek entered sparse trees that gradually became dense. Someone could get lost in those woods. Forever. But the trees at the edge revealed nothing. They stood as always, the wind orchestrating their motion.

Her ears rang as if someone had boxed them over and over. *What's happening?* She clutched her head, and the room spun fast before it slowed to a crawl. In the old living room she stared through a hole in the wall where the window used to be. The air turned viscous and shimmered in layers, like she was driving on a blacktop on a hot day. Noise of cars smashing, parts of buildings tumbling, like towers of children's blocks being kicked over.

She felt the heavy weight of her pack against her back. She reached behind her to check if she was wearing it, but she wasn't. She was sitting at her desk in the library in a West Virginia farmhouse. She'd made it. She hoped wherever her parents, brothers, and sisters lived, they were quick thinkers, and resourceful, too.

The pain in her head came back. She closed her eyes. Lack of motion helped. She forced herself to go over images until she found a fixed memory about the pain. The teenager yelling about bombs in the store, then moving lightning fast into her peripheral vision and screaming in her face. Then white linoleum. Spinning. Crashing. Lying on the ground and staring at her backpack, noticing that the top had been torn open. Then sitting on the curb outside, going through the pack, and discovering that her wallet was gone. No ID meant no last name. Without her name, how could she find her family?

That precise moment, sitting on the curb, was when her headaches had started.

Chapter 7

THE TALE OF
THE HORSE AND
THE SHELTER OF LEAVES

July 13, 2014.

Sabine was flipping through a magazine in the library when she heard Tommy yell, "Paul's hurt!"

Kate was already at the backdoor, carrying a bowl and the first-aid box. "Bring a clean rag," she ordered as Sabine entered the kitchen, running outside without waiting for a response.

Sabine snatched a clean dishrag out of a drawer and followed.

Kate set the bowl on the porch, and Hank and Tommy guided Paul to Kate. Blood covered his face, neck, and shirt. Kate took a fifth of bourbon out of the box and handed it to Paul. "Take a couple slugs. We don't have pain pills."

Sabine turned away while Kate cleaned the wound. "Not as bad as it looks," Kate said. "Facial wounds bleed a lot. But you need stitches."

Sabine made herself watch Kate sew Paul's cheek while her stomach churned.

Tommy kept his hand on Paul's shoulder and leaned in. He shook his finger at Paul. "Here's a joke. It's nasty, but no laughing. Don't you dare laugh." He launched in, and soon Paul's shoulders were shaking with silent laughter and tears were in his eyes.

"Hey man, no more jokes," Hank growled.

"Tommy, stop," Kate said. "If Paul wiggles, it'll take me twice as long."

"Just one more, a short one," Tommy said.

By the time Kate finished sewing up the wound, Hank's fists were balled up and he was glaring at Tommy.

In between laughing, Paul bit his lip but didn't cry out.

Tommy sat by Kate. She ruffled his hair. "You're a mess."

"But it worked, my darlin'." Tommy laughed his raucous laugh.

Kate stood and planted her hands on her hips and pouted, pretending to be irritated.

Paul gazed at Kate with admiration, perhaps sexual longing.

Sabine squatted behind him and put her hand on the boy's back. "Tommy, what happened?"

"Paul was on lookout. Hank and I were searching an abandoned garage. Three kids came out of the woods, and one jumped Paul and sliced his face. Paul had no time to pull his gun, or a knife. Paul yelled and punched the kid. Hank and I came running, and the kids ran like hell. We didn't go after them; they looked no older than twelve, maybe younger. They'd spotted our truck and come to check us out."

"Paul, you're brave," Sabine said. "I bet your father and grandfather would be proud. I am."

Paul cried a little.

"You miss your family," she stroked his hair. "I miss mine too, even though I don't know who they are. There's a hole and it feels weird."

Paul nodded. He remained a child. What business did a fifteen-year-old have hitchhiking halfway across the country after bombs fell? Sabine knew without asking that he wouldn't want her to reveal his family business in the log. She didn't blame him.

❧

They talked about the attack on Paul. Sabine and Jen fussed at him to be more careful, and tried to convince him to stay at the farm. "There's plenty to do in the garden," Jen reminded him. Paul appeared to listen, but said nothing.

Kate said little—admitted her worries, but said she'd go with whatever Hank said. He, Tommy, and Sharp hadn't said anything yet. Who knew what Lavinia thought?

They gathered after dinner. Crouched in a corner, Paul looked at his feet as if he'd done something wrong. Hank and Sharp stood in front of the fireplace. Hank declared the boy should be allowed to choose.

"Tell us what you want." Sharp nodded his encouragement to Paul.

"Grandpa and Pop taught me to shoot," Paul said. "I want to help. My gun helps out. Does it matter where we forage? When I was hitchhiking through a city, a guy picked me up. We hadn't gone more than a couple blocks when, fast as a snake, the guy grabbed my crotch. I punched the side of his face and he let go, and as soon as he slowed to make a turn, I jumped out. Nothing half that bad has happened while we've been foraging."

Sabine considered speaking up, but didn't want to embarrass Paul. He was trying to be a man. He hung out with Tommy the most, but he'd warmed up to the other men too, even Sol. When Paul licked his lips while staring at Kate, Sabine guessed what was on his mind.

"Sharp and I agree with Paul," Hank said. "We think it'll be good for all of us if Paul keeps foraging. We'll keep a closer eye out from now on."

Sabine was relieved the decision had been made, though she'd still worry.

⤳

In the log, Sabine wrote:

Out my bedroom window the mountains shift with shadow and light as if lumbering across the land. Afternoon sun streams in the window. When I was a kid, by early August trees dropped some of their green to save energy and water. Harsh light baked the southern clay. By October, leaves still clinging began falling, their acrid smell rising from fiery piles. In my neighborhood, burning leaves remained an autumn ritual.

Late-afternoon light spread butter across the wall. The attic room turned into a childhood room. This sad feeling is a warning. If I sit in childhood, I'll fall into misery. The cusp of a bad-memory train racing toward what I keep trying to forget.

She slammed the notebook shut. When she pulled her jacket off the chair, an image of the ornate coat given to her by the man she loved flashed into her mind. His forbidden name shadowed her while she hurried across the field. *Giles.*

At Giles's party, people had crowded close to catch his words. He'd leaned against a kitchen counter wearing a Jackson Pollock undershirt under an unbuttoned dress shirt. When he gestured, his white cuffs flopped around. Beer and bourbon and strong words about painters and poets, arguments about who'd become famous and who was doomed to obscurity. She argued with him in an elaborate flirt-dance. Later he followed her into the dining room. They pushed the bowls of party food to one end of the table and pulled up chairs. He launched into a description of stews.

"See that shelf?" he asked. "All cookbooks. I like making complicated stews and baking bread."

He reached out to grab chips from a bowl, exposing his left arm to the elbow. Needle marks and round scars. Her heartbeat picked up, and she pretended to study his bookcase.

"Tell me about your sculpture collection."

His voice turned soft, with a Southern lilt. "Not much traveling lately, too busy with university stuff. In grad school I used to make runs down to Mexico to hunt for good pieces."

Had he combined heroin trafficking with sculpture? Heroin was supposed to be cheaper south of the border.

"You like cookbooks?" he asked. "I'll be glad to lend you one or two. *Larousse Gastronomique* is a cookbook, also a cooking encyclopedia. I never lend it. The huge one with the red cover." He pointed to it, high on the shelf. "If you wanted to borrow it, though—"

"I'm not much of a cook," Sabine said. "But thanks for the offer."

This drug addict lives alone in a beautiful house full of fine art and cookbooks? How is that even possible?

She stumbled over a rock embedded in the field and almost fell. *You're a refugee living in West Virginia,* she reminded herself. *Watch where you're going. You're not at Giles's house.*

What else had she and Giles talked about? The early stuff faded. She'd left the party that night with the man who'd brought her, but tucked in her bra she'd carried a slip of paper with Giles's phone number on it. His piercing blue eyes had scared her. She knew they could mean the end of her single life.

On their first date they'd felt like a couple and talked for hours. He'd asked her to stay the night and they'd slept on the bedspread, fully clothed, holding hands. He taught philosophy at the university, but she didn't care where he worked. She liked his style. She didn't ask about the scars on his arms, decided they were old. She'd ignore them, pretend they weren't there.

Their good years played out—then came the worst. But if she dwelt on him, the nightmares would come back.

All the objects he'd given her, she saved. The glass-bead necklace, the blue sapphire engagement ring, and the antique stuffed dog, its coat rough, one plastic eye missing. Their first Christmas, he bought them both Moroccan sheepskin coats. Hers was orange suede with a circlet of leaves embroidered in red thread across the back. When the weather turned cold, they brought out their coats. He wore a fedora; she draped the necklace over a peasant blouse. After they split, she kept his coat and hung it by hers. Later she opened the closet door, and a flurry of moths swarmed the room. She wrapped both coats in a garbage bag and carried it to the trash across outstretched arms, as if carrying a corpse. Everything else was destroyed by the bomb.

During the years with Giles she wrote in notebooks, budget-binders, sketchbooks with black covers, and on the backs of envelopes. The stack grew. Story scraps, opinions, descriptions. Five or six decent poems out of hundreds of attempts.

Nothing was left, except what was in her backpack and her favorite shawl. And the machete, hidden somewhere in the farmhouse.

Startled by a birdcall, she reassured herself that the farmhouse was directly behind her, all she had to do was to turn around. Grass and weeds swayed in the breeze; bugs jumped on her ankles, but she didn't push them off. The bird sounds turned ominous, and she dared herself to walk among the wide-spaced trees into the darker woods but couldn't do it. She leaned against a rock outcrop and closed her eyes against the sun.

When she opened her eyes she wondered how long she'd stood there. By the time she reached the farmhouse, she could barely make out the shapes of the trees.

In her room she lit both candles. DC at night had never been this dark. The field outside her window lay in blackness, a stable piece of the world, while her equilibrium came and went. The candlelight fractured her reflection across the windowpanes. Since the bombs she kept discovering aspects of herself. Were they caused by the bombs, or had they been with her all along?

༚

Sabine sprawled in the living room with Sol, Tommy, and Paul, speculating about the bombs. They had no new information, but they all had opinions. They mostly agreed on the theory that the terrorist attack had been carefully planned and carried out by a large group of people with excellent computer skills and knowledge of buildings, airports, the electrical grid, naval bases, shipyards, bridges, trains, and subway tunnels. But they couldn't come close to agreeing who'd sponsored and carried out the attack.

"You gotta figure it was al-Qaeda," Tommy said. "Of course they'd target naval bases and hub airports. And cities like DC, Chicago, New York, and Miami, for the infrastructure and for the symbolism."

Paul picked up the poker and pushed ashes around in the fireplace. "DC and New York are government and communications. You got it wrong. The bombs must be a CIA plot. A setup so the Prez can bomb the hell out of any country he wants, in retaliation."

Tommy shook his head. "We could bomb Pakistan, Syria, Iran, Somalia, and Yemen—and maybe the scariest, North Korea—whenever we want. Not the CIA. How about homegrown terrorists? A group of antigovernment loners who got together."

"It's an interesting theory," Sabine said, "but I agree with Tommy." She leaned forward. "Think about Memorial Day's symbolism. A holiday honoring dead servicemen and women. The bombs spoke for al-Qaeda: 'Your military and civilians have died. More will die for what you did in Iraq and Afghanistan.' Doesn't al-Qaeda, or a similar group, make more sense?"

"You're misguided about the CIA, Paul." Tommy took off his cap, smoothed his hair, and pulled the cap back on. "You've been reading too many thrillers. But just maybe it could be homegrown terrorists. If the CIA didn't dig them out of their holes in time, then we're in trouble."

Sabine kept her tone soft. "What makes you think it's the CIA?"

"Maybe the plan got out of hand?" Paul said. "Like, the CIA meant to attack two or three places, but more cells got activated. They got their wires crossed." Paul hung the poker on a hook and rubbed his hands on his pants. His face shone. He enjoyed debating, and liked adults taking him seriously.

"Paul!" Sol erupted. "Tommy teaches history and geography. You're just a boy—you don't understand how the world works."

Paul's face fell. He ducked his head and headed toward the hall.

Sol tried to touch the boy's shoulder as he passed. "Paul. Look."

"Asshole," Paul muttered over his shoulder, and he left the room.

"You didn't have to do that," Sabine said. "He was just giving his opinion."

"He doesn't have a grasp," Sol said.

"And you?" she said, her voice rising.

"Better than a kid," Sol said.

Not wanting to argue with Sol, Sabine left, wondering why Tommy didn't defend Paul. Was he scared to confront Sol? She didn't think of him as a scary guy. He could listen without getting defensive. That kind of person was easier to confront than someone slippery, the kind who made jokes and put people down, like Tommy.

❧

Sabine asked Kate if she needed help making lunch. Kate shook her head.

"Okay, I'll clean the library till lunch."

On her way through the living room, she spotted magazines she hadn't noticed before under a pile of old newspapers. She stacked the newspapers by the fireplace. Old magazines were popular, so she slipped a few under her shirt and closed herself in the library, where she transferred them to her desk drawer.

She climbed on a chair and wiped down the top of the book-case. Books were piled on chairs and some lay on the floor. She dusted and shelved them, then dragged three chairs into the living room to make her room feel bigger. She positioned the dictionary on the top-left corner of the desk and laid a notebook and pencils in the center. One place where she could impose order.

When she was done cleaning, she headed to the kitchen for lunch. Kate sat at the head of the table, as always, with Tommy on her right. A few times he leaned over and whispered in her ear, then kissed the corner of her mouth. She responded each time with a lovely, slow smile, meant for him.

Sharp came in and sat without speaking. Between bites of food he stared at the map on the wall with a faraway look. Sabine rehearsed questions to ask him, but couldn't think of anything that sounded spontaneous.

After they finished eating, Kate repeated her usual spiel. "Vegetable scraps in the compost bucket. Scrap meat in the dog dishes."

Sharp pushed back his chair, nodded to Kate, and left. Sabine wasn't surprised Sharp didn't help out; his skills lay elsewhere. No one challenged him, or Hank, if they didn't do a household chore.

Tommy followed Kate to the sink, pressed against her back, and slipped his hands around her waist. She faced him and pushed him away. He left the room laughing. Paul watched from the doorway—wanting, Sabine assumed, to trade places with Tommy. She was sorry Paul was the only teenager at the farm.

The Tale of the Horse and the Shelter of Leaves

A shelter fashioned from summer's green leaves. Imagine a moving house, the interweaving leaves, the sun full to burning, the sparkle of leaves when the shelter swayed in summer wind. Not a house covered with leaves, but rather woven from leaves. A rustling shelter that wouldn't last. The horse shimmering from the angle of the sun. He switched his tail and faded into trees. Airborne, the horse flew straight and peered down at the swaying green mass. The leaves were weaving themselves, forming a wall that trapped him outside.

The horse longed to return to summer, to reverse the time machine, force it to reverse itself. The machine wouldn't stop.

Time never did. The horse offered to race with time and bragged
he'd win. Time showed the horse dreadful things: bug-sized
humans ran in circles and blocky buildings toppled to the ground.
  The horse flew low, back to the spot where his shelter of leaves
once stood. Not a leaf on the blackened ground. Nothing moved
on the ruined field. He told himself he was still in charge, the one
in command. With bravado he called, "Come back, Shelter of
Leaves, come back." But time did not bother to answer.

From the veranda Sabine watched the fog lift, followed by a sheet
of rain moving in from the east. Was that a shadow on the barn
yesterday, or a trick of light? She pulled her shawl close around her
shoulders. An animal moved at the edge of the trees then ventured
into the field. A brown and yellow dog, German shepherd–sized.
She hurried to the railing and squinted through the rain. *Sun Dog.*
Impossible, the original Sun Dog was dead. But the shape resembled
the dog she'd chased away on the road. She eased down the steps,
but the dog pricked up its ears and bolted into the woods. No point
in chasing a dog that didn't want to be found. He'd come again.

  The rain slowed; birds landed on the field and pecked in the
drizzle. The leaves on the maple trees by the house dripped and wind
gusts ripped off leaves. The birds charged each other and scattered
across the field with furious pecking and head bobbing, chasing
scarce food.

  She must brave the woods and investigate the barn. Perhaps it
was a refugee's shadow that had slid across the barn.

Sabine woke to an *Om* sound humming in her head. She knew it
was from a CD, but couldn't recall when or where she'd heard it. A
gentle sound, calling up the word "home."

Then, loud voices from the hallway. Over them all, Jen was yelling, "Yes, yes! I knew about it!"

Sabine dressed with haste and took the back steps to the kitchen. "What's happening?"

Hank held a piece of paper. "He's gone."

"Who? What?" Sabine's heart thudded.

"Paul," Hank said. "He ran off during the night. While he and Jen were on watch."

Kate frowned. "What does the note say?"

Hank handed the note to Kate. She read, "Thanks. You guys are great, but like I said, I gotta take care of business. Wherever you all go, good luck! Your friend, Paul."

Sabine felt deflated. Jen leaned against the counter, a mug of coffee shaking in her hand.

"You knew he was planning this?" Hank asked. "For how long?"

"A week or so," Jen said. "It wasn't anything any of us did. Course I tried to talk him out of it, but he kept saying he had business. I think it was about his mom. He talked some about her." Jen's face turned red, then came silent tears she tried to hold back. She gulped her coffee and checked her gun. "I'm still on watch. Anybody coming?" She put on her jacket.

"Why didn't you come to me?" Hank said. "I could've talked to him."

Jen laughed. "Well, Mr. Big Shot, not everyone wants your advice. Paul asked me not to tell anyone, including you, till after he'd gone."

Hank glared at her, wide-eyed.

"I'm on watch," Jen said. "Anybody coming?"

"Hold on, Jen," Sharp said. "I'll come." He took two pieces of toast from a stack on the table and spread them with peanut butter. Without a jacket, he ran out the door after her.

Sabine thought it was a good thing Sharp went with Jen. He was level-headed. He'd talk to her. She poured herself a cup of coffee.

"Tommy, did you suspect Paul was going to leave? You two spent a lot of time together."

"No idea," Tommy said. "He wouldn't tell me, though—he knew I'd try to talk him out of it. The roads are dangerous, especially on foot. And we don't even know where he's headed." His shoulders slumped. He focused on the serving bowl of oatmeal on the table. He rose. "I'm not hungry."

"Just eat it!" Kate said.

"No," Tommy said over his shoulder and left the room.

"Pouty dumbass," Kate muttered.

Jude came and sat by Sabine. She put her head on his shoulder and reached for his hand. She couldn't eat, either.

⁊

The following day no one sat in Paul's place at the table. They finished the oatmeal from the day before, ate tart apples, peanut butter, and bread. Afterward, Sabine headed to the library with a cup of coffee. Worry about Paul mixed with thoughts about her amnesia. Why couldn't she find the names of people in her family in her brain? Giles's was somehow linked with leaving her family in fury, then blocking them out. But how?

She swept the living room and glanced out the window. Kate sat alone on the veranda, making Sabine's plan more difficult; she didn't want an interrogation. She put away the broom and took a medium-sized knife and wrapped it in a dish towel. She slipped it in her belt.

In the living room she tiptoed to the wall of windows. Kate was still in the chair, her eyes closed. Sabine hurried along the side of the house. Once in the field she slowed her pace and swung her arms, hoping to look casual. Afraid of the woods, scared of the people who might lurk there, she allowed herself to glance back at the farm. Kate hadn't moved.

Sabine hadn't walked far before the trees grew closer together,

the thick canopy darkening the woods and obscuring details on the
ground. She spotted a deer path and walked along it, headed in the
opposite direction from where she and Jude had walked. With a
small flashlight aimed at the ground, she walked on leaf-covered
dirt to muffle her footsteps.

Tinny voices. A radio? She crept behind a tree. Garbled voices,
followed by Sharp's clear one. She inched around the tree, but
stopped when she glimpsed something red through the brush. Sharp
was crouched over a piece of equipment. His back was to her, a large
phone to his ear, "Dammit, man, I couldn't get through. A spike in
calls yesterday? What emergency?"

Silence while he listened. He rose, paced in a tight circle staring
at the ground. "Got it. We're movin' out. It's too hot here."

The second she realized he'd hung up, she inched backwards.
Sharp kept pacing, mumbling to himself. She thought he was saying, "Move, move, move."

She backed away until she felt safe to turn around. At the field's
edge she took a full breath. *What is he up to?*

Chapter 8

BLOOD MOON RISE

July 15, 2014.

The creak of Kate's rocking chair on the veranda was a relief; she might rock for half an hour or longer. Even though Sabine's hands were trembling from two cups of strong coffee, she slipped into the kitchen for a third. Scribes needed three coffees a day to stimulate thinking and writing.

Kate appeared. "The one-cup rule!"

Sabine jumped. "I have to have two or three cups to write. What's the big deal?"

Kate shook her finger. "Liar! Every day you drink more, even when you're not writing. I'm telling Hank."

"Go ahead. He won't care." Sabine laughed. "Most of us can barely stomach this coffee anyway."

Kate stomped out of the room.

Sabine took a gulp of the bitter brew. "Tasty," she said to the empty room. *What a bitch, wagging her finger at me. She must think I'm twelve.* Kate probably drank all the coffee she wanted. And Hank had better things to do than monitor the coffee pot.

Sabine prepared her defense. If Kate told Hank, maybe he'd spring an attack later. But she doubted Kate would tell him.

꙳

The following day Sabine woke agitated. After breakfast she carried her third cup of coffee to the living room. Today the coffee smelled burned—probably Kate did it on purpose, in retaliation. Sabine busied herself dusting furniture, telling herself the dread she felt might not be about the day but something else she couldn't put her finger on. She tried not to imagine what might have happened to Paul on the road. He was young, and good with a gun—but he was alone. She hoped he didn't have far to walk.

Just as she was telling herself she'd cut back to two cups of coffee tomorrow, she heard harsh, loud voices from the veranda. She crept to a window.

Jen and Sol stood far apart on the veranda. Jen made choppy movements, slicing the air for emphasis. "How dare you accuse me! Paul was my friend, like a brother."

Sol shook his head. Jen gave him the finger and spat over the railing. Sol stormed in the front door and glanced Sabine's way. His eyes fell on her coffee cup. "How many cups have you had today? You eat a lot, and now you're stealing coffee. Can't turn our backs on you for a minute."

Before Sabine could respond, Sol ran upstairs. Two minutes later he came down wearing his jacket; he sneered at her on his way out. She imagined tripping him. What kind of paranoid jerk would think Jen wanted Paul to leave? And why did Sol care about Paul, anyway?

If Kate couldn't make her stop drinking too much coffee, Sol sure couldn't. If Hank or Sharp told her to stop, she would. They were the ones who had rescued her. They held the power.

Either way, it was time to steal something critical: maps.

Kate tromped down the front hall.

Sabine gulped the rest of her coffee and hid the cup behind a lamp. She hurried to the second floor, but slowed her steps when she approached Kate and Tommy's room. She stopped in front of their door. No movement from inside the room or anywhere else in the hall. She slipped inside and shut the door.

The box of maps still sat by the chair. Virginia and West Virginia maps were in her pack; she needed the Eastern states. She found a map of the East Coast and took the back stairs to her room, where she lay the West Virginia map across her bed and pinpointed the farmhouse's location. While walking she'd seen a bullet-ridden road sign that read Big Brook. The next, smaller dot read: Little Brook. That must be where they were.

She read off names of towns near the interstate so they'd sound familiar when they left the farm. Then put the maps in a side pocket of her backpack.

Smooth it over with Kate. She needed information from her. She couldn't afford to make her an enemy.

She found her in the living room, flipping through the pages of a cookbook.

"What are you fixing to make?" Sabine asked, smiling.

Kate looked up. "If you're interested, I'm trying to find something new to do with canned tomatoes. We've done soups and stews, spaghetti sauce . . ."

"How about a succotash thing? Canned lima beans, corn, and fry up some onions. A few potatoes?"

"Good idea. Thanks."

"You're familiar with the area. I'd like directions to the nearest gas station."

Kate's eyes widened. "What for? There's no gas or kerosene. And no food."

"When I was walking, I avoided the interstate," Sabine said. "Walking to a station by the interstate might help me get a better sense of where I am."

"It's dangerous," Kate said, "and getting worse. I wish we'd leave for St. Augustine today. I bet things are fine down there. I haven't talked to my grandparents, but the town's small and wouldn't be a target."

"I walked by myself for three weeks," Sabine said. "I'm aware what's out there. Maybe there's less of a threat now because more people have died."

Kate shook her head. "No. Those who are left will be more desperate."

Sabine said nothing.

"You're gonna go whether or not I give you directions," Kate said and sighed. "All right. Take a right at the foot of the driveway. Head east a mile, and you'll hit an intersection with a nonworking stoplight, if someone hasn't torn it down. The station's on a corner there, next to what's left of the interstate on-ramp."

"Thanks," Sabine said. "But you're right, it's too dangerous. I'll stick to writing."

Before Kate could answer, Sabine headed to the library and sat down at her desk. She imagined herself walking to the station. A wild man jumping out of the bushes, swinging a machete. Her body felt numb. She looked out the window at nothing.

Stop worrying about machete man; stop worrying about what Kate thinks of you.

✖

At dinner Hank reminded them about the meeting, though no one needed reminding.

Sabine waited for Hank to say something nasty about her stealing coffee. His style would be to say it in front of everyone. But he didn't mention it.

She wondered when they'd give up the fantasy of FEMA, the National Guard, or the Red Cross sending help. While working in the garden, Lavinia, Jen, and Tommy reassured each other that help would come. Sabine kept quiet about her hunch they were wrong. Hank and Sharp had been at the farmhouse since the day after Memorial Day. Now it was mid-July, and no sign of help.

Once they gathered in the living room, Jen spoke first, her

words tumbling out. "Lemme tell you what we found today. Hank, Sharp, and I circled behind the farmhouse, pulled off the road, and walked northwest, toward the farm. The other truck headed northeast. A pincer move. We found fresh-cut branches and shells that didn't belong to us. Footprints led to several burned-out campfires. We've been breached!"

The word "breach" sounded humorous, as if they lived in a castle or a military installation. Sabine's mind skittered away from the worst: government in ruins, more bombs, radiation sickness, starvation, cannibalism.

Randolph's loud voice interrupted her reverie. He faced Hank. "A decision to leave the farm is foolhardy! The hill's a vantage point, plus we have guns and ammunition."

"We don't have enough guns and ammo," Hank said. "And some of us can't shoot worth a damn. If we stay together, we'll need more cropland. There are four women here, but not enough to build a self-sufficient community. We'll need women who want families. We're under forty and healthy, but we won't be if we stay here through the winter without enough food."

Sabine looked over at Lavinia's sunken cheeks and frail hands. An old woman's hands. She probably couldn't walk a mile. Sabine hadn't planned to say anything, but she jumped up. Her chair hit the floor and she kicked it out of the way. "What if some of us don't want to form a community or have babies?"

Everyone turned to her.

Randolph said, "Each of us is free to come and go."

"What I mean is," she said, "all of us might not want to build a community, because deep down, we're all hoping and waiting."

"For what?" Randolph asked.

"For the world to go back to the way it was. But guess what? No one's coming to rural West Virginia. Not FEMA, not the National Guard, not anybody! Hank told us how FEMA works: first they restore power, then communications, and finally transportation.

Anyone noticed these wonders happening around here? I sure haven't." She stopped trying to control her irritation. "On the road there were plenty of people who could've helped me, but they shunned me. No one helped till I met Sharp and Hank."

She waited for someone to challenge her, but no one spoke. They knew she was right. "We want someone to fix the chaos," she continued. "A stable food source. Safe roads. Working cell phone towers. News about what's happening in the world. But we're not going to get it."

She picked up her chair and sat back down. Her face felt feverish.

Hank repeated what he'd been saying before she interrupted. The farmhouse wasn't safe anymore. They needed to leave. Jen chimed in again with the evidence they'd found that refugees were encroaching on their land.

Sabine noticed that nobody mentioned the word cannibal. Was she the only person worried about it? With Hank and Jen repeating themselves, she grew bored; she dozed and dreamed about a pale man with a misshapen face. The man asked if she'd come to bed with him. A rattlesnake hiss sounded nearby, growing louder by the minute. Sabine raised her voice over the rattling and yelled she didn't have a home. The sound reverberated, the snakes were coiled under the living room furniture. She jerked awake.

She and Jude were the only ones left in the living room. The cessation of voices had woken her. Jude pulled her from her chair. She leaned against him, glad for his warm body. He kissed her forehead.

"What did you all decide?" She buried her head in his chest.

"You weren't following each word?" He chuckled. "Yesterday Tommy found tractor tracks running across our field, probably from a nearby farm. The tractor was gone by the time Sharp and Hank got there. Even if we hunted them and stole their tractor, it wouldn't matter. People have been glassing the farmhouse. Two days ago Kate caught binocular reflections from several places at the edge of the woods."

"Kate didn't tell me," Sabine said.

"She thinks you're unstable."

"I'm better. Can't you tell?"

He turned away. "I'm afraid they'll attack the farm during the day, while most of us are off in the trucks."

She moved until she could see his face. "Are we sure these people are enemies?"

Jude sighed. "How naive. If they weren't enemies, they'd drive up or walk up the driveway waving a white flag. This spying is about one thing. No. Two things."

"What?" She frowned.

"Our food stores aren't great, but they're better than no food. And we have a warm, well-fortified house. Winter's coming, and people are getting desperate for shelter."

"When do we leave?"

"It's Monday night. Tomorrow we harvest what we can from the garden and pack the trucks. We leave at five or six Wednesday morning, or tomorrow if we can get it together by then."

"And go where?"

"St. Augustine, Florida. The vote was unanimous, except for your vote. You were right about going south."

Sabine nodded. "You're positive we shouldn't stay and fight off any attackers who might come?"

"Hank keeps reminding us we're vulnerable. If a gang pinned us down, it wouldn't take long to starve us out, or take us out one by one."

"Let's check out the old pickup in the garage," Sabine said. "If we can get it running, you and I can take it."

"I don't know about going off without the others," he said.

"It's a mistake to trust everyone here. Hank and Sharp are secretive. Kate's hiding something. I'd rather go with you."

What was the point of falling in love, with so much uncertainty? She'd had enough instability with Giles.

"When you first got here, you were secretive too," Jude said. "Don't judge people for their secrets. We're in a crisis, and people are scared."

His face was haggard. She pulled him closer. "Come to bed."

He followed her up the stairs and closed her door. She lit the candle on the bedside table. He undressed her, looking at her body, yet he was distracted. His sad expression frightened her. She pulled off his work shirt, T-shirt, and pants. She took his penis in her mouth, aware of the bowie knife in a sheath strapped to his calf. She could take away his sadness, but only for a while.

When he was inside her, she enjoyed the soft sounds they made. But as soon as they pulled apart and lay without talking, her thoughts crowded back. Before she had a chance to talk more about the truck, she heard his regular breathing. She blew out the candle and curled up with her breasts pressed against his back. She hoped he'd be loyal. She'd told him she didn't want to come back to West Virginia. If he agreed to ride with her to St. Augustine, it meant he was willing to give up searching for his dad, and his old girlfriend, Laura.

She stroked his head, and he halfway opened his eyes and kissed her forehead before falling asleep again. If he wouldn't go along with the plan to go in the pickup truck, she'd abandon it. To leave him felt intolerable. People couldn't tell she was clingy because she didn't act it, but she felt its pull inside. Her own weakness revolted her, made her feel vulnerable, but she didn't know how to get rid of it.

She woke when she felt Jude tossing around. Half asleep she said, "Jude, you can fix the pickup in the garage. I'll help."

His face obscured by shadow. "You're serious about the two of us going?"

"I meant it when I said it before. We'll take maybe a rifle and a small gun. I'd rather bargain with my crotch than a gun."

"If guys are hungry," he said, "they won't care about sex. Or they'll take what they want. Besides, we don't have any 'small guns,' as you put it."

"My point, Jude, is we do what it takes to stay alive. I walked to the farmhouse. More miles than your fifty on horseback! I'm not naive about what most men want from women."

"You're a little crazy," he said.

"I'm practical. Sex becomes a means to an end, if we screw other people for food and information. We do what we have to," she said. "Despite machete man, I made it here, didn't I?"

"I get your point about surviving, but it still sounds slutty."

"No, sluts enjoy it," she said. "I'd whore for food, but I'd take scant pleasure in it."

She slept again and woke to a roomful of sun and automatically reached for Jude. He was gone. She groaned at the empty pillow. She didn't want him out foraging, didn't want any dreadful things to happen at the last minute.

❧

In the morning, Sabine dressed fast and put on her vest with pockets. Loud voices rose from downstairs. She crept down the front stairs, filled with an urge to get more maps. Hank and Sharp sat on the couch in the living room, their heads touching, whispering. Sharp glanced up, his eyes wide, and Sabine waved and kept moving, slipping out the front door. She jogged down the driveway, using the trees for cover. At the end of the drive, she scrambled over the fence and ripped the seat of her pants on a nail sticking out of a loose board.

She saw no one on the road, made it to the gas station faster than she thought she would. Even before she opened the glass door, the stench knocked her back. Five or six bodies lay inside. A swarm of flies spread out, their buzzing filling the room. From the doorway, she surveyed the room until she spotted what she wanted. She held her breath and ran. Instantly black bodies were on her. The buzzing roared in her ears. With lips pressed together, she moved to the map rack on the back wall and grabbed a handful of maps. Flies crawled over her face. She tried to brush them off. They flew back. She bolted out the door.

"Damn flies! What?" Sharp stood in front of her. She brushed flies off her arms; they flew off, but she kept rubbing her arms. She shook her head in case they were in her hair.

"I didn't mean to startle you," he said. "I'm on watch and saw you hop the fence. Why are you wandering around alone?"

"I walked twenty-one days before you and Hank found me," Sabine said. "I'm clear on what it's like out here. Did Hank pass on my machete-attack story? I killed the man."

Sharp nodded. "Hank may not have showed it, but he was impressed. Still, why risk going out alone?"

"Maps. For security."

Sharp laughed. "You like maps? That's it?" His eyes narrowed. "You don't have a plan to leave the farm without us?"

"Someone told me once that maps were essential to everything we do," Sabine said, avoiding Sharp's eyes. "And why would I leave the farm by myself? We're sort of a family. Anyway, you're the one with a sneaky plan, not me."

"Me?" He raised his eyebrows.

"What were you doing in the woods? Wandering around the other day, I heard tinny voices, saw you talking on some kind of phone. Camping out with marshmallows and graham crackers, were you?"

His face changed to a mask. "Spying on me, wiseass?"

She shook her head. Her gut hurt. She didn't want him mad at her. "Look, I'm just teasing. Don't worry. I don't care what you were doing, unless it could cause trouble for the group. What you do isn't my business." She didn't blink. "I haven't told anyone about you in the woods, and I won't. You and Hank have been good to me."

"You really haven't said anything to anyone?"

"Nope." Her hands were sweaty but she didn't wipe them on her jeans.

"Let's get back to the house." He didn't look at her.

"Together? Won't that look weird?" She tried to smile but was too edgy.

"Nah. I'll say I spotted you leaving the house and came with you, to keep you safe."

"The gas station was like some horror movie. Dead bodies, flies everywhere."

Sharp didn't respond, and they walked back to the farmhouse in silence. At the fence, he took her hand and boosted her over without a word.

"Thanks," Sabine said. "Now I have a serious question. Something I've been wondering. Did you find a sale on red shirts? It's like your costume, or something."

Sharp laughed so hard he bent over.

"Obviously you like red."

"It's a powerful color. And it hides dirt." He laughed some more.

"That's it?"

He cleared the fence. She took his hand and held it in both of hers. "Look, Sharp, you're hard to figure, you don't talk much. But I'd like us to be friends. We need each other; we'll need each other even more once we hit the road."

"Sure thing. I'm not much of a talker. Nothing personal."

When they got to the house he held the door for her. She was so surprised she forgot to say thank you.

They followed the sounds of laughter to the kitchen. Everyone except Jude and Jen were there. Sabine was glad that Jude was on the road. He might be jealous if he saw her walking with Sharp. Had she made a mistake telling him about bargaining with her crotch? She'd wanted to help him understand how she thought about survival. But her survival tactic didn't apply to any other man in the farmhouse. Sharp attracted her, but she cared about Jude.

Lavinia stirred a pot of oatmeal, humming, her sour expression gone. Yet yesterday at lunch Lavinia took tiny portions and pushed food around her plate, as usual.

Sabine ate a bowl of oatmeal, thinking about Sharp. Randolph stood in the pantry with Kate, pulling cans and jars off shelves and passing them to Tommy, who wrapped the jars in newspaper and set them in boxes. He was wearing his ball cap and whistling, like he was preparing for a Boy Scout camping trip.

Sabine finished the oatmeal and went to the living room, where she rummaged through a pile of clothes the foragers had pilfered from stores. A blue fleece vest that was too big but would fit over a sweater or jacket. She could toss her smelly vest. A knit cap with a red tassel that was childish but warm. Her backpack was ready and waiting in the armoire. She had winter clothes, prepared for whatever came. Who knew if they'd make it to Florida.

⁓

Midafternoon, Lavinia was still helping Kate, the two of them working in the garden, pulling up vegetables that were ripe or near ripe and putting them in boxes. Tommy and Sharp were walking the perimeter on watch. Randolph and Sol had taken the blue truck north to search for gas, and Jude and Jen had headed south and west on back roads, also looking for gas. Sabine was relieved Jen was riding shotgun with Jude. Jen was a good protector.

Sabinee paced the upstairs hall, worrying, still hoping Jude would travel with her in the third truck. She could fix it herself, if the problem wasn't complicated. An image of a teenaged boy flashed through her mind, the two of them side by side in a garage, leaning over a car engine. His pale hands hovered over the battery, he turned caps and explained something, patience in his voice. He was trying to teach her. Her brother, a boyfriend? She was younger than the boy, probably too young for a boyfriend. A radio blared a familiar rock-and-roll song she couldn't place. She'd been close with this boy. His face had drifted through a dream she'd had recently. In the dream he'd betrayed her, but she couldn't recall the betrayal.

Right now fixing the pickup was more important than images

and sounds. She headed for the garage, and was surprised to see as she approached that the door was halfway open. At the doorway, she heard someone breathing. She crept toward a flashlight beam and recognized Jude's butt, half inside the engine and half out, his feet just touching the floor.

A surge of happiness. "Hi! When did you get back? I didn't see the truck."

"Hey. I pulled way behind the house."

"What are you doing?" she asked.

"What does it look like?"

"Fixing the pickup," she said. "I thought we were going in a big truck."

"No corrosion on the battery," Jude said, sliding out from under the truck. "Let's see if it'll start. A few weeks ago Hank asked me to fix this thing anyway, so we'd have a third working truck, in case a big one broke down. But I've been slow getting to it. I've been distracted—well, it's all your fault." He chuckled.

"Amusing." Sabine didn't laugh.

He stood and reached for her hand. "You and I will take the pickup. With one change. I want another guy to come with us. In case we run into trouble."

"Who?" But she already knew.

Jude looked at her, and she nodded. She still didn't like Sol, but she'd make it work. She would.

Jude pulled her close. She kissed his cheek and laid her head on his shoulder.

"I keep going over lists of calamities," she said. "What if Kate won't give us food?"

"The food belongs to all of us," Jude said. "And it's three fewer people for her and Hank to manage, once we're on the road." He squeezed her. "The best plan would be to caravan. But we'll likely get separated on the road. Kate, Sharp, Hank, and I discussed this, and we figure the castle's a good rendezvous spot. A good Plan B, if we get separated. We hope Kate's grandparents will take us in, but won't know till we get there. The castle's a national monument, a tourist attraction. Easy to find."

"How big?" she asked.

"Kate says it's a fort that looks like a castle, with bastions and cannons. Even a moat. We'll find a place to camp and come to the castle at 8 p.m. the first night we get there. If no one meets us the first night, we keep coming back at the same time, night after night. We wait half an hour."

"Why all the spy stuff?"

"Sharp said we shouldn't wait around. Things could turn bad, quick, if people notice us."

"What things?"

"We could be attacked for the trucks. Or money."

"Why doesn't Kate just give everyone her grandparent's address?"

"She wants to check with them first. If they're still alive and agree to take us in, we'll all stay there. She says it's a big house on a few acres."

"I walked to the gas station and found some maps. Maybe they'll be some help."

"You tell Kate you were walking to the station? She's such a mother hen."

"She warned me it was dangerous. I almost laughed in her face."

"Yeah." He turned back to the engine. "I think I've fixed the problem. It's an '88, but it should roll along a while longer."

"I'll get in and start 'er up," Sabine said.

Jude handed her the keys and focused under the hood. She tried a few times before the engine turned over. The muffler didn't muffle well, but the engine sounded smooth. She jumped out and kissed the corner of his mouth. "You did it!"

"Hey," Jude said. "I wanted to tell you what I heard last night."

"What?" Expecting bad news, her heart beat faster.

"Randolph and Lavinia were arguing pretty loud. He was begging for sex, and she must've said no ten times. They both sounded tired."

"They're mismatched," she said. "Poor guy. He thinks he can't do any better. But he can."

He smiled. "Well, time's a wasting. I'll go talk with Sol."

"Hope it works out with him." *Lie.*

"You're packed?" he asked.

"Been packed for days."

Jude left, and relief pumped energy through her. She vowed to try harder not to judge Sol. On the road together, maybe she'd grow to like him.

She wet some rags under the faucet and wiped down the cab's interior. The pickup had been dark green once, but now the faded paint had a covering of bird poop and tree sap. Without hot water, she wouldn't take on the exterior. She found a tattered East Coast map printed in 1989, Virginia to Key West, under the front passenger seat. She shoved it in the glove box.

Chapter 9

BLOOD MOON SET

July 16, 2014.

Roused from sleep, Sabine bolted up and checked Jude's side of the bed. He wasn't there. Something felt wrong. What had woken her? Men talking in deep, low tones. Had she dreamed the voices? No, they were drifting through her open window. Unfamiliar. Urgent.

The full moon turned the field silver gray. An attack during a full moon? Unwise. Whoever they were, they must be desperate and probably amateurs.

She jerked open her bedroom door and hurried to a window overlooking the front yard. Two men crouched behind a big tree. More men might be hiding.

Jude wasn't on watch. Her mind buzzed. He'd said he was going to the garage to dig around for spare tires for the trip, but how long ago was that?

Her hands shook as she inched the window open. Who was on watch? For God's sake, she couldn't recall. Her bare feet were rooted to the floor, her breath was loud in her ears. She felt like a child lost in a strange city.

Hank walked around the corner of the house into the yard.

"Hank!" she screamed his name half a second before a single shot. A pause. Three more shots.

Hank cried out, spun around partway, and collapsed.

Footsteps pounded down the hall. Kate screamed. The sound of her voice released Sabine. She ran down the back stairs. Hank was dead. Hank was on watch. Who else. *Who cares? Hank is dead.*

Sabine hit the bottom step just as Kate ran into the kitchen. Sabine seized Kate's shoulder. "Stop! Stop! Don't go outside! No!"

Kate shook her off, threw open the door, and ran down the back steps. Sabine followed as far as the porch. The moon silhouetted Kate running across the lawn holding out a gun. She turned the corner toward the front yard yelling, "Hank, Hank! Darling!"

A quick volley of shots. Silence.

Sabine couldn't see Kate. Maybe she was hiding.

She doubled over with fear. The kitchen was dark except for a patch of moonlight shining through the open door. She leaned over the sink to vomit, but she didn't. Kate was a talker, if she was merely hurt she'd cry out. Kate was dead.

Hide in the pantry, curl up on the floor, wait for help. Who was on watch with Hank? Everyone would be running downstairs.

A hand on her shoulder. She spun around. Jude whispered "Shhh" in her ear, his finger to his lips. "Hide in the pantry," he whispered. "Jen and Sharp are scouting the field and the woods."

"Hank and Kate. I watched Hank fall after he was shot. They're not okay, are they?"

Jude stared at her like she was crazy. Her stomach knotted, but she held his stare, pretending strength she didn't feel. He shoved her into the pantry, then crept through the room and into the hall.

Barefoot, wearing nothing except underwear and a T-shirt, Sabine felt defenseless and ashamed. She had no gun. Someone shouted. She cringed, hands cupping her ears.

She imagined running across the fearsome yard, snow and ice

slowing her down, her bare feet oozing blood, trailing black splotches across the snow. Bolting across the yard to kill the men hiding behind the tree. She would raise her gun and shoot each one once, then stand over them and unload her gun into their limp bodies.

The fantasy's impact pushed her flat against the pantry wall.

No, she wouldn't let fear keep her hidden in the pantry. She'd handled machete man. And there was no snow or ice outside.

Loud footsteps tromped down the front stairs. She scurried to the living room. Randolph, Sol, and Tommy ran past her and out the front door, guns drawn. Randolph? Good, Hank had let him carry a gun; even with bad eyes, he might help. She crept through darkness to the window and glimpsed two people moving in the field, one taller and larger than the other. Jen and Sharp, she hoped.

At the other window, the moon illuminated Hank and Kate. Hank lay in the same position, his legs bent at unnatural angles. Kate's body lay nearby, a dark stain covering her chest. Part of her skull was missing, her blond hair lay loose on the grass, her night-gown was pulled up to her waist. Sabine wanted to run outside and cover her, hold her head in her lap, and comfort her. In the kitchen she should've grabbed Kate's shoulders with both hands, stopped her from running outside. Held on with all her strength. *It's my fault Kate got shot.*

The front door slammed. Sol yelled something about burying bodies. She made out Lavinia's voice, cut off by Randolph's gravelly one. They all talked at once. Sabine couldn't make out the conversation. She refused to think about burials yet. She wanted to hear Jude's voice. And the others' voices, too. Did Tommy know about Kate yet?

Sol called her name from the hall, but Sabine kept moving. In her room, she took her backpack out of the armoire, pulled on jeans, another shirt, shoes, and socks. In slow motion she washed her face and brushed her teeth. She watched her hand slide her toothpaste and toothbrush into a vest pocket. The Stephen Crane novel she'd been reading lay on the bedside table. She slipped the book, candles, and notebooks in her pack's side pockets. She patted the maps, safe in another pocket.

She cried out of guilt for every mean thought she'd ever had about Kate. Kate had given her food, water, and shampoo. At times she hadn't been kind. But who stayed the same day after day? She'd accused Kate of being suspicious, but it was the other way around. She was the one who'd been suspicious of Kate.

Kate had offered to pack boxes of food for her, Sol, and Jude to take in the small truck. Were the boxes ready to load? Sabine paced her room. And would the six who'd planned to travel with Kate and Hank still take two trucks? They wouldn't need two now, but the decision wasn't hers.

Quiet outside. The two shooters could be down the road or hiding in the woods. She went over what happened step by step, starting with unfamiliar voices in the yard. At the part when Kate ran outside, she closed her eyes to see the images clearly. Kate had yelled for Hank and called him "Darling."

Her body jerked each time she heard footsteps or a shout. If everyone was shot and killed, she didn't think she could go on. She'd wait for the shooters to come for her. No. She'd lived through a lot; she wouldn't give up. Even if there were three or four men, Sabine and the others still outnumbered them. If people were wounded, she'd help. She wanted to help.

She'd been tensing her body so long her muscles ached. To keep busy she made her bed, swept the floor, and dusted the bedside table with her shirttail. Tidy room, the same way she found it. But who cared?

She was glad she'd finally begun the log book—she'd been taking notes about the house and had conducted interviews with a few people. Once Jude had asked her when she'd interview him. She reminded him he'd already told her about his farm and family. "But I'm saving the best questions for last," she'd said, and they'd kissed and pulled off each other's clothes.

She'd never complete the log now.

Their lives would stay like this. Scrounging for food. Running, looking over their shoulders. Carrying guns. She gritted her teeth and a surge of hate filled her chest. If someone handed her a weapon and said, "Shoot that one," she'd pull the trigger without hesitating.

PART
TWO

Chapter 10

CRICKET MOON

August 1989.

Elaine mounted the church steps and released Sabine's hand to push open the brass door. Elaine loved the cheery feeling of a crowd walking up the steps, her family a part of something larger. She believed in God, when the belief was convenient. Church rituals were holdovers from her own parents. Even when inconvenient, which meant church every Sunday, even when she wanted to sleep, she went to keep up social ties.

She loved the relaxed, hormonal state of pregnancy but hoped her third child would be another boy so Frederick would stop nagging her to have more children. At forty-one she needed an exciting, meaningful project beyond her family.

Frederick still held Sabine's hand. He was an attentive father, unless a big case at work frustrated him. That past Friday night he'd yelled at their son Freddie for not mowing the lawn and taken away telephone privileges for the weekend. Freddie had mowed the back-yard Friday night under floodlights and mowed the front yard at six on Saturday morning.

Frederick preferred to yell at Sabine and Freddie, but if they weren't around he yelled at his wife. Elaine told herself he just needed to blow off steam. Usually his outbursts were short and he apologized with a kiss. Sometimes she pushed him away and called him a cruel jerk. She thought about her mantra, no sex for a week, and it made her laugh—she knew she wouldn't hold to it.

Elaine waited for Freddie, who was walking behind. Father and son studied the ground when they walked, keeping their bearings in silence. Freddie was a teenager; acting surly was expected. But Frederick was forty-one, overage for a moody attitude.

Elaine's lower back ached from walking the few blocks from their house to the church. She plopped down in the pew and opened the church bulletin, her thoughts on her husband. The new baby meant she'd be a house drudge and a butt-wiping milk machine yet again. She'd need friends to get through the day. Weekends with Frederick were usually fun, a respite until Monday's boredom.

She'd considered an abortion, but she'd convinced herself to have the baby. The doctor would do a C-section, which meant she could have a postpartum tubal ligation without a second surgery. She'd fulfill this promise to herself and wouldn't tell Frederick. A woman didn't need her husband's permission.

Again last night she and Frederick had exchanged words.

"If you're tired of staying home," he said, "hire a maid and a nanny. Take swimming lessons at the club."

She put her hands on her hips like a sitcom wife. "I play tennis. Maybe I'll get a maid. But I'm not having children for someone else to raise!"

Frederick, exasperated, gave her his usual frown. He still didn't understand how to make her happy. It sure wasn't having more kids. He ran his hand through his hair and left the room.

⚜

Sabine turned ten and entered fifth grade a month before her brother Jeffrey arrived. He was born at 7:00 a.m. on a brisk October morning. Her parents' wishes had come true. Her father couldn't stop smiling; he phoned her grandparents, then called their friends.

But the following day, no one was happy. Something was wrong with Jeffrey. The nurses couldn't wake him for feedings. Elaine whispered that the baby's lips kept turning blue. Sabine looked through the glass windows of the nursery, but couldn't see much. Jeffrey lay in a plastic box with tubes coming out of him. The bald baby with blue lips scared her.

Her brother Freddie came to the hospital to see Jeffrey the day he was born, just after the nurses put tubes in his little body. Freddie was seventeen, in high school. He didn't come to the hospital on school days. He got himself up, made breakfast, and caught rides to school with friends.

Jeffrey was moved out of the nursery into his own room.

From the sixth-floor window Sabine watched leaves blow and spin off trees. She tried to make up a story about leaves but couldn't concentrate. Her science teacher would be pleased if she showed interest in anything. The next day she'd bring the book about trees to the hospital.

If one of her parents left Jeffrey's room to take a break or to go home and sleep, the other stayed. She looked forward to weekends, when Freddie came. With him, she turned the elevator into a roller coaster, closed her eyes and leaned against him, giggling and groaning while they rode to the basement and rose to the top floor. Finally, Freddie would hit the button to the cafeteria floor, and he'd let her pick what she wanted to eat, usually pancakes, bacon, and orange juice. Most of the day, they sat under the cafeteria's bright lights and did homework.

"I'm reading about Leif Erikson," she told Freddie. "He was Norse, which means a person from the north, probably Iceland. Next I'll read about Captain James Cook. He made maps of unexplored places."

Freddie nodded while peeling an orange. "Maps are crucial to your life. Think about it. If you don't have a map, you can get lost. You should keep a map with you at all times, your whole life."

Some weekdays, Sabine sat in the waiting room reading about Leif Eriksson. Dad liked biographies about explorers and mountain climbers, which was why she'd picked explorers for her history essay. She brought her chair near the waiting room door so she could watch Jeffrey's door, and when a doctor went into his room, she crept over to listen. But she mostly forgot what the doctor said. The name of Jeffrey's condition was unpronounceable. She hated the word.

Once when the door was open, the doctor fussed at her mother, told her forty-one was too old to have a baby. Her mother cried.

Sabine couldn't help her mother. She ran back to the waiting room.

An hour later she'd figured out the doctors' problem. The doctors couldn't see enough of Jeffrey's insides. They couldn't fix him without a map.

Her three grandparents came to help out, but only Moomah paid much attention to her. If the doctors pronounced Jeffrey's condition stable, Sabine asked or demanded that one of her parents take her to school. Twice Moomah arranged for her to escape to a friend's house for the weekend. Three times she let her have sleepovers with friends. Moomah was her favorite grandmother.

One evening, on their way out, the dog that hung around the hospital dumpsters followed Sabine and Moomah back to the parking lot. She told Moomah a dog with clumps of missing hair was following them. Her grandmother scanned the area, then focused on Sabine as if she were crazy. One by one Sabine questioned all the adults, but none of them could see the dog.

Still, her father agreed to stop at the grocery store, where Sabine used her allowance money to buy two boxes of dog biscuits. Her father waited in the car. He held on to her shoulder when she got back, and rubbed his wet eyes.

Once Sabine found a hiking magazine in the waiting room and

brought it to her father, who sat in his usual spot in Jeffrey's room. When she gave him the magazine, he cried. All his crying scared her. She turned away so she wouldn't have to watch.

She forced herself to look at Jeffrey. Too small to be a baby, he looked like a pale doll without hair. She wanted to hold him and make special wishes for him to grow bigger, but couldn't pick him up because of the tubes. Her chest hurt each time she left his room.

Before breakfast she stuffed dog biscuits in her coat pockets. On her way in and out of the hospital she threw biscuits to the dog she'd named Sun Dog. When she was little, her mother had made up a story about six dogs the size of cars. The dogs raced across the flat surface of the moon, while hundreds of dogs lined the route and barked them on. When the six dogs picked up speed, their bodies shone. When they reached the finish line, the winning dog burst into flames, and this magnificent dog had the honor of bringing the dog villages fire for a year. But Sun Dog wasn't magnificent like a fiery sun. He was thin and mangy. If she fed him he'd get bigger and happier. Seeing Sun Dog turned into the best part of her day.

A month dragged by until one windy morning, two doctors walked into Jeffrey's room with their shoulders all hunched over. Sabine pressed her ear against the door. No words, just mumbling.

After the doctors left, she crept into Jeffrey's room, which always smelled like medicine. She stood by the crib with her parents, who were crying. She froze when Mom told her to say good-bye to Jeffrey.

They left the hospital late; the sky was black and full of stars. Sabine hated the hospital; but now they wouldn't be coming back, she was scared to leave. She felt a wrenching inside, had the panicky thought that Jeffrey would be all alone in the crib.

She followed her parents down the path and out of darkness. Sun Dog ran to her, his tail wagging. She squatted under a street-light and petted his back. He had a doggy smell, but she squeezed him tight and whispered that she'd always love him. She dropped all the biscuits she had in a heap. He gobbled the biscuits as if he were starving. She wanted to take him home, but there was no point in asking her mother, who was allergic to dogs and cats.

After walking a few steps, Sabine turned to wave, but Sun Dog had disappeared. Her parents were halfway to the parking deck and she ran to catch up. Her body felt heavy and numb, and even though her legs wobbled, she kept going. She wouldn't think about Jeffrey's pale body with tubes coming out. And wouldn't think about leaving him alone in the room. And wouldn't think about his body on a stretcher covered with a sheet. And wouldn't think about the funeral-parlor people taking him and putting him in a box, like Mom said they had with Grandma Cecily.

⤫

During the funeral at church Sabine wondered what would happen to Sun Dog. Who'd feed him and take him home? He'd be lonely for her.

Freddie didn't sit in his usual slouch. Today he wore a black suit and sat stiffly in the black limo. Even their dad remained quiet, a side of him they didn't see often. Her mother looked frozen in the backseat of the big, black car, rebuffing her husband's attempt to hold her hand.

Chapter 11

YOUNG MOON

August 1991.

Two years after Jeffrey died, Elaine was still letting housework pile up. She moved like a bug in molasses. Out the window over the sink there was nothing new to see. She tried to make herself get started by washing dishes. Memories of Jeffrey arrived unbidden. He no longer resembled a newborn; she'd aged him, making him resemble and act like Freddie at age two. Except she imagined Jeffrey as kinder and more obedient. Two-year-old Jeffrey played in the yard, laughing and splashing in a wash tub and running around with his favorite plastic boat. Sometimes Jeffrey assumed baby form as well, asleep in a crib, his belly rising and falling with life. No medicines, no tests, no mind-numbing machines.

Elaine leaned over the sink and gagged up eggs and coffee. She rinsed out her mouth and gulped a glass of water.

At a sharp laugh Elaine turned in surprise to see Sabine sitting at the table, two or three teen fan magazines at her elbow. Had she been sitting there long? Elaine hadn't noticed. She wondered for a second what else she hadn't been noticing. Sabine hadn't reacted when her mother threw up in the sink.

"Mom, look," Sabine said, pointing to a picture. "He's gorgeous."

Elaine glanced at the photo of a rail-thin singer with ringlets of dyed black hair. He wore a ripped T-shirt, dark glasses, and an earring. She had no idea who the boy was. She couldn't keep rock and pop stars straight. Didn't care to.

She reached for her new apron, a birthday present from Frederick. He'd tucked a box in the apron pocket with a diamond tennis bracelet in it. She enjoyed wearing the apron more than the bracelet. It was cream-colored, with pink and red cabbage roses. She turned. "Hey, Sabine. My new apron. Like it?"

"Daddy gave it to you, didn't he? It's old-fashioned. It looks beautiful on you."

Elaine tried to smile. "Yes, your daddy's birthday present to me. Cabbage roses are all the rage."

Sabine, always ready to heap praise on her mother, and others. The child who never disappointed. Soon after Jeffrey died, Elaine had a visit from a friend who brought along her three- and four-year-olds. Sabine, who was ten at the time, had taken the kids to her room, showed them her stuffed animals, and played with them.

At the sink Elaine lifted the soapy dishrag to her cheek, wondering, probably for the thousandth time, about the mystery of time. It dragged as if Jeffrey had been dead for decades instead of two years. Occasionally she thought the funeral had happened just a few days ago.

She turned the water on full force to drown Jeffrey's whimpers from his steel hospital crib.

She was living outside of time.

প্র

August 1993.

Elaine moved through the heat carrying a tray of frosty drinks into the pink dusk, a glass of lemonade for Sabine, gin and tonics for herself and Frederick.

Frederick sauntered onto the patio. He'd changed from office clothes into white pants and a faded madras shirt. His pants appeared vivid in the fading light as he lay on the lawn chair by Elaine. He leaned to kiss her cheek, then grinned at Sabine swinging in the hammock. She jumped up, hugged her father, and took the lemonade off the tray. Back in the hammock, she balanced the glass on her flat stomach, held it with one finger, then let go. She contracted her stomach muscles, relaxed, and did it again, watching to see if the glass tipped.

Elaine suspected her daughter had practiced this trick. She was glad Sabine had time left to be a child. The porch light shone across part of her daughter's face, reminding Elaine how beautiful this child-woman had become. The high cheek bones, the full lips, the wide blue eyes. She didn't have Elaine's curly dark hair, but rather her father's thick, brown hair. She'd stay lovely into adulthood.

Sabine's peaceful expression revealed someone who hoped nothing else would change. Elaine had overheard her on the phone once, saying, "I couldn't stand it if anyone else died. Freddie's a pain in the ass, but I don't wish him dead. The way he drives his car, he could kill himself."

Losing Jeffrey had left its mark on Sabine, on all of them. Elaine hoped she and Frederick appeared happy, the perfect husband and wife, murmuring with heads touching, side by side in lawn chairs.

Sometimes she and Frederick could be happy, despite Freddie. They were relieved that Freddie had gone to boarding school for the summer to study computers. Freddie's sole letter home had claimed he was too busy studying to write or call. Elaine didn't mind. Frederick claimed he didn't either. They reassured each other summer school would prepare Freddie for college in the fall. With their son launched and happy, she and Frederick could be guilt-free at last.

The trouble with Freddie had begun in eighth grade. Other mothers of teenaged sons complained of their moodiness, but none of their boys stole and wrecked his father's car; none of their boys was expelled for smoking pot in the bathroom and the parking lot. Elaine told herself Freddie was just going through a stage. Frederick had gotten his car repaired and they'd never called the police. They should've called the police and made Freddie pay for the repairs.

Frederick leaned over to Elaine's chair. "You're worried. What are you thinking about?"

An image of herself at the door, the cop on the porch saying, "Your son's dead. In a car wreck." Elaine smiled to reassure Frederick she wasn't worrying. She rubbed her glass, which was dripping with moisture, over her cheeks, a small relief from the stifling heat.

The sky lost its pink cast and turned deep blue. Stars came out as Elaine half-listened to Frederick talk about his day at the office. How did stars come into being? She wanted to read ancient creation tales about the cosmos, not scientific ones. She'd read more about the Native American tradition of naming the moons after the weather and crops.

When Sabine was small, Elaine had read her bedtime stories about chickens and bears and the moon. When she ran out of books, she made up stories, mostly about moon creatures. One story about blue-cheese mountains covering the moon, featured a gang of giant warty frogs living on the mountaintops and staging croaking competitions.

Elaine allowed cricket sounds to drown out her husband's words. She took his hand but didn't look at him, enjoying the distant sound of his voice. She hoped Sabine would hold moments like these against future pain. Elaine needed her daughter to believe in the safety of a summer night, for sometimes the illusion was what a parent could give. Even hope could be flimsy, though. This she knew.

She watched the old cricket moon rising. The burnt end of summer, the dry grating of male crickets' mating sounds. The crickets would die off, the late-September air would freshen, startling the leaves, forcing them to color and finally fall. The vibrant, dead leaves would scuttle across the two-lane suburban roads, propelled by autumn winds. An end to the nasty, sticky heat. Her favorite season was almost here.

In two weeks Freddie would enter his freshman year of college and Sabine would enter sixth grade, which meant more hours in school each day. Like in the early days of her marriage, before the children came, Elaine would have the house to herself.

No more cocktail parties, no more tennis, no more lunches with friends. No more grand ideas, no more pining for a mission. Nowhere to go. She'd talk out loud to dead Baby Jeffrey all day, if she wanted.

☙

August 1993.

Freddie patted his jeans pocket to reassure himself the bag was safe, then jogged down the hall to his dorm room, sweating—though not because the thermometer had hit ninety degrees. He locked the door, shoved a chair under the knob, and pulled a repp tie from his closet. Not a big bag. Still. His works waited in an old Godiva chocolate box in his dresser, hidden under T-shirts; he picked up golden Lady Godiva and headed for his desk.

He mixed the junk in a big spoon, lit a match, and stuck it under the spoon thinking how he loved the old '60s lingo. *Junk.* When he said the word, he sounded like a cool jazz musician.

He pulled the junk up in the needle, laid his arm on the desk, and tied off. He pushed the needle in the best vein, grateful it hadn't collapsed. Not yet. Ducky's arms were covered with abscesses and blown veins, but Freddie had promised himself to take better care of his own body. A secret way he'd stay superior to Ducky.

Good stuff. He nodded in the desk chair. His computer and schoolbooks sat in his line of vision, but they didn't register. An idle thought or two about homework drifted through his mind, but he didn't care about studying. Instead, he thought about the hot skank with dyed red hair who sat by him in class, watching her dark red fingernails fly across the keyboard. By day three they were getting it on in his room, so hot for each other they stayed half dressed.

But he couldn't hold the girl's image, and he floated over the ocean, rocking with the waves. His parents' smiling faces and lips moving, urging him to go to summer school. To spend the summer rotting away with boredom. Screw computer school.

From far away a knocking sound. Someone at the door—maybe the girl. Marlene. More likely his Ducky. "Be right there. Be cool."

Good old Ducky had just bought a new Beemer with the inheritance money he'd gotten after his mother died. They'd use his car for their next score. Where they were going, a fast car would be essential. Freddie pulled the chair away from the door and unlocked it.

Two large men filled the doorway, blocking escape. Zip rammed a gun into Freddie's cheek and pushed, backing him into the room. His lackey, Boots, kicked the door shut.

"Pay up, little rich boy," Zip wheezed. "You wanna score something today it's gonna be five hundred up front, and that ain't counting all the back money."

Zip slid the gun in his belt, grabbed Freddie by the shoulders, and pinned him against the wall. Boots swung hard and Freddie turned his head. Boots got him upside his nose. Freddie fell, holding his nose, bleeding like a stuck bitch. The heroin was wearing off, and his face burned.

Zip jabbed his pistol into Freddie's stomach. "You get nothing but our visits till you pay up."

Freddie wanted to take a deep breath, but blood pounded in his throat. He whispered, "Okay, man. Top dresser drawer."

Boots yanked on the drawer, pulled out a wad of bills, and counted them. "Two hundred twenty-seven dollars. We'll be back for the rest."

The dealers left, slamming the door. Their raucous laughter faded down the hall. Freddie stayed on the floor, figuring by night he'd feel like a piece of dead meat. He considered driving himself to the ER, but ice would work. He didn't want the ER hassle; since he was eighteen, he'd have to pay. Hospitals were expensive, and the cops would get involved. He struggled to the bathroom holding on to furniture and walls, washed his face, then stumbled to get a tray of ice. His nose hurt like a sonofabitch. He and Ducky would have to find a new dealer by sundown. No problem, he had some names.

Another knock. Freddie didn't move. "Who's there?"

"Who do ya think?" Ducky's irritated Southern drawl.

"Okay, coming."

"What happened to you?" Ducky groaned when Freddie opened the door. "You look terrible."

"Boots and Zip paid a visit, with a gun and a great big fist."

Ducky ambled to Freddie's little refrigerator for a beer while Freddie toweled off the fresh blood from his face with exaggerated care.

"Let's pack our stuff and leave sometime after midnight. School's over the end of next week anyway," Ducky said. "They'll never find us." Even his chuckle sounded Southern. He put his feet on the wobbly coffee table and lit a joint.

Freddie held the towel on one side of his nose, then the other. His nose looked crooked; it was probably broken. But once he was high, he wouldn't feel it. And what was a broken nose? His teeth were white and straight. A crooked nose would make him look tough. He walked out of the bathroom with his chin up and grinned at Ducky. Grabbing a clean shirt from the closet he said, "Let's score big before we leave. I got five hundred and fifty stuffed in the toaster. And I've made a decision: time to buy us some guns."

Chapter 12

SPLINTERED MOON

May 26, 2014. Memorial Day.

On Monday morning, Elaine's cell phone sounded, playing Bach. Freddie heard his mother answer, then pause for a long time. Then, "Frederick! What's happening?"

"Mom?" he called from the other room.

She didn't respond. He heard her pick up the wall phone and dial a number—probably his father's office, that's where he was, even though it was a holiday—but she soon slammed the phone in its cradle.

Freddie was playing with his seven-month-old daughter, lying on the floor, showing her how to stack cloth blocks. When his mother ran into the room, he stopped and looked up.

"What was the call about?" he asked.

A blast like the roar of jets colliding. Freddie scooped Lily off the floor and held her. Plates and cups rattled and slid out of an open cupboard; boxes and jars flew off pantry shelves.

"That sounded like a bomb! Come on!" Elaine ran to the kitchen.

Freddie put Lily in her carriage and pushed it to the middle of the dining room, away from the windows. He tried to jam a bottle in Lily's mouth. The baby turned her head and screamed.

Breathless, Elaine whispered, "It was your father on the phone. Something bad is happening downtown. We were cut off."

They had a beach house and knew how to prepare for weather emergencies. They went into hurricane mode. Elaine packed two ice buckets and several pitchers with ice. She rummaged through cabinets for more containers. Freddie slid the bolts on the doors and checked the locks on the downstairs windows. He ran upstairs, shouting, "I'll check the windows and fill the tub. We'll need water." They moved fast and ignored Lily's screams.

Freddie turned on the TV. Confirmed bombings in DC and New York. Most communications were down. No information about Richmond, or the beach. The TV screen went dark. He stared at the blank screen, waiting for it to come back on. It didn't. He went back upstairs and, feeling a surge of hysteria about Mags, he opened his cell phone—but nothing happened. Water gushed into the bathtub. He leaned out the bathroom window, tried his cell phone again. Nothing. When water splashed over the sides of the tub, he turned off the faucets.

"I'm taking Lily to the sunroom," his mother called from downstairs.

Freddie was grateful he had brought the baby over early to visit. If Mags didn't arrive by five, he might unravel. He depended on her to care for Lily. At least here, his mom would help. And he wouldn't have wanted her to be alone for this, either.

Freddie opened his old bedroom closet. The faint odor of Old Spice still clung to his high school clothes, a few shirts, and two out-of-date sport coats. His mother hadn't touched a thing; except for adding Lily's crib and baby stuff, his old room remained a relic. He patted coat pockets and found what he was searching for. He slipped on the brown tweed sport coat, took a box of ammo from his chest of drawers and studied his reflection in the mirror. The coat worked, no bulge in the pocket. Mother might freak, but later she'd be happy he had it.

His mother's eyebrows went up when he walked into the sun-room. "Why on earth are you wearing a wool sport coat?"

"It's chilly."

"It's May," she said.

Freddie shrugged.

Elaine pushed a bottle of milk into Lily's mouth. The baby sucked with vigor.

Freddie faced the yard. The oaks, taller than when he was a child. The familiar clumps of fading daffodils. Azalea blooms framed the windows, but it was too much pink for his taste. "I'm going out there." He slid his hand in and out of his pocket. The Glock was the one remainder of what he referred to as his "heroin summer." If he had a bag of heroin with him now, he'd shoot every damn bit. Where was Mags? She was in charge of the baby. Oh God, he hoped nothing had happened to her. She was visiting Addy; they'd been hospital roommates when they had their babies. He didn't know Addy's last name or where she lived.

"Did you reach Mags?" Elaine asked.

Freddie shook his head. "I want to try the landline from over at our house. Maybe she left her friend's number on the kitchen table."

"Freddie, everything's gonna be alright. Don't go outside. Let's get ourselves together, think about what we planned for today."

His mother's soothing tone felt empty. He looked at her, debating whether to say something snide about a barbecue in the midst of chaos or to thank her for the concern. He swallowed and said, "Thanks, Mom. I want to see Mags at the front door this minute. Dad will show up, too."

Elaine attempted a smile.

❧

Close to midnight, Elaine stopped by the window. Voices, then splintering wood and breaking glass. Five men ran up the sidewalk to the house next door. Two carried rifles, and the others carried tire irons or baseball bats. With her heartbeat in her ears she grabbed a flashlight, tiptoed into Freddie's room, and woke him.

They crept downstairs. Elaine put her finger to her lips, took a bottle of dish detergent, and squeezed two lines of liquid on the floor, starting from the legs of the sideboard to the front door. She pointed to the sideboard and put her hands under one end. Freddie took the other end. Together they slid the sideboard against the front door, then she wiped up the detergent near the door.

They sat at the dining room table. Freddie was trembling as much as she was.

"We have to get out," he whispered. "No phones, no electricity. No help."

"Early tomorrow morning," she whispered back. "Till then, let's sleep in four-hour shifts. Whoever keeps watch will feed and change the baby's diapers and pack the food. The family next door is vacationing in the Bahamas, there's nothing to do for them."

Freddie cocked his head. "Liquid detergent. Impressive move."

"It's what women do while sitting around the house. We invent stuff," she said. They smiled at each other. Elaine was surprised: in the midst of terror, she felt a surge of joy Freddie was with her.

Elaine opened the door to Jeffrey's unused nursery. She'd given away the baby clothes, but kept Jeffrey's crib hoping that one day Sabine, or even Freddie, might have a child. She selected the baby blankets she couldn't bear to part with, put them in a tote bag, and went to bed.

⁂

Freddie took first watch, until 4 a.m. He was at the kitchen sink when he spotted lights and shadows bobbing along the outside walls of a house across the alley. He pulled ammunition out of his coat pocket, hurried to the back porch, and loaded the Glock he should've loaded earlier. The shadows turned into two men with flashlights and rifles, and a third man carrying an axe. The man swung the axe, which shattered the glass sliding doors to the sunroom.

Freddie shot twice at the sky. He had a gun he wasn't skilled enough to use. Ducky was a better shot and had always been the one to do the heavy protecting when they negotiated with drug dealers; Freddie just slouched around trying to appear tough. Ducky helped him save face by calling him their lookout.

After what felt like hours, but was probably three minutes, the men ran out of the house and faded through the hedge. Maybe his shots had scared them off, or maybe they'd gotten what they wanted—food, guns, money, who knew. Frequent burglaries were the downside of living in a wealthy neighborhood.

Their house would be next.

He hurried to his bedroom and pulled half a box of ammo out of his chest of drawers. All the ammo he had left. Shooting in the air was stupid, but it was done. Like Dad was fond of saying, he'd acted before he thought. His father's voice in his head: "Stupid move, Freddie. Why are you so stupid?"

Freddie sat on his bed, facing the street. All quiet and dark. Almost time to wake up his mom for her turn at watch. He didn't want to wake her. He dozed off and slept until seven thirty.

❧

After Freddie woke Elaine, they ate stale bagels and talked in low tones so they wouldn't wake Lily.

"I'll walk around the neighborhood," he said. "See what has changed. Let's finish packing and go to the beach house."

"Thanks for letting me sleep. Please, be careful."

Lily started crying then, and Elaine ran upstairs to dress the baby and pack her clothes in the carryall. She fed Lily while watching the kitchen clock. Lily finished her bottle, and Elaine prepared another and put it with the supplies. She looked at the clock again. When she finally heard Freddie's key in the lock, she breathed her first deep breath in twenty minutes.

"I walked a few blocks south, then north," Freddie said. "Two strangers were walking down the middle of the next street over, scanning houses. A few blocks away three houses and a garage were burning. One house was complete rubble, with a giant crater where the lawn and the street used to be. But we know shortcuts, and there's almost no traffic. I heard cars in the distance. We'll make it to a main road." He checked their supplies. "We're running low on coffee and milk."

"Like I don't know it. We're almost out of baby formula and food." Elaine felt her irritation rising.

"You understand the big picture?"

"Meaning what?"

"No help's coming. Not yet, anyway," he said. "Leave a note for Dad and Mags. You finished packing?"

"The food and Lily's stuff is ready. Before we leave, we'll drive downtown, to your father's office. Maybe he hasn't left yet, and if he's not there, we can at least get information."

"Mother, driving down to the financial district right now is a totally insane idea. Two big cities and Richmond have been hit; I think we can assume this is a terrorist attack. Probably the bastards have hit the Federal Reserve Bank. We shouldn't go. Dad will come to the beach. It's our home as much as this place is."

"Don't take that tone with me, Freddie. We must pull together if we're going to make it."

"Dad and Mags will come to the beach," he said.

"I want to at least try to get to the financial district. I won't leave without trying to find your father."

"Okay, okay, we'll try. But if it looks sketchy, I'm not driving any farther."

"Your car or mine?" She tried to keep the snide tone out of her voice but couldn't help it.

He hesitated. "My car's smaller, but better on gas."

"Your Beemer can squeeze into tight spots in case we run into heavy traffic."

"Mother, in the last two days I haven't seen a single car drive down this street."

Elaine began crying. "We don't know what we'll find. It's scary."

"Pull yourself together and don't let Lily see you cry," Freddie said. "Your car's roomier, for all the boxes and totes."

"Plus the baby seat in my Volvo is better."

Freddie frowned. "My baby seat's fine."

"No, you bought a cheap car seat. It's unsafe. Besides, a roadster isn't meant for a family."

"I'll load the boxes," Freddie said. He sounded frustrated. Elaine couldn't bring herself to care.

She took the baby to her room, where she shoved shorts, slacks, shirts, bathing suits, and sweaters in a stylish weekend duffle. In her jewelry box she found Jeffrey's hospital bracelet. She slipped the bracelet into a pocket in her purse, then rummaged through the bathroom cabinet and put blood pressure pills, ibuprofen, and cough syrup in her purse. Also, Frederick's sleeping pills, for when he made it to the beach.

"Hurry up, Mother!" Freddie called.

Elaine wondered whether to add Sabine's name to the note. She'd been gone nearly three years; it was useless to add her name. With a red pen she wrote in big, attention-getting letters:

Dear Frederick, Mags, and Sabine,
May 27th
  Freddie, Lily, and I are driving to the beach house. It's not
safe here.
  Come to the beach. Quick as you can.
  My love to you all.
  Elaine

Maybe Sabine would come home after all. Elaine laid the note in the middle of the table and picked up sleeping Lily, curled in a blanket on the floor.

"Before we go," she said to Freddie in a low voice, "we have to check on the Gaskins. Don't tell them the government might not come. They're old. They need hope."

Freddie inhaled a long, slow breath. "We'll zip next door, stay a few minutes, and hit the road. I don't want to be on the road at night."

Elaine had a set of the Gaskins' house keys. She knocked and yelled out "Hellooo" before unlocking the front door.

The old couple sat in the living room. Mabel, in her rocking chair, glanced up but didn't acknowledge them. Harry held a newspaper in his lap and jumped up smiling.

Freddie asked Harry if they wanted to come to the beach, but Elaine knew persuading Harry was futile. Freddie was afraid, but rushing and pushing these two wouldn't work, he'd only scare them more.

"Freddie and I won't be next door any longer," Elaine said. "Please come with us? We have plenty of room and we'd love to have you."

Harry shook his head.

"Harry, we can't wait for Frederick and Mags. If you see any neighbors, please tell them where we've gone. Are you sure you don't want to come? We can help you pack."

Harry shook his head.

Freddie paced in front of the fireplace. Elaine pointed to the fireplace and Freddie brought in firewood from the pile by the backdoor.

Elaine noted the scrapes on Harry's arm and cleaned them with peroxide. While she worked, Harry glanced at his arm. "I got these scratches bringing in firewood. Just in case the weather turns. Us old folks get chilly at night."

Elaine nodded. "Good. Never can tell when you might need wood. Freddie, check to make sure their windows are locked."

Freddie parked the baby carriage in front of the couple and went to check on the windows. Harry made silly faces at Lily, who smiled. "Would you look?" Harry said. "I got a big smile." He laughed.

Elaine carried a tray with two glasses and a pitcher of orange juice to the coffee table.

Freddie ran down the steps. "All windows locked and the fire is set. All it needs is a match. I checked your pantry, too. It's pretty full."

"Why thank you, son," Harry said. "Mighty nice of you, and of course our dear Elaine. We just love her."

"Harry, please," Elaine said, "don't go outside unless you have an emergency. Strange men are walking around the neighborhood. Men broke down the door on the other side of us. Keep your blinds closed and the doors and windows locked. Help will be here soon." She felt a surge of guilt. Who knew when help would come?

She touched Harry's shoulder. The old man reached up and patted her hand. "Don't you worry about us. I'm fast on my feet." He lowered his voice. "It's Mabel I'm worried about. She doesn't understand what's going on. She won't leave, no matter what." His eyes filled with tears, but his voice sounded firm. "Don't worry, we'll make do till help arrives." He glanced up at Freddie. "Thanks to you both for your help."

"You and Mabel have been wonderful neighbors," Elaine said. "I've loved knowing you both."

"Same to you, Elaine, and you, too, Freddie. Take care of your daughter, Lily. God bless all of us. We'll see you when you get back home."

Elaine knelt in front of Mabel and kissed her soft cheek. "Thank you for everything. I'll miss you."

Mabel smiled at nothing.

❧

Freddie navigated side streets, inching toward his father's office downtown. He avoided the interstate, figuring it would be jammed. Taking shortcuts, he made it within a mile of his father's building before hitting solid traffic. Cars were headed away from downtown, so many that the congestion blocked side streets. People yelled and cursed out of their windows at other drivers to get out of the way. Freddie pushed the door lock and wiped his hands on his pants. Where was the Glock? In his jacket pocket, at the bottom of a tote. In the trunk. What an ass he was. He debated going to the trunk, but a gun in his lap would provoke another fight with his mother. He'd wait and see.

Elaine jiggled Lily on her lap. "Oh dear," she glanced at the gas gauge. "We're not moving at all."

"For ten minutes. As soon as people get out of their cars, things will get out of hand."

Elaine focused on something over her shoulder. "That office building on the corner? The one with the lawn? Back up far as you can and take a right over the curb, drive over the grass. Let's take a chance on the side street."

"We can't see. The street's probably blocked." Freddie wiped his hands again. A man wearing a cowboy hat jumped out of a camper with a rifle in his hands, red-faced and cursing. He waved the gun and fired in the air twice.

Another man eased out of a truck with a gun. He crouched, aimed at the rifle-toting man, and yelled, "Downtown's nothing but rubble. Turn your camper around so we can get outta here, idiot!"

"Crap! It's getting ugly." Freddie threw the car in reverse, gripped the steering wheel, and backed up to the car behind them. He made a sharp right turn. "Hold tight!" The car bounced over the curb and the lawn. He slammed on brakes at the edge of the side street, which was also blocked. Freddie pulled up the emergency brake and pushed open the door.

At the first car, Freddie yelled into the open driver's window. "Two guys with guns right around the corner. Please turn around."

The man frowned.

"Aw, come on." Freddie said. "We gotta work together to get out." He glared at the driver until he finally nodded.

Freddie ran to the next car, where a frightened woman was hunched over the wheel, several teenagers huddled in the backseat. Freddie smiled at her. "You gotta back up and turn around. Downtown's destroyed, and there's trouble!"

The woman nodded. "Thanks. Just debating what to do. I heard the shots!"

"You're welcome," he called back to her, already running to the Volvo. "Okay. Okay," he said as he jumped back in the car. "Soon as they're gone, we're outta here."

Elaine, pale-faced, clutched Lily, who cried.

Freddie reached behind the seat and pulled up a tote. "Her bottle's in here, right?"

Elaine nodded. When she gave Lily the bottle, the baby clutched it and sucked energetically.

Freddie exhaled loudly. "I love Volvos. They turn on a dime. It's gonna be okay. It's okay."

With a shaky hand Elaine patted Freddie's arm and smiled, but he could tell a ball of fear sat tight in her gut.

⁂

Forced by heavy local traffic to turn onto the interstate, Freddie managed thirty miles an hour. Up ahead, a semi had collided with a SUV, which had flipped and overturned, landing halfway on the median strip. Freddie maneuvered to the far-right lane, picked up speed, and gained a few miles, but a three-car pileup forced him to slow again minutes later. He eased off the road and drove on the right shoulder.

Elaine clenched the passenger door handle. "Freddie, careful. There's a ditch! There's no room on the right."

He slowed and they crept around the wreck. She noticed he avoided looking at the destroyed cars.

Across the median a military convoy proceeded west. Freddie barely glanced at the line of trucks with their headlights burning.

He focused straight ahead. "Four cars and a semi, wrecked within twenty minutes."

"You're doing fine, son," Elaine said, trying to sound calm. "People are panicked and not paying attention."

"Thanks." His voice sounded strained.

"Lily drank the entire bottle. She's milk-drunk and should sleep till we get to the beach house. I feel bad leaving Mabel and Harry, with no one to look after them."

"Well, they have each other, at least." Freddie's voice was low, sad.

"The day after Jeffrey's funeral, Mabel stood on my porch, so I gave her a cup of coffee figuring she'd say a few platitudes and leave. But she leaned back in her chair and said, 'I'm sorry. I can't imagine.'"

"Yeah," he said.

"Mabel didn't expect much, which made it easy to talk. For six months after Jeffrey died, she came over two or three times a week. She and Harry had tried to have children, but couldn't. They were too embarrassed to go to a doctor."

"They wouldn't say why?"

"Too embarrassed," Elaine said. "They're from the generation when people didn't talk about that sort of thing."

Freddie spun the steering wheel, overcorrecting to avoid a body sprawled half on the road, half on the shoulder. A man stood over the woman, hands covering his face.

"After Jeffrey died," Elaine plowed on, "you never asked how I was doing. Like most young people, you looked forward. Mabel helped me. I didn't expect a lot from you."

Freddie couldn't talk. He felt unworthy, caught. "I tried to be nice when Jeffrey got sick. After Jeffrey died, Dad got mean again. I just wanted to get away."

"I didn't agree with Mabel," she said, "that losing Jeffrey was about the loss of a dream. When I held Jeffrey, his presence was beyond an idea. But I understood how the absence must've felt to Mabel. Sometimes I felt worse for her than myself. I had you and

Sabine. Mabel revealed my own selfishness to me, though I don't think that was her intent. We grew to be more than neighbors."

Freddie wanted to scream a baby dying wasn't remotely the same as a baby who was never born. He was mad at everyone, mad at what was happening, and hated to be reminded of his selfishness. Still, at forty-two he wasn't as selfish as he used to be.

Elaine stopped talking. Freddie had retreated inside, ruminating, not hearing her. If he was going to make it, he had to become a better father.

And Sabine. Elaine was through talking to Freddie about Sabine. His whining, his "if only this, if only that." Concerning Sabine, what had been done could not be fixed.

❧

Freddie still had the wheel. Elaine cradled the baby. After all of her fussing about Freddie's car seat, she couldn't bear to leave Lily in it. He didn't mention it. She rationalized that the highway was less crowded. And Freddie was driving under the speed limit.

They obsessed about water, veered to another subject, and returned to water. The number of glasses they could drink. The body's reactions to various bacteria, what they'd read and experienced, the diarrhea and vomiting during their trips to Mexico and the Middle East. Ten two-gallon jugs full of water sat in the car trunk, along with three empty jugs. How would they purify the water? Bleach, if they couldn't buy purification pills? Water down the baby formula and give Lily juice?

"We have repairs at the beach house," she said. Work would help Freddie stay grounded. She felt afraid for him, thinking about his problems in high school and college. He was a computer programmer with a logical mind, but his mind was in splinters today.

Elaine watched the changed landscape out of the window. Few people were walking around or driving. Coffeehouses, a bowling alley, and a couple of stores they passed appeared burned out. Some others had smashed windows. Looters already? Yet some businesses looked open, with customers coming and going. In some spots the odor of smoke hung in the air.

When they spotted two open gas stations she said, "Freddie let's get gas while we can. We don't know what's open down the road."

Freddie topped off the tank and paid cash. Elaine smiled to see him carrying bottles of water to the car.

She thought about water, food, and medicine. Some people would die without their medications. Drugs found in the rubble with damaged labels would be a guessing game. They had to find a pharmacy for her blood pressure meds.

Freddie touched her hand. "Dad and Mags will find us. You left a note. And our neighbors are probably at their cottages, too."

Elaine felt overwhelmed, but crying would irritate Freddie. Sabine's disappearance wasn't Freddie's fault. Sabine, gone almost three years. Thousands of futile prayers for her safety and return. Freddie might be her only living child.

His rage be dammed, she let her tears come. The house in Richmond? Refugees would break in, vomit on her sofa, pee in their bed. And the teak headboard. She and Frederick just had to have that specific teak headboard. She remembered the furniture maker who'd made a pass at her when he delivered the headboard. Adorable. And half her age. Just the guy taking the time to talk with her, pay attention to her, had been nice. She'd probably never have sex again.

Her mission was to gather the family: Sabine and Freddie, Mags and baby Lily. And her dear, workaholic husband. But how to find her lost ones?

⌘

Freddie let Elaine drive the last leg of the trip, fifteen miles on familiar rural roads. She avoided broken-down cars, driving into shallow ditches and across lawns and fields. Freddie held Lily, whispering to her they'd be at the ocean soon. The baby smiled and laughed at his funny faces.

Elaine tamped down her irritation about Freddie's insistence on driving her car until now. She detested men's need to stay in charge. But she squirmed at her pettiness. They had survived the bombs in Richmond, what difference did it make who drove?

She reached across Freddie and adjusted Lily's bonnet to block the sun pouring in the window. She was happy to have sunglasses. She longed to sit on the beach, stretched out on a blanket in the sun, and then to swim in the ocean, even though the water would still be chilly. She yearned for ten glasses of water followed by ten rum and Cokes with crushed ice and lime twists.

"Once we get to the beach," Freddie said, "we'll have to be careful. Promise you won't go off in the car without me. Okay?"

"Yes, dear. That's wise."

"You're not listening," he said. "You're using your vague tone of voice."

"Yes, I am. I am." She felt on the verge of hysteria. They were driving into the beach village, but everything had changed. Street signs gone. Sand piled high as dunes over parts of the road. Windows boarded up at her favorite coffee shop.

"Would you look?" Freddie said. "Looting already. Just like in Richmond."

"Where's the main beach road?"

"Ignore the debris," he said. "Keep straight and cut over on Sanderling Lane."

She nodded, grateful he could discern where they were. She drove toward the ocean and took a deep breath, expecting clean air, but the air smelled rancid and fishy. Not far from their house the familiar low wall, meant to keep sand off the road, ran for blocks.

"I'm stopping. I want to see the ocean for a minute."

"Mother, it's not safe!"

"Just a minute." She stopped the car and jumped out. Happiness and gratitude flooded her. Freddie frowned but got out and put Lily in the stroller. High tide, a strip of sand visible, with choppy water beyond. Farther out something large moved: a cherry-red SUV, rocking in the waves. Water, almost up to the windows. A shape moved in the driver's seat. At the open window, a man's terrified face. "Help! Help!"

Elaine cupped her hands and shouted, "We'll help." She waved her arms. "We can save that man."

The wind took away Freddie's words, but Elaine thought he said, "Too late." Then he yelled, "Get in the fucking car!"

Elaine walked in a circle patting her clothes for her cell phone. "We're near the old grocery store."

Freddie shouted above the sound of the ocean. "And the Flirter Dunes, down by the pier. Anyway, I'll try."

Before she could stop him, he pulled off his shoes and tossed his wallet on the wall. He took the steps down to the beach two at a time, ran, and dove into the water and swam out. When he popped up he swam in a circle. She gave him the thumbs-up to show he was in the right place, but she couldn't see the SUV either.

The fast current pulled Freddie north. She feared he'd panic, and gestured with both arms for him to come ashore. Her gut hurt so bad she feared she'd throw up. She followed him with her eyes until he struggled to shore.

"The water's rough," he said when he came back up the stairs. He was shivering.

"Maybe we—"

"Mom, don't bother," he said, retrieving his wallet from the wall. "The SUV's gone."

She sighed. "People do crazy stuff when they're scared." Lily cried. Freddie shook the carriage side to side to quiet the baby. She glanced at the carriage. "Son. Rock the carriage, don't shake it." Her eyes back on the water, she opened her phone.

"Don't tell me how to take care of Lily. Cell towers don't work here, either. Why the fuck do you keep trying?" Freddie yanked the phone out of her hand and threw it hard. It slid into the water and disappeared.

She backed up to keep from pounding on his chest. She looked at Lily and stuck out her tongue and wiggled her eyebrows, hoping they both would stop crying. Lily sensed that everything was wrong, but didn't have words.

"Poor man," Elaine said. "The SUV will wash up on the beach three states away. Let's get to the cottage; you're soaking wet, and the wind's up."

They hurried to the car. Getting close to their cottage buoyed her. She must forgive Freddie for tossing her phone.

"Come on, dear, there are towels in the backseat. You want to drive?"

PART THREE

Chapter 13

GHOST MOON

July 17, 2014.

By four in the morning, everyone except Sharp had crowded into the living room. People were all talking at once, but no one knew much about what had happened. Jen said she and Sharp were on watch at the edge of the woods when they heard shots and separated to search for shooters. She'd last seen Sharp running across the field, toward the road.

Sabine hoped Jen wouldn't feel responsible for Sharp.

Sabine hurried to the kitchen, made a large pot of coffee, and poured herself a cup. She found stale bread and peanut butter and put them on the table, though food disgusted her. She returned to the living room. "I made coffee, and there's bread and peanut butter."

Sol, Lavinia, and Randolph leaned against the wall. Lavinia's red face shone from crying. Had the deaths triggered thoughts of events in her past? Lavinia had helped Kate a few times, but Sabine never noticed her talking with Hank. She must be suffering in a deep way, people didn't starve themselves and drag around depressed without reason.

Randolph patted Lavinia's arm with a faraway expression, unaware of what he was doing, then went to Tommy and laid his hand on Tommy's shoulder. "I'm sorry about Kate. I haven't the words."

Tommy looked frozen. He held his stomach as if a blow would crack him wide open. Not scared, more stunned. The worst had happened, and he couldn't allow himself to comprehend it. His expression was familiar. Sabine saw the same expression when she came upon her reflection in a mirror. Another reason she avoided mirrors.

She sat with her coffee, worrying about Sharp.

The backdoor banged. Sharp hurried in with a wild expression, his eyes darting around the room. "Is everybody safe?"

When no one answered, he said, "There were only two of them. I took care of it." His red shirt was dark with blood.

Sabine pointed to his chest. "We're all fine. Are you hurt?"

He touched his chest. "Oh. This must be from one of the guys. Soon as I shot one, the other guy came at me with a knife. I took it from him." He wiped his hands on his pants. "Is there coffee?"

Sabine hurried to the kitchen, poured him a cup, and added the powdered milk she'd watched him spoon into his coffee. She came back and gave him the cup.

Sharp nodded at her and paced, sloshing coffee on his jeans. He announced in a loud voice, "You-all gotta get on the road! More sons of bitches will come."

"What about you?" Jen asked.

"I have to bury Kate and Hank," Sharp said.

"We'll help," Sabine said.

Sharp shook his head. "I owe Hank everything. I'll stay and protect the farm."

Randolph opened his mouth to speak, but he didn't.

Why would Sharp protect the farm? She moved closer. "Sharp, I'm strong, I'll dig Kate's grave. You dig Hank's. Then we'll all leave together. We'll caravan."

Sharp shook his head, spilling more coffee on his jeans.

"If we're gone, what's left to protect?" Jen squinted.

With a bleak face, Sharp sucked in breath.

Sabine was close enough to touch his arm, but didn't. "If you'd rather come in the pickup with me and Jude, that's fine. You're welcome. I'm sure Sol won't mind switching."

She didn't have to look at Sol, she felt him glaring. But she wanted Sharp in the pickup with her, and could live with Sol's anger.

"Without Paul, Kate, and Hank," she said, "we fit in one big truck and the pickup."

Sharp focused on Sabine. "It's kind of you to offer help."

"If I may interject?" Randolph said. "Digging graves takes too long. Let's wrap the bodies and lay them side by side under a tree. Sabine's right, let's take the blue truck and the pickup. " Randolph looked around for agreement.

"Randolph's right," Jen said. "A quick burial, then we roll. The blue truck's in better shape. Randolph will drive, Lavinia in the middle. I'll ride shotgun. Sharp and Tommy will stay in the truck bed and cover the rear. We'll need both Labs. Gun can go in the pickup with you guys." Jen looked at Sabine.

"A solid plan," Sabine said. "Gun's a good watchdog."

"Nope, just changed my mind," Jen said. "Gun can't ride by himself. He'd be easy pickins and he'll miss his pals. We should have all three dogs."

"Okay, take all three." She wanted Gun, but lacked the energy to argue.

Jude took Sabine's hand. "That's fine, Jen."

"Sharp, it's okay for you to take my place in the pickup." Sol frowned. "There's nothing to do for Kate and Hank."

Sharp paced close to Sol, who backed away.

Randolph called to Sharp. "Please, we must go. We need you with us."

Sharp didn't break his stride as he walked out the front door.

"Let him go," Jude said in a low voice. "He needs time. Sometimes doing nothing is the most helpful thing."

Lavinia spoke up. "I'll get sheets to wrap the bodies."

"Use tablecloths," Sabine said. "There are some in the sideboard in the dining room."

Randolph kissed Lavinia on the cheek, like a father sending his daughter off to school.

"I'll help," Jen said, following Lavinia.

"Okay, we're off." Jude said. "See you guys in two weeks. Let's go." He waved to no one in particular and pulled Sabine toward the hall. His hand was clammy and shaking.

She pulled away. "Wait. We can't let Sharp walk off. I'm talking to him before we go."

Jude clenched firmly, pressing his hand to hers.

Sabine took his wrist with her free hand and pried herself away. "Stop." She ran out the front door and spotted a splotch of red by the barn. Sharp scowled when he spotted her. She followed when he moved inside the barn.

"Sharp, they're wrapping Hank and Kate in tablecloths. Then they'll put their bodies under the tree, the best we can do. Please come with us. You said more men will come soon. You want your throat slit?"

"I can't leave Hank."

"But Sharp, he's not here. He's gone."

Sharp's shoulders slumped.

"Hank was your good friend," she said. "It's terrible. But the farm's too dangerous. Please."

He stared at an empty horse stall.

"Do you want to stay because you and Hank were lovers?"

Sharp turned. "Lovers?" He laughed, paused, and laughed again. "You're weird. We're brothers. Half brothers with the same mother. For two years, when we were kids, Hank and I lived together. My dad was Cody Sharp, Hank's dad was called Jimbo."

"I never considered half brothers. You don't look alike."

"Hank and I will always be brothers." His hand moved to his chest.

"You two acted furtive together, always whispering."

"Yeah . . . ," his voice faded. "Too long a story. You-all have to get on the road. Here's the short version: Dad died. Mom married Jimbo Johnson and Hank was born. Mom and Jimbo fought because Jimbo didn't measure up to Dad."

"Little Hank was great. We raced trucks and played trains. Hank would stand at the screen door in his diaper, waiting for me to get off the school bus. One day, Mom was outside my school with the car all packed. She announced we were moving to Colorado. Hank would live with Jimbo. I was ten and Hank was two. Mom didn't let me tell Hank, or my friends, good-bye."

"She just drove off?" Sabine shook her head.

"Yep, like a maniac. Like the devil was chasing her. I had to live with her through high school, but a few days after graduation I loaded my car. We stood in front of our dumpy house, arguing. She accused me of abandoning her, but I drove back to Jimbo's anyway. Hank was nine. I stayed with Hank, Jimbo, and Jimbo's parents. Real hospitable country people. Hank and I went fishing, hiking, and swimming. Come fall, I drove him to school and picked him up after school. I job hunted, but couldn't find anything, so I moved to Quantico. Found a job and an apartment not far from Hank. I visited on weekends. Mom divorced Jimbo, married again. She wanted a man to cling on to.

"While in Colorado, I sent Hank letters and cards every week. We were each other's family." Sharp focused on his hands. "I can't believe he's gone."

"Hank's in your heart," Sabine said. "But you won't make it alone out here."

He shrugged.

"Thanks for trusting me," she said. "I understand Hank better now. You want me to keep quiet?"

"Yeah, keep all this to yourself."

She placed her hand on his arm. "You're sure you don't want to come with us?"

"Have a good life in St. Augustine. I hear it's a beautiful town.

Kate gave me her grandparents' address. I'll find you all if I change my mind."

"Okay. We'll hit the road."

Sharp tried to shake her hand, but she pushed past his hand and gave him a quick hug. She hurried to the house, where everyone stood around drinking coffee.

Jude was pacing and frowning. "Let's go," he said the second he caught sight of her. His eyes were wide. She'd never seen him so frightened.

"Okay," Sabine said. "See you all on the first of August. Have a safe trip."

Everyone muttered distracted good-byes, looking scared and jittery. She followed the men down the hall and through the backdoor. She turned away from the tree where white shrouds covered Hank and Kate.

Jude took the wheel. "Sol, cover Sabine while she gets the gate."

Sol wasn't a great shot. Sabine trembled as she unlocked and locked the padlocks. No one tried to kill her.

Once on the road she said, "I'll navigate. Keep an eye out for gas stations." She stuck her own maps in the glove box. They drove a mile and took a right onto the interstate, but the section wasn't cleared. Jude worked his way around the abandoned trucks and cars—they didn't bother to check them for gas, local folks would've siphoned them long ago—and got back onto a state road.

Sixty miles down the road, She and Jude kept watch while Sol put a handkerchief over his mouth and siphoned from a Cadillac lying in a ditch. Its big tank held enough to fill their tank and most of the gas can.

Their plan was to stay on state roads running parallel to the interstates. The state roads were narrow, and tedious to maneuver with all the abandoned cars around. They scanned the surroundings constantly for other people, but nothing moved except circling birds and grasses swaying in the fields. Monotony, laced with dread.

"I'm thinking," Sabine said, "that Kate and Hank could've been secret lovers. When they were killed, Kate ran outside calling his name, and called him 'darling.'"

Jude kept his hands on the steering wheel. "Never thought about it."

"No, they weren't lovers," Sol said. "But Hank and Sharp probably were."

"What?" Sabine said, like the thought had never crossed her mind.

"They probably lived together in DC. They were closeted because Hank was high up in the government."

"Get serious," she said. "This is 2014. Not 1954. No one cares who you sleep with." She felt guilty playing along with Sol, but she liked secrets. And she promised Sharp; he'd confided in her.

Sol barked out a laugh. "They might care if you're working out of the country. I think Hank was CIA."

Jude looked over at Sol. "CIA?"

"You mean it?" She shook her head.

Sol laughed. "It fits. When we did introductions? Hank wouldn't discuss his work."

"I didn't notice," she lied. "A lot was going on."

"Other times, he gave me bullshit answers. Claimed he traveled for an export company." Sol smirked. "Hank's room connected to Sharp's by a bathroom. I found a box of rifles under Sharp's bed. The box was covered by a tarp. Inside were .27 caliber rifles."

"Twenty-seven caliber?" Jude said. "What sniper teams use?"

"Yep," Sol said. "And next to the guns, a box of fifty glow sticks. I'll bet they weren't for a party. Plus, Sharp's bed always stayed made-up, like he never slept in it."

"How often did you check his room?" Sabine asked, her voice sharp. Sol was a snoop, like she was. His revelations surprised her.

"Often enough." Sol chuckled. "There was something about Hank and Sharp's connection, though." He cocked his head, thinking over the answer. "They were together a lot. Watching Sharp's reaction after Hank was killed, I was sure they were lovers."

"The family living at the farm; could it have been their stash of guns?" Jude glanced at Sol.

"Why would farm tenants have sniper guns?" Sol asked. "From Hank's description of finding the bodies, it doesn't sound likely. 'Course, we don't know how much of his story was true. Maybe it was made up."

"Hank kept on and on about leaving," Jude said. "Said we didn't have enough guns. Why lie? And why did he keep changing his mind about where to go?"

"Can you list where the Federal Reserve Banks are located?" Sol looked over at Jude.

"Federal Reserve Banks?"

"People might know where one or two are located," Sol said, "but Hank knew where all twelve were. We talked about it once, on watch. One's over in Richmond. Hank could've been involved with banks somehow."

"And you know about these banks because . . . ?" Sabine asked Sol.

"High school economics class," Sol said. "We memorized their locations."

"You think the CIA was after Hank," she said, "and Hank messed up something so they killed him? But we aren't trained people, only Hank, Sharp, Jen, Tommy, and Paul were even good with guns. "

Sol shrugged. "Hank and Sharp were professionals," Sol said. "I never told anyone, but one afternoon I came upon them in the woods. They didn't see me. Sharp was talking on a sat phone and Hank was pacing nearby. I went back to the spot twice, and both times a sleeping bag and field manuals were in the same place."

"Field manuals? Damn! I never suspected." Jude slapped the steering wheel. "Why didn't you tell me?"

"I was nervous about finding the stuff," Sol said. "It wasn't that I didn't trust you. I figured if I didn't say anything, you'd be safer. If you let something slip, who knows what they would've done to you. If they'd seen me, I bet they would've come after me."

"What's a sat phone? What kind of field manuals?" Sabine asked.

Sol sighed. "It's a satellite phone. People use them outdoors, in remote locations."

"Well, excuse me for not knowing every fact in the world," she said. "We'll never be sure what Hank and Sharp were doing "It's easy to attack dead people's character and make up things." No way she'd tell them she saw Sharp on the sat phone. She felt too protective of him.

Jude glared at Sol. "You should've told me, I would've confronted Hank and Sharp. I got along with them better than you."

"Did you ever go back and check out the manuals?" Sabine cut in.

"I did," Sol said, shooting a dirty look at Jude. "One on explosives and demolitions, an Army Survival Manual, an Army Special Ops Unconventional Warfare Manual, and one on booby traps. And a sketchpad with floor plans of buildings and subways, or maybe train tracks and a station. I didn't have an opportunity to study them much. I didn't want to take any; for sure they would've noticed."

"Jude," she said, "do you have a theory about Kate calling Hank 'darling' when she ran after him? I think she was in love with him. Sol shook his head. "If Hank was in love with Sharp, he wasn't messing with Kate. Jude tapped his chin. "Hank kept reminding the people on watch that when we reached St. Augustine we'd have to stay alert. Who'd be watching for us in St. Augustine? The town's way north of Miami."

Sol pulled a pack of cigarettes from his shirt pocket.

"I thought you were out of cigarettes," she said.

"I found two packs in my tool box." Sol tapped the pack against his palm. "I took a look at Hank's body, you know. A bullet in the middle of his forehead and another on the left side of his chest. Clean. Like a sniper did it."

"I heard three shots," Sabine said.

Sol nodded. "A third bullet in his thigh—for an artery, I guess. The bullet to the forehead was the kill shot. The other two were insurance."

"If they wanted Hank," Jude said, "why kill Kate?"

"My hunch is Kate got in the way," Sol said. "But there's no point going over this. I shouldn't have brought it up." He lit a cigarette and looked out the window.

Sol irritated her, but his assassination theory was worth considering. And if they wanted Hank, they wanted Sharp too.

"Why didn't you tell us about the guns under Sharp's bed," she said, "after Hank was killed? With more protection we could've stayed at the farm."

Jude scowled. "I thought you don't like guns."

"I don't," she said. "My feelings about guns keep changing though. I'm afraid of them. But lately I've been rethinking my attitude. Now they seem essential." When Hank took her foraging he'd had a gun tucked in his waistband. "Hank always had a gun on him and five or six stashed behind the front seat of the truck. But owning lots of guns doesn't mean he was CIA."

"Hank always worried we'd be ambushed when we foraged," Jude said. "But what about the fresh footprints and guns we found in the woods? CIA people wouldn't be clumsy . . . unless they planted the guns and faked the footprints. But why bother?"

They'd never find out who'd been watching the farm, or if Hank had been the sole target.

Her hunch was that Sharp knew he'd be next. Staying alone in the farmhouse, he was setting himself up as a target. Was he suicidal? He didn't appear to be the type to kill himself. But who knew anymore.

⟨≈⟩

"Stay on the lookout for a bigger truck we can grab," Sabine said. "One with good tires. We need to get better sleep in the truck bed." As it was, they had to squeeze in among food boxes, the Coleman stove, flashlights, the propane canister, sleeping bags, blankets, and tarps.

"We got it, Sabine, we got it," Sol said. "You've reminded us about the truck a bunch of times."

"We'll make St. Augustine in way less than two weeks," Jude said.

"We need the extra time," she said. "We have no clue what's ahead."

"You don't think we'll make it?" Jude said.

"We'll make it," she said. "But if the others run into trouble, who knows? At least they have Jen; she's a good shot and usually has a cool head. If Sharp goes with them and Tommy rallies, they'll be okay. Otherwise . . ."

"I'm keeping count of the days," Jude said. "A human calendar. Today's July17th."

"A glimpse of the boy inside." She kissed him full on the mouth. "You're dear," she whispered. Jude blushed, and she kissed him again.

Sol kept his eyes on the road. "What? No kiss for me?"

"Can you keep watch while I write?" she asked Jude.

"Sure." He squeezed her hand.

An image of the pond, with an abandoned boat she'd passed on the way to the farmhouse. No name for the place, but it didn't matter. She had the image. She pulled a notebook out of her pack and wrote for a while—a story for Jude. When she was done, she tore the paper out of the notebook and handed it to him. His face reddened as he studied it. He put it in his pants pocket and reached for her hand.

Writing made her think of the dictionary. No excuse for forgetting it. Maybe a dictionary could have jogged her memory, some word could have given her a clue about her family.

It was nearing dusk. Sol and Jude got out of the truck holding handkerchiefs to their faces to search for gas among a line of abandoned cars. Three cars had gas; they siphoned it into the can and poured it in their tank until the gauge registered almost full. They filled up the gas can for emergencies, then laughed and hugged each other. A victory. They were confident again.

Every fifty miles, she turned on the radio and moved the knob up and down the dial. She remained sure they'd get reception in areas with less damage.

"Sabine. Stop turning on the radio," Sol said. "There's nothing on."

"Events change, and we're farther south now. Radio stations could resume broadcasting any time, some have backup generators and multiple antennae." She intended to turn the knob until she was ready to stop.

"On rural roads there's less chance we'll find a station," Sol said.

"Not true," she said. "Transmission for FM stations is weaker. But being in the country shouldn't matter one way or the other."

"You sure?" Sol asked. "You're making this up."

She refused to answer.

❧

Their days took on a pattern. They avoided the interstate and cities if they could find an alternate route, preferring the two-lane roads through the country. When they came to abandoned cars blocking the lanes, they made U-turns or cut out a section of fencing with wire-cutters and drove through fields until the field and road diverged, then cut their way out of the field, and drove back onto the state road.

Often by sunset they were as punchy as kids. When it grew dark, they piled in the truck bed with flashlights and guns and slept. They avoided corpses, the buzzing flies, and the ever-present vultures circling, the black birds of death. They tried to stay frugal, but sometimes splurged and used propane to make morning coffee and cook a meal, if they had food.

When they ran out of propane, Sol said, "Let's ditch the cylinders."

"We absolutely will not get rid of empties," Sabine said. "If we find an adapter, we can refill them. A store like Home Depot should have adapters, if we see one."

"I'm no camper. You can refill these things?" Sol frowned.

"Yep. People with boats do it. It's not legal, but that doesn't matter much these days." More propane meant a future. Finding another open store meant a future. They couldn't stop thinking they had a future.

They drove by neglected fields, rows of shriveled beans, withered squashes, and rotted tomatoes. If they saw a back road sometimes they took it for a mile or so, and if they didn't spot any houses, they hid the pickup among the brush and slept on the ground. If they felt safe, they allowed themselves a fire. One evening, just as they were finishing a soup of stunted carrots and shriveled potatoes, trucks with bad mufflers came down the road.

Sabine scooped up handfuls of dirt, tossed the dirt on the fire, and waved her arms to dissipate the smoke. They crept to the edge of the brush and lay among rocks and brambles. The sun hadn't yet set.

Two trucks, a pickup and a flatbed, with about twelve men in all, slowed and stopped parallel to the field. A bearded man on the flatbed held a tall cross, another man brandished an axe. Since machete man attacked her, things like that—axes, knives—scared her more than guns. The rowdy, dirty group were probably recruits from neighboring farms. The men looked around, alert—searching for prey to rob and kill? Some of the men glanced at their empty pickup truck; they probably smelled smoke from the fire.

Her stomach lurched at the image: their bodies decapitated, skinned, and roasted on a spit like pigs.

The flatbed cab door opened. A burly man eased out and ambled to the rear of the flatbed, where he started arguing with two of the men. Arguing turned into shouting. The driver of the other truck, a skinny man wearing a yellow shirt, scrambled out of his pickup. He pulled knife out of a sheath lashed to his calf. Concealing the knife, he hustled over to the big man. In a flash the skinny guy grabbed the man's arm and sliced open his gut. The big guy fell on the road screaming.

Like angry bees, three men poured out of the flatbed, wielding two guns and a machete. The three took hold of the skinny guy and pinned him to the road. The one with the machete pulled down his zipper and peed in the guy's face, then swung the machete like he was going to chop off the guy's head. Instead, one of the other men shot the skinny guy in the stomach and chest. Within a minute, his yellow shirt turned red.

The burly man called out. One of his buddies leaned down to hear what he said and kept nodding. The big man's head fell to the side. The man yelled, "Chuck's gone. And Yella, too. Let's dump 'em in the ditch and vamoose before their families come after us."

More men left the flatbed, shouting and arguing over which two would drive the trucks. One man glanced in the direction where Sabine, Jude, and Sol lay, but he jumped back into the flatbed.

As the trucks pulled away, one man held the cross higher and launched into a familiar tune:

Onward Christian soldiers, marching as to war,
With the cross of Jesus going on before.
Christ the royal Master leads against the foe
Forward to feed our families, on to war we go!

The men sang the verse again, their voices fading.

"They're heading east, ahead of us." Jude's voice was shaking. He clutched his gun in his left hand, the truck key in his other.

They waited until the trucks were out of sight. "It happened so fast," Jude said. "Still, we knew this was a possibility."

"Knew what was a possibility," Sabine asked. Jude must mean the men could've come after them. She felt her voice rising. "They killed those two guys and dropped their bodies in a ditch. Their friends and neighbors. Why do that?"

Jude shook his head and didn't answer.

Too jumpy to sleep, they loaded the truck and took off. Jude drove ten to fifteen miles an hour to limit the bad muffler sound. He didn't turn on the headlights. When they reached an intersection of state roads, they studied the terrain. Nothing alarming. She shined her flashlight out the window, searching for an interstate ramp, but didn't see one. They drove until dawn without finding a ramp. They kept to their route; she insisted they not take detours.

At dawn they went half a mile down a dirt road. No houses, only a cul-de-sac for the county dump. Large dumpsters full of garbage, abandoned furniture, and appliances. They pulled the pickup away from the dumpsters. Before sleep, Sabine worried about their location—sitting there in plain sight. If those men in the flatbed had taken notice of the pickup and came back, they'd be trapped here. The hymn chilled her, the words went round and round in her head. A Christian war song.

⁊

They woke when the sun was high overhead. Sol pushed Jude away from the driver's side. "Move over. My turn. I'll get on the interstate first chance we get. With luck we'll find nice city people who can give us some news. Let's hope those guys were locals sticking to back roads near their farms."

"The cities could be just as bad," she said. "Maybe worse."

The truck's muffler sounded like it had even more holes. Sol ignored the roar and drove fast.

"Shouldn't we try to find another route?" Jude asked.

"Shut up, man. Let me handle this." Sol didn't take his eyes off the road. "Gimme a cigarette." He reached out his hand to Sabine.

"I found this pack when we rummaged through the store," she said. "I'm not giving it up. Besides, you said you found two packs in your tool box."

"Cigarettes make you cough, you're not a real smoker," Sol

muttered. "You're stingy. Just wait till you want something, then see what I give you."

"You two. Enough," Jude said. "Here, Sol, take one of mine."

Sol's voice was tight. "You smoke cheap, crappy brands. No thanks."

Jude lit a cigarette and jabbed it between Sol's lips. "Take it and shut the fuck up."

"No trucks behind us," she said. "Let's calm down." The cigarette smoke made her head pound. She used to smoke and loved to smoke. When the stress let up, she would stop. "We need something to take our minds off those men. I'll have nightmares." She put a hand on Jude's knee. "Have you all considered this? We could stop the next time we run out of gas. Set up a permanent camp near a river or creek. Florida could be a wasteland full of crazy people out to kill us.'"

"You don't mean it?" Jude scowled.

"We'll live off the land," she said. "Until things gets better. Let's drive around and pick a spot."

"We'd starve out here," Sol said. "We're driving to Florida so we can fend for ourselves. You said it yourself. With better climate and help from Kate's grandparents, we have a chance."

"We might be chasing a year-round warm-weather fantasy," she said. "What if the explosions have messed up the weather?"

"If things are worse in Florida, we'll go somewhere else," Jude said. "Sol's right. We can't just pick a spot of land that doesn't belong to us. We'll get shot. Besides, the climate isn't good here, and we're meeting the others."

"This talk is stupid," Sol said. "Let's stick to our plan."

No one disagreed. The men were being reasonable. She wasn't. The pit of her stomach ached. A respite from fear and uncertainty— she longed for that, and guessed all of them secretly hoped for happy surprises. She wanted to wake up to the miracle of unspoiled food in a working refrigerator, with cupboards filled with black bean and lentil soup and crackers. In this imaginary, vacant house, they'd find fresh towels, clean pillowcases and sheets, and a working bathroom. They could sleep as long as they wanted, roast hot dogs and potatoes in a living room fireplace stocked with plenty of cut wood in a brass holder. A radio would pour out music and never announce bad news.

In daylight, one of them would mention something small, like missing a cup of good coffee or a hamburger with fries, but they didn't talk big. No fantasies and unrealistic hopes, not even in the quiet of night huddled together in back of the pickup, for comfort more than warmth.

Yet she felt sure they each had a respite fantasy. They resembled dumb animals, waiting for exhaustion to lead them into the oblivion of dreamless sleep.

෩

Past Blacksburg, Virginia, signs for North Carolina appeared. Sabine longed for the coast and Wilmington beach, to show Jude the ocean. "Let's get past the cities the best we can," she said. On the outskirts of Greensboro, she gave Sol directions.

He said, "Tell me when to stop."

The sky darkened. They left the truck and sat on the curb in a suburb. They shared a box of stale cereal and an industrial-sized can of pears.

"Cereal and canned pears, like when I was a kid." Jude chuckled. "Let's move. We've been out in the open too long."

"Even in the suburbs I feel exposed," Sol said. "The country feels safer."

"We'll stay near here tonight and leave early tomorrow morning," Jude said.

Sabine felt silly doing it, but she insisted they looked for an apartment where she might've lived when she was younger. Her idea was based on a hunch or a wish, or nothing.

They drove four miles through a residential area, not using the headlights. Jude turned a corner and Sabine told him to stop. She clicked on a flashlight, left the truck, and inched her way through debris. A yellow-brick apartment building with a ripped green awning. The gold carpet with a green diamond pattern in the lobby looked familiar. The awning was the same forest green as the uniform her building's doorman—Samuel—had worn.

Jude stood beside her. She tugged his shirt. "See the awning?" She moved the flashlight beam over it. "The Lake Towers? Let's go!"

"Go where? This building's nothing but rubble." Sol glared at her; he thought she was crazy. "We're safer in the truck."

"I want to see."

"Let's camp out tonight, then take a look in the morning," Jude said.

They found slabs of smooth pavement and laid out their sleeping bags.

She slept fitfully, and when early morning came she turned in her sleeping bag to watch Jude's face—eyes closed in sleep, lids pale blue, cheeks pink, blanket warm, his fists curled at his neck like a little boy. Beyond him lay rubble. She wiggled out of her bag, put on shoes, then climbed the crumbling steps of the building and peered in through broken glass. The lobby looked like an earthquake had hit it. She watched the building, expecting that it would put itself back together, like in a cartoon.

Jude took her hand. "You got out in time. Wonder how many in your building made it out?" Was his question referring to DC? But this was North Carolina. She felt stupid and humiliated.

"I . . . I just don't know." She didn't feel like talking.

Sol sat up in his sleeping bag. "Christ Almighty. We're leaving. There's nothing here for us. I'll drive."

Sol had figured out the truth; Sabine could tell by his face. He understood that she wanted this building to be true, but it was only wishful thinking. Sweet Jude took her word that she might've lived here years ago, or that the buildings resembled each other. One of the differences between the two men.

Sol took charge, and she was relieved. He drove for hours while she kept her head on Jude's shoulder and tried not to think or feel. But a nasty thing crept around inside her. The building did resemble her old apartment building, but she'd never lived in Greensboro. Why make a big deal about coming here? Something about solving the memory puzzle. Jude hadn't contradicted her because he'd felt her distress. Maybe he loved her—didn't care if she lied, or if she was crazy, just hoped that when she calmed down, she'd tell the truth.

Lying was a different thing from crazy. She'd told him a lie when she insisted the scar on her stomach was an appendix scar. She hadn't wanted to think about it then. She shut it out again by closing her eyes.

They crossed a river, and the steel bridge made the truck tires hum. The sound turned into a woman's voice, and Sabine was a child again, sitting in a car with a woman. The woman turned the ignition key and said in a soft Southern voice, "Sabine, put on your seatbelt. You are precious cargo." The voice faded.

Since Greensboro, she'd slept poorly, and felt agitated and angry most of the time. Her body was sore from sitting squeezed between the men. She craved a solitary walk. Until Greensboro she'd taken the navigator job to heart, deciphering road signs damaged by target practice and cars smashing into them, but now she couldn't bring herself to care. Even abandoned cars with bodies inside were becoming routine. The muffler was an ongoing problem, so they kept driving slowly.

At dawn and dusk on country roads, she scanned with binoculars for rabbits, deer, and other game feeding in the open, but animals were scarce. One afternoon she saw quick movement among the trees. A doe? She signaled Jude, who pulled the car halfway into a ditch. Then each man took a rifle, climbed the fence, and walked through the field while she sat with a gun in her lap to wait.

Airplane engine sounds startled Sabine. She jumped out of the truck and gazed up. A small plane, flying toward the coast. An airport must be open nearby. She pointed to the plane as the men walked back.

"The plane's good news, but no game," Jude said. "It's more stale crackers, half-rotten tomatoes, and sour apples."

They drove on. Her excitement about the plane dwindled. Her stomach growled. More scrounging for clean water in creeks and rivers, scrounging for food. More disappointment wearing them down. She smelled a salty breeze blowing off an ocean that didn't exist.

Chapter 14

HAWK MOON

July 27, 2014.

Hawks soaring, gliding high. Their strong, sure movements belied the blustery air, thick with dust blowing off fallow fields. The three of them passed houses with trucks parked in driveways, people riding horses and walking along the roads. At times their pickup got stuck behind a slow-moving tractor. Sabine liked getting stuck; it felt ordinary, like they were merely going for a ride in the country. Before the bombs.

"I wanna see the beach." Jude fidgeted. "I'll drive through the night."

She sat close, her head on his shoulder, drifting in and out of sleep. Sol's head lay against the passenger's window. When she half-way woke during the night, Sol was snoring lightly.

The truck slowed, and Sabine woke to dawn in Wilmington. All three of them piled out of the truck and raced downhill to the deserted beach and across the sand to the water.

"Oh, no," she said.

The sand was stained with black and brown streaks. Debris was strewn along the tideline. Brown foam surf broke on the sand, and way out, the water was gun black. At the water's edge they dodged what the tide washed ashore: dead fish, globs of oil, slivers of wood from busted boats, shredded beach towels, a bloated human foot, plastic bags.

She took Jude's hand and squeezed it. He pulled free and wheeled around. She and Sol followed him to the pickup without a word. Jude settled himself in the driver's seat. He veered to the right, backtracking away from the coast.

"What if Florida's like this?" she asked, not expecting an answer.

They drove in silence. Jude stopped once so they could get food from the back of the truck and relieve themselves. After that, Sol took the wheel and kept his foot on the accelerator.

Sol slammed on brakes. "To the left. Bodies! Five or six lying near the fence."

"We should stop," she said. "They might've been walking when someone drove by and gunned them down."

"Not stopping," Jude said. "Too risky."

She was stunned he refused to stop, but stayed quiet. He was probably right. Hank's words: bombs turned everything into kill, or be killed. They drove on, and the sun moved low and lit up the fields, turning them golden brown, tinged with red. Sol took a rutted road running alongside a field. The fence had been cut in several places and lay flat on the ground.

Sol drove over the fencing into the field and climbed out of the truck. "I had to get out and stretch."

Sabine sat on the field stubble. She ate a sliver of cheese and an apple, but still felt queasy. Sol picked up a handful of dirt. "It's sandy. A good place to throw down sleeping bags and look at the stars. I'm sick to death of sleeping in the truck."

Jude came to her. "I've always wanted to see the ocean."

"Jude, I'm sorry. I described the beach as wonderful. It wasn't."

"I'm not twelve. I'll live." He laughed a little. "Maybe."

She pushed his shoulder. "Stop it. You'll live a long, wonderful life."

They sat on the ground, each thinking their own thoughts.

The ocean was the lowest point for Sabine, except for Kate and Hank's death, since the first bomb exploded in May. She suppressed the urge to keep apologizing for the beach, as if the filth and destruction were her fault. Even her memories, what few she had, felt stained.

"It's getting dark. Let's get it together." Sol pointed a flashlight at the ground to avoid detection while they searched for a level spot for sleeping bags.

Jude looked at something on the hill.

Two rapid shots. Another.

Jude gasped and fell to his knees as if he'd decided to sit.

She froze, then heard her own voice screaming. She and Sol pivoted toward the hill.

Sol drew his gun.

A house, visible from only one angle, hidden among shrubs and trees. They'd missed it when they'd checked out the spot.

Shadows fled through trees. More shots from that direction, close enough to kick up dirt nearby.

Sol shoved his gun into his belt, took Jude's arm, and dragged him toward the woods. Sabine darted ahead to clear a path, tossing tree limbs, stomping on brush. More danger in the woods? Put Jude in the truck bed and drive like hell to a hospital? The moon wasn't full, maybe they could get away.

Blood bloomed across Jude's thigh. Sol laid him on a bed of tags under a big pine, and Sabine knelt by him.

Sol handed her a Swiss Army knife. "Cut off his pants. I'll get blankets and a canteen."

"Also a bowl," Sabine said, grasping the thick fabric and cutting as fast as she could with unsteady hands. As soon as she ripped off the pants leg, the wound above Jude's kneecap gushed blood. She yanked off her jacket and T-shirt, sliced and ripped the shirt into strips, tied two strips above the bullet hole and laid the rest across the wound.

She hadn't seen a hospital sign since—well, she couldn't recall, except the sign had to be a long way back. They wouldn't make it to a hospital, and it might be deserted anyway.

Jude gasped in rapid breaths; something was wrong with his lungs. She crawled up to his chest. Blood seeped through his shirt. She pulled it off. Another bullet wound.

"Jude, can you hear me? You've been shot. Sol and I will take care of you." Jude didn't open his eyes.

Sol stood above them. "Did you see any hospital signs?"

She forced a whisper. "Way back. He's shot in two places. We won't make it to a hospital. But we can't take care of him here."

Sol didn't look at Jude.

She was naked from the waist up and Sol was staring. She slipped on her jacket and fumbled with the zipper. "The truck will jostle him. If we try to leave, the shooter will have another opportunity to shoot us all."

"The shooter will have to risk coming into the woods to get us here," Sol whispered. "Let's take turns on watch. We'll be ready."

She ran to the pickup for another shirt and a gun. She slipped the pistol in her jacket. *Aim at the shooter's chest. Riddle him with bullets.* Until machete man she'd never thought about killing, except the times she'd been so angry at Giles she wanted to kill him. But she never would've hurt him physically.

Maybe the shooter was a woman, scared, ready to puke, like she felt this moment. Sol sat by Jude's legs, holding the compress against the leg wound.

She held the dry shirt against Jude's chest wound. When it was soaked, she returned to the truck and rummaged through her pack for cloths. Nothing left except her beloved shawl. The only valuable thing she had left.

She ran back. "Sol! Got any rags or T-shirts?"

Sol rushed to the truck and came back with two dishtowels.

"Wrap one around his knee," she said. "Give me the other."

She pulled the soggy T-shirt off his chest and pressed the towel against the thigh wound. "Jude? Sol and I are here." No response. His eyes still halfway closed.

Sol took first watch in a thicket at the edge of the woods, a pistol in his belt, a rifle beside him. She imagined he was too tired to walk like he typically did when on a watch team. For two or three hours she sat with Jude. She trickled water into his mouth, but most of it ran out.

She looked up to see a dark shape sitting with his back against a tree, head bobbing.

"*Sol.*"

His head jerked up when she said his name. "Sorry," he said. "I must've drifted off."

"Nothing happened," she said. "I've got a pistol. Give me the rifle." With a bitter smile, she held out a shaky hand, and he gave her the rifle. He probably knew she was itching to use it.

The ugly house stood on the hill in darkness. The house with the ugly people who'd shot Jude for standing in their field. Their precious, stubble-filled, broken-down fenced field. The house didn't deserve the moon's beauty or the warmth of the sun.

Heedless of the noise she made, she kicked underbrush and stones and stomped along the edge of the woods muttering. The whole ugly world, falling deeper into chaos. Her feet hurt from kicking rocks. Sorrow replaced anger. She preferred anger, didn't want to feel anything tender. Rage had been a good shield.

Sol dozed on his jacket, close to Jude.

She knelt by Jude. His forehead was still hot, his breathing rapid and shallow. She went to the truck and pulled her shawl from the pack. She folded the shawl until it was thick and smaller, then wet it and laid it on his brow. When she kissed his cheek, her whole body shook. Unable to stay with him, she moved to the edge of the woods. The horizon was pinking.

Please, please, please, a miracle! Nothing, not a single thing, no other thing she could think to do for him.

Forty feet away a shadow turned into a silhouette: an animal creeping through the field. It slunk like a fox—but no, it was the wrong shape. It was a small German shepherd, lapping water from a creek. She walked toward the dog. The dog jerked its head. Palm down, she held out her hand and called in a soft voice. The dog stood motionless, water dripping from his mouth. *Sun Dog?* She inched close. No tags. He took off running across the road. *Fool. Standing in the field. Exposed.*

She hurried into the woods and found a clump of bushes to relieve herself behind.

Jude's face felt hot; he must have a fever of about 104 or 105. She crouched by him, took the shawl off his brow, doused it with cool water, wiped his hands and face, and dunked the shawl again. She laid the shawl on his forehead. His body radiated heat, his breath grew more rapid and shallow.

Oh God, please, a miracle.

Sol woke but didn't look at her. Instead he moved deeper into the woods.

Jude's lips moved, and she leaned in close. But no sound. She took his hand. "Jude, I'm so sorry. If we'd gone with the others, we'd be safe. This is my fault."

Jude's eyelids stayed half open, his eyes blank and fixed. No way to tell if he understood her words. He coughed and made gurgling sounds followed by a surge of clear fluid from his mouth. His little finger turned blue, followed by the other, and then all his fingers. She pulled off his boots. His toes were blue, his feet were turning blue.

Her teeth chattered and she laid kisses across his forehead. "I love you so much. Inside I've been calling you my bright man. And I never told you; I wish I'd told you again and again how much you mean. Without you I would've given up. You made me want to struggle to live. Please stay."

She squeezed tepid water out of her shawl and dumped it in cold water. She laid the shawl on his forehead. A small, ineffective gesture. Even with clenched teeth, she couldn't control the sound of her chattering teeth. She held Jude's hand between hers and focused on his chest, making sure his chest kept moving.

His mouth opened. His chest moved, stopped; moved slightly, and stopped. No sound except the chatter of her teeth.

Sol came toward her but didn't acknowledge her.

"He's gone," she said, but the words garbled. Sol wasn't looking at her, so perhaps he didn't hear. He handed her a cup of black instant coffee and stared off in the distance. Had he seen something dangerous? She couldn't talk. Or hold back tears.

Sol's expression was frozen.

Tears and mucus dripping, she wiped her face with the back of her hand and rubbed it into her jeans.

Sol reached over and put his cup of coffee on a log, as if the cup was a piece of fine china, not a cracked mug they'd dug out of a sink full of dishes at the last house they'd rummaged through.

He knelt by Jude. He pulled the shawl off Jude's forehead and studied his face. She found herself backing away, finished with both men. She wanted to run, but had nowhere to go.

"Jude and I have been buddies since third grade," Sol mumbled. "We rode the same school bus, ate lunch together, and traded food. Two hard-boiled eggs for a banana, an apple for my mom's half-stale cake that Jude loved. On weekends after chores, we met halfway between our houses and walked to the country store to buy licorice, raced our horses across the fields, and did stupid tricks in the river."

Sol's pants were splattered with blood. She glanced at her own jeans. Bloody, too. The same pants she'd worn for days. She rubbed the stain covering her thigh and said, "I don't know much about Jude's past. He and I stayed in the present."

Her jaw hurt. Her nose was still running; she raised her arm, then wondered why it was in the air—oh, she was going to scratch her nose. She rubbed her nose on her shoulder. "Not even your last name. You must've told me at the farmhouse, but I don't recall."

"Henley. Solomon Jacob Henley."

Sabine frowned. Jacob and Solomon. Biblical first and middle names.

"You're thinking my family's a Bible-toting bunch. You're half right, my parents love the Old Testament. But by high school my brothers and I stopped going to church. What a waste of time."

"I still can't recall my last name," Sabine said. "I hope I figure it out before a bullet gets me, too."

"Don't talk like that. After all, your last name might suck." Sol gulped coffee. "We've been here too long. Why hasn't the shooter come down the hill and picked us off?"

"Tell me about your God," she said. "He's sure busy protecting the world."

"Not how God works," Sol said.

"Sorry, I have no idea why I said that."

Sol tugged Jude's body until his friend lay against his chest. He murmured words to Jude, words she couldn't hear.

"Time to dig." She had to move or she'd go crazy. She got the shovel from the truck.

"It's not safe here. Never was," Sol said. "We have to go, now."

"You and your safety. Screw safety. I'm not leaving till Jude's in the ground."

"I meant we carry him in the truck until we find a safe space."

"No. We bury him here, or farther into the woods."

He took the shovel from her and began spading in a soft spot. "Okay, here. Hurry."

She dug with her hands and brought the sandy brown dirt up to her face. A pine aroma mixed with decaying things. Not the feel and smell of her childhood dirt, the wonderful red clay, its heavy stickiness in her hand. Something from home to hold.

When they'd dug about six inches, she said, "Let's leave him open to the trees and sky. Animals and vultures will get him anyway."

Her stomach hurt thinking about the dog she'd seen earlier eating Jude's body.

Sol grimaced. "Since we're doing this, we should make a real grave. Go deeper."

"No. Jude would want this. I'm sure." She pulled off what was left of Jude's jeans. They laid one of their valuable blankets beside Jude and slid him onto it. Sabine unbuckled his sheath and bowie knife and tossed them on the ground. They slid Jude's torso onto the blanket. One leg bloody and ruined, one young and whole.

Together, they slid the blanket into the shallow spot and pulled it around him. Sabine adjusted the blanket over Jude's face. She pulled the strip of leather out of his long, dirty hair and slipped it in her pocket. She wrapped his head with one end of her shawl and spread it out as far as it would reach, to his knees. His crimson shroud.

Sol threw shovelfuls of dirt, and she threw handfuls. At first she counted handfuls but stopped as soon as she understood counting distracted her. She wanted to stay present, not run away by spacing out.

A thin layer of dirt covered Jude's body.

"Be right back," Sol said.

Before she could say, "No, don't leave me," he'd disappeared farther into the woods. She grabbed the sheath and bowie knife off the ground and fastened the sheath to the waist of her jeans.

Minutes later Sol came back dragging a small tree limb. She held the branch steady while he sawed off two small pieces and tied them to the limb. He fashioned a rough approximation of a cross and wiggled it in the dirt.

She didn't think Jude would want a cross, but since Sol hadn't insisted they dig six feet down, she wouldn't object. She didn't want to fight with Sol.

Since the sky had turned light, she'd been scanning for birch trees, but hadn't seen any. Nothing like the ones growing at the farm. She searched for another sentinel, a substantial tree. Her gaze fell on a big pine reaching toward the sun, its lower branches broken off. It looked sturdy enough. She could find the tree again. One day, she would return.

Without thought she folded her hands while Sol recited the Lord's Prayer. A natural gesture—she must've prayed in another life. While she didn't believe a word of the prayer itself, the rhythm of the words felt ancient and soothing.

They sat in silence a minute until Sol touched her arm.

She took his meaning. Together they rose, brushed off the dirt, and carried the saw and shovel and bloody rags to the truck, as if they were a couple instead of two strangers thrown together during a surreal time.

The sun sat well above the horizon by the time they'd finished loading the truck. Sol turned the truck around. They didn't speak but nodded, reassuring each other. Sol drove across the field crouched low over the steering wheel. Sabine cringed in the passenger's seat, expecting a rage of bullets to slam the pickup. Once they hit the road she straightened up, and Sol put his foot to the floor until the speedometer hit fifty miles an hour. She kept her eyes on the back window to memorize the look of the woods and location of the sentinel tree, but the pickup moved too fast.

❧

Somewhere outside of Piney Springs, North Carolina, she wrote:

The Bone Woman's Tale

A crone known as Bone Woman visited Baby Jeffrey in his dream. The woman's bones were held together with twine, her pallid face and wild gray hair, fearful. But her face softened gazing at him sleeping.

She leaned over his crib and swayed, her bead necklace hit the crib bars. To a rattling rhythm, she whispered, "Mystery shadows slide where critters search for rock shadows or tunnels

under cool sand. A storm signals excitement about the Cere-
mony of Fire."

She laid her gnarled hand on his head and left the room. He
cooed in the quiet of the day.

The Bone Woman returned. "Child, I'll teach you how to
put on your yellow headband and red beads and chant, your face
to the moon.

"You flew among people, your hair glowed like dawnlight.
But your light could not last. Our Ceremony of Fire will help
you transform. You fly around the circle and ask for kisses and
we will watch your fire disappear."

She said to Baby Jeffrey, "The chant goes like this: The raven
make friends with cacti and smoke, who make the potion and
call down the moon. The brave raven stares at death. Once you
reach the safe place, you will see the ocean take on the color of
sky. The Ceremony of Fire is for those who look straight at dan-
ger, straight at death, at pain in the imagination and at the pain
in the real."

Bone Woman vowed not to weep and cradled Jeffrey against
her bony shoulder. His smooth face close to her wrinkled one.
She wept and carried him toward the fire.

She took the potion bottle from her pocket. "Dear Jeffrey,"
she whispered, and poured the potion, "may you discover secrets,
what wolves sense about the land, how smoke drifts, and how the
ocean pulls its color from the sky."

Sabine closed her eyes, weary of vigilance. She didn't care what
threat lurked on the road. So much had happened since leaving the
farmhouse. The farm felt far in the past now. Yet she could measure
the time in days since leaving West Virginia.

After what she'd discovered about country men since her first
conversation with Jude, her old stereotypes angered her now. How
unkind and superficial. She and Jude had helped each other stand
up to what they feared. He'd been her life a short time, yet he'd filled

many parts of her. Not only her body. His raucous, abrupt laugh; his curiosity about animals, woodlands, and horses, and places he'd never been. His playfulness and humor, his respect. Kind, and unlike her, not a gossip. Jude found ways to say things that helped people to like themselves.

When he'd talked about his disappointment with the ocean, he'd said, "I'll live. Maybe." He'd been joking, of course. Would she have recalled his words if he hadn't been shot? Probably not. The words reminded her how Jude had loved his life. She was glad they'd interred him unprotected.

Dusk came, and Sol pulled over and left the truck to fill two water jugs at a creek. A gun lay on the dashboard and a notebook lay in her lap. She'd become casual around guns. Not like the day Hank handed her a gun, then took it away before they went inside the mall. Her face had probably told him she couldn't handle a gun.

She missed the place where the sky took on the color of oyster shells and merged with the sea. The dunes, waves, the pound and spray she may never see again. Blurred images of walking by the ocean with adults as a child—with family.

The ocean she'd shown Jude had turned sluggish, fetid, was possibly dying. She thought of Jude, his bloody lungs in shreds. Would his death pull Giles's death close again? Now she'd mourn two men. And still the hole where her family should be.

Chapter 15

NUT MOON

July 28, 2014.

The following morning the engine started knocking, worse than the muffler full of holes. People could hear them. Dangerous, but she didn't say anything, hoped the noise would stop. Sol drove his usual way, with his body hunched over the steering wheel.

"If the truck's thrown a rod that's serious. But it could be something simple." When did she learn about cars? A teenage boy had taught her.

Sol looked rough—dirty shirt, shaggy hair, and scraggly beard. He didn't respond. A half hour later the truck slowed. He wrestled with the stiff wheel and turned it to the right, toward a ditch. His face red with effort, he managed to guide it off the road and turn off the ignition. "All I know about trucks is how to fill them up with oil and gas. C'mon. We're ditching it."

She shook her head.

He hit the steering wheel. "Goddamn it, Sabine. This truck has served its purpose."

"Jude worked hard on this truck. Let's not give up yet."

"Savannah's not far. Let's walk."

She groaned. "We don't want to get trapped in a city." She jumped out of the truck and opened the hood. "I can do a bit of engine work," she said with false confidence. The oil was dirty but not low. No battery corrosion. She wiggled wires to make sure they felt secure. She sniffed the engine but didn't smell anything leaking. "Okay, try to start it."

Sol turned the key. Nothing happened.

Back under the hood, she wiggled wires.

"Sabine."

She hated him saying her name in a parental tone. A familiar, icky feeling; did her father talk that way? "The truck's all we have left of Jude."

"You can't be serious. It's just a pickup. Let's walk while it's still light. We can come back here if we don't find anything."

Being alone terrified her. Without a word she pulled Jude's pack from behind the seat and rummaged through it. His wallet with twenty dollars, pictures of his old girlfriend and family, and his driver's license. She stuffed the wallet in her own pack, checked the bowie knife on her waist, and slipped on Jude's jacket.

Sol stuck his gun in the back of his belt and covered it with his jacket. He packed tools from the truck. Maybe he was thinking to sell them to make money. They tied sleeping bags across the bottom of their packs and walked a few yards.

The maps. She ran back to the truck, emptied the glove box, and tucked the maps into her pack. They set off at a quick pace.

Half an hour later Sol took her arm and they stopped. "Hear it? Planes are flying again." They searched the sky and didn't see anything, yet the sound was unmistakable.

They walked until she spotted a creek that was deep in spots and not murky.

"The creek looks okay." Sol didn't answer. She drank, filled a water bottle, and splashed water on her face. Sol did the same, but mostly just streaked his dirty face. They walked again. Sabine felt jittery, needed to talk, but Sol was still mad at her about the truck.

"I haven't read a newspaper or listened to a radio in ages," she said. "Do we still have states, or have they been divided into territories with names like The Swamps of Florbama?"

Sol didn't laugh. He probably wanted to punish her. Giles had never punished with silence; he hadn't played mind games. Giles's silences had come from deep inside, had little to do with her. He'd been ten years old when his mother died, and he'd grappled with the empty place, his memories scant and exaggerated. During the drive to Florida, Giles had receded into Sabine's past like a long-ago film character. But now, with Jude's death, Giles's death drew close again. The loss of both men wove and tangled together.

She lost herself in words. *Giles, while shadows elongated across the snow and tinged it the palest blue, I suppose you drank your last shot of bourbon and put a string of black warrior beads around your neck. You tasted frigid air and lay in the soft bed of snow. With your face fixed on the moon, did you pray for a quick death? Before your lungs filled with frost crystals, did you sing praises for your life?*

Sol yanked her arm. They were walking past a strip mall into a residential area, mostly apartment buildings. An occasional moving car.

"Did you see those gas trucks?" he asked.

She nodded. "A good sign. Airplanes and now gas trucks."

The few pedestrians they passed kept their heads down, disinterested in two dirty strangers wearing backpacks. Sol slowed his pace and glanced in car windows, checking for keys in ignitions, while she played lookout. The area felt familiar. Most beach towns felt the same.

Her stomach cramped. Polluted creek water? The next cramp made her double over. How far could she walk? Trying to have a conversation with Sol wasn't working. *You're fine. Jude's dead. No, you are not fine.* She wouldn't take off Jude's jacket, even though she was sweating and not soothed by the jacket.

There was no evidence of explosions in the city or suburbs. At intersections they checked route signs to figure out the fastest way out of the city. They'd take US 12 over the Savannah River, but not today. She felt tired, about to collapse.

They came to a park bordered by waist-high shrubbery. Deserted, but too exposed. They walked a block to a construction site and threw down sleeping bags behind a pile of lumber and earth-moving equipment.

Voices close by. The construction site stood on a hill, above a neighborhood. She and Sol peered down. People in a backyard, picnic tables full of food, and the smell of hot dogs grilling. Children chased each other behind large white houses without trees or grass.

Sol groaned. "Am I insane? Are those people having a picnic? A fucking picnic?"

"The grocery stores here must be stocked. Either this area wasn't hit, or they got back on their feet quickly." She waited for Sol to say something, but he didn't. "Let's go down there and try our luck?"

He shook his head.

"Those hot dogs smell so good. I could eat five," she said.

"You haven't seen yourself in a mirror. Blood all over your jeans, not to mention the bulge of a gun and Bowie knife at your waist. They're liable to call the cops on us."

"You're filthy too. Take a look in the mirror." She patted his back, but he didn't respond.

⁂

Early the following morning, she woke retching. She made it to some bushes before vomiting. There was soap, water in her canteen, and a toothbrush, but no toothpaste. She popped a piece of gum in her mouth.

When Sol woke, they set off walking.

"The sun's high," he said. "We slept a long time. I feel lucky. Today we'll find a car. Yesterday, walking by those apartment buildings? We were being watched."

"Watched? Why didn't you say anything?"

"I didn't want to worry you, so I waited to see what would happen. Nothing did. But if people are holed up in their apartments, why?"

"Yeah," Sabine said. "Not many people are walking around."

"What about radiation? Or maybe some kinda plague?"

"But near the construction site those people were in their yards. They didn't act scared." Maybe her nausea was radiation sickness. But her breasts felt sore. And this morning was the second time she'd thrown up. Familiar. Morning sickness.

"Yeah, all those happy people, eating in their yards." He heaved a big sigh.

She didn't want to talk to him. Sol still breathed while Jude was down in the dirt. If the shooter had aimed two or three feet to the left, Sol would be gone, and Jude would still be there. Her gut lurched; it was a terrible thing to think. She didn't want Sol dead. She just wanted Jude alive.

They turned onto a main residential street. Sol draped his arm around her shoulder and pulled her close. "Stay close. Don't look up. To our left, somebody's glassing us from a window. Nine or ten floors up. Keep walking."

Too surprised to resist, she speculated about radiation and disease. Would people think they were contaminated? The urge to look up was almost overwhelming. Several times she touched Jude's bowie knife.

Sol took her hand so he could set a faster pace through city blocks. But whenever they passed people huddled on the sidewalks, she pulled on his arm to slow their pace. People were fairly clean and appeared healthy. She smiled, but received no more than a rapid glance from anyone. Walking slowly, they picked up snatches of conversation about electricity problems and gas station deliveries. A few stations had gas—that was still big news. Trucks were running; supply lines were open. They looked like derelicts, but people on the street were tense, they had bigger worries than dealing with two ragged strangers.

They came upon a residential block with stately brick houses. Trees along the curb were surrounded by owner-planted flowers, edged with paving stones. Sol wiggled a stone out of the dirt and dropped it in his pocket.

"Is the rock to break a car window?"

"Aren't you clever," he said. "But I don't have hot-wiring tools, or a slim jim. The ideal would be an unlocked car with a key in the ignition and a full tank of gas. We can jump in like we own the car." He grinned as if he believed stealing a car could be easy. She suspected he was too pragmatic to believe this. Had the news of gas deliveries cheered him up, and he wanted her to feel happy?

Whenever she slowed, he stopped and gave her water, then took her hand as if he expected her to want to hold his. They came upon several blocks of shops and slipped inside a deli, gold lettering still visible on the shattered front window. The glass cases in the front were stripped bare. They searched a storage area in the back. They found two bags of crackers that weren't too stale and old-fashioned celery sodas in green glass bottles. Someone had probably stashed them and never came back. They sat on the curb. She pulled a jar of peanut butter out of her pack; they spread peanut butter on the crackers and chugged the sodas. They shared the third soda. Peanut butter made her happy enough to smile at Sol. He laughed.

They walked beside parked cars, and by late afternoon she said, "Enough" and pointed at a grassy lawn in front of a post office. Before he could stop her, she lay on the grass.

"It's not safe. While it's light, we have to keep moving. We're almost to the highway."

"We still don't have a car. I'm not going any farther till morning."

"Okay. I'll look for cover." He went around to the back of the post office and returned. He tried to help her up but she shook him off and stood on her own. In the back of the building, about fifty postal trucks were parked in lines across the lot.

Sol grinned. "We'll hide in plain sight."

They rattled truck doors in search of an unlocked truck. How many people still received mail? Speedy mail delivery and computers might be gone. Out of habit, she pushed a button on her smartphone, aware the battery was dead. She checked the useless device less and less these days; she preferred talking face to face. This new reality probably resembled how it had been for her parents and grandparents at her age.

"You miss your phone?" she asked.

"Not as much as I thought I would."

Finally, a truck with an unlocked door. They slipped inside. Without mail bags there was enough space for two sleeping bags. Sol rummaged in his pack and discovered some Nabs. He handed her two cheddar crackers. She shoved both in her mouth.

"Too bad we can't steal one of these trucks," he said.

"Why? We'd stick out on the highway—plus, this isn't comfortable. And I'm guessing they don't go fast."

"You're probably right."

"Something I've been thinking about," Sabine said. "Jude's father. From what he told me, his dad was the only family he had left. When we find a phone, you should try to call him and tell him about Jude."

"I'll ask my parents. They'll find him. Good thinking."

"We can't forget to do that."

"This morning? You threw up again," Sol said. "I bet you're pregnant. Trust old Jude to leave his mark, the sly son of a bitch." He rustled as he wiggled down in his bag. "You're kinda old to be having a kid."

"Late twenties, that isn't old." She'd never seen Jude as sly. He wasn't sly, was he?

"Really? Late twenties?"

"What?"

"You hold the maps at arm's length and squint to read them. The long-arm is a problem people get at forty. And your thighs jiggle. Granted, not much, but my mother wore bathing suits."

She wanted to slap his smirky mouth.

"And something else. The apartment building in Greensboro? You never lived in Greensboro. You're a liar, and not a good one— your face gives you away. But for the life of me I can't figure out why you lied."

She hated Sol. She didn't bother to take off her shoes before sliding into her sleeping bag. With her back to him, she closed her eyes, right away regretting her decision. Wiggling around didn't help her discomfort. Determined to sleep, she closed her eyes.

She dreamed she had the body of a young girl. An old woman wearing a necklace of blue beads reached for her through thick fog. Sabine ran full-out and thought she'd escaped, but the woman jumped in front of her and opened her mouth, and a rattler surged out and writhed on the ground toward her. No matter how fast Sabine ran, the rattling monster stayed close. She fell on a plot of coffin-shaped dirt. When she rolled on her back, her belly swelled, becoming huge; she feared her body would burst.

A woman's face appeared in the helicopter door. The helicopter spun like a child's top, fast then slow. The woman aimed a rifle at Sabine's giant belly. But she dodged the shot.

She woke in a panic, found herself coiled around Sol's back and rolled away. How dare he say those things! With gritted teeth she lay in her bag, wanting to rant out loud about his bad qualities and how he'd hurt her feelings. Dammit, hormones were taking over her body again. She muffled her crying, missing Giles. Missing Jude.

Somewhere a dog barked. She looked out the small window. No wind, even the trees stood hushed. White postal trucks lined up in rows, a surreal landscape. Sun Dog wasn't there, she'd left him back at the hospital to comfort other children. If he were still alive, he'd be old, with a gray muzzle and stiff legs. Young or old, she needed him.

Back in her sleeping bag, she worried about age. She wanted her twenties again. Not to change her appearance. No, more important, to do life over and make decisions that didn't hurt her. She'd willed away thoughts about her age for so long she couldn't recall when she hadn't lied. But even as she pushed away the truth, she did recall most of her earlier life, more than she acknowledged out loud. Was she ready to unravel the years, especially the final months with Giles? Most events had become clearer. She could puzzle out the rest. Writing was no longer enough. She had to talk with someone. *If Jude were here*—no. Even if he were alive, it would be unkind to tell him about Giles.

A wave of exhaustion. She slept again.

Sol shook her arm, speaking in an eager voice. "The sun says it's five. Let's go. We don't wanna get caught sleeping here."

They stumbled out of the truck. "A bathroom would be nice," she muttered.

"I wouldn't mind seeing water run out of a faucet."

They walked a block.

"Look at the sign!" Sol pointed to a hand-lettered sign propped by a gas pump. "We got electric. Gas. Food. Hot coffee."

They headed for the bathrooms. She was grateful for running water even though it ran cold and there were no hand towels. She dried her hands and face with toilet paper.

While waiting for Sol to come out of the restroom, she spotted a policeman near the door, his gun prominent on his hip. He eyed Sabine and she gave him her most innocent-looking smile. As soon as Sol came out of the bathroom, she pulled her jacket over her gun and took his hand. He was startled but kept hold of her hand as he pushed open the door to the smell of hazelnut coffee.

"What was that about?" he whispered.

"The cop kept eyeing me. You think he can tell that this is blood on my jeans? I wanted us to look as normal as possible."

"Good thinking."

A long line in front of a counter with coffee carafes. "I'll get us big coffees. Check out the food. Buy everything!"

"Lots of real cream," he said. "If they have it."

The tall man in front of her looked around. He had a wide, friendly face.

"Hi," she said. "My friend and I are traveling. I'm trying to understand what happened here. I don't see any evidence of bombs."

The man looked directly at her. "Hey, sweetie, you sure look all tuckered out. I can tell you been traveling." He laughed, showing cigarette-stained teeth. "No bombs around here. Got wind that one fell 'bout forty miles away, but there's rumor's flying every whicha way. And big problems with trucks delivering stuff. Sometimes the electric don't work. We got cleanup crews over on the beaches. Been going to the beach myself to help out, when I can. Some folks left town to go to their friends and families. Our block is half empty, kinda weird, half a ghost town."

The line inched closer to the coffee stand.

"You-all have mail service," Sabine said. "Any word on the president and vice president? Are the airports open? Has any group even claimed they did all this?"

"Sure, the President's around. I didn't vote for the man, understand, but I sure didn't want nothing bad to happen. Now the Vice President, well, he's not so hot, at fifty-two he had a heart attack, so he's in the hospital. Think about the stress, you know. Myself, I'd never want to work in government of any kind. Nope, no group has said anything. So, the enemy's a mystery. Makes me think they aren't finished with us yet."

"That's more scary! What about the airports?"

"The little one up the road's open. Don't think the big ones are working." He reached for a carafe and poured a large cup of coffee.

She spoke louder. "You don't get any papers?"

He turned, sloshing coffee, holding the lid in his other hand. "Gotta get me some sugar and cream. Yeah, we get the county paper, it's about three pages long. But that's it."

"Out on the road we can't always get coffee. Sure smells great." Sabine smiled. "My friend and I are traveling south. How are the roads?"

"Again, you got rumors of roving gangs. I ain't setting foot outside this county. You heard bombs hit Miami?"

"Yeah, we did. Thanks so much for the information. I appreciate it." She nodded.

"You bet. Well, good luck out there." He touched her shoulder and left.

She poured two coffees and paid double the usual price, feeling relieved the man hadn't asked her about what had happened farther north, especially at the farmhouse. Too much explaining she didn't want to do, and she was too tired to make up a good lie.

Outside, Sol sat at a picnic table behind the station. He held up a new can opener like it was a prize. Five cans of pinto beans, granola bars, and beef jerky were laid out on the table.

She laughed at his display. They feasted on hot dogs topped with chili and cheese, and she told him what the man in the gas station had told her.

"You got a lot of news." Sol frowned when a blob of chili fell on his shirt. He dug in the bag for a napkin. "Don't know why I bother with napkins." He eyed his dirty shirt. They finished off a large bag of potato chips.

"Maybe things aren't so bad down South," she said. "Long as we don't go as far as Miami, we should be fine." She smiled, then remembered she was mad at him for calling her a liar.

He didn't respond.

"Aren't you happy? This is the best news we've gotten in a long time. In some places, things are getting back to normal."

"Yeah. Good news." But his low voice told her he was troubled by something.

They loaded their backpacks with food and set off. They came upon an older neighborhood with brick houses and lawns with large oaks. The grass grew knee-high in some yards. No cars were parked along the first block. They hurried around the back of one house and peered through windows. It was full of furniture and unwashed dishes in the sink. At the next house, a jug of milk sat on the dining room table, along with a pile of laundry.

Then they came to a house with a wide dining room window that was partway open.

Sol looked at her. "I could climb in the window. What do you think?"

"No, no. Look." By the dining room table, a large black cat lay still, its legs stiff and unmoving. "I bet the cat starved. The family must've left in a hurry and abandoned it. Poor thing. It's creepy."

"Or the cat came through the window looking for food, then couldn't get out?"

"I don't know," she said. "But I won't go in there. Let's keep looking. There are lots of houses to check out."

They walked down the alley, past abandoned trampolines, basketballs, and kids' toys. Gardens taken over by weeds with a few wilted flowers. A silent jungle gym. In the next block, a whitewashed brick house took up half the block. The rooms downstairs were sparsely furnished. No dishes or laundry or other signs of people. Sol put a finger to his lips and took hold of the backdoor knob. The door swung open. "Lock's busted," he whispered. "We're not the first people to do this."

He pulled his gun from his waistband. "Anybody home?" he called.

The house smelled musty, but nothing reeked.

He called out again and flipped the light switch. "Electricity. Great." They moved down the hall, alert for sounds.

"I'm showering, even if the water's ice cold," she whispered. "It doesn't feel like anyone's here."

"Let me check before you go upstairs," Sol said.

Only large pieces of furniture remained in the dining room. The living room and den had sofas and not much else. The litter on the floor suggested the family had sorted possessions, dropped their discards, and left in a hurry.

Sol bounded down the steps. "All clear."

She ran upstairs into a bathroom. At the tepid water she laughed, giddy to be standing under flowing water with a whole bar of soap instead of crouching by a river with a soap scrap. She left the bathroom wearing dirty clothes and followed the noise Sol made opening and closing drawers. The master bedroom was spacious enough for a mahogany four-poster bed, two antique bedside tables, and two large chests of drawers.

"I'm trying to find some clothes, but this guy was short and fat." He rummaged through the walk-in closet.

"Maybe they had skinny teenagers." She pointed to his head. "Your hair's awful, stiff and greasy."

His neck flushed pink.

Sorry for her words, she handed him her shampoo—one of her prized possessions. "Here, it was in the bathroom. I didn't mean anything by it. My hair was awful, too."

Sol headed for the shower, and she explored the other rooms. The family hadn't taken large furniture, which meant they hadn't been sure where they were going. A bedroom with basketball posters tacked on the wall and schoolbooks on the floor. No computer. In the walk-in closet, dress shirts, two pairs of jeans, and one clean work shirt. T-shirts in the drawers. Two hockey sticks, a basketball, and tennis shoes piled in a corner.

She took both pairs of jeans, some T-shirts, and the work shirt, and put them by the bathroom door. "I found some clothes," she called through the door. Without waiting for a response, she went back to the master bedroom closet. She found two long-sleeved women's T-shirts. None of the jeans fit. She put on a clean shirt and stuffed the other in her pack. She'd stay in jeans stained with Jude's blood. Maybe she wanted to stay bloodied.

The towels in the linen closet were musty, but she found two small bottles of shampoo and a basket of scented soaps. She dropped the soap and shampoo into a pouch in her backpack.

Downstairs she rummaged, no longer feeling intrusive; snooping seemed natural now. Bookcases full of books in most rooms, including the large bathroom. A giant TV, a music system, nothing dirty or broken. No photographs. The family had taken time to pack photographs.

Sol came downstairs wearing new clothes.

Sabine laughed. "They fit. Looking good, skinny boy."

Sol flushed. Someone had ransacked the kitchen cabinets, but he found a can of garbanzo beans, opened it, handed her the can and a spoon. "Eat up. You need extra food. Before dark we have to find a car." He whispered even though they were alone.

She gobbled the beans and thanked him twice.

"I'm gonna go upstairs," he said. "Maybe somebody stashed food under the bed or in a closet."

He came downstairs with a big bag of walnuts. "Found this under the boy's bed." He opened the bag and offered it to her. She put a few in her mouth: not too stale. He ate a few and handed her the bag. "For you."

She touched his arm. He gazed at the floor.

"I like this house," she said. "Can we stay a few days? I could wash and dry our dirty stuff. I hate wearing bloody jeans. A respite from the road—it'll still be easy to make St. Augustine by August 1st."

As she predicted, he shook his head. "Too risky. Someone could come in and corner us. We'd lose time, or worse. And we might run into more trouble down the road."

"You're right. Just hoping."

He put his hand on her shoulder. "Sorry."

They slipped out the backdoor and stood on the patio, taking in the neighborhood. They walked south two blocks, passed more empty yards, then reached a wide side street. They turned onto it and moved slowly, checking cars. Sol spotted keys in two cars' ignitions, but both were out of gas. Two other locked cars had less than a quarter of a tank.

They came upon a late-model Buick with keys in the ignition. The body of a well-dressed man sat propped against the open driver's side door, as if he were relaxing on the curb. The open car door had dug into the grass. The dead man had white whiskers, white hair, and soft-looking hands. A swath of dried blood along the side of his head—and a bullet hole just above his ear.

Sabine backed up at the smell of death. She surveyed the area. Deserted.

"Help me," Sol said.

She held her breath as they took the old man by the shoulders and pulled his body several feet to a bus stop sign. Sol propped the man up with care. She wondered how long he'd been dead, but didn't know how to tell.

Sol slipped into the driver's seat and turned on the ignition. "Look. A full tank!"

She moved away from the dead man, trying not to vomit. "A full tank when gas is short?"

"That's why he had a full tank." Sol pointed to the backseat. "A stack of rifles, two boxes of ammo on the floorboards, and a case of liquor."

Who was the man? A gunrunner? A vigilante? A bootlegger?

"Why didn't the people who killed him take the guns?" Sol wondered aloud.

Sabine opened the trunk. Empty. "Maybe the trunk was full of guns, too, and whoever killed him emptied the trunk first. They'll come back for the rest. Let's go. Now."

"Give me your pack."

She handed it to him, and he wedged it on top of the bottles with his.

Sabine said, "If I'd known about the guns Sharp and Hank stashed at the farm . . . we could've stayed there. And Jude would be alive. Why didn't you tell Jude about the guns under Sharp's bed?"

Sol didn't answer. He pulled out a cigarette and lit it. "We can make it to St. Augustine."

Chapter 16

WILD ORANGE MOON

July 31, 2014.

Sol sped through residential neighborhoods toward the interstate. Sabine lay her head back on the leather seat, relieved to leave the city. A nice car with a full tank of gas, and soon they'd be on the highway.

"The castle should be easy to find," he said. "We'll locate the O'Malleys with an old-fashioned phone book, they'll have a landline like most old folks. And if the phone book doesn't work, we'll ask around. The town's isn't big." His voice sounded confident and unruffled.

"Why did you shoot Jude's horse?" she asked, caught up in her own thoughts. "I asked Jude, but he changed the subject."

With one hand on the wheel, Sol blew two smoke rings. "Jude loved his horse. He said he had to put down his horse, but he couldn't do it, so he gave me the gun, knowing I would."

"Jude was soft-hearted."

"One way to look at it," Sol said.

"What?"

"Jude was a coward, but I didn't say it. He was broken up over the horse. Most of his family had been wiped out."

Sabine felt squirmy. Jude had acted cowardly when he persuaded her to leave without helping to bury Kate and Hank. But she understood why he was in a hurry. Mostly she resented Sol understanding Jude better than she did.

"Something else," she said.

"Fire away." Sol kept his eyes on the road.

"At the farm, you stared at me at meals."

"I liked to look at you. Between you, Kate, Jen, and the scarecrow Lavinia, there weren't many women. Kate was with Tommy, and Jen acted like a guy." He gave an embarrassed laugh.

She nodded. "I was your default."

"You were never my default," Sol said. "I'd always pick you. I watched over you, but you never caught me. When you walked outside, alone, if I was around, I got nervous. I didn't want anything to happen to you. That day you were sitting by the barn I thought for sure you'd spotted me."

"That shadow was you? It scared me. I never thought about someone protecting me."

"People kill on the streets and in the country. It's ordinary since the bombs."

"Don't say ordinary." She touched his elbow. "Thanks for watching out for me."

He didn't answer.

"The field where Jude died, did you see a dog? Medium sized, drinking from the creek. When I got closer, he ran away."

"I haven't seen any dogs on the road," he said. "You suppose folks are killing them for food?"

"Probably. When I was a kid, I had a dog friend. I gave him biscuits and named him Sun Dog."

"You know what 'sundogs' are, right?"

She shook her head. "The name just came to me. I needed something sunny to happen at the time."

"Sundogs are like halos—rings or spots that appear around

the sun. I've seen them twice, in the winter, in the late afternoon. Nothing you'd see in the city."

"Never heard of a sundog." She slid toward the passenger's window, closed her eyes and dozed. She dreamed of running through a cemetery, chasing Jude's jittery shadow. It turned into a human-sized black flag, fluttering, urging her on. She leapt over gravestones and wrought-iron fences until a wall encircled her, obliterating the cemetery. She woke just before slamming into the wall. Her forehead felt wet; her heart pounded.

Sol was still draped over the steering wheel, a cigarette dangling from his mouth. When he spoke the cigarette bobbed up and down. "Sure was a quick nap."

She couldn't talk and gobbled nuts. She hated this early, primitive part of pregnancy when food and sleep mattered most. And Sol was confusing her: first he called her a liar, then said he watched over her. Jude had bragged about Sol's intelligence; he'd been right. Sol was smart. Traveling with him made her feel safe. And sometimes he was good company. Thank goodness, because they were stuck with each other until St. Augustine.

She dozed again. In this dream she walked between two adults who held her hands and talked over her head in grown-up gibberish. Red tennis shoes on her feet. She bent over to admire them. A boy walked behind her, scuffing his shiny black shoes on the sidewalk. Up ahead a church, its golden dome gleaming in the sunlight.

Someone called, "Hey Frederick. Hey Elaine. How you-all doing?"

Sabine jerked awake. "Frederick and Elaine! Those are my parents' first names. And I have a brother, too. His name's Freddie."

Sol looked at her. "You dreamed all that just now?"

"New red tennis shoes. My legs were skinny, like a kid's. I must've been six or seven. I think we were in a suburb of DC walking toward St. Giles Episcopal." Her stomach fluttered. How weird. She had not thought about the name connection before. Giles.

"My parents wouldn't have let me wear tennis shoes to church," Sol said.

"I was just thinking that. But dreams aren't replicas of our waking life, dreams send messages—"

"My God! Behind us!" Sol yelled, and the Buick lurched forward as he jammed on the gas. Sabine twisted in her seat. A big truck was coming up behind them, gaining fast. She searched both sides of the road for a way out, but the rural road was straight, with no exits.

"Outrun them!" she cried. She held her stomach. *Oh please, I don't want to die on this road.*

The speedometer hit seventy, too fast for a country road. "They'll run us off the road," Sol said, fear in his voice.

Without thinking, Sabine took her gun, rolled down the window, and leaned out as far as she could. Aimed for the truck's front tires. The first bullets hit the grill. She aimed higher and fired over and over, until the windshield glass cracked into stars.

The truck swerved, fishtailed all over the road, and slowed.

"I hit the windshield! Maybe the driver, maybe not."

"My God, Sabine. You did it. I'll get off this road soon as I can."

They drove until they reached a town. Within a few blocks Sol found an intersection with highway signs. "Okay. Four choices. One road goes straight south, okay? The symbol shows a four-lane highway."

"No more back roads. Too many crazies." She stuck her head out the window to make her head stop spinning, tears falling. She rubbed her face with her jacket. The road widened into a pull-off, and Sol eased the car off the road and drove behind tall bushes.

She couldn't stop crying. "Why are you stopping?"

"We need a break from the road," he said. "Here's a park, if you need to walk around. Picnic tables and grills, even a creek. I'll be right back." He headed toward a stand of trees.

She got out to stretch. Her legs shook, and her knees almost buckled as she stood. Dark trees draped with Spanish moss, a creek littered with condoms, diapers, and beer cans. The place felt sluggish, fetid. Dusk was coming on, but the feel came from the dank air more than darkness.

She had truly thought they were going to die. The image of her and Sol thrown like rag dolls from the Buick onto the road filled her head. Jude had trusted Sol. Now Sol was all she had.

"May I talk to you?" she asked when he got back, hoping for his answer before they were both just memories inside the minds of strangers. She stayed alert for strangers with guns.

Hands in his pocket, Sol moved with deliberation. "This place might not be safe. I shouldn't have stopped."

"Come sit at the table. I have something I need to say out loud." She expected him to resist, but he followed. She slid her hands under her thighs to stop them from shaking. "In case we die in ten minutes or the day after tomorrow, I want to tell you what happened to me. It's about my big love, the person who caused my memory problem."

"Okay," Sol said.

"Giles and I met at a party. He was a philosophy professor, ten years older. We fell crazy in love and married seven months later. I was twenty-four." She stopped. "A cigarette?"

He handed her one and lit it.

"Some years later, bad stuff happened, we divorced." She sat motionless.

"For a storyteller that sure is a short story."

"Gearing up for the middle."

"The part where something happens," he said.

"After the divorce I heard nothing about Giles at first. I didn't contact his friends, assuming they blamed me for the split. I still lived at my parents' when a friend of Giles called me."

She clenched her stomach, but nothing happened.

"You all right?"

"My head's spinning. It's the cigarette. Telling this stuff feels awful." Her voice came out stiff; it was a voice she recognized from a time when all she did was cry.

"Take it slow." He came around the table and sat beside her. "I'll sit by you so you won't have to look at me."

Her fingers moved over the table; she found a loose piece of wood and tugged at it. "Giles's students—I said he was a philosophy professor, didn't I?—his students had been complaining to the department chair, saying he came to class reeking of alcohol. Even at eight in the morning, he was high. Maybe still drunk from the night before. He didn't dismiss his class till long after the bell rang, going on with some rambling, nonsensical lecture."

"Sounds like he was in trouble." He lit a cigarette and blew the smoke away from her.

"Unraveling, yes. So, when his friend Charlie called, it was to tell me that the university had fired Giles. And he'd disappeared. Nobody could find him at the usual bars. Rumors were he'd moved to New York, or gone to Mexico to hunt for pottery. I told Charlie I was moving out of my parents' house and gave him my cell number.

"Two years later, I heard from Charlie again. Giles had made contact with him a couple months earlier. Charlie said Giles sounded okay, was living in New Mexico, working on a philosophy essay and taking walks, trying to get his head straight. Charlie thought Giles was struggling to stop drinking. Sometimes Giles slurred and was incoherent, sometimes not. When Giles didn't answer his phone, Charlie called day and night for several days."

She held her stomach until the urge to vomit passed.

"You're doing fine," Sol said.

"A backpacker found Giles in jeans, a T-shirt, and windbreaker, frozen in a snow bank. The hiker called police. They found information on Giles's body and contacted his father, who then called Charlie. Charlie flew to New Mexico. Giles's father picked him up at the airport and they drove straight to Giles's house.

"When I heard I felt glad Giles's mother was dead. What mother wants her son to die before she does? And in such an awful way. When the cops found him, his BAC was .25. Charlie said his house was filthy: dishes in the sink, empty fifths, smelly garbage. But he'd left some odd, lovely scribbles thumbtacked on the walls. Charlie mailed me one piece Giles wrote. It's in one of my notebooks."

Images of them in Giles's bedroom, holding each other, sweating in summer heat. A window fan whirring, a red-framed mirror throwing back their reflection, their nude-dancing mirror selves. A white iron double bed covered in a crazy quilt. On the table, a pre-Columbian statue Giles bought in Mexico, a grimacing baby's head.

"Two years after we married, I had a son. Giles, Jr. We nicknamed him Mick. That summer, when he was nine months old, we drove to Albuquerque intending to visit Giles's father and show off Mick. We camped cross-country, and by the time we reached New Mexico, we were fed up with camping with a cranky baby.

"Before Albuquerque, we parked our camper on the edge of the desert. Giles set up the tent. I cooked hot dogs and pinto beans. Giles took a beer out of the cooler. I asked him not to drink, figuring he'd been sneaking brandy shots all morning. He didn't listen, and I was sick of nagging, so I gave up. After lunch I crawled in my sleeping bag and laid the baby on his blanket beside me. If only I hadn't been so tired."

Sol's head kept moving, probably scanning the area. The woods and stream were falling into shadow. No cars passed on the road.

"When I woke, Giles and Mick were gone. I called and called, then drove up and down the highway and finally went to the ranger station. The ranger took me into the desert. We heard a baby screaming. Giles ran to the Jeep holding the baby, shouting, 'Get us to a hospital, something's wrong!' The ranger sped off. Giles said Mick had started fussing, so he took him for a walk. Giles stumbled into a hole and hurt himself, so he laid Mick on the ground to examine his foot. Giles said the baby wasn't three feet away when the rattling started."

Sabine laid her hand on Sol's arm. "Cigarette?"

He lit a cigarette and handed it to her.

"Guess what happened next."

"I don't want to guess." He put his hand on her back and rubbed gently.

"In the truck Mick screamed, then went limp. His lips turned blue. His cheek puffed up where the snake bit him."

She coughed and Sol lifted his hand off her back. "At first the nurses tried to keep me out of the room, but I kept opening the curtain, so a nurse let me in. Mick's face was covered with an oxygen mask and there was a tube in his leg. A nurse yelled out numbers while a woman stood by a medicine cart. When a nurse yelled fifty-eight an alarm went off, a nurse put a tube down Mick's throat, and a doctor started pressing on Mick's chest.

"Mick and the clock. I looked back and forth. They worked on him almost an hour, but I knew he died in the first ten minutes. I turned on Giles, screaming, calling him a drunk. Someone took my arm, I felt a prick, and things turned slow. I fell asleep saying Giles killed Mick."

Sol cleared his throat. "Where did you bury Mick?"

"Mick's coffin came on the plane with me on the flight to DC. I was in a fog. My parents and brother met me at the airport. Giles drove our camper back. I deliberately timed the funeral so Giles couldn't be there. When he got back in town he came to my parents' house, but I wouldn't let him in. He called and called, but I never answered. I returned his letters unopened.

"I was a tiger without forgiveness. I froze him out. I suppose he grew numb until he didn't care whether he lived or died. His drinking got worse and my bet is he started shooting heroin again."

Sol murmured how sorry he was. His voice soothed her.

"I forgot to eat and couldn't sleep. Mother drove me to a psychiatrist. She told the doctor about our family, and my brother Jeffrey dying when I was ten. I wrote 'The Bone Woman' about Jeffrey's death. His death was when I started losing my memory, bits, and only sometimes. The doctor helped me to figure out 'Bone Woman.'

"The doctor called my symptoms 'complicated grief.' But I said it wasn't complicated. It was simple. If Giles hadn't been drinking and drugging, he wouldn't have taken our baby into the desert, fallen in a hole, and hurt his ankle.

"After that I didn't much care about anything. The doctor and I talked once a week, for about four months. It felt good to cry and holler. Sleeping pills helped, too. The doctor explained how Jeffrey's death affected me, years before I lost Giles and Mick. My parents pretended their marriage was fine. We were all fine, which meant of course we didn't talk about Jeffrey. I confabulate—make up things to fill the holes—because of memory gaps." She sniffed. "After a few months I stopped seeing the doctor."

"Why?" Sol's voice was soft.

"He kept pushing me to forgive Giles, and I wasn't ready. Maybe never would be ready. I liked the doctor, but I didn't want to waste more time arguing with him. I broke my next appointment and never went back."

She looked up through the trees, blinking. "It wasn't up to the doctor to tell me to forgive. Maybe I feared Giles. More likely I feared what I'd do to him if we got together. I dreamed about stabbing the baby's killer, but the person didn't have a face. Screw forgiveness—I wanted revenge." Her chest started hurting as soon as she said the word. *Revenge.*

"When was the last time you went to Mick's grave?" Sol asked.

She hung her head.

"You've never been?" Sol asked.

He put his hand on her back and the warmth came through Jude's jacket.

She tried to see his face in the dark. "I'm so tired. No more talking."

"Ready to get back on the road?"

She nodded and he followed her to the Buick. They drove in silence. Sol pointed through the windshield. "Look, the moon's up." It glowed soft orange low on the horizon, revealing trees draped with Spanish moss. The cooling air filled with small animal sounds.

She'd told Sol the worst. Not all, but the worst. And she'd been honest. She'd made up nothing, not painting a better picture than she deserved. But memory was complex, too mutable to allow for talking about all the pieces at once. She leaned against the window, but sleep would not come.

She opened her notebook and looked at Giles's scrap of paper, written in his boxy handwriting. The car was too dark to read his words. No matter, she'd memorized them:

New Mexico: Among the red rock cliffs, dwarf trees, and dry wood, like driftwood scattered across the sand. The sun fell, the moon soared. By moonlight I followed Sabine's prints for miles across the sand, an endless trail, heading east. Why walk? She's gone.

Giles had loved Mick; he hadn't meant to hurt their boy. But for all of it, it was too late to fix.

Sol's startling voice, gruff and raspy: "Let's look for food. And deal with the guns. We've waited too long to get them off the backseat. It's dangerous riding around with guns in plain sight."

PART
FOUR

Chapter 17

BITTER ORANGE MOON

June 22, 2014.

Elaine stood at the door of Freddie's room and watched her son sleep. They'd arrived at the beach over three weeks ago, but the ocean had not relaxed her. She watched her kind, smart, handsome, headstrong boy.

During his childhood, her feelings about him had fluctuated between anger and pride. But no matter how she'd felt about him through his middle and high school years, she'd stood in his doorway every morning, then tiptoed to his bed to tickle his feet. Even after Jeffrey died she'd kept up the ritual. She'd say, "You sleep in a rat's nest. How do you stand it? You're old enough to wash and change your sheets. I showed you how, why won't you do it?" She wouldn't stop tickling until, barely containing a laugh, he'd yank his feet away and pull a pillow over his head. But before he could go back to sleep, she'd pat his back. "Breakfast in twenty minutes." Usually he'd appear at the table on time.

Freddie at five; his skinny, shivery body leaping out of the bathtub, jumping foot to foot while she toweled him dry. He'd fidgeted when she read him bedtime stories. When she finally put the book down and asked him what he wanted to do, he scrambled under his bed and pulled out a yellow box. From then on at bedtime, they sat on Freddie's bed and played robots, dinosaurs, and aliens with the plastic figures who lived in the yellow box. He taught her about the creatures and complimented her on realistic growls and facial expressions. He always took charge of their games and she loved watching him happy.

Leaning against the doorjamb, looking at her forty-two-year-old son, she wondered if he'd be insulted if she tickled him.

She took her coffee out on the deck. The ocean was rough; huge rolling waves pounded the sand. As a child, Freddie had been fearless. No matter how rough the surf he'd run headlong into the water, pulling his child-sized surfboard, laughing and sputtering when he got dragged under. But Freddie had lost his verve over the years, turned sorrowful like his father. Now he matched his father in stature and mannerisms.

She cried thinking of her husband when he was about Freddie's age. The passage of time made her chest ache. She couldn't risk talking about Frederick for fear of sobbing, which might well lead to unending screaming. She'd act strong, push it down and bury it deep, otherwise she'd be no help to Freddie and Lily.

Each day she prepared herself: Frederick wasn't coming. There would be no news on TV about Richmond's downtown office buildings. He knew the beach house phone number, and if he could get to the beach, he would have. The beach was his favorite place—he'd told her earlier that year that he didn't care if he ever traveled again, the only walking he wanted to do was with her, on the beach. Frederick was physically and mentally strong, which gave her hope. She missed him every minute.

News at the beach was mixed. Electricity flowed, and the naval base, as far as they'd heard, was okay. The beach cottages were forty miles from the base. The poor road conditions, the disruption of fuel and supply lines, meant few deliveries and sparse inventories. Only a few stores had reopened; food and fresh water remained scarce. A neighbor told Freddie a food riot had broken out in North Carolina, maybe in Raleigh. But maybe that was just a rumor.

She and Freddie figured riots, if they came, wouldn't break out until late winter around the beach area. There were plenty of small farms around. But if local farmers couldn't grow enough food and didn't have enough feed for their cattle, or enough fuel for their equipment, there would be trouble.

"Riots depend on population density," she'd told Freddie, making up the facts as she went along. "Fewer people means more food for the rest of us, but we don't have numbers. Strange there's nothing about food riots on the news." These words would've sounded foreign in her former life, when she'd kept the pantry loaded and the refrigerator full of food, and donated regularly to the food bank and victims of earthquakes, wildfires, hurricanes, famines, and floods.

They turned on the TV while making morning coffee, and left it on until they went to bed. The news the cable channels broadcasted was half credible. Sometimes they couldn't separate accuracy from rumor. Since Memorial Day, explosions inside buildings had been reported, but not confirmed.

The biggest news was from the International Atomic Energy Agency—the IAEA. They announced that most, and possibly all, of the Memorial Day bombs weren't nuclear devices, and assured viewers the radiation threat was low. Gleeful reporters reiterated that so far none of the bombs had been discovered to be nuclear. Rather they were the smaller IEDs—improvised explosive devices. But the following day the reporters backtracked and reiterated that the findings were preliminary, required more investigation.

She scanned the beach with binoculars: the sand was less streaked now, and less debris floated near the shoreline, but farther out a mass of boards, plastic bags, and miscellaneous trash floated south. Freddie spent most days working with other volunteers to clear the beach. He came home exhausted and sweaty, full of descriptions of what had washed up, including body parts. She was revolted by his stories, but grateful he was engaging in something useful. Some volunteers were Freddie's acquaintances from the neighborhood, but he hadn't yet encountered any childhood friends.

The phone rang for the first time since they'd arrived, and she froze. Frederick, calling from the office? Unable to pick up the phone in time, she listened: "Hello. You've reached Elaine and Frederick. Leave a message, if you wish. We'll call you back. Thank you for calling." Her chipper, controlled voice. She no longer felt she was either of those things. Irritated she'd forgotten to change the recording, she listened as a man apologized for dialing the wrong number. She had no idea what to do about her outgoing message and left it as it was.

The baby would wake any minute. She poured herself more coffee and waited for her heart to take up its normal rhythm. She'd walk on the beach, then drive around and search for an open pharmacy. Not much gas, but there was enough to drive to the mall and back.

꩜

She smoothed sunblock on Lily's face, hands, and arms, tied her bonnet, and settled her in the cloth carrier. She slid the glass door closed behind her but didn't lock it. She wasn't going far.

A stiff wind blew from the ocean and dry sand stung her legs. She slipped on her designer sunglasses. Lily scowled and swatted at the bonnet with chubby fists; Elaine pulled the bonnet lower. She took off in the opposite direction from what she'd intended, to keep her back to the blowing sand.

If the food situation didn't change, Lily wouldn't stay rosy and healthy for long. What if they couldn't find blood pressure meds and baby formula at the mall? She kept up a brisk pace, dodging trash on the sand, trying to outwalk fear. After fifteen minutes, she headed back to the cottage, facing the blowing sand. As she walked up the steps to the deck, she found herself shivering.

Freddie's jacket hung on a chair in the dining room. She slipped it on and checked her watch. At least her watch battery still worked. She scribbled a note telling him she'd be home by ten thirty, then strapped Lily into the car seat. Should she try to hide the car when she returned from town? Not many cars were on the road these days, and her silver Volvo was just two years old, ripe for stealing. But hide it where? Dammit, whenever she turned around she saw another problem. She was overwhelmed. She had never really cursed before, but now she cursed everything—a smile on the outside, curses on the inside.

The idea of a trip to the mall flooded her with fear. Might as well be driving into the Canadian wilds with a toothbrush and a sweater. For the first time in years, she worried about running out of gas. How many stations were open? What would she find at the mall? Guns and looting? The steering wheel felt slick in her hands. For distraction she turned on the radio, but couldn't find classical or easy listening, only raucous gibberish; nevertheless, she was grateful for the distraction. She'd turned into a news junkie, keeping the radio on in her bedroom at all hours in case there was important news.

At the first gas station she slowed, looking for a sign stating when it would reopen, but there wasn't one. In front of the next station a sign said they'd get a gas delivery on June 25th. A three-day wait.

Most of the strip mall's stores were still closed, their fronts covered with grating. The twenty-four-hour pharmacy was shuttered. But a Patient First had lights on and a parking lot full of cars. The seats in the waiting room were taken. She wrote her name on the sign-in sheet and parked Lily's stroller by a wall. Lily wiggled and whimpered until Elaine took her out and stood in front of a fish tank. Lily, immediately entranced, pointed to the fish and squealed.

A few people had pulled chairs in a semicircle over in a corner. They were sharing news about gas stations, stores, and rumors about mercenaries walking in their neighborhoods, openly carrying guns. Other patients were burying their faces in fashion magazines. She'd like to join them in their escape. But she had an obligation to Lily and Freddie to stay informed.

Her watch read 9:43. More people arrived. Was it worth the wait? Did their pharmacy even have meds? She rearranged Lily on her hip and went to the receptionist. "Excuse me. I'm wondering if your pharmacy has any meds? I suppose I will have to be examined to get a prescription for blood pressure meds. If you're already out, there's no point in my waiting."

The girl at the desk appeared to be about fifteen, with multiple ear piercings and dyed red hair. "Say again?"

Elaine repeated herself.

"I'll check," the girl said. "I'm a temp because my dad is one of the doctors here. I just answer the phone and get people to sign in." The girl returned a few minutes later. "Dad says sorry, the pharmacy is out of blood pressure meds. We're one of the few places open and crowded since Memorial Day. Hospitals are swamped. But we should be getting a shipment in a few days, so come on back."

"Thank you. One more question: Do you have information about stores carrying baby formula and diapers that are open?"

"Twenty-five, maybe thirty miles up the road, near the base, there's a Target."

Elaine nodded. "I know where it is. Could you call them for me before I drive all that way?" The store meant a round trip of fifty or sixty miles. She probably didn't have enough gas.

"No way. I'm swamped." The girl pointed to two people standing behind Elaine, waiting to register.

"Okay," Elaine said. "Thanks."

"No problem."

Elaine wheeled Lily back out to the car. Just as she was finishing strapping her into her seat, a shrill voice came out of nowhere—"Hey lady, I need help!"

Elaine emerged from the backseat. A skinny teenaged boy stood by her car, hopping on one foot, a panicked look on his face.

Elaine slammed the door shut and positioned herself in front of the window. "What do you want?"

"I hurt my leg and need money to see the doctor," the boy said.

Elaine shook her head. "No money. Sorry."

His eyes bulged. "I need money to see the doctor!" Quick as lightning, he reached into his boot and pulled out a knife.

She slid her hand into Freddie's jacket pocket. "Get away from my car or I'll shoot you."

The boy ran his hand through his hair and laughed. "Yeah sure, lady, you're gonna shoot me." He moved closer, waving the knife near her face, using a back-and-forth motion, as if to hypnotize her.

"Don't do this." She pulled out the Glock. "Go inside. Even if you don't have money, they'll help you."

His eyes flicked to the gun. "That your husband's gun? Bet you don't know how to use it." He reached for her arm.

She shook him off and yelled, "Don't touch me again, or I'll shoot."

With a lazy grin he lowered the knife until it touched the place between her breasts. With his free hand he pulled her away from the car and peered into the back window. "How old's the baby? She's really cute, she's something special."

Elaine released the safety, aimed at his right ankle, and pulled the trigger. The boy screamed and fell. Lily started to cry and banged a fist against her ear.

Ears ringing, Elaine backed away, ran around to the driver's side, unlocked the car, and stuck the key in the ignition. As she pulled out of the parking lot, faces looked out the waiting room windows.

On the beach road she picked up speed. The doctors would help the boy. She had to get back to her beach house. Oh God, she'd shot him. At a hairpin curve she tapped the brake to take it at thirty. Seventy in a thirty-mile zone—she had to get a hold of herself. She'd call the police soon as she got home.

When the cottage came into sight, she started crying. Freddie paced the driveway. He jumped out of the way as she pulled in. Her whole body vibrating, she slid out of her seat and felt the solid drive-way under her feet. "Freddie, I shot a boy who threatened me and Lily with a knife and left him bleeding in the parking lot. He had a knife. Oh, I already said."

"Is Lily okay? She's crying." He opened the door and unbuckled the car seat. "Are you okay, Lily? How's my girl?" Lily stopped crying and squealed as he held her close. "Okay," he said, his voice quiet. "Let's go in the house and you can tell me what happened."

Freddie put Lily on a blanket on the floor. The baby rubbed her ears and closed her eyes. He rushed to make coffee, and Elaine sat on the couch where she could see through the dunes, farther out to the strip of blue. Pelicans flew by in formation and two ravens landed on the deck railing. The ubiquitous cries of gulls calmed her. The birds hadn't flown away.

Once my ears stop ringing, I'll be okay. She covered them with her hands, but it didn't help.

Freddie handed her a mug of coffee and sat close. "Okay. Tell me again. Slowly."

"My ears are still ringing. I was leaving Patient First. I'd just put Lily in her car seat when a boy appeared and claimed his leg was hurt, and asked for money. I didn't see anything wrong. I refused. He pulled a knife out of his boot and waved it in my face. He pointed it at my chest and moved closer. But it wasn't the knife that made me pull the trigger. It was when he looked through the window at Lily and said she was cute—then I shot him in the foot with your Glock. My hand still hurts from the damn gun."

Freddie's mouth hung open. "You shot him with my Glock?"

"I wore your jacket today because I knew the gun was in the pocket. I've known since Richmond."

"And you're trained to use a gun?"

"When your father and I were in college, we backpacked in

wilderness areas. Each of us wore a whistle to scare off bears, but in case a whistle wasn't enough, your father carried a gun, too. I asked him to teach me to shoot. It wasn't a Glock. I don't recall the kind of gun."

Freddie closed his eyes. "I don't believe what I'm hearing."

"You can't imagine me backpacking with a forty-pound pack, can you?" Elaine smiled. "Your father and I would go out for a week or two at a time. Long enough to get away from studying. Hiking and camping together—that's when we fell in love."

"Okay. I suppose I can see you two on top of a mountain in a tent. Did anyone see you shoot the boy?"

"Only a whole waiting room full of people. Ever had that feeling of time grinding to a halt in a crisis?" She pursed her lips. "I chose his foot on purpose—so he couldn't walk and threaten anybody else."

"What kind of car did he have?"

"I don't know if he even had a car. I was buckling Lily in the car seat when he appeared. I didn't hear a car. Maybe a bicycle? Maybe he was just hanging around the parking lot waiting for someone small or old to attack?" She shuddered. "You think I'll get arrested?"

"My guess is the police have bigger worries. But all those witnesses, someone must've got your license plate."

"This morning I was thinking we should hide my car anyway. People need cars. And now the police will recognize my car in the driveway from the witnesses' descriptions. But where could we hide it? There aren't many garages with locked doors around here, it's mostly carports."

Lily crawled to the doors leading to the deck. She raised her arm toward the ravens and spoke in gibberish.

"Yes, Lily," Freddie said. "Birds—ravens." He drummed his fingers on his knee. "I need to think where we can hide the car."

Elaine touched his hand. "I shouldn't have gone off without you, but you looked so peaceful sleeping. I didn't want to wake you."

"Don't you remember what I said? When we were driving here?"

"No. What?"

"I told you not to go out alone," he said. "It's not safe. And I was right. And why did you go to Patient First, anyway? Lily's fine."

"Ah. Yes, you told me. And my mission to the mall failed. No diapers, no baby formula, and no meds. And I shot that poor boy."

"Meds?"

"For my blood pressure. The receptionist said they'd be getting more in a few days—but damn it, the receptionist will recognize me. And I signed in. And two summers ago when I sprained my wrist and went there? Patient First has it all: address, phone, Social Security."

"Let's think this through. It's complicated."

"It's not complicated, Freddie. I have to call the police."

Freddie's eyes widened. "Let's not do anything until we've had time to think. For now, let's talk about where to hide your car."

"Forget hiding the car, the police will find me. It won't matter. We're home a lot and no one will steal my car."

"Of course someone will steal your car," Freddie said. "We have to hide it."

"Where? There are people all up and down the road, rummaging through trash cans and trespassing. If you can come up with something clever, I'll go along with it. Otherwise, let's not worry about something we can't solve. Are you going to help with the beach cleanup tomorrow? I took a walk this morning, and it's looking cleaner. You volunteers are doing a great job."

"Maybe," he said. "I found something resembling a big toe and more rotted fish and birds yesterday. It's disgusting work." He got up. "Why don't we eat something, and then we'll talk about this some more?"

Elaine forced a smile. "No lunch for me. I'm going to lie down. Later I'll fix a nice dinner. Canned tuna spiced with dill pickles, served with a side of stale crackers. For dessert, we have a choice between the canned succulent oranges or some half-rotten banana slices imported from scenic Richmond."

When Freddie didn't respond, she felt deflated. "Will you take over with Lily? I'm so tired."

"Sure," he said. "Try not to worry."

⁓

Freddie fed Lily a bottle, thinking what a loving and attentive mother Mags was. Even in the middle of the night, she struggled out of bed when Lily cried.

He sat on the deck with Lily, holding her and showing her the stars, until she fell asleep. She was beginning to look more like Mags: her eyes were turning hazel, and her hair was still silky blond like Mags's hair. He liked the resemblance, even though it made him sad. His fun-loving, humorous Mags.

He took Lily to the nursery, a small room next to his room. Not wanting to wake her, he laid her in the crib without changing her diaper. He flicked his finger at the mobile over the crib and watched elephants, smiling mice, and kittens bounce.

What changes were coming in the world? He'd changed since the bombs—a little, at least. He took care of Lily now more than he ever had. He watched his mother fix formula and change diapers, and practiced to improve. He often glanced out the window overlooking their street, thinking he heard Mags's car pulling in the driveway. Each day without news felt worse than the day before. He was driving himself nuts.

His useless computer sat on a table in the living room. What was going on at his office? He'd lost count of the times he'd called and gotten a dead line. His volunteer work felt endless, probably useless. The sand was still oil-stained, and there was always more debris floating out beyond the breakers.

CNN's Matt Morris was reporting from DC on the TV. Freddie turned up the sound and settled on the sofa. Morris said the president hadn't been seen. The DC Metro wasn't working, commuters were making do with buses and cars. The few government agencies that were up and running were short-staffed because of the disabled subway. Rubble still littered the beltway, but work was progressing.

Endless investigations made people feel as if the agencies were in control. But Freddie doubted anyone had full control. How could a president vanish? He was probably hiding in some "undisclosed location."

A camera panned across a line of people waiting for a grocery store to open in DC. There! A slim girl with tangled, dark hair, shifting from foot to foot, not talking. The sad face, the shifting feet . . . Sabine? No, it couldn't be. She would have taken off when she spotted the TV camera. Running was her style. The last postcard she'd sent had come months ago and been postmarked from DC. But no way was that her. She wouldn't stay after the bombs. He stared at the TV, hoping to see the line of people again, but Morris switched to a weather report.

Freddie turned off the TV and hurried to the kitchen. His heart bumped around in his chest as he searched until he found the two fifths of bourbon stashed in the back of one of the cabinets. He filled a glass halfway and went back on the deck. The sky had lost its pink, and the placid ocean shone as if a layer of liquid silver had been poured over it.

He tasted the bourbon. He didn't want to drink. He took another sip and savored it on his tongue.

Would he see Mags again? His kid sister? He was the main reason Sabine wouldn't ever come home. He was the one who must find her. The lost ones: Mags and Dad and Sabine. And before them, Baby Jeffrey and Mick. Who would be next? Lily? Mom? Him? He'd lost so many people, and he was only forty-two.

The Glock caused him trouble back when he used drugs, and today it caused trouble for his mother. He gulped a mouthful of bourbon, and then another. He found himself crying, wrenching sobs that hurt his stomach, enough that he feared he'd puke. Finally, the tears slowed, and he wiped his face on his sleeve. Damn. He'd just blown his nose on his shirt like a kid. This feeling reminded him of his father. Three months after Jeffrey's funeral, his father had turned back into his usual, angry self, spouting snide remarks.

Freddie hated going over these thoughts. Such old business. He willed himself to think about the time he rode the Ferris wheel with his father. They laughed in the swaying car, rocking high in the air, the lit-up fair and city spread below. Listening to his father laugh, he'd felt free.

He growled at the ocean. *Screw happy Ferris wheel thoughts.* Holding his glass under his nose, he sniffed before chugging the inch of bourbon left at the bottom. He couldn't remember his last drink, which was a good thing. But with the whole country falling apart, there were plenty of reasons to start drinking again. He should pour the bottle down the sink, and never do heroin again. He was a real father now. He looked to see if the neighbors were on their decks, watching him crying and drinking.

≈

June 23, 2014.

Glad morning had finally arrived, Elaine sat up in a tangle of sheets. Her head hurt from dread, lack of sleep, thoughts of prison, and her horror at having shot a child. She'd shot some woman's child to protect Freddie's child. Some woman who'd raised an idiot boy. Freddie had acted like an idiot when he was younger. How could she help with Lily if she went to prison? Since the bombs had fallen, she hardly recognized herself.

Wearing her fluffy white robe, she made a pot of coffee. They didn't have fresh cream or milk but did have two jumbo-sized packages of dried milk. She went onto the deck and sat in a lounge chair still damp from the ocean air. The sky hung low over the water, gray on gray.

Soon Lily would wake and break the early-morning silence. Elaine hoped Freddie would change the baby's diaper and feed her breakfast. As if on cue Lily cried, followed by Freddie's heavy foot-steps stumbling to her room.

Elaine took another sip of coffee. Good. Freddie was becoming more responsible.

Ten minutes later Freddie emerged on the deck with Lily in his arms. "Hi Mom. We're all clean and ready to start the day." He gave Lily the bottle, which she managed herself. "How did you sleep?"

She shook her head and rubbed her eyes. "I'm calling the police. The longer I wait the worse it'll get."

"Are you sure?"

"Well, what do you suggest?"

"Let's get on with our lives. We have more important worries, like getting more supplies while we still can. There might be more bombings. And any number of things could get worse. You need your medicine, and Lily needs diapers and formula. I should put up storm windows on the second floor and buy sturdier locks for the storage unit. And an extra one for the front door. After the errands, we'll hide your car."

"Why don't you want me to call the police? The truth, Freddie."

He leaned against the railing. "I'll buy some new faucet handles for the outside shower. The ones we have are so old, they don't even make them anymore."

"This house has three full bathrooms and a half bath. How often do we use the outside shower? Stop stalling."

He focused on the ocean for a long time. Then he faced her. "The summer I went to computer school? And Ducky was there? We got into some trouble."

"Drugs. You told your father and me about it."

"Not all of it. We weren't smoking pot. It was heroin. Near the end of school, two dealers came after us. Ducky and I owed them money, and of course we didn't have it. We left school a week early, in the middle of the night, and drove straight to the beach. Don't worry, we didn't come to the cottage. We stayed in a cheap motel,

The Waves or The Dunes, some name like that. We lay on the beach and laughed at how we'd gotten away with using and had fun. We weren't ever going back to that school. Later Ducky heard one of the dealers hadn't stopped looking for us. The other dealer got busted and gave my name to the police in some kind of bargain, but the dealer only knew Ducky by his nickname. Ducky was smarter."

He looked at his mother. She was gripping the edge of her chair.

"How much heroin did we do? You don't wanna know."

"How much do you owe those dealers?"

"About $10,000, well, more like $20,000. I don't know why the cops didn't come after me for possession and distribution, but I finally stopped looking over my shoulder ten years ago."

She turned away. "I'm getting a refill. Want some?" She didn't wait for an answer. Her hands weren't steady when she mixed the powdered milk with warm water. She hated powdered milk, how it clumped if she poured it directly into the coffee. She resisted an impulse to run and hop in the car and leave Freddie to deal with Lily and the house. The impulse was strong. After beating the milk into a froth, she poured it into the cup and watched the white swirls mix with the dark. The task helped her quiet her breathing. Her headache was worse now.

Lily whimpered. On the deck, Freddie sat unmoving. Elaine pulled a blanket and wooden blocks from the baby carriage and spread the blanket on the deck. She put Lily on the blanket and put the blocks down next to her. Lily reached for a block.

With some luck, this would keep Lily occupied long enough for Freddie and her to talk for a few minutes.

She said, "Son, come sit down."

Freddie took the chair next to her.

"The two events aren't connected," she said. "The police will be interested in me. Not you."

"But what if the police run both our names through a computer system?"

"Why would they?"

He didn't answer.

"You're acting paranoid," she said. "I know nothing about police procedure, and I suspect you don't either. But I have to report what I did to the boy." She laid her hand on his arm.

"I hate it," he said. "They could have a warrant out on me. Soon as you call the police, I'm leaving."

"What do you mean leaving?"

"I'll walk on the beach. Don't worry, I'll come back when their car is gone."

Elaine shook her head. A warrant, after all these years? Before she could talk herself out of it, she went in the kitchen and picked up the wall phone.

Freddie hovered behind her. She ignored him and dialed the non-emergency number. She spoke with an officer for a few minutes, gave him her name, address, and phone number, and described the boy she shot. She said there were lots of witnesses. The officer gave no indication when the police would talk with her. He was casual, as if she were reporting a stolen bicycle.

She put down the phone. "Stop worrying. It'll be fine." She wasn't going to tell Freddie any more than what he heard. Let him worry.

Freddie left the room. Five minutes later, he came back with the baby. "Maybe I was right to begin with: the cops have more important things to do with people ransacking malls and breaking in to homes, especially in wealthy neighborhoods. We're far from town. Nobody will bother with these beach cottages, they're pretty basic."

Her eyebrows went up. "Are you serious? These cottages cost a bundle."

"But they don't have a lot worth stealing."

"Maybe not our cottage. But many of the cottages have elegant interiors."

She left the room, retrieved the Glock from the top shelf in her bedroom, and took it into the bathroom. She wiped the gun with care, making sure her prints and Freddie's were off of it. She held it to make sure only her prints would be on it. Then she put the Glock back on the top shelf, far out of Lily's reach.

Standing in front of her open closet, she wondered when Freddie had become so dismissive of their family's wealth, acting as if owning a large suburban house as well as an ocean-front house was no big deal. Freddie gave no thought to how others suffered, no thought to the people who had lost their homes to the bombs and had nothing to eat and no place to stay. He gave no thought to the world beyond his own small one. She was still irritated he'd thrown her cell phone in the ocean.

His voice buoyant, he called to her, "I'll get Lily's bonnet. Let's all drive into town. Go to the hardware store, get your meds and baby stuff, then find a nice place for lunch."

She didn't answer. Their conversation still buzzed in her mind. By the time she'd put on a shirt and long pants and tied the laces on her walking shoes, she'd reconstructed a conversation with Freddie from years before. He'd come home from summer school tired and thin, and with his nose so swollen it looked like a potato. When she'd suggested he make a doctor's appointment, he'd shrugged, said he'd bumped his nose against a doorframe. She watched the mail for the letter containing his summer school grades, but the letter never came. And she was too tired, too lazy, too something to make him search his car. If he'd ever put the letter in his car.

She wondered what else Freddie had lied about. Had he cheated all through college? He'd been a top student, but had he deserved it? She didn't want to ask. The conversation would end with Freddie hollering. They needed each other, and she needed time to calm down.

After Jeffrey died, she'd stopped thinking about God but continued to pray out of childhood habit, just in case a listening presence could hear. Now she said silent prayers for the boy with the knife,

praying he got good medical care and learned something about violence begetting violence.

Miserable, she went into the living room. Morning light lit
up the white upholstery on the sofa and chairs; a strong gust blew
through the sliding doors and sent the shell mobile over the dining
room table clacking. Wild wind and cloudless sky, the kind of day
she and Frederick loved. After a morning beach walk, they would
stop at a little ocean-front place for lunch. Despite a cap and suntan
lotion, Frederick's face always turned scarlet by lunchtime. The two
of them at a glass table at The Ocean View, waiting for lunch. He
told a dumb joke and laughed—one of his endearing traits, laughing
at his own jokes. His booming laugh turned heads.

She covered his hand with both of hers. "I love you more than
I did yesterday."

Frederick grinned. "Right back at you, lovely Elaine."

Freddie's voice interrupted. "Mother! Have you turned to stone?
Come on out. I'm teaching Lily about birds."

She opened her eyes, glanced at Freddie, and realized she didn't
want to go anywhere with him. She was mad all over again for the
years he took away from her and Frederick and Sabine, the years
when their lives revolved around his needs, his wants, his moods.
Even if she needed meds and diapers, she didn't want to ride in the
car with Freddie.

"You don't want to go to town."

She shook her head.

"Okay. I'm going down to the beach with the volunteers."
He cleared his throat. "Since last night I've been thinking about
Sabine."

"Sabine. What about her?"

"I thought I saw her on TV last night. Standing in a grocery
store line in DC."

"You what?"

"Sabine. I thought it was her on TV. I thought about it later and decided it wasn't, but the resemblance . . . When bombs hit DC she would've run, probably headed for a beach. I'll find her. First, by trying to find out how the beaches down the coast fared with the bombs."

Elaine shook her head. "This country's in chaos and you want to look for your sister. You realize most cell phones don't work? We have no idea where she is." Tears were thick in her throat. "Sabine's been gone nearly three years. Don't you think your father and I tried to find her? We hired a detective too late. She'd been gone for six or seven months."

"I'm sure she made it out of DC when the bombs hit," Freddie said, not listening. "She's resourceful. Remember how she snooped to get information? She hated feeling left out because she was younger. There was that summer she camped in the backyard with that smelly old sleeping bag, a Swiss Army knife, and a Girl Scout canteen, and dragged around Dad's old backpack—"

"She was eight the summer she camped in the yard." Elaine wiped her face with a handkerchief.

"Mom, in a crisis, if she could, Sabine would head to the beach. I have no idea which beach, but that's where she'd go."

"So many thunderstorms that summer." Elaine nodded. "She'd come in the kitchen, dry off, wait till the storm passed, and drag her stuff back outside."

Freddie laughed. The sound set Elaine on edge.

She forced a smile. "Go volunteer. I'll take the baby. Try not to make noise when you come back. I'll try to get Lily to nap, so I can nap."

Freddie took three water bottles from the pantry, then grabbed an old beach towel, and dropped them all in a daypack. In a loud voice he called, "See you later!" He took the wooden steps down to the beach two at a time.

Elaine carried Lily into the master bedroom, put her down by her side and laid her hand on the baby's stomach. Lily looked around and closed her eyes. Elaine thought about the stories she created about Jeffrey after he died—a baby prince without flaws. How thin her fantasies about dead Jeffrey were, compared to this living child.

She picked up sleeping Lily, took her to her crib, and placed her on her back. She left the door open and went to her own bed. She ruminated on Frederick's last phone call, before the bombs hit. It had left her with the same old frustration: all he did was work, work, work, weekends and holidays.

The month Jeffrey was born and died, joy and grief pulled them closer. In the days after the funeral, Frederick had left work at two o'clock. Sabine and Freddie didn't come home from school until four-thirty. With the house to themselves, Elaine and Frederick held each other, yelled, sobbed, and talked more than usual. Sometimes after their feelings were spent, they could be tender and sexual, drink coffee together and talk about other things. They were filled with gratitude for each other, and their love had grown stronger than when they dated in college.

Today she admitted to herself she'd been smug about their ability to weather losing a child. As the months wore on, Frederick reverted to longer hours at the office and she reverted to staying alone, speculating what to do when Sabine left for college. She prepared by calling schools and agencies about volunteer work. She also taught herself to knit and made baby blankets to sell at church bazaars. Sometimes a ball of panic lodged in her chest; to combat it, she kept moving.

This was the year Frederick was going to cut back on clients. In April, they'd talked about transitioning to living in the city house part-time and spending the rest of the time at the beach. They'd planned to live at the beach full-time by December.

Now Elaine made no plans except helping Lily, Freddie, and herself survive. Filled with the sound of "no" wherever she turned, she stared at the wall until sleep carried her away.

❧

Freddie raked sand, separated out sludge, and bagged it. Others dragged plastic garbage bags along the beach, filling them with trash. At lunchtime an old guy drove a Jeep onto the beach, bringing a cooler filled with thin sandwiches and water bottles. They sat on towels in a circle and ate. Freddie threw out questions about beach conditions as far south as Myrtle Beach. He doubted Sabine could have traveled any farther south. Two volunteers told him they'd heard of riots over drinking water. These bits of information could be rumors.

After lunch they worked nonstop until 4 p.m., when the trucks arrived to pick up the garbage bags.

Freddie arrived at the cottage relaxed and proud of his hard work. He tiptoed inside. Lily was asleep in her crib, and his mother's door was closed.

Without company to distract him, Freddie felt like a trapped wolf eating its own leg to get free. All his stored-up guilt about Sabine gnawed at him. Why hadn't he searched for her sooner? He hurried to his computer, then turned away. Where were the legal pads? Dad was a lawyer; there must be a stash somewhere. He eyed the cabinet that held the liquor and moved his chair so he couldn't see it.

A legal pad and pencils were in the living room desk. He pulled a floor lamp close to the dining room table, wrote the word "bourbon" at the top of the page, and scratched it out. He had to pour out the bourbon. He tore out the page.

At the top of the new, he wrote "Finding Sabine." He started a list below:

#1. Hire a private investigator: discuss finding Dad, Mags, and Sabine. Cost?

#2. Look around the cottage for a large map of the East Coast. Or buy one.

#3. Buy pushpins to mark beach towns that weren't bombed.

#4. Likely places: the Outer Banks, Emerald Isle, Topsail, and Atlantic Beach—all beaches in North Carolina—could be okay. Myrtle Beach, SC is probably okay. (I don't know for sure. But they aren't big cities.)

What if Sabine made it farther than South Carolina? Should he find out about Georgia beaches? No, that was too far. Her postcards to their parents came two or three times a year, postmarked Seattle, Albuquerque, DC, or Houston. Each postcard said, "I'm working in DC (or Raleigh or Seattle or Albuquerque). I have an apartment. Don't worry. I'm fine. S." Never a return address. Freddie didn't believe she'd moved to Houston or Albuquerque or Seattle. She loved the South and the ocean. Maybe she'd asked friends to mail the postcards.

The whole family could live here in the cottage. Freddie saw himself fixing up a haven for when Dad, Mags, and Sabine arrived.

At the top of the second page he wrote "Cottage Repairs," and made another list:

#1. Install eight storm windows upstairs.

#2. Buy and install a storage-room door padlock. Bigger and stronger than the one we have.

#3. Buy and install a front-door lock, to supplement the one we have.

#4. Buy and install faucet handles for the outside shower.

#5. Buy and install motion sensor floodlights for front and back of the house.

Tomorrow he'd call the private investigator, but finding Mags would be nearly as hard as locating Sabine. He didn't recall her friend Addy's last name. They'd met in the hospital when they had their babies, and they'd called each other daily to talk about nursing and sleep schedules and hormones and crying and whatever else new mothers talked about. He supposed the investigator could start with the hospital; Addy's baby was born the same day as Lily.

Freddie had a feeling Mags was still alive. She'd come to the beach looking for him and Lily. If she could. Perhaps she'd been wounded and couldn't contact him. He couldn't think about that possibility.

The investigator would tell him the odds of finding either of them. He still had most of the $900 he'd discovered in a box in his closet. Drug money, but he must have been high when he hid it, and like many things, he'd forgotten all about it. He also had three pairs of gold cuff links, one pair with diamond chips, and a Rolex. All this he would use for bargaining with an investigator.

He snatched the phone book out of the desk drawer. When he reached the I's, he stopped. Mags would have identification, he hoped. But what if Sabine didn't have a driver's license, credit cards, or a cell phone? Maybe she was a waitress who dealt in cash and didn't have a bank account. Maybe she had a pile of money stashed and used prepaid phone cards and credit cards. She'd been gone almost three years. Sly and smart, she was the kind of person who could maneuver herself off the grid because she was capable of cutting people off. He and the investigator could hunt for her, but if she didn't want to be found, could she ever be?

His parents hadn't searched for Sabine at first—they hadn't realized she was missing. They'd just assumed she needed time alone after Mick died; they'd expected she'd contact them in a month or so. They didn't understand how much she hated Freddie, how she blamed him for what happened with Giles and Mick.

His wife, his little sister, his little brother, his nephew. His hands shook. Nausea hit and he just made it to the sink. He vomited and felt better. *Mags and Sabine could arrive anytime. He'd find them both, and his dad was on his way. They'd all be together again.*

He scrubbed the sink, brushed his teeth, and washed his face, avoiding the bathroom mirror. At the table he glanced at the pad, but couldn't think of anything else to write. He wandered by the TV and out of habit reached for the remote, then changed his mind. He walked to him room, fell across his bed, and pulled a pillow over his head, wishing he were dead.

_____

June 30, 2014.

Elaine stumbled into the living room without a bathrobe. Morning sun blazed off the deck and the rooms felt stifling. She slid open the doors to a burst of cool ocean wind. Almost a full pot of coffee, still warm. Too tired to premix the powdered milk, she poured a cup and mixed the powder in. It clumped on the bottom. She stabbed the blob with a spoon.

By the sun's position, it was around eleven o'clock. Amazed at how long she'd slept, she felt rested, even cheerful. A wave of gratitude for Freddie and Lily.

Freddie's note sat on the table: "Lily and I are going for a walk on the beach. Back around lunchtime."

Three loud knocks on the front door. Her heart jumped. Frederick? Mags? Sabine? She ran down the three steps to the landing. Two men in uniform stood in the doorway.

"Elaine Owen?"

"Yes, yes. That's me."

"Mrs. Owen, I'm Officer Sorrento, and this is Officer Smythe. We'd like to ask you a few questions pertaining to June 22nd when you allegedly shot and wounded James Hudson in front of the Patient First in the Sea Breeze Mall."

"Come in." The men followed her into the living room. She realized she had on her nightgown. "Let me put on a robe. Feel free to sit at the dining room table. Would you care for coffee? There's a pot already made." She hoped they couldn't see her heart thumping.

"No thank you," Smythe said. "This shouldn't take long. We have a few questions."

"Be right back." She smiled. "Going to get my robe." Before he could stop her she ran to her room and grabbed her robe off a closet hook. She hurried to the dining room and sat at the table. "Okay. I'm ready for questions."

"Was the gun yours?" Sorrento looked into her eyes. His face was blank.

"The gun belonged to Frederick. My husband."

"May we see the permit?" Sorrento asked.

She shook her head. "It's at our house in Richmond. Or what's left of our house. The house was still standing when I left, but there were looters all over our neighborhood. That's why I'm here. On Memorial Day Frederick called me from his office. Something bad was happening downtown. We got cut off. Then there were two explosions in our neighborhood. My husband never called back. I still have no idea where he is."

She felt the sting of tears. *My God. Shut up. I'm going on and on.* "I reported the incident with the boy at Patient First on June 23rd. Some people in the waiting room watched the whole thing from the windows. A few were rushing out just as I pulled away. There wasn't anything wrong with the boy's leg. He wanted money. He pulled out a knife and grabbed me. I panicked." Was she talking too much, too fast?

Officer Smythe consulted his clipboard. "Yes, ma'am. We have the record of your call. We've been busy."

"We need to see the gun," Sorrento said.

Elaine got the gun and laid it on the table. "It's a Glock. But you know that." What if Freddie walked in? He was paranoid. He'd either tell them the gun was his, or worse, he'd run out the door. And get himself arrested.

She glanced at the clock—11:15. Freddie's note said they'd be back at lunchtime.

Smythe inspected the gun and wrote down the serial number. "Thank you."

"The boy? How is he?" The room had grown warmer. Elaine felt sweaty.

"His foot is going to be fine," Officer Smythe said. "He broke probation carrying a weapon and threatening you. He's a minor with priors. We'll inform you."

The men stood and she jumped up. She heard a man's voice: Freddie coming up the beach stairs? *Take a deep breath. Stay calm.*

At the landing she faced them. Even if Freddie came in the other door, she had to say this: "Please understand, I don't go around shooting people. Since the bombs I haven't been—I haven't been myself. My husband's missing, my daughter's missing, my daughter-in-law's missing. I can't sleep. I'm. Well. Nothing's the same."

"It's true, ma'am. Nothing's the same." Smythe smiled and Sorrento nodded. Elaine mumbled good-bye with her head down, hoping neighbors weren't wondering why a police car was parked in front of her house. Most of all, hoping they'd leave before Freddie got back. She leaned on the closed door, and sighed when she heard the police car pull away.

From the deck she searched up and down the beach. No sign of Freddie. The voice she heard must've been a neighbor on his own deck. *Oh, my God, what if Freddie ran away with Lily?* Elaine checked the driveway. Her car was there. The clock read twelve. She had to get air. She found underwear, shorts, and a T-shirt, ran to the bathroom, and struggled into her clothes. No time for makeup. Clutching her house keys, she ran down the deck steps to the beach.

Chapter 18

FRUIT MOON

August 1, 2014.

Sol and Sabine drove an hour through banyans and trees festooned with Spanish moss crowding the edge of the road. A billboard appeared, featuring a pretty woman holding a shrimp dripping butter and smiling. Lawler's Seafood.

"A restaurant, just three miles away," Sabine said. "It has been ages since I had a nice piece of fish. You like seafood?"

"I've had lake trout, but not shellfish. Nothing fresh anyway."

"In Florida we can eat all the fish we want." She stretched, surprised her muscles felt relaxed. Then it occurred to her the ocean could be polluted. She wouldn't mention it to Sol.

"I've been thinking about what I took from my apartment. Did you manage to grab something special before you left? I took my shawl and notebooks, that's it. Jude has the shawl now."

Sol shook his head. "I thought I'd only be gone two or three days and would be bringing Jude back to my house to stay. I have a picture of me, my parents, and my brothers from a picnic last fall, though. We stopped a hiker and asked him to take it. It's in my wallet."

"With my building crumbling and things blowing up," Sabine

said, "I felt lucky to get out alive. Today, I wish I had anything—a snapshot, my gold bracelet, some object from my old life."

Sol pointed up ahead. "There's the restaurant," he said. "Let's hope this place is open, and cheap."

Lawler's parking lot was half full, which they took as a sign the food would be decent. The building was long and narrow, with a low ceiling. Windows ran along one wall facing a lake. Tiki torches lined a walkway down to the water. The moon and torches threw shards of light on dark water made choppy by the wind.

By the cash register, a sign read: Sorry! Our Credit Card Machine Isn't Working. Cash Only. Only Local Fish Available. Don't Worry, They're Florida's Best!

They ordered. Sabine said, "Thank you for listening, about me and Giles. You're a good listener."

Sol shifted in his chair, kept his eyes on the table. "A question. You met Giles when you were twenty-four?"

"Yep, twenty-four. Giles was thirty-four. I was twenty-seven when Mick died, and twenty-nine when Giles died," she said in a rush. "Since you like to try to figure stuff out, I'm thirty-five. Not forty. My eyesight could be failing, though, and I guess my thighs are getting bigger."

"I exaggerated because I was mad. You're beautiful. Thanks for telling me the truth."

She nodded, unsure what to say.

"You think I listen well?" Sol asked. "Sometimes I hear myself lecturing people and later I feel bad."

"You may feel bad, but you still think you're right."

"You caught me," he said. "But when people won't talk to me after I've lectured them, I realize I should've kept my mouth shut. Like the stupid argument I started with Paul."

"At least you're honest with yourself," she said. "I hide the truth from myself. And I don't get the same kick out of being right that I used to."

Sol pointed at the wall of windows. "The light's fading. I can barely see the lake."

"I love the blond wood," she said. "And the lake, right outside." She leaned across the table. "We have to get rid of the guns in the car before they bring trouble."

"I was thinking the opposite. The farm folks don't have many guns among them. Maybe we should keep them for when we get to St. A."

"No."

"Let's take a walk after dinner," he said. "I'm glad you brought your jacket, it's windy."

The waitress put their plates on the table.

"A walk would be nice," Sabine said, distracted by the pile of steamed shrimp, broccoli, and french fries.

Sol shoved fries in his mouth, then dug into the coleslaw. He gazed at the red snapper. "It's big."

She laughed. "Hope it's good."

His first bite was tentative; then he ate with enthusiasm.

For dessert, she ordered apple cobbler and he, the key lime pie.

She pointed her fork at the cobbler. "The first fruit we've had since those bitter apples at the farm. Even if this isn't fresh, the apples are sweet."

"Best meal since the farmhouse."

"Still want to take a walk? I'm getting sleepy." She took Jude's wallet out of her jacket. "Here's what's left of his money. Five dollars." She pushed the money across the table, then held the wallet to her chest.

Sol laid down more cash. They walked around the side of the building and followed the lake path.

"Two months ago I was putting toppings on pizza dough and planning my big move to Charlottesville," Sol said.

"I was an assistant manager," she said.

"What did you manage?"

"A sporting goods store. I drifted from job to job, sometimes they blur together. I was in charge of reordering stuff—baseball mitts, tennis racquets, and basketballs. I was there about six months, right before the bombs."

She slid on the path and he reached out to keep her from falling. She moved away. "I'm fine, thanks."

His expression made her think he was trying to determine if she was lying about her job. They walked halfway around the lake in silence. It was smaller than it appeared from the restaurant windows. Would Sol ever trust her? She wanted to behave better, to catch up to her chronological age. Pieces of herself were floating back, which made her proud. Even in the chaos, she found herself feeling safer.

"I thought we'd see the blue truck on our way down," she said. "Maybe they took another route?"

"Maybe." He touched her arm. "Did Jude tell you about Laura?"

"What?"

"He broke things off with Laura before the bombs. After he started seeing her, he kept going to the bars and usually picked up some girl. We only had two bars in town, so of course Laura's friends spotted Jude and told Laura, and of course she made a scene. He admitted to her he didn't want to settle down, told her good-bye. After the bomb, he went to her house to check on her, but nobody was there." Sol scuffed the ground with his foot. "Laura was cute, but boring, not too smart. She had no sense of humor, and you know how Jude loved a laugh."

"Jude never talked about Laura." Sabine felt her voice shake.

"If he loved her, he wouldn't have been picking up girls, out in the open. He wanted her to find out."

"Makes sense, although his strategy stinks," she said.

"I figured Jude didn't tell you. After the bomb, he claimed he'd try to find her after things settled down. I asked if it was guilt talking, but he didn't answer. I knew I was right. He talked about his mom, little brothers, and older sister like they weren't dead." Sol lit a cigarette and held out the pack. "Want one? Oops, you shouldn't be smoking."

"You're right. No cigarettes. It would be miserable to start and have to quit again."

"You're way different than Laura," he said. "From watching Jude with you, I'd say he loved you, for real."

Sabine's mind stopped. Hadn't she cared more for Jude than he cared her? At the farm, she'd wondered if Jude would leave her to search for Laura and his father once the turmoil subsided. The feeling was stronger than wondering, more like worry. That's why she'd never asked Jude how he felt about Laura. As usual, she feared the truth.

This information shouldn't matter, since Jude was gone. But it did matter. She felt worse, losing him felt bigger, for hearing how much he cared. Overwhelmed, she leaned against Sol and he put his arm around her.

"Maybe I shouldn't have told you about Laura. Jude was my best buddy. I should've kept his secrets. I'm not sure anymore. You confuse me, Sabine."

"Why?"

"You just do."

"You don't want to talk about it?"

"Let's get to the car," he said.

They walked toward the parking lot. She was relieved to see the Buick intact, still in the parking lot.

"We have to move the guns off the backseat. No more waiting." Sol slid into the driver's seat and started the car.

"Not off the backseat. Let's dump them. I assume your rifle and pistol are registered? And Jude's rifle and pistol?"

"I suppose Jude registered his," he said. "He was straight arrow about things like that."

"Let's keep the registered guns." She spotted a narrow road off to the right. "Turn over there. It's a state road with scrub and trees."

Sol parked far off the road. She opened the trunk and found

the cooler with cola and beer cans sitting in water. She emptied the dirty water and put back the cooler while Sol paced.

"We can maybe, just maybe, justify stealing the Buick," Sabine said. "But driving around with stolen guns? The police would think we killed the old man and stole his car and the guns."

He lit a cigarette. "No one is gonna care about an old man. That town's in chaos."

She waited.

"You aren't going to budge on this?" He paced again.

"It's a deal breaker."

"What do you mean?" His eyes opened wide.

"I haven't thought it through, but I just might take off. "

"You'd go off by yourself, just like that?" He blew cigarette smoke skyward. "I don't believe you. It doesn't make sense; we're in a stolen car, and that's worse."

She flushed with anger. "Believe it." She pulled a pair of gloves out of her backpack, wishing for a cigarette.

He took a few more drags off the cigarette before grinding it out. "Okay. Okay."

"Put on your gloves," she said. "Throw the guns in the bushes. Over there. I'll help."

"You will not. You keep watch. Any car slowing to check us out, or anybody coming on foot, come tell me." He pulled on gloves.

Since she'd won about the guns, she kept watch without fussing. Sol carried three rifles at a time into the bushes, checking each one to make sure it wasn't loaded before tossing it into the scrub.

She found a plastic bag in the trunk and handed it to him. "Put the ammo boxes in here. We'll drop the bag in a trash can some- where else."

"No. We'll keep ammo for our guns and what we don't keep, we sell. Ammo will be worth a lot." He moved the liquor bottles to the trunk. "We can sleep in the car. You want to stay here?"

"No. It's creepy," she said. "Let's keep driving."

"Yep, this place makes me nervous too."

"Sorry I'm acting nutty. But you grew up with guns. I didn't. And I have just three words about guns: Kate. Hank. Jude."

They got in the car, and she balled up Jude's jacket and laid it against the window. "I'm falling asleep. Stop when you see a safe place." He pulled onto the highway. The last she heard was the engine's steady hum.

The car slowed and stopped, the radio and heater went silent. She didn't open her eyes. He moved closer and lifted her left hand. His lips grazed her hand. A whisper: "I love you, crazy, beautiful Sabine."

A car door opened and closed with a thunk. Rustling sounds, then something soft fell over her. She pulled the softness inside, weaving it into a dream.

☙

August 2, 2014.

Before dawn they were back on the road. Sabine puzzled over what to say about the night before. Had Sol said what she thought he said? She must've dreamed it. But why would she dream he said he loved her? She'd spent a lot of time telling herself he was a jerk. One part she was sure about: a sleeping bag covered her when she woke.

She glanced out the rear window, a new habit since they'd been followed. No cars behind them. "Ready for coffee," she said.

"Two meals in a row we don't have to fix—I could get used to that."

"I'm excited about seeing the farm people. Aren't you?"

"Not particularly." Sol drove in his usual position. He reminded her of some old movie gangster: the hunch, the cigarette hanging out his mouth, the scowl.

"I hope everyone's okay. You worried whether we'll find them?"

"Not particularly."

She pulled the East Coast map from the glove box. "We're almost to Yulee, then Jacksonville. After Jacksonville we turn east onto the coastal road, 1A. Then straight down to St. Augustine. Almost there!"

Sol didn't answer.

"You didn't get enough sleep?"

No response.

Out the window, horses grazed on flat land. Horses this far south were a surprise. Kentucky, Tennessee, and Virginia were the real horse country. What was wrong with Sol? Had she said something mean? She didn't think she had.

The Buick slowed and stopped.

The Florida Line Diner had a silver top and wooden steps up to the door. Wonderful smells—coffee, bacon, and sausages sizzling on a grill. They sat on dark-red vinyl seats, the rips mended with duct tape, at a brown Formica tabletop with salt and pepper shakers and plastic flowers. She ordered a large coffee, sausages, two eggs over easy, and tomato juice. Then she added hash browns.

"Whoa, eating for two," Sol said.

A jolt ran through her body. For a few days she'd managed to dodge the fact of her pregnancy. "This place is almost full. See those guys in hard hats? If any bombs hit here, they're on top of the cleanup. I hope St. Augustine is alright."

"Sabine, stop it. You're avoiding the situation."

"You're right. Sorry. I am trying to live up to my real age."

The waitress brought the coffee and juice.

"What are you going to do?" he asked. "About the baby? If you're not keeping it, you better do something. We should look for a clinic when we get to St. Augustine."

"I have no idea how I'll manage, but I am having this baby. And I am keeping this baby."

Sol's eyes filled, and his face flushed. "Good. That's good," he whispered.

His response startled her. Did he care? Of course, she was carrying Jude's baby. "Once we get there, I'll find a doctor and start on prenatal vitamins—better late than never. I'm so malnourished I'm surprised I could even get pregnant."

His eyes widened. "Too skinny? I didn't know that. My parents didn't talk about such things. I learned about women and sex from my brothers and school friends."

"Did you date much?"

"Two girls in high school—one in my junior year, then Mary Lee, who was smart. After we graduated she took off to a real college, not a community college, and never came back. I was seeing a girl three months before the bombs, but we didn't fit."

"You don't want city life?"

"I like country living," Sol said, "but I want an education more than a farm. Sandy wanted me to forget college and get a job driving a truck. One of my brothers is a car mechanic, the other's an electrician. Neither job is for me."

"You didn't inherit their mechanical ability?" She remembered his puzzled face when he stared at the pickup truck's engine and giggled.

"I take after Dad. He's quiet and bookish. He could've been a college professor; instead, he delivers mail. He reads all the time and loves to lecture about what he reads."

"Ah, that's where your lecturing talent comes from."

Sol grimaced. "About seven in the morning, Memorial Day, my brothers and I arrived at our parents' to prepare the barbecue pit for the picnic. An explosion came from the Barnville area, but I couldn't get anything on the radio or TV. When Jude didn't answer his phone, I got worried. I got a pack together and walked over to Barnville. And here comes Jude riding his horse down the road. His family, except for his missing dad, all dead, and his home place mostly destroyed. He was panicky about more bombs, said we needed to get out of there. I called my parents to check on them. They were fine, so I told them I was leaving with Jude, I'd probably be home in a day or two. Hope they're still okay."

"It sucks that there are no phones." Sabine wrapped toast and butter cubes in napkins. They ordered sausages and three bottles of orange juice to go. "Want me to drive? I haven't driven in a long time."

"Driving makes me feel I'm taking care of you."

"You have been, since Jude died. Strange, since you think I'm a liar. And you thought I didn't treat Jude well enough. And you think I'm cold for ignoring you at the farmhouse."

"So, among your many talents you read minds?"

"Tell me I'm wrong."

"You're half wrong and half right," he said. "You were important to Jude, so you're important to me."

"I've been on my own for a long time."

"I'm trying to imagine you working in sporting goods," he said. "It doesn't fit."

"What did you think I'd be doing?"

"Working in a library," he said. "A bookstore. Maybe teaching high school English."

"In high school I toyed with drama. Thought I'd be famous, act and sing and dance on Broadway. I also considered culinary school."

"I don't understand you." He shook his head.

"You don't understand because you hardly know me. I had two years of college as an English major, then switched to drama and finally dropped out. Before I could go back and finish, I met Giles. After Mick died, I drifted job to job and didn't consider going back to college. If I could pay rent, go to movies and plays, have a drink with friends, I was okay. I couldn't make myself care about jobs. Just getting by.

"With Jude, for the first time I began thinking about the future, feeling there could be one. How stupid, right? Nothing's stable. In DC my notebooks sat empty, waiting for inspiration that never came. The two tales about Jeffrey and the horse are the first stories I've written in years."

A mileage sign for St. Augustine appeared as soon as they turned east, toward the coast. Sabine felt restless, eager to get off the road and see everyone from the farm. She felt caged in the car, panicked, like a woman with her hair on fire scrambling for water.

PART FIVE

Chapter 19

HUNTING MOON

August 2, 2014.

They reached the outskirts of St. Augustine around lunchtime. They drove past a strip of motels, but agreed to sleep in the car in a residential neighborhood instead. They'd find a campground tomorrow.

She peered out the window, and was relieved to see people coming out of stores and pumping gas. People walked along the sidewalks, not hurrying. Maybe Florida hadn't been attacked. No, the man in the coffee line said it had been. Miami in ruins and Cape Canaveral also hit. She wanted a newspaper less than three days old, or a motel room with a television that worked.

They drove through a neighborhood of large two-story houses with red-tiled roofs sitting along wide streets lined with giant palms. She pointed to a yellow stucco house. "This is an old neighborhood. Older wealthy people still read newspapers. Let's sleep here and take off before people open their doors and find their paper gone."

Sol chuckled. They backtracked to the IHOP on Route 1. No newspaper boxes on the sidewalks. The restaurant, a fake colonial, was half full. They picked a booth overlooking a main street.

"Do you-all get newspaper deliveries?" Sabine asked the wait-ress. "I don't see any damage. Ya'll survived the bombs okay?"

The waitress grinned. "Sure did. We lost phone and lights for maybe a week. People with wells got no water, the pumps didn't work. Sometimes the motels get newspapers, from big cities up north. The boss is smart, bought himself a generator so we could keep feeding people, made triple money since most places closed. What can I get you folks?"

"What about farther south?" Sol asked.

"What about it?" The waitress frowned.

"Don't play dumb." Sol glared. "Did any bombs hit farther south?"

The waitress sighed. "Miami and Cape Canaveral. But we'll sur-vive. So, what can I get you folks?" Her false grin stayed on her face. Talking about bombs was bad for business.

They ordered.

"Why Cape Canaveral?" Sabine asked.

"You know, cause of satellites," the waitress said. She walked away.

Sabine stared at the street, teetering between nausea and hun-ger. The same queasy feeling she'd had when pregnant with Mick. She nursed a large coffee, then ate the cereal she'd ordered. Ten minutes later, she barely made it to the bathroom. After her stom-ach was empty she lay on the bathroom floor, still nauseous. She needed a comfortable bed and lots more sleep.

Tapping on the bathroom door. "Sabine, are you alright?"

"Just sick to my stomach. I'll be out in a minute." She rinsed her mouth, washed her face the best she could, and stuck gum in her mouth.

Sol stood at the entrance, frowning. "What do you want to do? You look sorta green."

"Could we find a nice spot and park, so I can sleep?"

"I'll stop at a drugstore and grab something to read, then we'll hunt for someplace green."

He ran into a drugstore and came out with a paperback and a

bag. He drove around until she noticed a city park sign and they found a spot under some trees. He handed her the bag. "Here, orange juice, vegetable soup, and crackers. And Pepsis."

"Oh, that's so sweet. Thanks." She pointed toward the lake and trees. "It's so lush—all the colors, all the flowers."

"A foreign land after West Virginia." He laughed.

She crawled into the backseat. "I appreciate your thinking of me." The breeze through the windows soothed her. The rendezvous, the castle at eight tonight, she had to remind Sol. But sleep took her away.

She woke to strong late-afternoon heat. Sol dozed in the front passenger seat. She sipped the soup and looked out the window, grateful the car wasn't moving. She left the car in search of a bathroom. Trails and a lake in the distance, but no facilities. She camouflaged herself behind a tree. *Don't get too comfortable, we're not safe, even in this lovely, quiet place.* She went back to the car, lay on the backseat, and waited for Sol to wake.

When he did, he actually smiled.

Startled he looked happy, she said, "Hey, have a good nap? You must be so sick of driving. I'll be glad to take a turn."

"Feeling better?" He ran a hand through his hair.

"Fine. We should go to the castle soon."

He groaned. "It's nice to be off the road. I didn't realize how tired I was."

"Camping and driving's hard even in good circumstances. And it hasn't exactly been a relaxing trip."

"It's only August 2nd," he said. "Let's go to the castle tomorrow night. I'm not up for a bunch of people."

"I'd rather go to the castle tonight . . ." Seeing Sol's face, she took a deep breath. "Okay, okay, tomorrow night. What should we do for dinner?"

"Let's find a fast-food place, bring food back here, and watch the sunset."

They brought food back to the park and sat at a picnic table.

"It's all my fault that my best friend's gone," Sol said suddenly. "I've always been the cautious one. Jude was always impulsive. He ran from his homeplace after the bomb, just took off. He made moves on you right away. That's the kind of guy he was."

"I could say something cliché, like, 'It wasn't your fault.' But it won't help. You have to forgive yourself. Did you intend to get Jude killed? No. I don't think you wanted your best friend dead. Giles didn't intend for Mick to die. Everything's about intent."

Sol looked at his hamburger, but his eyes jerked around, seeing something internal. They ate in silence, then she carried the trash to a garbage can. Dusk was deepening the color of the lake, and she wanted to leave before the sky turned dark.

Sol came to her and took her hand. In the dim light she saw his eyes were red. "Thank you."

Without words she nodded. In the Buick, he lit a cigarette and stuck it in his mouth, hunched over the wheel, and started the engine.

He drove slowly to the neighborhood they'd picked. He had a good sense of direction—didn't hesitate once, even though the streets were dark. When he found a spot away from lights where the Buick wouldn't be noticeable, he flicked off the headlights, crept along the curb, and turned off the engine.

"You take the backseat," he said. "We have to leave early in the morning."

෴

August 3, 2014.

They woke at first light, rolled up their sleeping bags, and stowed their backpacks. Instead of slouching over the wheel, Sol sat upright and glanced out of the windshield every few seconds.

"Should I run and grab that newspaper? There, on the lawn." She pointed to a house.

"What if someone's watching?"

"When was the last time we got real news? The man in the coffee line?"

"No clue. And that's not the point." He inched the Buick down the street.

She rolled down the passenger window. "The newspaper's turning brown, it's old anyway. The family's away and didn't stop delivery."

Sol said nothing.

"Forget it," she said. "Let's get breakfast."

They went back to the IHOP and ordered breakfast from the same waitress. Sabine ate dry toast and scrambled eggs. She was afraid to drink coffee, but ordered it anyway.

A black Jeep convertible pulled up to the intersection and stopped. A man wearing a red shirt and dark glasses sat in the driver's seat. A familiar profile. "Sol, look! At the light. Sharp."

"Yep, it's Sharp. What's he doing driving a Jeep?"

The light changed and the Jeep sped away. Her heart hammered in her chest, and she gobbled toast to settle her stomach. The first cup of coffee sloshed around in her stomach, but she drank a second anyway.

"Soon as we finish eating, let's look for the castle," he said. "It shouldn't be too hard to find."

They paid their bill and headed out. They hadn't driven far before they spotted the castle on the bay front at Castillo Drive. They parked a few blocks away.

"I wonder if Sharp talked with the O'Malleys," she said. "Maybe all of us will be together again soon."

They walked until they stood across the street from the castle.

Sol touched her arm. "You okay?"

"My stomach isn't good. I keep thinking about Jude, Hank, and Kate. It doesn't end." She rubbed her stomach.

"The price of caring about people," Sol said.

She pointed to the castle. "Remarkable, isn't it? It's built on

a rise for protection, just like the farm. It was built as a fort. But
I imagined a country castle rising up at the end of the long drive-
way, lined with stately trees. Sheep grazing on brilliant green grass.
Bucolic, like England."

"Sounds like you've watched too many of those British PBS
movies." Sol chuckled.

"Austen and the Brontë sisters," she said.

"Or Evelyn Waugh."

"You studied Waugh in a West Virginia high school?"

"Careful with your West Virginia stereotypes."

"Sorry. I do fall into stereotypes." She looked at the castle.
"Want to check it out? People are walking over the footbridge." She
started to cross the street.

Sol caught her arm. "Let's not take a tour. We need to look for
Sharp's Jeep and the blue truck. We'll find a campground, then find
the O'Malleys."

Sol, ever the practical man, was right. His suggestions had kept
them safe. Except. Except it was Sol who'd been driving that terrible
day, spotted the field with the broken fence, and drove it. It had
been Sol's idea to throw down their sleeping bags. *Unfair, any one of
us could've been driving. And he's already hammering himself with guilt.*

"Let's head to the beaches," she said. "On the map there's Anas-
tasia State Park, St. Augustine Beach, and Faver-Dykes State Park.
Let's spend an hour or two at the first beach. Even before we look for
a campground. I'm sick of riding in this car."

Relief filled her when he nodded.

⤜

She held a water bottle above her head, letting water pour over her
scalp and down her shirt. Heat radiated off the sand and the wool
blanket. Her jeans were stiff with Jude's blood. A big straw hat, a
bathing suit, and sunglasses would make her happy. Sol lay facing
away from her. He'd taken off his jacket, shoes, and socks. From

his regular breathing she assumed he'd fallen asleep. The tide was out; sun, wind, and distance blurred the faces of people swimming. Restless and sweaty, she rolled her jeans to her knees and walked to the water's edge. Debris floated beyond the breakers, but the sand looked clean, no sign of oil or tar.

Joy moved through her. Jude would've loved this beach. *Jude.* After he was shot, she and Sol should've put him in the back of the pickup and made a dash back to where she'd seen the hospital sign. Maybe he would be alive. *Maybe. Probably not. Stop second-guessing.* Her joy at being on the beach evaporated.

She squeezed her own hand, trying to feel his corporeal flesh, or even her own body.

A familiar, melodious voice behind her. She turned. Sharp, walking in animated conversation with a young woman in a pink bikini.

"Sharp! You made it." Sabine couldn't help smiling. He looked splendid in green bathing trunks, a towel slung over his shoulders. For a few seconds he stared before registering who she was.

"How are you?" She moved toward him.

"All right. Where are Jude and Sol?" He pushed his sunglasses up on his head. Finally, a smile. Not wanting to talk about Jude in front of a stranger, she pointed in the direction of the blanket where Sol was sleeping. Sabine introduced herself to the girl. Without looking at Sabine, the frowning girl muttered, "Barbara."

"When did you get here?" Sabine asked. "Where are you staying? Have you seen the farm folks?"

"I'm at the KOA campground," Sharp said. "I came down by train."

"I'm happy to see you." A train? What about the Jeep?

The girl giggled and reached for Sharp's hand, but when he didn't respond, the girl's hand fell to her side. Sharp glanced at the girl. "It's been fun chatting. See you around."

The girl's mouth drooped. "I'll be at the Hot Dog Hut, 9 to 9. I gotta work all weekend."

"Okay. See ya." Sharp turned his back on the girl.

"Sorry to interrupt," Sabine said.

"Just some girl."

"There's a train station near the farm?"

"I hitched a ride to the station," Sharp said. "After you all left, Jen, Tommy, and I dug a hole for Kate and Hank. While we were digging Lavinia and Randolph loaded the truck and checked the house to make sure no one left anything. We said a few words over the grave, then they all left in the truck."

"How are you doing?"

"Okay," he said. "How about you?"

"I'm glad to get out of the car and happy we're finally here. But there's bad news." Sabine's eyes filled with tears. "In North Carolina . . . well, we were getting ready to throw down sleeping bags for the night. The area looked safe—then *bam, bam*. Shots from a house on a hill. They hit Jude. We did what we could, but . . ."

"What do you mean?" Sharp asked. "Where's Jude?"

"Jude's gone. We couldn't stop the blood. So much blood."

Sharp focused on the ocean, bare-chested. When his breath quickened, she imagined she saw his pounding heart. He sat on the sand. She sat close to him.

"Sol put up a marker," she said. "I memorized the route numbers so I could come back and find his grave. It was dusk when we drove into the field. We got careless. We didn't notice the house up on a hill because there were tall bushes and scrub." Her voice sounded like a robot's. She dug her feet in the damp sand, which anchored her a little.

"I'm sorry, damn sorry," Sharp said. "Jude was a real good guy."

"Can I ask you something?" *Don't put your hand on him.*

Sharp nodded. "Where's Sol?"

"Asleep on the blanket. Over there." She pointed behind them. "This morning Sol and I saw you driving a black Jeep."

Sharp's slate-gray eyes were inscrutable. His voice came out soft when he squinted at the sun. "That Jeep was Hank's. I loved it, always drove it when my truck was in the shop. Later, when Hank and I lived together in DC we shared stuff. Now what was Hank's is all mine. And I don't care."

She pulled her feet out of the sand; water filled the holes. The tide was rushing inland. She angled her legs and dug her heels in the sand again. "If you had a Jeep, why take a train? If you don't care what happens next, why aren't you telling me the truth?" She could ask Sharp a million questions. If he wouldn't answer, she'd ask other questions. With him she sensed there would always be more secrets. "At the farm, you told me your father died."

"First, he had a motorcycle accident," he said. "Then he lost his job for drinking. Mother could be a bitch. When he lost his job, she nagged even more. Dad killed himself. I think he never married her because she was mean." He cleared his throat. "I called my mother to tell her about Hank."

"You used the sat phone?"

Sharp didn't answer.

Sabine took a handful of sand, let it free, and watched the wind send it in all directions.

"Oh, right," he said, "you spied on me with my sat phone in the woods. When I told Mother Hank was dead, she screamed and cried. I felt bad, and said I'd visit soon. Since high school I've blown her off. When Dad killed himself, I halfway blamed her. She could've been kind when he struggled. After he died, she started dating Jimbo real quick. Still, her worst stunt was leaving Hank behind when she dragged me off to Colorado. I still don't like her, but I see a bigger picture. She had two sons. Now she has none. I'll never visit her."

Sabine nodded. This felt like the truth. "I think if we're lucky, someday we see a bigger picture." She tossed a handful of sand. "Her dumb mistakes. Losses."

"More losses are coming," he said.

"What losses?"

"Celestial intel. Hank knew bombs were coming, just not when. Memorial Day was only the first wave."

She couldn't breathe. "What's Celestial?"

Sharp shrugged.

"The first wave. You're sure?"

"Yeah. Hank knew more bombs were coming. Celestial pretended they weren't aware Hank knew all he knew, asked him to accept a raise and a higher position. But Hank already had lots of money stashed. He took all his vacation days and stalled Celestial while we scrambled to leave DC. We sold our condo and furniture. We stockpiled food and guns. He gave the farm family notice we were coming and told them we'd stay in the attic till they found another place to rent.

"Hank had his own sources outside Celestial. He found out that several al-Qaeda–trained groups and others had planned large-scale missions. The day of the bombs we arrived at the farm and hid the Jeep. Found the tenants dead and the house ransacked. Celestial guys had searched for something they didn't find. They left their mark. Why else slit the family's throats and thighs and leave the bodies scattered around? Nothing was missing in the house or the grounds.

"The farm was a gift to Hank from his father, Jimbo Johnson. Jimbo's eighty-two, too old for farming. Hank didn't want the place sitting empty, so he rented the farm. He didn't know he was putting the tenants in danger. He should've been more cautious."

"Why kill him?"

"Celestial's media image is important to them. Hank knew way too much," Sharp grinned. "But Hank will get those bastards from his grave."

"What were they looking for that they didn't find?" Sabine asked.

"Some papers. The farm wasn't safe, so Hank and I revised our plan. We'd gather refugees with various survival skills and resources and see how we all got along. Then move to a safer place with whoever wanted to join us. Hank was more outgoing than I am. We wanted to build a community, start over. But Celestial's after me."

"What's Celestial, exactly?"

"Who's after you?" Sol's voice from behind them.

Sabine turned. "Hi, Sol. Have a seat. Sharp's filling me in."

"Good to see you, man." Sharp stood and gave Sol a brief hug.

Sol reacted with an embarrassed grin. "Same here, Sharp. Glad you made it." He frowned. "Who did you say was after you?"

Sharp edged away from Sabine. "Celestial. A private military contract company. Mercenaries. Hank fought for them all over the world. The past few years he'd been gathering information about murder and corruption at the top, big money graft, and fraud. He planned to expose the top man to the media and the military."

Sol settled next to Sabine, moving close until their shoulders touched. He smelled like sweat and cigarettes; his familiarity comforted her.

"Over the years, I took on three, maybe four, mechanical jobs for them," Sharp said. "But Hank wasn't small-time like me. Celestial's guys killed the farmhouse tenants, trashed the house looking for something. Kate . . . she just got in their way."

"Celestial means?" Sol asked.

Sharp's voice sounded tight. "'Celestial: We cover every place on the planet.' Or some similar shit. The morning we heard the first explosion, Hank and I left DC. Fast. We kept our cells off. Well out of DC, Hank pulled off the road, wiped his cell, stomped it to death, and tossed it in the woods. I disconnected the Jeep's GPS and searched till I found a bug, courtesy of Celestial."

"How did Celestial find out about the farm?" Sol said.

"Celestial could've found my brother if he'd flown to the moon." Sharp shrugged. "What they didn't find were Hank's and my statements with supporting documents."

"You have a lotta secrets." She kicked at the sand.

Sharp frowned at her. "Hank and I cleaned up the mess that same day. Knowing Celestial would come back soon would've scared good people away."

"Mercenaries," Sol said, shaking his head. "I want to hear more, but I'm hot and sweaty. I got to jump in the ocean."

"The water's great," Sharp said. He lay on the sand and pulled his sunglasses over his eyes. His face became a mask.

Sol pulled off his shirt and walked to the water's edge.

Swimming in jeans didn't sound like fun, but she'd walk in to her knees. Sol stood at the edge, small waves covering his ankles. After studying the water he moved beyond the breakers and swam north. He kept parallel to the shore, then allowed the current to pull him south, until he was opposite where she and Sharp sat. He walked to shore grinning. "Rougher than lake swimming. Great."

She was impressed with how he'd studied the currents, his strategy. He'd never swum in an ocean before. Sharp sat up and kept on his sunglasses.

"Sharp, here's something small," she said. "But I wondered. Did you drive the green pickup at the farm?"

"Yeah. When Hank and I visited, we drove the pickup. The farm family probably used it, too. Why?"

"Jude and I tinkered with it, expecting the battery to be dead. But the pickup started right up."

Engrossed in talking they didn't notice the gigantic wave until it was on top of them.

She yelled, "We're gonna get wet!" The wave crashed over them. She scrambled to stand, laughing. Her nose burned from inhaling salt water. Sharp's laugh sounded genuine, which made her feel better.

Grateful for a break from Sharp's intensity, she stood watching the water and mulled over what he'd just said. How much of his story was made up? He'd lied about taking the train. The Celestial company sounded strange. She had read mercenaries were a shadow military, but didn't know much else.

Sol was partly right: Hank and Sharp weren't CIA. But Celestial probably did jobs with the CIA, or for the CIA. *Stop. Let the wind clear away your thoughts.*

She ran into the water. The waves washed some of Jude's blood off her jeans. A symbol of a beginning in St. Augustine. No. A lie. Washing off blood didn't wash away a memory. Every time she tried to get rid of unpleasant memories by covering them with a lie, she got irritated with herself, which made her depressed. Farther out, she spread her legs to keep from getting knocked over by the current's push and pull.

Sol came up beside her and whispered, "Sharp has quite a story. I always knew he and Hank were plotting something. But there's a hell of a lot Sharp will never tell, not to anyone, much less us."

"I suppose he told us enough to stop our questions," she said.

Sharp ran past them and dove under a breaker. He swam straight out until she couldn't see him. A powerful man taking on the ocean with a vengeance, thinking he could tame it. A haunted man. She suspected women had tried, and failed, to cuddle and soothe him, to fix what had been broken. Coupled with his good looks, his sadness and silence must make him irresistible to women who loved rescuing wounded men. A doomed choice for a long-term mate. Like Giles, maybe worse. But he didn't appear to use drugs. She'd never even seen him have a drink.

Tears about Giles were coming; she leaned over and splashed water on her face.

Sol moved closer. Did he sense her thoughts?

"Sharp said he rode the train to St. Augustine, till I told him you and I recognized him driving a Jeep," she said. "He admitted the lie right away. One night in the living room, Hank alluded to turning away refugees from the farm. Hank told me I was brave to leave DC alone and walk all that way. Did he pick me because of bravery?"

"Maybe because you're beautiful," Sol said. "We'll never know. But I knew something was up. The satellite phone in the woods and padlocks on the gate? What city person carries padlocks around?"

"When Hank and Sharp found me in the field, I looked terrible. Filthy, matted hair, and a scrawny dirt face. Not beautiful."

"They saw the woman under the dirt." Sol laughed.

She elbowed him. "Shut up. Anyway, Sharp would've brought his sat phone, right? You can call your parents and brothers, tell them about what happened to Jude, so Jude's dad will know."

"Good thinking. I'll ask him."

"I'm sick of speculating how the pieces fit together," she said. "But I need to understand the big picture. The rifles under Sharp's bed? I'll bet he brought them down here in the Jeep."

"Sharp's trouble. Big trouble." Sol kicked the sand. "You think so?" *Liar. Of course Sharp spelled trouble.*

"Enough danger talk. I'm starting to sound like you. I definitely sound like you when I say my jeans are sticking to me."

She laughed. "Saltwater's sticky. Sharp's staying at a KOA campground. Hot water and soap, washers and dryers."

They waited for Sharp to finish his swim. They followed his Jeep in their Buick to the campground a few miles away.

⁂

Sabine woke beneath a palm tree by their campsite, sweaty and logy. A breeze brought the pungent smell of flowers. In the strange interlude just before falling asleep, Jude's voice had come to her. He'd said, "Hank's a beast."

Was Sharp also a beast? Jude had known Hank and Sharp better than she did. He'd walked the watch with them both; they'd hunted and foraged together. Jude could read people, but he'd never said Sharp was a beast. Jude had admired Sharp.

Could she trust Sharp when he talked about his father and being Hank's half brother? At the farm he and Hank had looked out for all of them. Yet they'd lied from the start and put everyone in danger.

The campground soothed her. Children's laughter sounded from the playground and the pool, country music and campfire smoke drifted through the trees. The well-maintained grounds felt luxurious compared to how she and Sol had been living.

On her way to the bathhouse, she spotted Sol in the laundry room. "Hey. Did you take a nap?"

"No nap. I'm washing our sleeping bags and blankets. And my clothes. These big machines make it easy."

"Where's Sharp?"

"He had errands in town." Sol frowned. "We talked a little. He drove by Kate's grandparents' house, but didn't visit."

She didn't want to think about the O'Malleys, or what Sol thought of Sharp. "Off to the showers. Making up for all the ones I missed."

∽

Sharp hadn't come back to the campground by the time Sabine and Sol left for dinner.

"Okay with you if we go back to the diner?" Sol asked.

Sabine nodded. "But let's hunt for a newspaper stand. What did Sharp say about the phone?"

"He gave me his extra set of Jeep keys," Sol said. "He was fine with my using his phone."

"Excellent."

"He has Kate's grandparents' address. He says the house is a big, rambling place on the edge of town. He didn't go to the door because he's a coward and couldn't face the O'Malleys with news about Kate."

"Come on, he just lost his brother," she said. "His father killed himself and he's estranged from his mother. I don't think he has a girlfriend. Your whole family's alive. He's alone."

"You're part right." Sol crossed his arms high over his chest.

"Do we have time after dinner to talk with the grandparents?"

"No, it's nearly seven. Let's hope the farm folks come to the castle at eight. We can all stay at the campground tonight and talk with the O'Malleys tomorrow."

"Only two people should tell the O'Malleys that Kate's dead. The part about all of us descending on them comes later."

"I guess you want to talk with them," Sol said.

"You and I should be the ones."

"I'm flattered," he said. "You're choosing the man who lectures people."

After a quick dinner, they drove to the castle. Sol searched for a parking place. At 7:35 there was still no sign of Sharp's Jeep, or the farm truck. Sol parked on the bay front, a block away from the castle gate. When he lit a cigarette, Sabine rolled down the window. The strong smoke made her queasy.

Sol stubbed out his cigarette. "There! Sharp. Moving fast over the footbridge."

"Where?"

"He's gone around toward the back."

Sabine opened the door. "Let's go."

"Let's wait and see if the blue truck shows up," Sol said. "It's almost eight. Rendezvous time."

"I'm going," she said. "Get your gun."

Sol took her arm. "Are you crazy? This is a public place."

"I have a bad feeling. Sharp's skulking around. Get your gun. If you won't, I will." Hitting the car windshield had been a fluke, but maybe she'd get lucky again. And Sol was a decent shot.

She paced the sidewalk while Sol stuck the gun in his belt and dropped a box of ammo in his jacket pocket. "Okay."

Sabine scanned the area for the blue truck. "No sign of the others."

Crossing the footbridge, they heard a popping sound. Sol took her arm and they stopped. Moonlight blended with the lights of the city flickering over the inky water of the bay. She tried to focus on the bay, hoping for calm, but terror filled her. Only a few people were walking near the waterfront. "Let's go back to the car and watch for the blue truck from there," she said.

"Let's hope the popping sounds were firecrackers," Sol whispered. "Stay behind me."

Sol inched forward. She ignored his words and moved up beside him. A man crouched in the shadows along the castle. She tugged Sol's jacket. They stopped.

From behind, one shot, and another. The man by the wall yelled, "Sabine, get down! Get out of here!" Sharp.

Three more shots whizzed past. Sol shoved her to the ground and whirled around. Another volley and Sol fell. In the shadow of the castle wall, Sharp toppled.

From behind, footsteps running—perhaps fading, she didn't know. Maybe three people. Celestial's men? Sabine heard herself screaming.

A night watchman ran toward them, talking fast on a phone.

Sabine crouched by Sol. He held his arm in his lap, covering a bloody place with his other hand. "Sol! Sol!" He didn't respond. "Look at me! The watchman's calling for help. Sol, can you hear me?" She held his chin, turned his head toward her. "Sol, an ambulance is coming."

His face almost touched hers, but he didn't see her.

The watchman jogged closer. She scooped up Sol's gun and jammed it in her jacket, then pocketed the box of ammunition, the Buick keys, and Sol's wallet. Before the watchman could stop her, she ran to Sharp. He was curled up by the wall, his hands laid across his stomach, a dark stain spreading under his hands. "Sharp, can you hear me?"

"Oh, Sabine," he moaned. "Why in hell are you here? Not your fight."

"I'm so sorry." She fell to her knees and cradled him. "We came to meet the others, like we planned. The watchman called for help, ambulances and police are on the way."

"Cops won't matter," he mumbled. "There's a bandana in my pocket. I'm sweating like a pig."

She found the bandana and patted his face. She gently rocked him. Moving closer, she whispered, "Sharp, help's coming. Hang on. Please, please don't die."

From Sol to Sharp and back to Sol, muttering, "Hurry, hurry, hurry." A crowd gathered on the sidewalk. Sirens. A police officer pushed back the gawkers. Another officer ran to Sol, who wasn't moving.

The officer asked for Sol's name and address, then hers. He cocked his head and asked, "What happened here?"

"I didn't see the shooters," she said. "Our friend Sharp, the guy over there, was running toward the castle. All the shots came from behind. I didn't turn around, but I'd guess two or three people were shooting."

Sirens came closer, then stopped. "I gotta go to the hospital with my friends."

EMTs ran toward them. Sol and Sharp were loaded onto stretchers. The police officer let her go. She ran to the curb and shouted to an EMT, "Where are you taking them?"

"Flagler! Don't try to follow, we'll be running red lights."

"We're from West Virginia. Where's the hospital?" She jiggled the car keys against her thigh.

The sirens blared. The EMTs didn't answer. Racing to the Buick, Sabine fumbled with the key, hands shaking. Finally, she got the key in the ignition. The ambulance's taillight guided her. She passed cars and flew through orange and red lights. Cars up ahead swerved out of their way.

At the emergency room entrance, a huge parking lot was all lit up. She parked and surveyed the lot. *Full of cars. No people. Think this through. No mistakes.* She pulled out Sol's gun and box of ammo. Sol's gun had no smell because he'd never fired it. He hadn't had the chance. She locked the car, opened the trunk, wiped off the gun and box, and dropped them in the trunk, then covered them with a blanket.

She made it to the ER behind an EMT pushing a stretcher through swinging doors to an elevator. "GSW to the abdomen," the EMT shouted to the woman at the desk, and kept moving.

Chapter 20

BLOOD-POPPY MOON

August 3, 2014.

In the cacophony of the ER, Sabine took a few breaths to calm herself, then gave her name to the registrar. Half in a trance, perched on the edge of an orange plastic chair, she waited to be called to fill out forms. A crowd filled the waiting room, sitting or wandering to the phones and snack machines.

What was on the floor? Spots on the linoleum, starting at the entrance, blooming larger in a path to the swinging doors. A trail of red poppies. Some small, most large and smeared by shoes. Her stomach heaved. Probably Sharp's blood. People walked over the blood and spread it further. She closed her eyes and wished she was anywhere else.

"Sabine Sharp," the loudspeaker blared. "Cubicle number four." The woman behind the desk nodded and picked up a pen. Before she could ask questions, Sabine said she knew two people being treated in the ER. She opened Sol's wallet and gave the clerk his address and insurance information. She claimed he was her boyfriend.

Sharp would go to the OR for surgery, then to the ICU. No visiting unless she pretended to be a relative. She made Sharp her cousin, but said she didn't have his wallet. The clerk told her not to worry, a nurse would get his wallet and information.

"I don't have a pen." The clerk handed her a pen. Without a second thought, she signed a paper guaranteeing payment for Malcolm Sharp. *How can I pay for this?*

At the bottom of the page by the big X, she signed her name. Sabine Owen.

She stared at her signature. Owen. Her last name had just rolled out. Owen. Mother Elaine. Father Frederick. Her big brother Freddie. The facts had been there all along. Even 757!

The registration clerk cleared her throat and raised her voice, "So, is it Ms. Sharp? Or Ms. Owen?"

"Don't know why I said Sharp. Malcolm Sharp's my cousin and my last name's Owen. I'm so stressed."

The clerk nodded. "That's all the information I need. Thank you." Sabine's legs shook. At the emergency room door she rang the bell. An orderly led her to Sol's cubicle, where a nurse was bandaging him. He lay with his eyes closed while the nurse finished with the dressing. She left, and beyond the curtain Sabine listened to the nurse talking with the attending doctor. She told the doctor Sol's x-ray looked okay.

Sol opened his eyes. Maybe he recognized her, but he didn't say anything.

The nurse returned. "Mr. Henley, your wound's superficial. The doctor will be here in a minute. Do you have any questions?"

Sol nodded at the nurse. "Thanks. No questions."

After the nurse left, Sabine pulled a chair close to him and launched into a description of chasing the ambulances, exaggerating how she blared her horn nonstop at cars and pedestrians, dodged traffic, and ran red lights, like a stunt driver.

"Sabine. Thanks." He reached to take her hand, but his right arm was immobile. "Just imagine I'm holding your hand."

"Okay." Amazing what a gunfight could do. Mr. Straight-Laced had changed into Mr. Sweetie-Pie.

The attending doctor came in. "Mr. Henley, you won't need surgery, but you'll stay the night for observation. We've given you something to help you sleep. We've started you on a course of antibiotics. Please be sure to take them all. You also have a prescription for pain tablets when you leave. We'll get you into a bed as fast as possible."

"May I stay with him tonight?" Sabine asked, using her most polite smile.

The doctor nodded. "Certainly. The rooms have reclining chairs. Extra blankets are in the closet."

"Thanks a lot." Again, her best smile.

The doctor left.

"Sol, you're all right. It's just one night."

"I'm glad the doc said you could stay. Otherwise I'd make them." His laugh was giddy. "You're with me, I'll be fine."

Sabine followed as an orderly wheeled him to a room. Despite the beeping monitors and a tube in his arm, Sol fell asleep quickly.

The machines on the wall behind his bed illuminated the room with soft light. Too agitated to sleep, she gazed at the fluctuating numbers on the monitors. By now a surgeon might've finished operating on Sharp. They'd probably taken him right to the ICU; maybe he was on a machine to help him breathe.

Her last name. Her parents' names. And Freddie. And their faces were clear. She'd never been so exhausted.

☙

She jerked awake at dawn when a nurse came in to take Sol's blood pressure and give him pills in a small pleated cup. Sol barely roused, and as soon as the nurse left, he dozed off.

Awake, jittery, Sabine asked at the nurses' station where she could get coffee. The nurse showed her a little room with snacks, juice, and a coffee pot.

With a large cup of coffee caked with disgusting creamer, she went back to his room. The rattle of a meal cart came down the hall and a woman in blue brought in Sol's breakfast. Bleary-eyed, he tried to sit. Sabine hurried to help him.

"I'm hungry," Sol said.

"What can you recall?"

"I took my gun out of the backpack before we went to the castle," he said between bites of hard-boiled egg. "I put the gun in my belt. Nothing much after that."

"You never fired your gun. After you and Sharp were shot, I found your gun on the ground. The night watchman never saw it. I put it in the trunk of the Buick. Sol, are you listening? This is important: you never fired the gun."

He focused on the window. "I'm trying to understand. My head's jumbled."

"Shock. Trauma." She shook her head. This was all too familiar. "Tell me about it."

"What?" He gazed at her with a blank look.

"Nothing."

He held toast in his left hand; he opened a packet of grape jelly and spread it on the toast with his finger.

"The nurse said police will come and ask you questions. Before you're discharged. Tell the truth. We came to the castle to meet our friends. We weren't aware Sharp was going to come to the castle. Don't mention you even had a gun."

"It's true. We didn't think Sharp would be there."

"Eat your breakfast. I'm going to the cafeteria. Want me to bring you anything?"

He shook his head.

"Don't mention the gun."

On the elevator, her mind buzzed with all she had to do. More nauseated than hungry, she hurried through the line and avoided the eggs. She put dry toast, oatmeal, and bacon on her tray. She'd eat meals whether or not she wanted food. She paid with Sol's money, ate a few bites of toast, and threw the rest away. Then she took the elevator to the ICU.

A wall phone was by the swinging doors. A nurse answered and said she had ten minutes for a visit before buzzing her in. Sharp's room was number seven.

She paused at Sharp's door, intimidated by the tubes and machines. Trying to the turn the machines' sounds into something else. Oh, to be back at the farm lying in the field, listening to the rhythmic ticking of small insects buried in the grass, enlivened by the sun.

Sharp's eyes were closed, his face pale. A thin oxygen tube curved over his ears.

"Sharp?" she whispered. "It's Sabine. You're going to be okay. Sol's right downstairs in a room. He'll be okay too. They're only letting me stay a few minutes."

Should she touch him? Finally she moved close enough to touch his hand. And jerked back. His hand felt warm and limp. His fingernails were ragged and chewed. Had his nails been bitten up when they talked on the beach? She couldn't recall. At the farm he'd acted confident, at times serene, surely not a nail-biter. But back then she'd seen him from a distance.

She pulled a chair close to the bed so he could hear her. She fixed her eyes on his hand.

Images flooded in: constantly clicking machines. The small white crib dwarfed by the large room. A baby hidden under tubes. The somber doctor, the crying woman, the crying man. Unable to stand the noise, she watched the little girl run out of the room and flatten herself against a wall. The girl tried to catch her breath. The baby's name was not Mick. The baby in the crib was a tiny, red newborn, born years before Mick. The crying people, her parents: Elaine and Frederick Owen. The crying child, herself. When she wrote "The Bone Woman's Tale," the familiar baby was clear. "Briefly you flew among people, your hair glowed like dawn light.

But the light could not last." She'd been ten years old; she felt ten all over again.

A nurse stood over her. "Ms. Owen. Time's up. You're welcome to visit again after three today."

Sabine dried her face on Jude's jacket sleeve, but the jacket gave no comfort. "Thank you. If he wakes, please tell him Sabine was here. I'll come later."

When the elevator opened, a policemen and a man wearing shiny shoes stepped out. They headed toward the ICU doors, on their way to question Sharp.

In the elevator, she longed to ride to the first floor, walk out, leave this hospital, and all hospitals, forever. *Buy a bathing suit and towel. Go to the beach, watch the ocean, and don't think about anything.*

When she got to his room, he was sitting up, alert.

"The police had some questions. The nurse said I'll be discharged as soon as they give me some papers. I can't wear these clothes." He held up a plastic bag with blood-splattered jeans and a bloody shirt. "A nurse cut my shirt off when they brought me in."

Sabine tossed his shirt in a trash can. "Put on the jeans. And your jacket. I'll wait in the hall." She paced the hall, unable to calm down. *Get Sol settled. Visit Sharp later. Go alone to the castle tonight and hope to God everybody will be there.*

At the nurses' station, she asked about Sol's discharge instructions. A clerk said they were waiting for the doctor to sign them. Probably twenty more minutes.

Sol sat by the window, fully dressed.

"You're not as pasty as before," she said. "How do you feel?"

"My arm hurts when I move it. I'll have to come back to the clinic here, in a few days."

She sat on the edge of the bed and moved until their knees nearly touched. "How did it go with the police?"

"You and I went to meet our friends from West Virginia, unaware Sharp would be there. You and I drove down here to start a new life.

I didn't mention a gun. The police asked where I was from and I told them. They didn't stay long."

"Soon as the discharge papers come, they'll put you in a wheelchair and take you to the entrance. You wait while I get the car. We'll drive to the pharmacy, then the campground."

"You're taking care of me," he said.

"You took care of me. We're friends."

"Just friends?" When he looked at her, she felt her neck turning red. Before she could answer, a nurse brought discharge papers and two prescriptions. An orderly appeared in the doorway with a wheelchair.

On her way to get the car, she glanced back at Sol, sitting on a concrete bench. He looked thin and forlorn as he waved with his left arm. She was taken over by an image of Sol as an old man. Her eyes burned and she wasn't exactly sure why. A sort of tenderness for him.

Her face felt wet, she sat in the Buick trying to collect herself. The sun shone and beaches were nearby. Sol was fine, and Sharp would be fine too. Jude's jacket lay on the backseat. She felt in a pocket for Kleenex and pulled out a red bandana. Sharp's bandana. Stiff with dried blood. She pushed it back in the pocket and started the engine.

She helped Sol maneuver into the car. He was clumsy; she put on his seat belt for him. "The nurse gave me directions to the closest pharmacy. You haven't asked about Sharp."

"Sharp. How's he doing?"

"I only visited a few minutes. They took out the bullets. He's stable. Let's hope the farm folks show up tonight."

"Oh shit. We have to go back to the castle." Sol patted his jacket pockets. "Cigarettes?"

"We'll buy some." The sun disappeared, the sky grew thick with dark clouds. "Would you look at that? Three minutes ago the sun was shining. It's gonna pour."

"I wish we were back at the farm," he said. "I want an ordinary life."

"Things are bad if you think our farm life was ordinary." She laughed and turned on the windshield wipers. "I can't face sleeping on wet ground, or in the car. Your arm needs to heal. Do you have enough money for a night in a motel?"

"Two nights, if it's cheap. I'll call my folks and ask them to wire money."

"They'll be happy to hear you're okay." She wouldn't tell him about discovering her last name, or talk about 757.

In the pharmacy parking lot she told him, "Wait here, I'll get prescriptions and cigarettes."

"You have my wallet?"

She nodded.

"Good. A new toothbrush and toothpaste? Shaving cream and a razor? I'm sick of this mess." He rubbed his scraggly beard.

She dropped off the prescriptions and zipped down the aisles. She had no idea which shaving cream and razors to buy; she made quick decisions based on the packages, choosing the ones with the handsomest men. She bought a carton of cigarettes, picked up the prescriptions. She passed a newspaper rack on the way out and scanned the front page of the local paper. Nothing about shootings at the castle. Then she noticed the paper was three days old.

In the car she said, "Let's find Sharp's Jeep and get the sat phone." Rain pounded the roof and the wind picked up. She drove slowly around the castle until she spotted the Jeep. She pulled up alongside it, helped Sol out of the Buick and into the Jeep, then ran back to the Buick. Dripping wet, she closed her eyes and tried to empty her crowded mind.

Twenty minutes later Sol tapped the window and stumbled into the car, drenched. He held up the phone. "Everything's fine with my parents. There's a Western Union here. They'll send money on a prepaid credit card. We can pick it up tonight or tomorrow."

"Were they upset? It has been over two months."

"Dad was pissed, and Mom cried. I couldn't get off the phone till I promised to call again in three days. I said nothing about Kate and Hank. I told them about Jude and asked them to find Jude's dad."

"You have enough money for a few nights at a motel, then?"

"Yes."

"Then let's check out of the campground. Just think, a motel. Luxuries any time we want."

Palm trees thrashed in the wind. The windshield wipers couldn't keep up with the torrent. She drove slowly. At their campsite, she said, "I should've gotten the sat phone for you. Anyway, you shouldn't get your bandages any wetter. Stay here." Before he could argue, she jumped out of the car. She snatched towels, clothes, and sleeping bags off the picnic table and dumped them all in the trunk. At Sharp's site, the tent stakes pulled up easily. With the tent flat on the ground, she threw the stakes and Sharp's soggy sleeping bag in the middle. She rolled up the tent and shoved it onto the backseat.

"You're speedy," Sol said when she jumped in the Buick.

"Sharp travels as light as we do."

By early afternoon they'd found a motel room with two double beds. The walls were an ugly shade of green and the room smelled like pine air freshener, but the air conditioner worked. They brought their packs to the room and Sol put on a clean shirt. Only a drizzle was left from the storm, so they walked to a nearby burger place. They devoured greasy fried flounder, fries, and salads with iceberg lettuce and shredded, stick-hard carrots.

"You look tired," she said.

"But I haven't done anything. It's only lunchtime."

"You were shot. With a bullet. From a gun. Let's go back to the motel."

In the room she flipped on the TV in search of news. The local news didn't mention the shooting at the castle, only a story about Miami's bomb cleanup. Fish and dolphins still dying at the Seaquarium. Volunteers were working with the birds and mammals at Zoo Miami. More people were needed to care for the surviving animals.

A news ticker crawled across the bottom of the screen, 20,000 estimated dead from the bombs in Miami and surrounding areas, and similar numbers around Minneapolis, Chicago, and Detroit. Numbers closer to 50,000 for DC, the Los Angeles area, and New York City. Volunteers had stopped looking for survivors long ago. Now they searched for bodies.

CNN national news came on. Her hope turned to misery when a reporter said at least 25,000 people had died from the flu and other airborne diseases. The numbers clustered around Chicago and New York City. So far.

She clicked off the TV and lay on the bed thinking about dying people, sea animals, and Sun Dog. That day on the road she chased the dog away, the fault of her muddled mind. Sun Dog could be playing with Gun and the Labs now. Ridiculous. She was ten when she played with Sun Dog at the hospital.

Unable to comprehend so many deaths, she grew numb and sleepy and made herself slide under the covers. Rain drowned out the air conditioner, but it couldn't drown out the terror.

Warm and cozy, she woke with Sol's arm lying across her stomach. He lay on his back, close to her. What was he doing in her bed? What did most men want when they got in your bed? She tried to move away but was too tangled in the sheets. The curtains were thick and she couldn't see if it was light outside. The air conditioner still roared and the rain had stopped.

She lifted Sol's arm off her stomach and inched her way to the edge of the bed.

Sol grimaced. "Oh God. Time for a pain pill. What time is it?"

"Five. We slept all afternoon." She brought the pill with a glass of water.

He swallowed the pill and patted the bed. "Come sit by me. I want to talk."

"I told the nurse I'd come back to see Sharp."

"This won't take long."

She sat at his feet.

"This isn't good timing," he said, "but the shooting at the castle shocked me into seeing what's important. You probably know how I feel, because I'm not a cool guy. I tried not to like you back at the farm. You were Jude's girl, which was obvious pretty quickly. And you made it clear you couldn't stand me. After Jude was killed— well, not immediately after, but when you started asking if I was excited to get to St. Augustine, I wondered why I wasn't. And now I know why. I wanted you. Only us, together."

She took an audible breath. "Oh, Sol. You're right, at the farm-house, you mostly irritated me. But after all that driving together, under bad circumstances, learning about you . . . I see more of who you are now. I trust you."

"I think I can trust you not to tell me lies," he said. "I hope you're done with lies."

"Here's a truth," she said. "I loved Jude."

"I can't believe I'm saying this," he said. "But part of the reason why—the baby. You're going to need help. You don't have a job, and we don't know yet if we even have a place to live. We all hope we'll have a place, but if Sharp's information is right, the crisis isn't over, and we're still in survival mode."

"I try not to look too far ahead," she said. "My thinking could get muddy again. I want to focus on the baby, but thinking about a baby feels like a luxury. I can't wait to settle down, find a doctor."

"If you eat right and sleep enough, the baby should be fine." He gave her a friendly pat on her leg. "I'm a good planner. Once I make up my mind, I rarely change it. When Dad asked me how much money to send, I'd planned to say $700, but $5,000 came out of my mouth." He frowned. "That's when Dad said I should be home, packing for UVa. The ten thousand in my account is money I'd saved from my pizza job for living expenses and books."

"Ten thousand dollars?" Sabine's eyes widened. "That's a lot of pizzas. I've been preoccupied, worrying about survival for myself. And for you, and the others. I forgot you were supposed to start school. You're throwing away the opportunity?"

"Thing are different now." He sighed. "Whatever happens, I want to stay with you. You don't want to live in the mountains, so we'll stay in St. Augustine, as long as it's safe. Or go somewhere else."

"Sol . . ." She didn't know what to say.

"If you'd told Jude you were pregnant, he'd have asked you to marry him the same day."

"We have no idea how it would've turned out between me and Jude," she said. "I don't want to marry anyone, if that's what you want. I need time to figure things out. I want to work, to be of use."

He face sagged, but he didn't look at her.

"All I'm sure of is keeping the baby."

"A yes to staying with me would be the best answer." His voice trembled. "You miss Jude. Still, I had to tell you how I felt."

❧

A middle-aged nurse wearing glasses greeted Sabine at the ICU doors and led her into a small office. "I'm Claire Cooper, head nurse. I'd like to ask some questions." She sat behind the desk. "Take a seat."

The wooden chair hurt Sabine's back; she shifted and waited for Claire to say something.

"Ms. Owen, are you Mr. Sharp's cousin?"

"Actually, I'm not. I said that so I could visit him. You wouldn't have let me in otherwise, and he doesn't have anyone else."

Claire steepled her hands. The fluorescent lights reflected off her glasses and hid her eyes. "To your knowledge, does he have any living relatives?"

"His mother lives in Colorado, but he never told me her last name. She's been married a few times. She and he don't talk. I'm guessing he wouldn't want her notified. No sisters, and his only brother died recently."

When Claire listened, her face lost its animation and fell into lines of sadness. No wonder. In the ICU, she must watch people struggle and die day after day.

"Mr. Sharp refused to give us information about his mother, or anyone. We have to operate again, but he has refused permission."

"I'll give permission." Sabine put her hands together to stop them from shaking. "What's wrong?"

"He's bleeding internally, in his stomach. He's young and strong. With this surgery, he'll probably do fine—but we need to move quickly."

"May I visit? I'll try to talk him into it."

"He's awake. I appreciate your honesty, Ms. Owen."

"Sorry I lied about being related to him, but I'm familiar with ICU rules."

"I understand."

Sharp's room was still noisy with machines beeping and clicking. His eyes were closed, but he had color in his face.

"Hi there." She moved to his bed.

His eyes flew open. "So, cousin, you came."

"Think we'd make good cousins? I had no choice. I guess I could've called you my husband or brother, but you and Sol were both here. It all happened so fast."

"It's cool. How are you doing?"

"Freaked," she said. "By the gunfight and the race to the hospital. But the worst is spending time in hospitals. They aren't my favorite places. Thanks for letting Sol use your sat phone. We have the phone with us, hope that's okay."

"Fine." He shifted his position and grimaced.

"Sol's parents were relieved to hear from him. Thank you." She touched his hand.

"Glad to help. I need a favor from you. I told you about Celestial wrecking the farmhouse looking for something? And they didn't find what they wanted? I left some papers there. Not smart to bring them to St. Augustine. When you go back to the farm, make two copies. Put one set in a manila envelope and mail it to the editor of *The New York Times*. The other set goes to the *Washington Post's* editor. The return address should read Hank Johnson at the farm address. You'll do that?"

"But I'm not going back to the farmhouse."

"Someone will go back. Swear you'll find someone to copy and mail those papers. They're Hank's evidence against Celestial. It's not much to ask."

"What if someone has already found them?"

"The Celestial guys aren't as smart as they think. The papers are in a dead drop spike, a few inches under the ground in the northeast corner of the garden. The broccoli patch. Along with some documents and the deed to the house. I hope one of the farm people will want the house and keep the deed. If there's anything left after refugee gangs get through with it. Supposing deeds still mean anything anymore."

"Once you're well, you'll want the farmhouse." She tried to get him to look at her, but he wouldn't.

"In my Jeep there's a big metal box. The key to the box is on the key ring I gave Sol. My duffel bag is in the metal box and in the duffel there's a wad of money. Take the money and the Jeep. Celestial followed me, so there's got to be another GPS, or a bug, still hidden on the Jeep. Most likely the underside. Get rid of it before you drive it."

"I don't want your money, or the Jeep," Sabine said. "I'll keep your stuff safe till you're out of here, though. Your tent's on the backseat of the Buick Sol and I are driving. It was raining like crazy, so I checked us out of the campground. I'll air out your tent soon as I get time. I'll search the Jeep and get rid of anything identifying you too. You have guns in there?"

"Hank and I brought fifteen rifles and fifteen shotguns when we left DC," Sharp whispered. "I ditched some on the way down, but I have a few." He yawned. "Sorry, my gut hurts. The cops were here and tired me out." His forehead dripped with sweat. "They took the bullets from my surgery and one of my guns. Scratched their heads when I told them my gun was registered to Celestial. Guess they didn't figure me as the military contractor type."

His eyes fluttered, closed, and he appeared to sleep. Then he jerked awake. "I'm so tired."

"You have to get that surgery," she said. "People in ICU get infections. Your insides are leaking. You want to get out of here healthy."

"No. I don't."

"You could tell the police the whole story. I'll help you get away from Celestial. Do more than abandoning the Jeep and changing your name. You could disappear in this town. The key is to cut people off. You've already done that with your mother. Stop being predictable—change driving routes, where you live and work, your clothes. Pay cash. Blend in."

"Giving the cops information about Celestial is a terrible idea. I gotta admit, though, you make disappearing sound easy."

"Almost three years ago I fought with my parents and brother and swore I'd never see them again. When the bombs came, my memory already had a few blanks. Yesterday in the ER my last name slid out. I'm Sabine Owen."

"It's good to know who you are," he said. "Your family?"

"We lived in Richmond and had a cottage in Sandbridge Beach. Or did before the bombs. The paper said two bombs exploded in Richmond. My brother Freddie's older and my parents are in their sixties."

"Freddie's married?"

"No idea. He used to date a girl named Margaret. Why do you wanna know?"

"Just curious. You've been gone almost three years? That's impressive. At the farm, I wondered about the mysterious woman from DC. Disappearing is a skill."

"You gotta give up a lot. Apparently, I willed even my surname to disappear. But my name sat in my brain waiting to return. Owen. Owen. Owen."

"It's easy to disappear, if you have nothing to lose." He closed his eyes and his face lost its animation.

"You have a lot to live for, Sharp."

"If only. Mother should've let me stay in West Virginia with Hank. Jimbo would've taken me in. I could've grown up with Hank and had grandparents, even."

"All of us at the farm," she said, "we helped each other. Except for Paul each of us chose to take a risk and drive to St. Augustine. To build something together. Does that mean anything to you?" Her throat felt thick.

A long silence—then, finally, "No."

Her face filled with heat. "I don't believe you. Damn it, Sharp! You must decide why your life means something. You're grieving for Hank and the childhood you didn't have. But you can move on."

"You were quiet at the farm, till you smacked Tommy—which amused me, by the way. You've turned into a feisty bitch."

"You ain't seen nothing yet," she said, pitching her voice low and mean. "Tomorrow, I expect you to be in this bed, all groggy from surgery." She pointed to the bed. "You need a Sun Dog to cuddle."

"Huh?"

"My pretend dog. When I was a kid, he arrived outside the hospital to comfort me while something bad dragged on and on. Later, he showed up on the road to the farm, but I chased him away."

"Along with feisty you're still a bit crazy, Sabine Owen." He closed his eyes.

She picked up his hand and shook it. "Open your eyes. Look at me."

He opened his eyes to slits.

"See you tomorrow. And I mean it. Please be groggy from surgery." She stomped out of the room and waved to Claire, who was in the nurses' station. Sabine waited by the nurse's office door. Claire strode over. "So?"

"It didn't go well," Sabine said. "I tried to talk him into surgery, but he's hell-bent on refusing. He needs a psychiatrist. He doesn't have anything to live for. His father committed suicide. If there's an emergency, I'm in room 202 at the Starlight Motel."

Claire made notes. "I'll make sure the nurses release information to you. Thank you, Ms. Owen."

❧

Sol was watching the news when she unlocked the door. He clicked off the TV, his forehead wrinkled. "Hey. How's Sharp?"

"His gut's bleeding, but he's refusing more surgery, says he has nothing to live for," she said, stomping in. "He lost Hank. I suppose since his father killed himself, he thinks suicide's a good way out."

"I can't imagine," Sol said. "I've been thinking about how you stayed with me. You could've gone off on your own. You're strong enough. Are you in love with Sharp?"

"What?"

"Forget it," he said.

"You're kidding. No, your frown says you're not. Sharp's beautiful to look at. He's like a big hunk of cake with caramel frosting. Easy to climb in bed with and gobble right up. But after the cake and frosting, all that sweet on the lips, comes bitterness."

"Got it. Okay, let's eat, then go to Western Union. I have the address."

After dinner in a deli filled with loud music and people, they drove to Western Union. Sabine waited in the car. Sol came out smiling. "Got the credit card and some cash. I'll open a bank account soon as we have a real address."

She parked a block from the castle. "You're wiped out. It's nearly eight. I'm tired, too. Stay here. I won't wait for the farm folks but a few minutes."

"I don't like you going alone." He touched her arm.

"I'll run if I have to. I'll stay on the sidewalk and won't cross the bridge."

He tapped the clock on the dashboard. "If you're not back in fifteen minutes, I'm coming after you."

"Okay." She jumped out of the car, thinking it felt nice to have someone care whether or not she died. No one had for a long time until Jude.

The castle loomed dark, and the streetlights and moon cast eerie shadows. Just beyond the castle, she spotted a blue truck. She squinted and read the license plates. West Virginia. Tommy's rolling gait, walking toward the castle with five other people. A kid with red hair. Paul! How did they find Paul?

Sabine ran to them. "Hey, everybody!"

Lavinia pointed. "Look. There's Sabine!"

PART
SIX

Chapter 21

PLANTING MOON

August 4, 2014.

Sabine led them to the Buick. Sol eased out of the car smiling, and grimaced when Jen hugged him with gusto.

"You made it! How are you doing?" Sabine asked.

"Where's Jude? Out getting drunk?" Tommy chuckled.

Her throat tightened. "Sol?"

Sol leaned against the Buick. His eyes drooped—exhaustion and pain. In a tired voice he said, "We were getting ready to camp in a field by a road, when out of nowhere some lunatic shot Jude. We never got a look at the shooter."

Paul's cheeks flushed red. He threw his hands over his face.

"My God! Oh God," Randolph muttered. He took Lavinia's hand. Lavinia hung her head.

"Goddamn!" Jen yelled. "The world has turned to shit."

Tommy gagged and hurried to some bushes. Sabine considered going after him, but left him alone. She'd hate for someone to watch her throw up. Tommy moved slowly back to the group, his face ashen. He leaned against Paul's shoulder, and Paul patted his back.

"Episcopalians say the twenty-third psalm at funerals," Randolph said. "We're sheep in dire need of a shepherd. We humans have made a mess; this catastrophe could be the end."

Sabine held her breath, not allowing herself to cry.

"Where are the dogs?" Sol asked.

"Little Gun's napping on my jacket in the front seat of the truck, but we lost the Labs," Randolph said. "On the way down, we let them swim in a pond to exercise and cool off. We were out stretching our legs, waiting for the dogs to tire out, when suddenly, gunfire. Both Labs fell. Gun was on a leash. I picked him up, and we scrambled behind the truck."

"While we argued about whether to bury the dogs, a man and a kid came out of the woods and fished them out of the water."

"What for?" Sabine asked.

"To eat them," Jen said.

Randolph took off his glasses, wiped them on his shirt, and set them on his nose. "Yes, Jen, you're correct. I just don't want to believe it." The trip had aged him; dark smudges were under his eyes, and his hands trembled.

To keep from crying, Sabine changed the subject. "Sol and I are staying at a nice motel. The Starlight. We'll hope for vacancies. If they don't have any, you all can bring sleeping bags to our room. Follow us?"

She and Sol led the way. Randolph strode into the motel lobby and came out a few minutes later with both thumbs up. He and Lavinia took a room with two double beds, Tommy and Paul took another room. Sabine stared at her shoes while they discussed where Jen, who had no money, would sleep. No one offered to take her in, or pay for her room.

Sabine didn't want loud-mouthed Jen in their room. Sol's eyes were closed; he leaned against the car, half asleep. After an awkward silence, Lavinia offered Jen the other double bed in her and Randolph's room. Jen put her arm around Lavinia and squeezed her shoulder. Lavinia giggled and turned red. Randolph jammed his hands in his pocket and said nothing.

Lavinia picked Gun up off the front seat of the truck and wrapped him in her sweater.

Randolph sighed loudly. "No, Lala. This is not a pet-friendly motel."

"Don't Lala me! I'll keep him close and zip through the lobby. Nobody will notice."

"Let's meet for breakfast and catch up?" Tommy said.

Randolph glared at Lavinia. "Damn it, Lala, the dog will be fine in the truck."

"Fuck off, Randolph. Stop bossing me around." Lavinia marched toward the rear lobby door with Jen close behind.

"Good plan," Sol said to Tommy. "Let's meet in the lobby tomorrow at nine. Sabine and I will take you to The Generic Pancake Place."

In the lobby Sabine checked the date before she bought the last newspaper in the rack. She held Sol's good arm as they walked to their room. Sol fell on the bed and closed his eyes. She gave him a pain pill, relieved he hadn't lain down on the bed she'd chosen. No one had asked about Sharp, or what happened to Sol's arm. They must've assumed that Sharp had stayed at the farm.

She didn't turn on the TV. On the front page of the morning paper, she read that gang members had been arrested at five truck stops along the Florida interstates. All of the men and the few women had a red rose tattooed on their right hands. A larger gang of about a hundred had been discovered operating in south Florida. National Guardsmen had arrested a few of the men when they attacked residents still trying to escape Miami. The arrests had led them to a warehouse stockpiled with stolen food and water, guns, ammunition, cars, and car parts. The Guardsmen and the gang had fought over the warehouse food and guns. The Guardsmen won.

Sol slept soundly. She called the ICU. The nurse said Sharp was still refusing surgery and would have a psych consult in the morning. If he was found mentally competent and still refused surgery, they couldn't operate.

ॐ

August 5, 2014.

At the Generic Pancake Place, everyone squeezed into a round booth.

"Somewhere in South Carolina," Tommy said, "after the dogs died, a car came up, practically on our bumper. I floored it and the truck rattled till I thought it would fall apart. Randolph watched out the back window and saw a tire fly off the car chasing us. The kind of thing that only happens in movies."

"Yep, like a movie." Randolph scowled. "Quite harrowing. I thought we were goners."

Tommy's face fell. His hand was unsteady when he took a swig of water. His jeans hung loose and his face looked different, gaunt. The effort to tell stories and make people laugh was draining him. Perhaps he'd discovered that humor couldn't ease deep pain.

"Stay vigilant. Every minute," Randolph said in a stern voice. "Those people killed the dogs in seconds."

Sabine thought about Jude in the field.

Lavinia shot Randolph a nasty look. "Let's call Gunther by his real name, not 'Gun.' I'm sick of guns. Gunther's a noble name."

Jen sat on one side of Lavinia. She laid her hand on Lavinia's arm and said, "I used to love messing with guns and hunting. Now it's a job that must be done." Lavinia smiled at Jen. Lavinia had traded her long skirt for jeans and a blue cowgirl shirt with mother-of-pearl buttons. For the first time, Sabine noticed that her eyes were sky blue.

"I've seen enough guns to last a lifetime," Sabine said. "I'm a crappy shot and I don't care. If guns are the future—well, I hope they're not."

The waitress brought their orders: plates piled with sausage and eggs, cups of coffee, glasses of water and juice. The abundance made Sabine's eyes well up.

Lavinia picked up a piece of toast, spread margarine on it, and nibbled with reluctance, but not revulsion. She sipped the orange juice.

The food riots in northern cities worried Sabine, but so far there were no reports of riots in the Mid-Atlantic or the South. There were more farms in the South, and the weather was warmer. If cities were bombed again, riots would spread. If Lavinia bothered to read the news, she'd discover people were experiencing hunger, and not by choice. Would the information change her deliberate starvation?

Jen took a link sausage off her own plate, patted it with a napkin, and put it under Lavinia's nose. In a soft voice, she said, "Here, try this. I got the grease off. "

Lavinia took a tentative bite, then another. "That's good. In a minute, I'll finish it." Lavinia laid the sausage carefully on her own plate and edged toward Jen until their shoulders touched.

"Lavinia's going to give me riding lessons," Jen said, "so we can ride together. There's a lot of horse breeding in Florida."

Covertly, Sabine studied Randolph, who sat on Lavinia's other side. He appeared intent on talking with Paul, but Sabine wondered if he was eavesdropping on Lavinia. He must be trying his best to ignore what was unfolding between Lavinia and Jen.

Jen was beaming. "You guys are gloomy. I'll tell you a happy story about Paul! We were on the road when he called my cell because things hadn't worked out. He wanted to come with us. I said we were already on the road and I'd call back after we discussed it. We stopped the truck so the guys in the back could get in the conversation. Randolph said yes right away. We all voted to turn around and get him. I told Paul to hang tight. 'Make your mom give you money and fix you something to eat.' That's what I told him."

"My big secret." Paul sighed. "Mom left Dad and me a long time ago. After the bombs, I worried I'd never see her again, so I made Dad give me her address. When I left the farmhouse, I hitched and walked till I found her house. Dad warned me she had a boyfriend and two little kids. I was two years old when she left me and Dad. She wasn't glad to see me. She let me spend the night, but told me I had to get on my way soon. When I asked why, she kept staring at the sofa. Finally she said, 'Your showing up's an ugly surprise. Got me a new man and a whole new life here.' Nothing to say to that, huh? After I called Jen I sat on the porch and looked at the mountains wondering why my dad picked such a mean, ugly woman. I didn't say good-bye."

"We backtracked almost a hundred miles to get him," Randolph said. "A fuel challenge, but worth it." He nudged Paul, who broke into a grin. "Found him curled up in a ditch, on the lookout for our truck."

"We're happy he's back." Tommy smoothed his mustache and looked around the table.

Paul's eyes shone. "Pop always called my mother a she-devil and said I'd be better off living with him and Grandpa. Meeting you guys made me a lucky guy!" His face was more freckled from the sun, and his red hair looked shaggy. Kate used to cut his hair.

A shudder went through Sabine as she thought about the terrible words she'd shouted at Freddie and her parents on the way home from the airport. The helpless panic she'd felt knowing that ahead of their car, a hearse carried Mick's body from the airport to the funeral home.

The restaurant clock read ten. She crumpled her napkin. "Couple nights ago, there was a shooting at the castle. Sol was shot. So was Sharp. He's here, in St. Augustine, in intensive care."

"Sharp's here? In the hospital? How's he doing?" Jen's eyes widened. Paul and Tommy were open-mouthed. Randolph, glaring at Lavinia, paid no attention to the news.

"Not good," Sabine said. "He got shot; had surgery, but he needs more, and he's refusing."

"Can I go see him?" Jen frowned.

"Sure." Sabine smiled. "I pretended to be his cousin to get into ICU. Let's talk about it later."

"Another thing," Sabine said. "The O'Malleys. Sol and I thought two people should break the news. What do you think, Tommy?"

"Tell us about the O'Malleys," Sol said.

Tommy crossed his arms. "Last summer Kate and I stayed with them about ten days. They're old, the grandfather's losing his memory. Sabine's right, only one of you should come with me. They adored Kate and her death will be a horrible shock."

"Sol's a good choice," Sabine said.

Tommy's eyebrows went up. "Sol? Okay, if that's all right with him."

"Sabine and I had planned to go," Sol said. "But the shootings changed things. Here's a quick rundown of what happened when Sabine and I got to the castle."

∾

The nurse who let Sabine into the ICU barely glanced at her. Harried and distracted, the nurses and orderlies were moving furniture and equipment into the hall, apparently setting up a patient's room for a procedure. Sabine hoped the room was for Sharp. If so, she'd have to talk fast.

Sharp sat in bed staring at the wall.

"How you doing?" She stood in the doorway, uncertain.

"Sane and competent. The doc told me that, so it must be true. Come on in."

She chose a chair near his bed. "Everybody's here and we're all staying at the Starlight Motel. We met at the castle last night. And Paul's back!"

Sharp smiled. "Glad to hear it. He's a good kid."

"Turns out he was looking for his mother who abandoned him."

"Don't tell me. His mother has a new family and doesn't give a shit about him." Sharp smirked.

"Yes, about right. He's a lovable kid. His deepest secret turned out to be the one he kept from himself."

"What do you mean?"

"Paul figured she wouldn't have left him if she loved him. Thought it was his fault, like maybe he was unlovable. He was only two years old when she took off."

"Even after Dad killed himself, I knew he wanted me," Sharp said. "He loved me even when he was drinking, after the motorcycle accident changed him. His friend died. Dad got a concussion and a broken leg. Out of the hospital, he drank himself to sleep. After showing up drunk at work and calling in sick, he lost his job. His nightmares got so loud you could hear him holler all over the house. Finally, Mom pushed him in the car and drove him to the psych hospital. They kept him a month. The doctor told Mom it was a stress reaction—Dad felt responsible for his friend's death."

Sabine nodded.

"When Dad had a nightmare, I'd sit with him. He'd light up the backyard with floodlights, his eyes darting to the window. He'd say, 'Don't worry, son, I'm a little keyed up is all,' and he'd light a cigarette and talk with the cigarette hanging out his mouth. Finally he'd say, 'I took some of those pills the doc gave me. Get on to bed, son. You got school.'"

"Did he ever talk about his nightmares?" Sabine asked.

Sharp shook his head. "Said he had no memory of the accident, or the nightmares when he woke up. One morning he was gone, no note, backpack on the closet floor. He always took his backpack. Soon as Mom saw the backpack, she called the cops.

"Mom wasn't there when I got home from school. Then she was walking slowly up the stairs, unusual for her. Before she got to my bedroom door, I knew.

"She said, 'I just identified your father's body. The police found him on the Blue Ridge Parkway. Behind the wheel, at an overlook.'"

"I'm so sorry," Sabine said, lost for words.

"I'd just turned nine. Things dragged on before he killed himself, then things changed fast. Nothing's safe."

She looked at the floor.

"Paul's everybody's kid brother." Sharp gazed out the window, where there was nothing to see besides another wing of the hospital.

Sabine touched his arm. "Paul called Jen. They all agreed to turn around and drove a hundred miles to get him." Her eyes lit up. "When's your surgery?"

"No surgery," he said, looking down at her hand. "They're discharging me. AMA, against medical advice. Soon as they finish doing whatever they're doing in the room across the hall."

"You won't have surgery?"

"No point. What's the name of your motel again?"

"The Starlight. Sol and I are in room 202."

Sharp raised his eyebrows. "Oh, really?" A brief smile.

"It's nothing like that. Sol and I are just friends. We got to know each other on the trip. We've been through a lot. I see him differently now. Please have the surgery and then come to the motel and rest up. I'll get you a room, or you can stay with me and Sol."

A young doctor with a harried expression appeared at the door. Sharp asked Sabine, "Can you come back later?"

"Sure. Sometime this afternoon." What else could she say? She had no leverage. Creeping into her gut, more than frustration, was the fear of what Sharp would do after being discharged. He probably wouldn't be at the hospital when she came back.

❧

Sabine wanted to talk about Sharp, but Sol wasn't in the motel room. His note on her pillow said he and Tommy were going to talk with the O'Malleys. A fifty-dollar bill lay next to the note. His generosity made her smile. What could she buy him?

She washed Sharp's bandana in cold water and soap, then stuck it wet in her pocket. By eleven thirty she was at the beach, lying close enough to the ocean to hear surf lapping the sand. She spread out the bandana on the towel, close to her. The bathing suit fit fine, though soon it wouldn't accommodate her growing belly. She drank water, ate a ham sandwich and an apple. She napped then crossed the sand to the noisy ocean. Even choppy and gray she loved the familiar feel. With the sea as background, images flashed like a

movie. Her trek to the farm, the three of them driving to Florida
to start a new life. Jude bleeding in the field. Sleeping in the motel
room with Sol. His willingness to let go of college plans after working hard. His petty complaints, his kindnesses. He still surprised her.
She liked surprises.

A woman strolling by gave her the time—1:24. Sabine folded
the bandana into a small square, put it in her jeans pocket, and
drove to the motel. She washed her hair twice. While toweling off
she noticed a blinking light on the phone. A message from the desk
clerk, saying someone had left a letter for Sabine Owen. She halfway dried her hair, slipped on a shirt and jeans. Hurrying to the
lobby, her heart revved up. Had something happened to Sol? But
if something had happened she wouldn't get a letter. She couldn't
think.

At the desk, a young girl handed her an envelope. "Sabine
Owen, Room 202," was printed in large block letters across the front.

Sabine sat in a wingback chair near the front desk. Inside the
envelope, a single sheet of paper read:

Sabine,

When I was a kid Dad and Mother took me to the beach
every summer. The best times were on the beach. This was
before he died, before Mother dragged me to Colorado.

Please get rid of the GPS and search for another bug on
the Jeep.

I've done things that can't be forgiven. I can't forgive
myself. I'm tired.

Thank you, dear Sabine.

Good-bye.

Sharp

Sabine walked outside with the urge to hop in the car and go,
perhaps to search for Sharp, or drive around and calm down. It
wasn't until she stood by the Buick that she realized she had nothing

besides a room key and Sharp's note. Back in the room she paced, thoughts flying and disconnected. She turned on the desk lamp, opened her notebook, and wrote until she couldn't write any more. Then she closed the notebook and waited for something to happen.

Sometime later—she couldn't tell how long it had been—the door opened. She yawned and realized she'd dozed off.

Sol stood over the bed. "Hey. How's it going?" He rocked on his feet, energized, smiling.

"Look." She pointed to Sharp's note on the bedside table.

Sol read it and dropped it on the bed.

"No surprise, Sharp's mixed up. I'm not touching his Jeep—Celestial tracked him in that thing, and we sure don't want to get mixed up with them. But we should get the money."

"The box is for you." She pointed to the bedside table.

"Salt water taffy." Sol smiled. "I haven't had taffy but once, when I was a kid. Thanks."

"Thanks for the money. I bought a bathing suit and towel. Maybe I should've bought you a suit?"

He glanced at the desk. "I'll buy a suit as soon as things settle down. Writing in your notebook? You haven't done that in a while."

"Things keep moving fast," she said. "I hardly have time to think, much less write. Sharp was struggling, but I didn't think he'd kill himself." She sniffed back tears.

"You were good to him," Sol said.

"I didn't do enough. Don't give me credit. I'm just trying to undo how I treated Giles. Besides, it's easier to be kind to a man you aren't intimate with. Kinda weird, huh?"

Sol sat beside her. "Come here." He edged closer and took her face in his hands. "Look at me. Things will get better. You're going to have a baby." He kissed her lightly on the lips. "I should apologize for the kiss, but I won't." His laugh came out as a titter.

"You look happy, which means the O'Malley visit must have gone well, right? I want to hear. But I need to sleep a few more minutes." The bed moved with Sol's shifting weight. The door opened and closed.

❧

Sabine looked at the clock when she woke and saw that she'd slept an hour. She drank three big cups of water and went to the lobby, where Sol sat reading a newspaper.

"Mrs. O'Malley's crumb cake wasn't sufficient," he said. "I'm hungry."

"These days I can always eat," she said, laughing.

They walked to The Captain of the Sea, near the motel. It was full of nautical decor, including saltwater fish tanks. Once they were seated she said, "So, the O'Malleys?"

"They were shocked to hear about Kate. Tommy spared them the gory details, but still. For a few minutes no one said anything. Finally, Mrs. O'Malley said, 'Friends of Kate's are our friends. Tell us about this farm and why you came down here. I'll get coffee and the crumb cake I made yesterday.'

"She brought in a tray, and Tommy told them about the farm and Kate's important work. He said she was competent and kind. He said she was buried with a friend who'd also been killed, and that we had a service. Before Tommy even asked, Mrs. O'Malley offered us a place to stay. Said the house was too big for them. Mr. O'Malley is in his eighties, but she looks younger. We came back to the motel and got everyone together. It'll take all of us to do a deep clean before we move in."

"We'll have to work out sleeping arrangements," Sabine said, half to herself.

"Lavinia and Randolph won't be together," he said. "They looked daggers at each other while we were talking."

"They're breaking up?"

"They already have. Tommy said they fought all the way to Florida."

"How much space is there?"

"Four unused rooms on the second floor. And about five or six acres of land, all weeds. Maybe we can grow enough produce for a truck garden. Mr. O'Malley's confused; we'll end up looking after them."

"Considering what they've offered us," she said, "we owe it to them." She waved to attract the waitress's attention.

After they ordered Sabine smiled. "It's working out with the O'Malleys. And it's probably for the best with Randolph and Lavinia. Can you picture him hauling dirt, tilling the garden, or working construction? He acts more like Lavinia's father than her fiancé. Maybe he'll go back to Richmond and a safe life."

"Safe?" Sol shrugged. "Randolph may go home and try for comfort, but what's safe these days? Maybe he'll stay and be Paul's surrogate father. Paul won't try to get back to the Upper Peninsula. He came a long way on the roads."

"Can we move in tomorrow?" Sabine fiddled with her napkin.

"We'll clean the upstairs tomorrow. It'll take at least a day. Then we'll need to figure out room sharing before we move furniture. It'll be the motel for two more nights."

"Finally, something more than temporary shelter. And I have news. Don't ask why I waited to tell you, but at the hospital when I filled out and signed forms, without thinking I wrote 'Sabine Owen.' My last name's Owen! My brother's name is Freddie, and my parents are Elaine and Frederick. And the numbers 757 came in a dream, like cartoon numbers bouncing around. The area code of the beach house. The phone number's here." She tapped her head. "I wrote it in my notebook, in case my memory goes again. I don't think it will, but you never know."

"Information about your family. Finally!" Sol grinned.

"I want to find them," she said. "At least two bombs hit Richmond. If they were able to get out, they'd go to the beach. But if I have to, I'll search in whatever's left of Richmond."

"I'll help you look. This is important." He covered her hand with his.

Chapter 22

SNAKE MOON

August 6, 2014.

Tommy drove the blue truck through quiet residential streets. Sabine followed at the wheel of the Buick, intent on the truck and noting street names. "Have you given any more thought to how we should divide up the bedrooms?"

"We could do two guys to a room," Sol said. "And you could pair up with Jen or Lavinia. Or the three of you in a room, which leaves a spare."

"I feel sick to my stomach," she said. "You have any crackers?"

"I stuck some in the glove box." He opened the cellophane and handed her two saltines.

She ticked off names. She didn't want to room with either one of the women. Plus, they liked each other, they'd want to be together. Paul would want to room with Tommy and vice versa. Would they be willing to room with Randolph? She hoped they would, so Randolph wouldn't be alone. His money couldn't cushion him against losing Lavinia, or really his whole world. But that arrangement left her and Sol as roommates. And her feelings about him were mixed.

"You know who I want as a roommate."

"I do?"

He touched her shoulder. "Yes, you do."

She didn't look at him.

Tommy's left blinker went on, and he turned down a long gravel driveway. A large stucco house with a red-tiled roof stood at the end of the drive. Sol hit it right: knee-high grass, hedges covered with vines, broken tree branches littered the ground.

"Forgot to tell you their house is pink!" Sol laughed.

"West Virginia must be fresh out of pink houses." Sabine smiled. "Pastel houses are a beach thing."

They followed Tommy up the steps. He grasped the brass knocker and tapped with a gentle touch. Mrs. O'Malley must've been on watch; she swung open the door, a smile brightening her round face. "I'm Sara O'Malley. Oh, look at all of you. James and I have been getting ready. And of course our Darlene helps." She let out a deep-throated chuckle and ran her hand through disheveled white hair.

They all sat in the large living room—except Paul, who stopped in the doorway, mouth agape. Mrs. O'Malley hurried to a Victorian sofa, sat, and smoothed her blue cotton dress. She spotted Paul. "What's your name, boy? Come sit. These old chairs will hold you, even if you don't think they will."

Paul grinned. "My name's Paul Higgins, I'm from Michigan. What a super house."

"Thank you, dear. Come sit by me." She patted the spot next to her, jumped up, and hurried to the door. She cupped her hands and yelled, "James, bring cookies. There's a boy here needing cookies." She motioned to Paul again.

Paul sat by her. "Thanks for letting us come." He flashed his charming, lopsided smile.

"I have to yell," she said. "Unless we're in the same room, I must yell for James to hear me. I'm thrilled to have you all."

"Paul and I will run out and get the food boxes," Tommy said.

"There's not much left, but no sense letting it sit in the sun. Be right back."

Mrs. O'Malley nodded. "Take them to the kitchen, Darlene will unpack them. Then come back so we can get acquainted."

During introductions, Sabine watched the slow-moving ceiling fan. The room felt stuffy. The house must have air-conditioning, but it was either broken or turned off. She had trouble sleeping when the air felt stifling. She hoped the bedrooms would have a cross breeze and ceiling fans.

They'd just finished introductions when Mr. O'Malley shuffled into the room holding a plate of cookies out in front of him like a waiter. With a grunt, he leaned over the coffee table and set the plate down. He stood over six feet and had long, bony arms. His white hair came to his shoulders. He wore a purple smoking jacket over gray sweat pants and blue high-tops.

Tommy, at the door, clamped his hand over his mouth. Sabine turned away and pushed down a laugh.

Mr. O'Malley headed for a wingback chair and settled in it with such ease Sabine figured it must be "his" chair.

"James," Mrs. O'Malley said, "here are Kate's friends! They lived on a farm with Kate. You'll get to be friends with them, because they're going to live with us."

James nodded, his face blank. "No, they're not."

"We'll discuss it later, dear." Mrs. O'Malley looked at Tommy. "Sorry. Sometimes James has trouble with remembering words."

Paul took a few cookies off the plate and passed the plate around. Sabine took three. Peanut butter and oatmeal. Delicious.

"Kate? Come over and give Grandpa a kiss?" James stared at Sabine.

"I'm not Kate. My name's Sabine."

"Come on over, gimme me one right here." He patted his cheek.

"James! Stop, this young woman is not Kate." Mrs. O'Malley's face turned red. "Remember, we talked about Kate? She went to heaven." She pulled a handkerchief out of her apron pocket and dabbed her eyes. "So Tommy, what's first? Darlene will be working downstairs. I should get her to come more often. The upstairs is yours. James and I don't go upstairs anymore."

"Don't worry, Mrs. O'Malley," Tommy said. "We'll be careful moving furniture. May we borrow the vacuum? Or if the electricity's off, a broom, or two?"

"Darlene will fix you up," Mrs. O'Malley said. "Call me Sara. It'll make me feel young."

No one answered.

Sabine put on a relaxed face when Mrs. O'Malley turned in her direction. Poor James. She didn't look a bit like Kate.

❧

August 8, 2014.

When the rooms in the O'Malley's house were cleaned and the furniture rearranged, they checked out of the motel and brought in their backpacks. They gathered in the living room.

Sol stood. "Sabine and I will clean up the front. Everything's overgrown out there."

"No," Jen said. "Cleaning the front yard's a waste. We need vegetables and fruit. We should work out back. We hardly have any money. It'll take all of us to clear the backyard jungle and put in a garden."

Before Sol could argue, Randolph cleared his throat. "Two days ago I received a cash infusion. We'll live well, if we're frugal. I won't be working in the yard with the rest of you. I'll be job hunting. Engineering work, if I can find it, with banking as a fallback."

"Engineering suits you. Can't see you doing heavy work. Yard work is real work." Jen crossed her arms.

"What about Paul, Jen, Sol, and I putting in the garden?" Tommy smiled. "The four of us will be enough."

Sol nodded. "I'll help in back soon as I finish with the front yard."

"What about me?" Lavinia's soft voice sounded like a child's.

"I haven't forgotten you, Lala," Tommy said. In a gentle voice he asked, "What about doing the shopping and cooking meals?"

Sabine stifled a laugh. Sol squeezed her hand to shut her up.

Lavinia glared at Randolph, as if her being stuck in the kitchen were his idea. "Around food all day?" she whined.

"If Lala wants to help put in the garden," Jen said, "she can. We'll all take turns making meals."

"Okay," Lavinia said. "I'll cook one day a week." Sabine noticed that her face had gained some color and she'd put on a few pounds. Jen the miracle worker.

Randolph rolled his eyes.

"Sol and I will make the front beautiful," Sabine said. "Then help with the back."

"It's safer to leave the front in shambles." Randolph walked to the fireplace and rested an elbow on the mantle. "For now, this town's safe. Only a few refugees. But the situation could change."

"We have guns and ammo stashed all over the house," Sabine said. "We'll be fine."

Paul jumped up. "Living here might be the last thing we do. Back at the farm we wanted to come here, but we can't predict how long we'll be safe."

Sara stood in the hall. "Good morning, you all. I made a batch of cookies last night."

"Thanks, Sara," Paul said. "Right now we're in a meeting."

"Is there anything I can do to help?" Sara asked.

"Do you have some pitchers we can take outside for water when we get to work on the garden?"

Sara beamed. "Certainly, dear. I'll fix you up."

"Be there in a few minutes," Paul said.

"I'm good at making schedules," Jen said. "I'll make one for shopping, meals, and chores. We're about out of food. I think Sabine should shop today, then fix something for lunch and dinner. I checked the tool shed. We're in luck, they have plenty of garden tools."

"Make sure you put yourself on the schedule," Randolph grumbled, not looking at Jen.

Jen gave Randolph the finger and grinned at Lavinia, who gave her a thumbs up.

"Sabine." Randolph moved toward her. He pulled a silver money clip out of his pocket. He handed her the clip. "This is around nine hundred dollars. No looting, okay? We're citizens here."

"You think I've forgotten the difference?" Sabine put her hands on her hips.

"Sorry. I didn't intend to be abrasive." Randolph touched her arm. "You know me well enough to know I'm a worrier, especially when it comes to money."

"You're a banker, I get it," Sabine said. "You feel responsible for us. I'll spend three or four hundred today, depending on prices. I'll bring you the receipts. But I'll have a lot of groceries to haul, can someone come with me?"

"I will," Sol said.

"Don't worry, Randolph," Sabine said. "I'll make the money last."

He nodded and adjusted his glasses.

"Damn," Paul said. "It's only nine o'clock and already my shirt's sticking to me. Almost makes me miss the Upper Peninsula; this time of year it's cool."

"Get used to the weather." Randolph focused on Paul. "I doubt the schools will use electricity to power air-conditioning."

"What schools?" Paul's lip went out.

"Next week, I'm registering you for school," Randolph said. "They'll be opening in September, I checked. You're a rising junior, correct?"

"Yeah. I 'spose." Paul looked at Jen.

"You have to finish high school," Jen said. "Randolph's right."

"But if something happens," Paul said, "I need to be at the house, to help protect you guys."

"You can't think like that, Paul," Randolph said. "You need to be relaxed to learn."

Sabine recalled all the times she went to school tense and miserable about Jeffrey. Her terrible grades had showed it.

"In a crisis I'll come get you, if I can, otherwise you'll walk," Randolph said. The high school's only six blocks away."

"You might learn more about what's going on in the world," Sol said.

Paul crossed his arms over his chest. Sabine imagined he was giving Sol the finger in his mind.

⁂

After visiting an OB/GYN later that week, Sabine started taking prenatal vitamins and carrying two bottles of water outside with her at all times.

The first morning she and Sol worked together, she felt inept when Sol handed her a small saw to cut the thick vines overtaking the row of hedges along the driveway. "This thing's too wobbly, gimme the clippers. I'll work on the skinny vines."

"You've never done yard work?" Sol snorted.

"I pruned rose bushes. Mother showed me. Mostly I clipped flowers and put them in vases."

"What can you do?" He grinned, but his tone was patronizing.

"Don't be stupid. I can make stewed chicken and dumplings, potato salad, Sally Lunn bread, fried chicken, and fried apples. I can fry up grits, make waffles, and pancakes from scratch. I can swim a long way and ride horses, though maybe not as well as you."

Sol shook his head. "How did you walk from DC to West Virginia and survive?"

"I'm stubborn."

He took the saw. She watched his careful, slow movement as he worked one side of the driveway, cutting the big vines and tossing them in a pile.

She crossed to the other side and clipped the thin vines. She should smack him and his condescending tone. She'd agreed to share a room with him even though she knew it meant sex eventually. She avoided him when she could.

There was one empty bedroom, if things got any worse between them. Her doubts about him were growing daily. She was still grateful to him for everything, but that wasn't enough.

Sol finished his side of the hedge and started on hers. "After we strip off the leaves and let them dry, we'll burn the big pieces in the fireplace. That is, if it's ever cool enough here to need a fire."

Focused on work, she didn't answer. She finished and carried a pile of small vines toward the backyard.

A sharp scream. Lavinia yelled and kept yelling. Sabine dropped the vines and ran to the back. Lavinia was edging away from a brush pile, holding a rake in front of her.

Sabine saw the snake coiled, ready to strike. "Get away, get away from it!" Her own voice screaming, her face full of heat.

From opposite sides of the yard, Tommy and Jen hurried toward Lavinia, brandishing sticks.

"Stop. Jen, back up," Tommy said. He dropped his stick. "It's a diamondback rattler. The rattling's a warning. Just let it be."

"You sure?" Jen dropped her stick, pulled out her blade, and pretended to lunge. "I could wrestle it, like people do with gators down here. The thing could be harmless. Where's Paul, he'll help."

Sabine ran to Jen and yelled in her face. "For once, listen! Paul's from Michigan. That's not even remotely like Florida."

Jen gave Sabine the finger but sheathed her knife and backed away.

Lavinia smiled at Jen as if she were some kind of hero. Tommy poured himself a cup of water.

"What's up?" Paul ambled onto the back porch. "Why's Sabine hollering?"

"A rattlesnake came out of the brush." Sabine pointed. "They like to nest there. Don't mess with them." She stomped off, picked up the vines she'd dropped, and set them near the porch, far from the brush. She had to sit. Her head thundered. Snakes in the desert, snakes in the brush. Sunning on a rock in the desert, the snake does what it does. *My Mick. A quick bite. Stop. You didn't see the snake biting Mick.* But she'd imagined each part. And she'd seen how the doctor and nurses rushed, called out words, crowded each other in the small room. The big clock throwing away precious minutes. Tiny Mick on the big white bed. Tubes and noxious smells.

Under the tree's shade she gulped water. Could she live in Florida, the land of snakes, and go outside day after day?

"What's wrong?" Sol stood over her.

"Go away."

"What happened?"

"I said go away!"

"After you tell me."

"Leave me the fuck alone!" She threw the water bottle at him, hitting him in the stomach.

"Sabine, what?" He picked up the bottle and set it beside her.

She lowered her head and waited for him to leave. *Oblivious dumbshit.*

When Sol finally left, she crept into the empty room upstairs and locked the door. She skipped lunch, lay on the floor, and stared at the ceiling. Dust motes hung in the air and she tried to follow them. The motes floated randomly, without planning, only drifting. What if Sharp and Hank hadn't picked her up in that field? What if she'd knocked on the door of a different farmhouse?

Sol's knock interrupted her. She was relieved she'd locked the door. When he asked if she was okay, she didn't answer. Later she dragged a chair to the window and watched the still trees, which didn't lift her mood. There were no ceiling fans in the upstairs bedrooms. The downstairs was a bit cooler, but no one ever turned on the energy-sucking air-conditioners. She was living with strangers, far from home in a threatening landscape that could be bombed any minute. And dear Sharp had killed himself.

The air cooled at dusk. Hunger drove her to the dinner table. Sol stared at her with a sad face, like he used to at the farm. His staring still creeped her out, but she felt no anger toward him. He was basically kind and wanted to help her. He had not yet risked asking why she didn't want to sleep with him, and she was relieved about that.

After dinner, she grabbed her sleeping bag and pack and slipped back into the vacant room across the hall. At the bottom of the pack she felt for Sharp's bandana and the leather string Jude had used to tie his hair. She smoothed out the soft cotton on the floor and put Jude's leather string on top. She laid her sleeping bag on the bed. While staring at the ceiling, she thought about asking Randolph to lend her money. When the baby was older, she would go to work and pay him back. A sketchy plan, but worth exploring. Randolph was kind, and she thought he would lend her money. Living expenses at the house were low, but having a baby would be expensive.

At dawn she woke to voices. She stuffed her treasures deep in her pack, dressed, and dragged herself to breakfast. After eating, she forced herself to show up at the hedge to work. She and Sol finished up clearing the vines, and Sol used the lawn mower he'd rented for the afternoon. He insisted on being the only one to ride it. Sabine didn't mind; she was content to pull weeds and clean up flower beds. While they worked they didn't talk, though once in a while they smiled at each other.

At the end of the day, he asked, "Tell me, why were you so upset?"

"I hate snakes."

"When are you coming back to our room?"

"It's not working between us. You can't be surprised. I can't take your money when the baby comes. I've been making another plan."

He bent over as if she had kicked him. "I have to take the lawn mower back to the rental place."

She nodded and went inside.

Chapter 23

WATER MOON

September 19, 2014.

A t eight in the morning Elaine answered the landline. A male voice identified himself as a Richmond police officer. Workers clearing debris from Frederick's office building had found his remains. Elaine heard herself say she wanted Frederick's body cremated. The officer said the funeral home would take care of the remains and send them, but transportation wasn't reliable, so he couldn't say when the urn would arrive.

After the call she sat at the dining room table, trying to catch her breath and avoid thinking about his mangled body. Of course, his body was all she could see.

Fed Ex delivered the urn ten days later. She felt scooped out; crying over Frederick since Memorial Day had drained her. Her pain over losing him felt different than the pain she felt about Freddie's unlived life. Her husband had lived where he wanted and done what he wanted. He'd become a lawyer, and with her he'd hiked many mountains and made enough money to buy a cottage at the beach. A rich, well-lived life.

Missing him overwhelmed her. She missed their activities, as

well as doing nothing with him: reading on the deck, drinking coffee, and marveling at the sun surging over the horizon. Working
in the yard in Richmond, resting with drinks on the patio while
evening came on and the wind slowed and finally stillness came to
the thrashing pines.

She took the urn out of the shipping box and stared at the ugly,
ornate green jar. People put urns on their mantles. Their stone fireplace didn't have a mantle, and even if it did, she'd never give an
urn a prominent place. A creepy idea. She stuck the vulgar thing in
the middle of the dining room table. Later she held it, then set it on
the coffee table.

Freddie walked by, picked it up. "Let's wait for a calm sunrise."
He set it back on the coffee table and walked away.

She tried to find humor in Frederick ending up in a hideous,
fake Chinese vase on the coffee table they'd bought together years
ago. Maybe someone else would laugh, but she could not.

After weeks of limiting the news, she and Freddie were watching
more television. The first relief concerned the government, which
had stabilized. Elections were scheduled for November to replace
senators and house members who'd died in the bomb attacks. Two
airlines had gone bankrupt, but other airline companies were flying
again—on reduced schedules, but still. Maybe she'd buy a new cell
phone. They were working in some parts of the country now. But who
would she call? None of her friends had called the beach house phone.

When a reporter began talking about illness, Elaine turned off
the TV, but seconds later she switched it back on. She jiggled her
foot and stared out at the ocean, barely able to listen. A viral airborne disease similar to SARS from Asia, had been sickening people.
Exotic diseases like visceral leishmaniasis had appeared in large cities, brought in by foreign aid workers and the military. The usual flu
outbreaks had begun, but the year's vaccine supply was quite low.
And worse, the bombs could've damaged peoples' immune systems.

She turned off the TV and paced. When her children were

young they'd gotten all the right vaccinations and she'd tended to
them like honored guests when they were sick. She thought she'd
done a good job with them, until Freddie had started coming home
drunk in high school. Then there was the heroin.

She went to bed early. During the night she sat upright, gasping
out of a nightmare of shredded birthday cards, each strip stamped
with numbers. The strips flew around, a terrible confetti taking
away her air till she couldn't breathe. "We're all going to die!" She
clamped her hand over her mouth. Oh God, had she spoken out
loud? Was she still dreaming? Sweat on her brow, she stared at the
dark wall, fearing they'd all be dead soon.

So far she and Freddie hadn't learned about any flu cases in
the beach area. Still, they avoided crowds when they went to buy
supplies. On the beach, she avoided strangers. Most days only a few
people walked along the sand.

Elaine's list of worries kept growing. First it was starvation and
inadequate medication, then robbery and terrorists, now diseases.
Regular TV programs were interrupted by grim-faced reporters issu-
ing updates on thwarted bomb plots in the US, hijacker arrests, and
raids on terrorist camps in the Middle East and Africa, and probably
in the US, too.

When she and Freddie sat on the deck, she casually mentioned
that the disease reports worried her. He didn't try to reassure her; he
agreed the crisis would get worse. They discussed plagues, poisoned
reservoirs, and bombs—dropped from planes and planted in vans,
subways, and tunnels.

"Who will take care of Lily," he wondered, "if we both die of
some disease?"

"Stop it!" She crossed her arms and stared at the sunset. Clouds
scuttled across the sky, birds skittered over the dunes, and waves
lapped the sand. Outside in the breeze, anticipating the moon and
stars, life felt familiar and ordinary—this small patch of earth still
sublime.

Freddie had finally reconnected with his computer company, which was up and running again, and started back at his old programming job. As a single parent, they were allowing him to telecommute. He soon figured out how to finish his assignments in three to five hours a day, which led him to wonder about the time he'd wasted while working in the Richmond office. Before the bombs he'd chatted with colleagues, sat in tedious meetings, texted Mags, and e-mailed friends throughout the day. He rarely chatted with anyone now. He kept up with house repairs, took care of Lily, and continued to volunteer with the beach cleanup crew.

He felt more confident taking care of his child by himself now; he devised games, they built cities of sand on the beach, and he read her stories. He slept through the night and didn't crave brandy or other poisons. Spending that time with Lily, unfamiliar feelings rose up; slowly, he realized the foreign feeling was contentment.

If he did crave a hit of heroin, a bump of coke, or a shot of whiskey, he rolled up his sleeve and inspected his arm. Despite his best efforts to use clean needles, his thighs and arms, especially the left arm, had ended up like Ducky's. There were remedies for tracks and abscess scars, but he needed to keep the scars to remind himself where he'd been. Luckily, his pale skin gave him a ready-made excuse to wear long sleeves, even when he swam.

One night, after he put Lily in her crib, he joined his mother on the deck. Her eyes were closed; he debated waking her.

"Ready for bed? It's only eight."

Her eyes flew open. "What's wrong?"

"Nothing, except it's unusual to see you sleeping so early."

She sat up in the chaise. "My book put me to sleep. Romances are fake and silly. They don't work for escape, I don't know why I bother. This one's going in the trash."

"You know, I adored Dad, right? Till sixth grade, when he started yelling at me and he never stopped."

"Back then, I could see both sides," Elaine said. "In some ways you're like your father. Guess your dad didn't like looking in the mirror. But neither did you."

Freddie felt heat in his face. "I suppose." Fear took hold of his gut, an urge to run; the old trapped feelings. He didn't yell as much as his dad did, but his anger flared when he didn't want it to. While working with the beach volunteers, he'd rehearsed what to tell his mother about the Glock, the dealers, and the drugs, but now his confidence felt shaky. He wanted to sound clearheaded and intelligent.

He paced the deck. "I tore up the letter with my grades from computer school. Ducky and I used drugs the whole time and hardly went to class. I failed both classes. Your money was completely wasted."

Elaine didn't respond.

He gulped to hold in tears. He hadn't planned to cry like a kid, sobbing out apologies for the trouble he'd caused her and Dad. He felt her staring and faced her. "In a weird way the bombs have been a blessing. I haven't forgiven myself for what I did to Sabine and Ducky, but I'm not the person I used to be. I'm curious about the world again—at least, what's left of it. I'm more confident. I'm glad to live with you and Lily. I haven't given up hope on Sabine and Mags."

Elaine took his hand. "You're learning what you needed to learn." She gave him a long hug. "Thank you for the truth."

❧

The next morning, his mother was washing breakfast dishes when Freddie came to the kitchen door.

"The urn." He pointed to the living room. "It's time."

"Yes. I'm finishing up." She dried her hands and collected the urn.

The ocean and sky were the color of crushed pearls. His mother helped him put Lily in the carrier on his back, and then they trudged down to the pier, Elaine holding the urn near her chest with both hands. Out on the pier, he covered her hand to help steady the urn while she broke the seal. Before she tilted it, the wind picked up some of the ashes and tiny bone fragments and whipped them away. Together they upended the urn, and the wind took the rest toward the sky. They stood in silence for a few minutes, then they walked toward the cottage, silent but for Lily's gibberish as she pointed at the ocean.

Freddie tried to stay busy, but thoughts of Mags and Sabine and his father came often. Ordinary smells—chicken roasting when he came home, or the shower running when he woke in the morning— reminded him of Mags. When he slept late and rolled to the other side of the bed, and found her gone, he cried. He missed their lazy morning sex before Lily was born. He changed his mind about her daily: she was alive and trying to get to the beach; she'd died and he'd never know where, or how, it had happened.

When he couldn't stop thinking about her, he yearned for a brandy. But if he drank one brandy, why not two, and in no time they'd turn into ten or twelve. He'd stay drunk, and heroin would follow.

From the deck he'd hear a low-pitched girl's voice growling and be transported to the old kitchen, listening to Sabine the teenager arguing with their father. Working on the beach with volunteers, several times he'd heard her raucous laugh, but when he'd turned, no one on the beach or in the water had remotely resembled her. One day he'd spotted an older man walking briskly toward the house wearing a sailor's cap and he'd had to force himself not to lean over the railing and yell hello. Maybe he'd see the man again tomorrow. The ashes he and his mother had scattered could be someone else's.

Lost people came to his dreams. He hurried through unfamiliar cities, searching for a face he recognized. Mags, Dad, Sabine, and Ducky. But seeing them caused them to disappear, and it was all his fault. Surrounded by strangers closing in with murderous expressions, he tried to answer their insistent questions, but they spoke in unknown tongues.

Often he chased Ducky through tunnels until his friend fell, arms flailing, trying to stop himself from hitting the concrete. Before he could help, Ducky's body contracted into a white ball and winked out.

After they'd left computer school, Freddie's drug use had skyrocketed. At first he'd told himself he could quit whenever he wanted, then he'd given up the excuses and rolled with the addict life.

But not Ducky. He'd struggled and managed to stay clean for about two weeks at a time, going to class and staying in the library to research his dissertation. Then Freddie would stop by his apartment with a bag of heroin, a mason jar full of pills, a bottle of Scotch. A real Pied Piper.

One morning he stopped by Ducky's apartment to share some good smack he'd scored. He handed a packet to Ducky, but Ducky threw the packet at him and pushed him out the door so hard he fell and cut his lip. Freddie played it up, begging to come in for ice and a towel. Ducky called him a son of a bitch, his hateful laugh booming through the door. He kept pleading, but Ducky had resisted that day and each day for the next few weeks.

Finally, he'd forced himself to stop going to Ducky's. Sometimes he'd found himself on a park bench, staring across the street at Ducky's building. Waiting for what?

No one else on the planet could make him laugh like Ducky. In seventh and eighth grade when neither of them could sleep, they snuck out of their houses and met at their corner dressed in black jeans and T-shirts, adding black gloves and wool scarves in winter. They let cigarettes hang out of their mouths pretending to be gangsters. They smoked pot and strolled through the world of wide lawns and safe houses. They stopped at a deserted elementary school yard. They hung off the jungle gyms, swinging and yelling; they pumped hard on the swings, let go and flew out, laughing hysterically.

They raced to a grassy ball field where one would grab the other with a whoop and take him down. Ducky's face illuminated by streetlights, Freddie held his friend's strong body close, wishing he could be more like him. They'd wrestle until one of them called

stop. His feelings for Ducky had been confused and he hadn't understood them. But Freddie figured whatever it was would pass, once
he had a regular girlfriend. When he and Ducky drifted apart, his
adoration subsided. Well, not quite. The intensity subsided, but the
longing never left. He couldn't forget when they wandered through
their domain, strong and powerful, as if the night world belonged
to them, as if they'd always wander together. Just the two of them.

He'd betrayed Ducky. Sick with envy, he'd tried to derail his best
friend, as if that would save his own life. Ducky had earned a PhD,
had a short career in academia, and died. In Freddie's quick version.
But the truth stayed curled tight inside, a stunted bud, rotting.

Chapter 24

———— ✦ ————

HURRICANE MOON

October 10, 2014.

B y two thirty the afternoon sky was dusky. Freddie switched on a
lamp to keep reading a detective novel. When he and his mother
went to the mall they visited a used bookstore, and each bought
three or four books. None of his detective stories gave him answers
about Mags or Sabine. Yet he couldn't stop reading.

Elaine appeared at his door. "Want to walk on the beach before
bad weather sets in?"

"Is it safe?" he asked. "I don't want Lily breathing in sand."

"I'll put a thick scarf around her mouth."

Dressing Lily wasn't a subject he wanted to argue about, so he
said, "Sure. Let me put on warmer clothes."

Elaine put Lily in a front pack and adjusted the straps. She and
Freddie walked north, the wind at their backs.

"This hurricane is gonna be at least a Cat 2," he said.

"I hate when the sand blows like this."

"I've been thinking how strange it was."

"What?" Elaine turned to him.

"Strange how my two worlds collided. Sabine and Ducky."

"To Sabine, he was never Ducky. He was Dr. Giles Duckworth." Elaine smiled.

"When Ducky and I started hanging out, Sabine wasn't even a teenager. She didn't know him except to say hi when she answered the door. Then Ducky got it together, so Sabine never knew about our heroin days."

"Of course she did, Freddie! She figured it out the night she met him. She saw the scars on his arms, the track marks. Giles told her he'd quit drugs, and she wanted to believe him. But he couldn't quit drinking for long."

"Huh, didn't know she figured out the heroin part. Their wedding was agony. Now they're both gone. And Mick, too."

He must've watched them standing at the front of the church, but the ceremony was a blur. He'd refused to join the wedding party for pictures; later, a few shots showed him off to the side, glowering. He'd made it through the reception on a few glasses of champagne— and a flask of bourbon. His heart full of grief and love for them both. He remembered watching them dance. They'd barely noticed him.

"The old saying about time healing all wounds isn't true," Elaine said. "You have to talk about Ducky and Sabine, cry about it, whatever works. And it'll still be inside you, but you'll be able to stand it."

"Thanks a lot."

His tone was so sarcastic, she stopped walking. "Freddie, if you do nothing, you'll get worse."

"I called the investigator," he said, "and told him to stop searching for Sabine but to keep doing anything possible to find Mags."

"Let's turn back," his mother said. "It's too windy. We'd best secure the deck furniture."

Back at the house, he felt too tired to move furniture. He picked up his latest detective novel and threw it across his room, then looked around for something else to throw. He had another book in his hand when he heard Lily jabbering in the hallway.

Embarrassed, he put the book on the bedside table, and took a deep breath. The hurricane was due to make a direct hit along the coast as a Cat 1, but from the strength of the wind, he figured for at least a Cat 2.

"Okay, let's move furniture, then I'll check the house."

They hauled the deck furniture, the grill, and three large potted cacti to the storage unit. He checked the windows. Under the house, he made sure the enclosure around the outdoor shower was tight. The pilings felt sturdy. He dragged pieces of wood to the dunes and buried them so they wouldn't turn into projectiles.

The hurricane hit during the night. Lily howled and abruptly stopped. Finally Freddie slept, until a loud noise woke him. He hurried to the sliding doors and edged onto the deck. He bent low, struggled to the railing, clutched it and watched shredded clouds stream by and dark roaring waves and foam crash on the beach. In a crouch he lurched inside and slid the doors closed. Grateful to have a dry, safe retreat, he checked on his mother and Lily. They were asleep in the old rocking chair in Lily's room, lit by a circle of light. He laid Lily on her back in the crib, and helped his mother out of the chair. She waved on her way to bed.

❧

In the morning rain fell in sheets, slowed, and started up again. Elaine wasn't worried, she'd been through many hurricanes. Freddie's repairs had made the cottage sturdier. She must thank him.

She was staring at the cabinet, deciding what to cook for dinner, when the landline rang. She lunged for the phone.

"Hello?"

Silence.

"Hello, hello, anybody there?"

Silence, followed by a click.

She shrugged and finished undressing.

The following day the butcher shop reopened. She managed third place in line. The butcher, a short man with a generous smile, seemed glad to see a loyal customer, and allowed her to buy two turkeys. She also bought baking powder, two bags of oranges, and fresh spinach. The drugstore had gotten a shipment of drugs. She bought a three-month supply of blood pressure medication, diapers, and a case of baby formula. On impulse, she bought a floppy cloth doll for Lily too.

On the drive home, the windshield wipers on high, she marveled that for the first time since Memorial Day she'd been able to buy produce, medicine, formula, even a toy, on the same day. The wind matched her soaring spirits. When the beach grasses dried out, she'd collect some and arrange them in her favorite vase, the purple glass one. Tonight she'd fix a proper dinner. Soon she'd invite the couple from next door over for drinks and dinner, if she could find more fresh vegetables.

Freddie had left a note saying he'd taken Lily to the beach. She didn't wait for him to help her carry in the bags. She made two trips and put away the groceries. On the deck with a glass of ice water, she felt time moving again; she was no longer outside of time, not like after Jeffrey died. Today felt precious, to be savored, each day no longer a space to fill by staring at the wall.

The muscles in her neck hurt when she woke the next morning. She threw on a robe and made coffee. Dizzy, she spilled the first cup all down her robe. She managed to pour another cup and make it to the deck. Freddie was supposed to go work on the beach. She had Lily for the day. Should she ask him not to go out? Silly, she'd be fine.

She skipped a shower and dressed slowly, then wandered into the kitchen.

Freddie was stirring oatmeal. "You okay? You look droopy."

"Not a hundred percent. Probably allergies. Not sick enough to stay in bed."

"I could stay here, there's always my office work."

"No, you planned to volunteer. I'll be okay."

The cottage felt deserted after Freddie left. Lily ran around the living room, sometimes pulling herself up on furniture and standing briefly before plopping on the floor. She'd walk soon. Elaine fixed on Lily, fighting to keep her eyes open. Had she locked the sliding doors to the deck? She didn't know. Her body felt heavy and sweaty.

Something hit her leg and screeched. She opened her eyes to Lily, screaming and red-faced. Elaine bolted off the sofa and staggered to the kitchen. Where was the phone? She had to call Freddie, but first she'd feed Lily, who clutched her leg and cried while she opened a jar of spinach. She found a bottle in the refrigerator. She sat Lily on the sofa and spooned spinach into her mouth, then propped her on a pillow with the bottle. Freddie's cell phone wasn't working. Maybe she'd just . . .

"Goddamn it! Mom, wake up! Lily's not in her crib." Freddie fingers dug into her shoulder.

"I must've drifted off while she was drinking her bottle," Elaine said, disoriented, still groggy.

"It's two thirty." He checked the sliding doors. "At least you locked the doors. She's gotta be here." He ran down the hall. "Lily, Lily, where are you, sweetie? Lily?"

Elaine poured herself a glass of water to cool off. She crept down the hall and peeked into the guest bathroom. No Lily. Her head hurt and her heart felt like thunder in her chest. She stumbled and grabbed a doorknob to steady herself. She fell. To stop the urge to vomit, she closed her eyes and took deep breaths. She managed to stand and lean against the wall to steady herself.

"Mom, I found her! Asleep under your bed. She has a big bump on her forehead."

Elaine edged into her room and sat on the bed.

Freddie held Lily and rocked her. "We're sorry, sweetie, so sorry." He glared at Elaine. "Look, Mom, that's going to bruise. Why didn't you tell me to stay home?"

"I got sicker, but I couldn't call you. I gave her spinach and a bottle. Sorry."

"She must've fallen. Should we take her to the doctor?"

"Freddie, if I'd taken you and Sabine to the doctor whenever one of you fell, I wouldn't have gotten anything done. Give her to me."

Freddie put Lily in her arms and stood over them, frowning.

"Don't worry, I won't drop her. Her eyes are clear, she isn't feverish. The bed has a metal frame. She probably bumped into it crawling around."

"I'll put her in her crib," he said.

"I have to rest. Take Lily and go away."

She woke hours later with a pounding headache and extreme thirst. She splashed cold water on her hot face and stuck a thermometer in her mouth. Only 103, not so bad. She gulped several glasses of water and chewed up three aspirin, wondering if the thermometer was broken. Before she reached the bed, the room spun and the dresser slid away. Hunched over, trying to still her own heavy breathing, she waited for the dresser to return to its proper place. She took hold of the dresser edge with both hands and gathered strength. Call Freddie? No. Her voice didn't feel strong, and she didn't want to alarm him. Flat on her back, safe in bed, she closed her eyes and begged for sleep.

No fever in the morning, and it was only 101 in the afternoon. She slept most of the next three days. On the fourth day, she felt well enough to sit on the deck. Her body was strong enough to kick the flu—this time, at least.

The hurricane had brought in new trash. Depending on the number of volunteers, it might take six or seven days for the beach crew to clear a mile, working their way the four and a half miles down to the pier. Once they cleared the beach they'd go north and work their way down again. At the end of the day, Freddie was often bone tired.

But the exhaustion and fresh air helped him sleep without drinking. He woke each morning feeling energetic. But today beach cleanup was cancelled, and even his Richmond office was closed.

He'd intended to spend the morning reading a detective novel. Instead he walked around the house aimlessly. Finally he settled on the couch and stared at the hurricane's remnants. He fixed his eyes on the wild waves and racing clouds, and hidden memories flooded in.

The day Sabine flew home from New Mexico, he and his parents had met her at the airport. Stone-faced, they'd waited for her plane, pacing and watching through giant glass windows; then they'd waited for the hearse; then they'd waited for Mick's casket to be unloaded from the plane; then they'd waited for men from the funeral parlor to slide it into the back of the hearse.

Sabine had taken the front seat in her dad's car. As soon as he turned onto the interstate, she'd erupted. She'd leaned over the seat. "You're a real shit, Freddie. If you couldn't get clean, you could've at least left Giles alone. But no, you urged him on, trying to ruin him, getting him to sink into the muck with you." Then she'd whipped her head around, faced Mom, and yelled, "You and Dad raised a selfish, spoiled brat. Freddie will fail at everything! You'll end up supporting him the rest of your lives. You deserve the misery!"

Freddie hadn't spoken, had kept his hand over his mouth to keep from lashing out at his sister. Their parents hadn't said a word. Sabine had the righteous power of a mother with a dead child. In her mind, they were all culpable. She was at least half right.

Chapter 25

HARVEST MOON

November 15, 2014.

Sabine slipped out of bed and dressed. An early-morning stroll around the grounds had become her solitary ritual. She moved slowly down the driveway, admiring the lush bushes and trees rustling in autumn's cool breeze. She was pleased with the work she and Sol had done.

"Sabine!"

She turned.

Sharp emerged from the shade of a tree and hurried toward her wearing cargo pants and a black T-shirt.

"You're here? I can't believe it!" Why wasn't he wearing his usual red shirt? A stupid, random thought for a time like this.

"I was headed to the house to find you. Everyone okay?"

"Everyone's okay. How did you get here?"

"I walked."

"Don't be literal, you know what I mean. I thought you were dead!"

"You're all okay, that is good news."

"Yep." Sabine smiled. "We settled in, put in a big garden; the vegetables are thriving. Now we're repairing the back steps and washing windows, that sort of thing. James is frail and has lost his memory. Tommy takes walks with him. Sara can't drive because of bad eyes. She acts like Paul's surrogate grandmother. They seem to enjoy talking and taking walks around the grounds; he holds her arm so she can't fall. I'm not sure how they managed before we came."

"Sounds like you all are getting along."

"It feels homey. Sometimes." She pointed to the house, the mowed lawn and trimmed hedges. "I'm trying to adjust to you standing here. Hard to believe you're here."

He moved closer. "Listen, there are more gangs on the road. Yesterday I heard chatter about more bombs and several nasty bugs. Most likely they'll be airborne and easy to transmit."

Her stomach turned. A plague? What about the baby? "I left your Jeep in the same place you left it. I searched it, but didn't find any surveillance stuff. We didn't want to drive it."

"I figured. It's cool. A friend took care of it. I'm driving another car now. What do you think about coming with me?"

"You mean take a walk?"

"Not a walk. I want you come live with me."

"Where? You just said the roads aren't safe."

"You'd be safe with me. I've rented a house near here, I like this town. When I have to travel, I could bring you back here, if you wanted. Or you could stay at the house. There's an alarm system, and I adopted two German shepherds."

Flooded with emotions, she stuttered, "I still can't believe you're alive. Come inside, have some coffee and cake, and see everybody? They'll be happy to see you. Everyone thinks you're dead."

"Not right now. I came to talk to you." He took her hand and she let him. "I went back to the hospital and had surgery. I wanted to come sooner, but once my body got stronger, I went back to work."

"Sol and I shared a bedroom, at first."

"You're sleeping with him?"

She pulled her sweater closer. "Not anymore. Only for a little while."

"You love him?"

"No, I don't. But I care about him and sometimes enjoy his company. I miss Jude."

Sharp ran his fingers through his curls with a shaky hand. "But you like me, don't you? You have feelings for me. I think you do."

"I won't deny it." Her neck felt hot. "But whatever your work is, I'm guessing you go away often. At the farm, you were secretive. I never knew what you were up to, or thinking."

"What I told you about Dad and my family was true. I am secretive—it's my training, and I guess part of who I am, until I trust a person."

"I think about you," she said, fiddling with her hands. *Stop fidgeting.* "I try to fit the pieces together."

He pulled her close and put his arms around her waist. "I'm happy you think about me. I've been thinking about you since I saw you standing in the field. You've put on weight, you're looking healthy."

She opened her big, baggy sweater. "I'm pregnant." She tried to stifle a nervous laugh. "It's Jude's. Sol offered to support me after the baby's born, but I won't let him. I'll borrow money from Randolph. I sleep alone in an empty bedroom."

He loosened his embrace. "Can I compete with Jude's memory?"

"If I wasn't pregnant, you could. But if I really understood what you do for a living, I'd probably freak. A military contractor? I don't think that's the kind of life I want. Plus, you might leave, walk away like you did with the girl on the beach."

"I'd just met her," Sharp said. "Come live with me and we'll see how it goes. About my work, I'll say this much: it's important, and I'm trying to make things better in this country, not worse. I'm a decent enough guy. I don't go out drinking and carousing. When I don't have to travel, I'm a stay-at-home kind of guy."

"In June I killed a man with a machete." She gulped a deep breath. "Then Hank and Kate were killed. On the road, Sol and I watched a standoff between two trucks full of farmers. They knew each other, still, they argued and fought. The guy from the flatbed was gutted and the one from the pickup was shot. Both of them died, right there on the road, and the other farmers left them lying there. Then Jude died. And then a car chased us and tried to ram our bumper. I shot out their windshield. I shot a gun at people!" She twisted her hands. "The killings at the farm, then dead people on the road . . . it's too much. You're tougher than I am." She shifted from one foot to the other. "You convinced me you were going to kill yourself and now you're here, expecting me to go with you. What if we did live together, and you went away and disappeared? And I couldn't find out what happened, and couldn't find you? I've done that to my family. It's horrible."

He touched her shoulder. "In the hospital I thought about what you said. It helped clear my mind. We might not have much time, but we'd be together." His eyes watered. "I admire you, leaving DC and walking miles alone. I want you."

She tried to smile, but tears came instead. She rubbed her eyes. "Are you grateful to me? Is that why you want me to live with you?"

"No, gratitude isn't why. Maybe a little. When I saw you that first day, I wondered about this woman alone in a field. You have been keeping yourself together."

"I wish I wasn't bringing a child into this chaos. That's probably a cliché most expectant women say."

"I can't see you as a mother. You're right, a terrible time for having kids."

"I was a mother. Still am, in my heart. My Mick died when he was nine months old. I want to have this baby, even though the timing's bad."

Sharp's chin dropped. "You had a child. I'm sorry, I had no idea. I didn't."

"I haven't talked about it. There's no way you could've known. Please come inside, they'll be happy to see you're alive."

He turned toward the trees and wiped his eyes.

"Not now. I should go." He looked into her eyes and stroked her cheek. "Please, don't travel. And take care of yourself." He pulled a grocery receipt out of his pocket and scribbled on the back. "Here's my address and sat phone number. My house is only a few blocks away, in case you change your mind. Leave a note. If I'm not home, I'll get back to you as fast as I can."

She slipped the paper in her pocket. "Sharp." She stumbled after him. "Come back and visit. Please stay safe." She reached to hug him, but he backed away.

He trotted to the end of the driveway and disappeared.

The empty space and her shaking legs forced her to sit. He's alive. He'd held her hand and stroked her cheek. He'd come for her, and she'd told him the truth.

He'd given her a thread to pull her closer. Could she make herself stop thinking about him? She hadn't stopped so far. Tears leaked out of her closed eyes. She'd made a mistake, letting him leave. Now he'd go away again, and maybe disappear forever.

꙳

November 19, 2014.

Freddie sat in bed engrossed in another detective novel about the kidnapping of a boy. The character didn't resemble him, or Ducky. But he liked the fast pace.

The thunk of a car door closing. The clock on his bedside table read 11:45. He hurried to the window. Without streetlights, the wind and full moon threw moving shadows onto the cottages and the street. He didn't recognize the car parked next to his mother's

Volvo. His stomach seized. The police, finally here to arrest him? A neighbor with a medical emergency? Did the Volvo have enough gas to get to a hospital?

Wearing pajama bottoms, not bothering with shoes, he hurried to the front door and peered through the small window by the door.

Chapter 26

THANKSGIVING MOON

Sharp pulled into the driveway, next to her mother's Volvo. They had discussed her going in by herself, and Sharp had agreed to wait in the car until she came for him. She needed to face her family alone.

There's still time to turn around and go back to St. Augustine, I don't have to do this. She leaned toward Sharp and kissed him on the cheek.

She hesitated. Her heart thudded and her hands shook.

In slow motion she opened the car door, climbed the wooden steps, and knocked. The door swung open immediately. Her brother, smiling in the light. She grabbed him and cried into his shoulder. "Freddie. Sorry, sorry, sorry."

He held her. She felt his body shaking, and took his face in her hands. "Freddie, sweet Freddie. I missed you so much."

He whispered, "Sabine, Sabine!"

She followed him into the living room—the same old furniture, the faint coffee smell, and the bowlful of shells, some broken, some whole, that she'd collected when she was a kid. Through the sliding doors, the muffled, rhythmic breaking of the waves.

Home, at last. Her family, Sharp, the people she loved.

She hoped they would have enough time.

ACKNOWLEDGMENTS

Thank you to:

Virginia Center for the Creative Arts (VCCA) for your time and support.

Blackbird Online Journal of Literature and the Arts for the opportunity to work on a wonderful journal and learn from editors Mary Flinn, Gregory Donovan, Michael Keller, and Randy Marshall; to Fine Arts Work Center, Provincetown, MA for workshops led by inspiring teachers Marie Howe and Victoria Redel; and to Elizabeth Cox at Bennington Summer Writing Workshops, for her encouragement.

The Rappahannock Fiction Writer's Workshop and my teacher, Bob Olmstead, who pointed the way to my first novel.

My teachers: Sally Doud, Gloria Wade Gayles, Susan Hankla, Elizabeth Hodges, Paule Marshall, David Robbins, and Leslie Shiel.

David Nolan, architectural historian, for helpful information about St. Augustine, Florida.

Brooke Warner, Cait Levin, and Krissa Lagos of She Writes Press. I've appreciated their accessibility and kind guidance all the way through.

Ken Hopson, Mitchell Craft, David Muessig, and Amy Coleman for the wonderful book trailer.

My friend and writing mentor of many years, Jamie Fueglein.

My faithful friends in my writing group—Ron Andrea, Danny Cox, Helen Foster, Jean Huets, and Laura Jones—and my writing friends Norma Clarke, Chuck Cleary, Karla Helbert, Taigen Dan

Leighton, Cheryl Pallant, Will Paoletto, Bill Tate, Pam Webber, and Anne Westrick.

My friend Jill Wilson, a former literature professor, who listened and gave smart suggestions.

My daughter, Sasha Gay-Overstreet, and friend Cyn Mathews for helpful information on hospital emergency room procedures, and for listening.

And my grandson, Cy, who buries himself in books, draws cartoons, and writes stories. His enthusiasm inspires me.

ABOUT THE AUTHOR

Lenore Gay is a Licensed Professional Counselor with a Masters in Sociology, as well as in Rehabilitation Counseling. She has worked in several agencies, psychiatric hospitals and for ten years she maintained a private practice. She was on the faculty of the Rehabilitation Counseling Department of Virginia Commonwealth University. She taught graduate students and coordinated the internship program.

The Virginia Center of the Creative Arts (VCCA) has awarded her two writing fellowships. Her poems and short stories have appeared in several small journals. Her essay "Mistresses of Magic" was published in the anthology IN PRAISE OF OUR TEACHERS (Beacon Press). Her short story "The Hobo" won first place in *Style Weekly's* annual fiction contest. She is a volunteer reader at *Blackbird, An Online Journal for Literature & the Arts*.

ABOUT THE PUBLISHER

SHE WRITES PRESS is a publishing company, a division of Spark Point Studio, LLC, a multi-media parent company. The press is for authors who want the freedom, control, and financial rewards of investing in their own books up front, without sacrificing the credibility and status that come with publishing under a highly selective imprint. The publisher uses traditional distribution and has an experienced editorial and production team, while allowing the author to retain full ownership of their project and earnings.

SELECTED TITLES FROM SHE WRITES PRESS

*She Writes Press is an independent publishing company
founded to serve women writers everywhere.
Visit us at **www.shewritespress.com**.*

Things Unsaid by Diana Y. Paul. $16.95, 978-1-63152-812-5. A family saga of three generations fighting over money and obligation—and a tale of survival, resilience, and recovery.

The End of Miracles by Monica Starkman. $16.95, 978-1-63152-054-9. When a pregnancy following years of infertility ends in late miscarriage, Margo Kerber sinks into a depression—one that leads her, when she encounters a briefly unattended baby, to commit an unthinkable crime.

True Stories at the Smoky View by Jill McCroskey Coupe. $16.95, 978-1-63152-051-8. The lives of a librarian and a ten-year-old boy are changed forever when they become stranded by a blizzard in a Tennessee motel and join forces in a very personal search for justice.

How to Grow an Addict by J.A. Wright. $16.95, 978-1-63152-991-7. Raised by an abusive father, a detached mother, and a loving aunt and uncle, Randall Grange is built for addiction. By twenty-three, she knows that together, pills and booze have the power to cure just about any problem she could possibly have . . . right?

Trespassers by Andrea Miles. $16.95, 978-1-63152-903-0. Sexual abuse survivor Melanie must make a choice: choose forgiveness and begin to heal from her emotional wounds, or exact revenge for the crimes committed against her—even if it destroys her family.

What is Found, What is Lost by Anne Leigh Parrish. $16.95, 978-1-938314-95-7. After her husband passes away, a series of family crises forces Freddie, a woman raised on religion, to confront long-held questions about her faith.